Rachel

Thank you for all your support and help to make this book possible.

May we both have success in all we do.

Thank you

Wallace Jane Eddy

THE LAST CELTIC ANGEL
AND SPIRITS FROM THE PAST

Wallace Jan Ecklof

AuthorHouse™
1663 Liberty Drive
Bloomington, IN 47403
www.authorhouse.com
Phone: 1-800-839-8640

This book is a work of fiction. People, places, events, and situations are the product of the author's imagination. Any resemblance to actual persons, living or dead, or historical events, is purely coincidental.

© 2010 Wallace Jan Ecklof. All rights reserved.

No part of this book may be reproduced, stored in a retrieval system, or transmitted by any means without the written permission of the author.

First published by AuthorHouse   7/26/2010

ISBN: 978-1-4490-9720-2 (e)
ISBN: 978-1-4490-9718-9 (sc)
ISBN: 978-1-4490-9719-6 (hc)

Library of Congress Control Number: 2010909227

Printed in the United States of America
Bloomington, Indiana

This book is printed on acid-free paper.

Cover by Kim Gledhill www.kimgledhill.com
Photography by Nicole Hymowitz nicolehymowitzphotography@gmail.com

"Legend Of The Celtic Angel"

Once a long time ago in the beginning of the time there were two races of beings one was as old as time itself, and possessed extraordinary powers, and they lived in the world of the Sidhe under the mound of Tara in ancient Ireland. They were known as the fairy folk, and they were as gods before the coming of the One God. The other race was new and was of the human kind called Man whose destiny was to overcome the older races and rule Middle Earth as was foretold by the runes of the Seers.

It was at this time that a prince of the old race called Tuatha De Danaan angered the Fairy King with his mischief-making of the people of Man. I came to pass that he was brought before his lord for punishment. The Lord commanded that he be sent to dwell among mankind on Middle earth and to live as one of them. He thought the prince would learn humility.

The Prince in his anger rose up against his lord and was vanquished along with his followers. When he was again brought forth before the King of Kings, the Lord said to him. "Thou art banished from the world of Magic and the heavens most high. You and all your people shall be doomed until you shall find a way to redeem them and so set them free.

As the centuries sped past, the Prince forgot the purpose he was exiled and soon all memories of who he was faded with each new reincarnation.

Because of what he was he became a loner, and outcast. He still retained certain powers that he no longer understood. He was as a freak, someone to be feared and suspicious of. He could talk to animals bend them to his will, in battle he had no equal, but he had no friends, no one to share his victories or pain. He was alone and haunted by dreams he did not comprehend.

One day he met someone who did not fear him, and shared with him his exploits and adventures. He now possessed a friend and confident that he could share with, and he grew to love him. His dreams began to take substance in his mind and for the first time in over two millennia he remembered who he was.

He strode forth to walk once again with those whom he had rejected, to touch and be touched with laughter and gratitude. Love now filled his heart, he accepted his fate, watching and waiting for the deliverance before it was too late. He had to fulfill his destiny, to reach the stars and hold once again the warmth of goodness, to dream the dreams of the gods and not of men.

On that day, he discovered what he was meant to do, but at the cost of his friend's life. The Prince lost him because his friend took his place in battle and so gave up the most precious of his possessions, his life. He wandered the world from that time until he came upon a female of the world of Man, the Prince found earthly love, this human emotion was like none he had ever known in the world he knew and began a new era for him.

In time, the woman became his wife, one that would become his soul mate, and he cherished her every single day, but she, being of the human kind, aged and grew sickly and in the end she was taken from him.

In his grief, he remembered who he was and why he existed. He cried out to the Lord, his king and asked, "Why did you take her, why could you not take me?"

The Lord's voice answered, "Your penance is not done and your work is not finished. You must learn from the pain you now feel in your heart, a real sense of loss before you may come to the path to forgiveness."

With a heart that was now broken and feeling that his soul was empty, he begins the search for forgiveness. He must find those of his kind and return them to the path of light and glory. He now knows his penance is to find the Children of Danu and return them to their conciseness and destinies.

Again he cried out to his kinsman. "When I have done this Lord, may I come home for I have suffered greatly?"

The Lord spoke to him, "When your time, there is done, you will once again sit at my table and take your place among your brethren. It was love that brought you back, and it will be love that will set you free, but only tears can cleanse your soul."

"When will I know," asked the prince?

The Lord and King of Kings replied. "When love suffers you to cry for all the innocents, and you sacrifice your immortality, then shall I set you free to commence the journey and return?"

Prolog

I was making my first trip back to Ireland since leaving there as a boy to immigrate to America. My business in Belfast researching old Celtic myths would keep me in Ireland a while before returning home. I must know if my friend, who helped me redirect my life and the destinies of so many others, is the last descendant of a mythical and ancient tribe. They landed on the island over two thousand years ago from Spain and conquered Ireland, also known as the second invasion. I have to know if these legends are based, in fact, so I can then begin to explain to myself the events of the last twenty five years.

Upon leaving the hotel in London, I hail a cab and head for Kings Cross Station for the train that will take me to Edinburgh. The cabby drops me off at the platform nearest a waiting train. Hearing a loud speaker call for all aboard to Edinburgh; I head toward the platform indicating my train. Before stepping aboard the car nearest me, I ask the conductor where my cabin is located. He looks at my ticket and says, "Cabin number twenty two sir, it's ahead two cars." Thanking him, I proceed to the car he's indicated.

The stewards are passing by the cabins calling out that dinner will be served in the main dining car. Brought back from my revelry of the past I realize that I was a little hungry and proceed there straight away. Passing through a few cars I notice there aren't many passengers taking advantage of the opportunity to alleviate their hunger pains, with many deciding to catch some sleep instead. Upon arriving at a car that serves as a dining car, I'm shown to a booth and given a menu. The selection through small provides a nice selection of five entrees, selecting the lamb chops I ask the steward for a glass of water.

"Father, excuse me would you care for some company for dinner." Says a young man accompanied by a beautiful woman.

"By all means please sit down I detest eating alone." I soon learn that their names are Shawn and Tara, and they're on a return to Ireland from their honeymoon. Shawn asks about my itinerary.

"I'm taking the ferry from Stranraer to Ireland then on to Belfast by train."

Shawn says, "That's wonderful we shall enjoy each other's company as we are going the same way."

We talk through dinner and finally after tea, Shawn suggests we retire to the Club Car and enjoy a few drinks, as we have some hours before reaching Edinburgh.

That's seemed to be a marvelous idea, as I did not desire to spend the next few hours peering out a window. They were such a charming young couple, so I agree.

I observe upon entering the Club Car that there's a middle age sonorous gentleman, a policeman, a middle age woman and a well dressed man in his early forties; sitting around imbibing some drinks engaged in conversation.

Stepping up to the bar I order water with a twist and some wine for my two dinner companions. We sit down and listen to our other fellow traveler's conversations.

"These trips are utterly boring lately with so many taking the air shuttle," expresses the rotund man.

The middle aged woman chimes in. "I just don't feel safe in one of those air planes. I rather enjoy the train, its old fashioned and a traditional way to enjoy one's travel. Don't you think Mr. Ives?" She refers to the well dressed gentleman.

"Well Mrs. Marklund, I take the train because me company does not pay for travel and the coach is more economical. I do wish they would put in some of those new movie machines, as I do agree with Mr. Montague that it can be a wee bit boring." The man called Ives complains to her.

Mrs. Marklund turns toward us smiling. "Hello there, Vicar you must be excusing us, please allow me to introduce our fellow traveling companions. My name is Mrs. Marklund and that stern looking gentleman in uniform is Officer Mac Swain, the Line's answer to security with so much terrorism." Mac Swain gets up and tips his hat toward us. Mr. Ives and Mr. Montague each stand as she introduces them to us as well.

"May I present Mr. Shawn Ryan and his bride Tara; they're on their way home to Ireland. My name is Tom Scanlon, tis a pleasure to make your acquaintance, I'm sure." After shaking hands, we're invited to join with them. Thanking her, we find seats.

Mrs. Marklund is quick to point out that they all have traveled together for some time, commuting from London to Edinburgh on business.

I explain that I've been in America for the past sixty years, and am returning to Dublin for the first time since leaving as a small babe.

"We've all traveled so long together we've run out of interesting stories to alleviate the monotony. Perhaps you might share one with us of America." Mr. Ives asks me.

"Well if it's a tale you'd be wanting, have you never heard of the Celtic Angel? They all say no, but Mr. Montague says if it's a religious one he'd not be interested.

"No it's not a religious story, but one from an old Celtic legend played out in modern times. It's about people who come together to form a family, that learns friendship, loyalty, love, sacrifice and faith. They also face tragedy, greed and murder, it's not necessarily about the Almighty, but how their lives are impacted one upon the other. Sit yourselves down and make your selves comfortable, for it may take while if you care to listen." They all want to hear my tale even Mr. Montague.

"I will have to start me story in the middle and then must go to the past, before I may proceed to the present. I'll mind you that this is a true story, although some among you may not believe.

The story takes place in Florida in the US of A. It's a place of almost endless sunshine, tourism, and wealth and the International Horse Show."

Mr. Mac Swain asks "Is Florida not where the Yanks have Disney World?"

"Yes it tis, but this story is about a place in and around the Palm Beaches, where the fabled wealthy from around the world gather." I can't help noticing now, all my listeners have inched up a little further forward with anticipation, as I begin my tale.

chapter 1

"The Job Interview"

Frank Collins, Desk Editor of Pro Horseman's Magazine is sitting at his office when the intercom screams, "Collins, come to my office!" He looks at the lighted switch blinking and sees that it's Old Man Ellsworth. Punching the answer button he answers, "I'll be right up sir." Collins picks up his assignment book and hurries down the hall toward the elevator to the Publisher's office on the double.

Entering the elevator for the short ride upstairs he wonders what's got Ellsworth the Publisher, so heated up this morning. Walking briskly he enters the publisher's executive suite and greets him. "Yes sir, Good morning, how was your weekend?"

."Good thank you, have a seat Frank." Ellsworth's answers briskly and gestures toward the conference table at the rear of the office. Ellsworth is a large man standing almost six feet four and weighing around two hundred and sixty pounds with salt and pepper hair, he doesn't look near his sixty six years.

Ellsworth is standing looking out the penthouse suite's windows that over look Palm Beach while he waits for Collins to take his seat. Turning toward Collins he asks, "Frank, what have we got on this Rancho de Los Angeles business?"

"Well sir not much, I've sent over three staff writers to try to interview this Doyle guy, but we can't get past the front gate. Research has turned up nothing on him except, he seems to be independently wealthy with some very good connections, both locally and nationally. He has a license to board and train horses, they also picked up some rumors that he has some kind of special ability to work with unmanageable animals. We're still working on that angle, but nothing specific. We've dug up something else; he was given a Rehab license about a year ago." Frank knows how the old man likes concise reports, so he leaves nothing out, something that the old man carried over from his old newspaper days.

"What are you telling me, he's turning that place into some kind of drug and alcoholic half way house? No wonder my phone's been ringing off the hook. That's all my wife and her society crowd will have to hear. Listen Frank, find out what's going on out there, and if it is one of those camps for no-hopers than let's see if we can apply some pressure to get him to move it somewhere else. Melody and some of her snobbish friends will drive me nuts if we don't, she thinks the power of the press can do anything. Keep me on top of this will you, I don't want to be the last to know, or hear it from one of her parasitic friends, ok." The look on Ellsworth's face tells Collins how serious the old man is.

"Yes sir, Mr. Ellsworth, I'll get right on it and see what my friend at PBSO can dig up for me, he owes us some favors for the concert tickets you got for him last month." Frank tries to reassure him, He realizes the meeting is over and gets up to leave when Ellsworth's phone rings.

"Yes, I'll take the call," Ellsworth tells his secretary, and motions Frank to stay.

"Hello Honey what's up?"......Yes in fact, we were going over the whole issue just now...Frank is taking care of it right now...He was just leaving... Of course we're giving it a priority...... No honey it won't be necessary for you to call her... Just as soon as I can find out anything you will know honey... Well it seems the man is quite wealthy, and has some very influential friends, so we must proceed carefully, but if he's doing what you heard... Of course we have to put a stop to it... Rest assured Darling, I'm aware of where we live…Yes…. Goodbye, see you tonight"…

"You see what I'm putting up with; they're fixating on this. Run this stat you hear me, she's driving me nuts." He's almost pleading with Collins to help get her off his back.

Upon leaving Ellsworth's office, Collins goes to the coffee shop for a cup of java and Danish then walks to his office. He can't help thinking how the old man dotes on his wife who happens to be twenty five years younger than him. He thanks God Ellsworth is married to her and not him. That still leaves a huge problem, how to find out what's going on, and does it fit into the format of an equestrian upscale photo magazine. The whole thing seems to be a newspaper story or at least one for the supermarket rag tabloids. Ellsworth still thinks he's the editor and chief of one of his wife's family papers like the Herald, even if they get the scoop. How does it fit with the National Horse Show story? Collins knows it's not for him to reason why, just get it done then it's up to The Old Man, he's the publisher.

"Good morning Mr. Collins," his receptionist greets him respectfully. "Your ten o'clock appointment is here, will you see her now? She's been waiting for forty minutes, I told her you were in a conference upstairs with Mr. Ellsworth." Agnes hands him the applicant's folder, and frowns at her boss. Collins thinks to himself, that she really could use a boyfriend to mellow her out.

"Give me a minute to look over her resume, and application, and then send her in."

Opening the folder and reading over a well written and concise resume, he notices she has some great qualities that the Magazine is looking for as far as background, and the application looks to be good as well. He hits the intercom and tells Agnes to send her in.

There's a knock on his door. "Come in." Collins answers and looks up as an attractive woman enters his office, and walks over to him and sticks out her hand.

"Hello Mr. Collins, I'm Deanna Gaynor it's a pleasure to meet you. I would like to thank you for giving me this opportunity to interview with the Magazine." Taking her hand, Collins is impressed immediately with her and invites her to sit down.

"Ms. Gaynor your resume says that you were a junior and colligate equestrian and you also attended Sweet Briar College in Virginia. I see you wrote for the college newspaper and year book, but you've not worked in the last twelve years, why don't you bring me up to speed with that?" Collins sits back in his overstuffed chair and waits for her response.

"The short version is I got married, my first husband was killed in the Gulf War, and I had a young son to care for. A few years later I remarried a local attorney and gave birth to a daughter; I moved here to Florida and got divorced. I run a boarding barn, and I am trying to stay current with the mortgage on my horse farm. Right now I need a full time position, or I might lose it.

I can be a wonderful asset to this organization. I'm dedicated and focused; I know many of the equestrians in the area and those that travel here from the Virginia and the New York training barns. I grew up with many top horse people in the country, plus my father had a great rapport in the Hunter Jumper and Fox Hunting circles. All I'm asking for is a chance to prove to you that I can do the job." Deanna's states with confidence, but she has butterflies in her stomach waiting for Collins to speak.

Collins knits his eye brows together thinking about his conversation with Ellsworth this morning, when suddenly an idea comes to him. He looks over her resume one more time, and he thinks that she could be just what they're looking for.

"Ms. Gaynor I think we may have something that you may be able to accomplish for us, and if you do, I will assure you of a permanent position with this Magazine. Would that be of any consideration for you?" He asks, hoping she says yes.

Leaning forward in her chair Deanna replies with enthusiasm without even asking what it is, "Yes Mr. Collins that would be great, if you think I'm really qualified to handle it, I won't let you down."

He reaches over to the corner of his desk and picks up the folder that he had placed there when he returned from Ellsworth's office. "Here is all we have on a piece we're trying to do on a place called Rancho de Los Angeles, it's located on the edge of the green belt, just west of the show grounds. As you know they have been fighting the development of that area for years trying to keep it for the National Horse Show people. Three years ago a man by the name of James Doyle purchased a three hundred and fifty acre estate there. No one thought too much about it at the time, but now with the rezoning it may well be the most important land acquisition in this entire county. It will hold up the promoter's of the equestrian development of over two thousand acres west of that ranch.

We do know that the owner is equitably well off with connections to influential people, one of whom you may be acquainted with, Edward Haskell is his name. I believe he hails from your old area of Virginia, and sat on the board of your college. This Doyle fellow has an Animal Care and Control license for a boarding and training facility as well as a State license to operate a Rehab facility. Ms. Gaynor I cannot stress to you how important this story is to the owner and publisher of this Magazine except, that should you get this story you might be able to write your own ticket with this organization." He sits back awaiting her response as she reads the sketchy material that he just handed her.

"Mr. Collins you've got a deal, I'll get on this right away. May I have use of the Magazine's resources for research? Oh, when is the dead line on this?"

"You will have everything we can give you; Mr. Ellsworth would like to have this before the Christmas Holiday Issue, which means about a month." He shakes her hand and welcomes her aboard. With that done, he buzzes Agnes.

"Yes Mr. Collins," Agnes professionally answers. He asks her to come in. He tells her to show Deanna to her desk and to get the necessary paper work and ID Badge, also to introduce her around the office.

"Oh Agnes, assign Tim as her photographer, I want color on this as well." Collins wishes Deanna well and tells her to keep him up to date on the progress daily.

Deanna leaves Collins's office and Agnes is waiting for her, " Ms. Gaynor, please come with me." Deanna follows her down the hall to a series of offices until they come to one that says staff writers on it. Opening the door Agnes herds Deanna over to what looks to be an empty desk with a computer and phone on it.

"This will be yours to use, any work that you do on it must be backed up, and then saved on a rewritable disk they're in the drawer. Here are forms that you will have to fill out and return to me. I shall forward them on to Human Resources. Please select a password for this computer, and I'll get you in, please don't give it to anyone and don't forget it," Agnes says. Deanna thinks that she is the perfect assistant as Agnes turns and exits out of the office.

Having now gotten her first assignment, she sits down to see where to begin. Reading the report that Collin's has given her, Deanna notice's the name he mentioned, Ed Haskell it's next to the handwritten scrawl of principle. Wondering did that mean a principle in the Rancho or principle in this story. She decides to contact him and feel her way, hoping it would turn out to be the Haskell who married her mother's oldest childhood and college friend, Moina McCann back in Virginia.

Her Mother and Moina worked in the Capital together after college, Moina married her boss. He was a Senator or something if she remembers correctly, that was before Mom married Deanna's Dad.

Dialing the number next to Haskell's name, she can't help having butterflies and feel her palms sweating.

"Hello, Haskell here," the voice on the other end of the phone replies then waits for her response.

"Hello Mr. Haskell, my name is Deanna Quinn; I'm calling from Pro Horseman's Magazine. The reason for my call is, I was told you're a principal owner in Rancho de Los Angeles. I'd like to stop by an interview you for the Magazine, sometime soon." Deanna asks him in her most professional manner.

"Well Ms. Quinn, you're mistaken, I'm not a principle in that operation at all, I do know and am acquainted with the owner James Doyle. Any interviews would have to be given by him," he states firmly.

Deanna has to think of something quickly, and she tells him, "I'm so sorry I was apparently misinformed." Before he can answer her, she asks him was he the same Edward Haskell that sat on the board of Sweetbriar College from the Haskell family in Virginia.

"Yes, as a matter of fact, I did sit on the board for a number of years with that institution."

"Well isn't that a coincidence I graduated from their nineteen years ago, I was from Lynchburg," Deanna tries to sound rather excited and surprised.

"Lynchburg, was your father by any chance Robert Quinn the Fox Hunter from Red Fox Farm?"

"Yes sir, that was my Dad," There's a pause on his end of the phone, and she hopes she hasn't queered the chance.

After the momentary pause, he apologizes to her. "I'm sorry I had a senior moment, how is he and your Mother? I knew them well, years ago in my younger days and my daughter was riding. He was my Mary's riding instructor and my friend." Deanna notes a touch of sadness in his voice.

Well, it was wonderful talking with you. I'm sorry about the misunderstanding; I just started with the Magazine and was hoping to do my first interview."

"Well hold on, maybe I can help you after all, I knew your people, and us Virginian's have to stick together you know. Jot down this number, its Jamie's cell number. I can't guarantee that you will get an interview, but tell him who gave you the number, and maybe he will. He's a very private person and protective of what he is doing.

Call me and we'll have lunch sometime, we can talk over some of the old times. Deanna you had beautiful red hair if I remember correctly, is it still like a sunset." Deanna hears him chuckle.

"Yes sir it is, and I would like to get together sometime very soon and discuss old times. I will tell Mother when I talk to her that we spoke and tell her you said, "Hello, if that's alright?"

"Absolutely Deanna, lot's of luck with the story, look forward to seeing you… Goodbye."

How lucky is this, she now has a way of meeting the mysterious James Doyle?

Chapter 2

Roberto Fills In Some Missing Gaps

Reading over Doyle's bio sheet Deanna's getting a feel for this assignment, along with what Collins had told her about the geographic aspect, Doyle could wind up with the richest piece of property in the country. The property is located in the remote southwestern section of Wellington almost next to Southwest Properties; they're the developers of Horse Show Acres. That's the proposed mini equestrian estates consisting of ten or more acres in the green zone of the county. If he's successful he could block that advancement plus development west of the Village. That alone would get some people upset not to mention if he were to move in undesirables like drunks or addicts, he could wind being the most hated man in all of Palm Beach County.

She decides to call him tomorrow, but first she must try to find out more about him. The report says he's not been very social in the right circles nor does he have political affiliations, and he doesn't play golf. He supposedly trains horses and raises pure blood cattle, but it offers nothing about how he's earned his substantial wealth.

Deanna's has a friend who is high up with the equestrian elite, she wonders if Roberto would know anything about him. Maybe Roberto can shed some light or is at least acquainted with other people that might know him. Dialing him, she listens to it ring; jotting down some more notes on some of the questions she wishes to ask, if Doyle grants her an interview.

"Ola Roberto here, who is speaking please," she hears him ask.

"Roberto, its Deanna Gaynor, do you have a moment... Yes, I'm excellent, how are you? It has been a long time, How is the family?____ Wonderful, yes Katy is taking lessons, but I'm afraid still not doing well.____ Jonah is doing wonderful thank God; he will be a graduate this year and is looking toward Notre Dame or Harvard.____ The reason for my call is, I've been hired by Pro Horseman's Magazine, and I've been given a tough assignment. Would you know anything about James Doyle or Rancho de Los Angeles?____ You do, oh that's great, can you meet me this afternoon?____ Where?____Ok, Bit Bits and Saddles, yes I know the place.____ One o'clock, perfect, I'll see you there.____Bye, bye." Deanna knew she could count on him, then knows everyone from owners to grooms if it has to do with horses in this area.

"Ms. Gaynor, Tim would like to know when you would need him for photos," Agnes announces standing once more in the doorway to the office.

"Not until at least Wednesday, I haven't gotten the interview set up yet, but I'm hopeful, just got some great leads that may work out. Please tell Mr. Collins that I'm off to meet someone who may shed some more light on our mysterious Mr. Doyle." She tells Agnes as she grabs her bag and rushes past her to meet Roberto.

Driving over to meet with Roberto, Deanne feels like she did in college, exciting challenges, and new adventures, confident in her own abilities again. Steve was such a depressant, she could never do anything right, and now he is doing it to her daughter Katy too. Suddenly, she remembers Katy's appointment with Dr. Winmien, Is it three thirty or four? She must remember to call after meeting with Roberto.

Pulling into the restaurant's parking lot, she see's Roberto standing out front waiting.

"Hey, how you doing I just got here," Deanna calls to him.

"Buenos Diaz my friend, let us go in and get something to drink and have some of their fine food." Roberto says with a warm smile. He kisses her hand with that old world Spanish style. He is a consummate gentleman always, and of course a ladies man.

Roberto takes her arm and together they enter the restaurant. The hostess greets them both and guides them to a quiet table overlooking a small man made lake. Roberto holds her chair and then takes his seat across from her smiling.

"Now tell me all about this wonderful opportunity you have, to work for Pro Horseman. This seems like a great thing for you, no?"

"It's wonderful, but I have to prove to them that I can write a good article that's why I called you. I have been given the assignment to do a story on Rancho De Los Angeles and James Doyle in particular. No one seems to know much about him and if anyone would, I thought it might be you."

"You are right Senora, he is a very private man, no one knows much of him at all, but I have heard things from some of my people that might help you. He mostly has Hispanics working for him, and they think he is like a saint; he also sponsors a small Mission out in Loxahatchee run by an old padre. You know free medical for the woman and children, teaching English and providing some housing and finding work for them. He is much thought of by these people. He hosts parties for the little ones and brings them gifts. He is their patron and protector; he sometimes even drives the bus when the old padre is sick. To these people, he is a hero against those that would exploit them, but they will not talk to you because you are an Anglo," Roberto further explains.

"Roberto I have heard that he is a trainer of horses as well, horses that are very difficult." Hoping he can give her some information other than what she already has from the magazine.

"I have not seen any of the horses he has trained, but the Argentines say that he talks to the horses, and they talk to him. I will make some inquiries around with some of the caballeros[1] and see if I can find out

---

1 Means Gentleman or cowboy

something more for you. I must tell you, they are not very talkative when it comes to him Senora."

"Please Roberto, anything that's true will help me with the article I am doing. I am going to call him today to try and set up an interview. So far, no one from the magazine has been successful. Wish me luck, it's getting late, and I have to take Katy somewhere. As always, my friend it has been wonderful, we must get together more often." Deanna apologizes to him as she rises to get up.

"Si, that is true, if only you would have the eyes for me, I would be a happy man," he smiles and laughs.

She waves goodbye and hurries to her truck, looking at the clock and realizes that she has only minutes to get to the school and get Katy. Pulling up on the side of the school she see's her walking slowly toward the truck her head hanging down in one of her moods again she supposes.

"Hi, sorry to be late, I got a new job today and was doing an interview. I was hired by Pro Horseman as a writer, and they gave me my first assignment, isn't that great." Deanna tries to involve Katy into some dialog with her.

"Yea Mom that's wonderful does that mean, we are all going to be happy again, or we just see less of you." She answers sarcastically.

"No, it means maybe I can keep the farm and try to help you be happy again," she answers her, trying to keep from losing her temper.

"No, it just means that Daddy is going to be asking me more questions and giving me bullshit about how you married him for his money and all you cared about is the farm. I'm so sick of all this. I may go live with him, so I don't have to hear how you favor only Jonah, and I'm your mistake."

Deanna tries to hold her anger in, but she's sure it shows in her face. How can she explain to her that her father's anger was in getting caught cheating and the divorce was his fault? It was his ego that was hurt because he didn't win; he's trying to turn her against her and screwing her up emotionally as well. She doesn't realize that having to go to the psychiatrist is a court ordered requirement now because of him. Deanna feels her pain and she doesn't know how to reach her,

They are almost at the Doctor's office. "Do you want me to go up with you?" Deanna hopes that Katy will say yes just once.

"No, I hate when you do that I'm not a baby just leave me alone," she opens the door then slams it and stomps up the stairs.

She has been seeing this guy for six months and is getting worse and still no answers from him, but Deanna had no choice as Steve received a court order and the judge picked this quack. Deanna wishes she could have her doctor look at her, but she knows Katy wouldn't stand for that.

Deanna has forty minutes to kill; she might as well call this Doyle person and see if he will see her. Dialing the number, it rings six times without any response or answering machine picking up. She is about to hang up when a man's voice answers.

"Hello Jamie here, how can I help you?"

"Hello Mr. Doyle, My name is Deanna Quinn," using her maiden name just in case Haskell mentioned her to him.

"Mr. Haskell gave me your cell phone number; I hope I have not caught you at a bad time. I work for Pro Magazine, and we would like to have an interview with you about Rancho de Los Angeles," Deanna holds her breath waiting for him to respond.

"Oh yes, Ed called me and mentioned you, I would be happy to speak with you, but for the life of me, I can't imagine why we would be of interest to such a celebrated magazine as yours. How about tomorrow say around one, we can chat over a light lunch? Do you know how to get out here or do you need directions?"

"No I don't; in fact, you are only about a mile from my farm in Loxahatchee." She answers him.

"Wonderful that makes us neighbors, just pull up to the gate and tell who ever answer's the intercom who you are. They'll know you're there to see me and buzz you in. Just follow the main drive to the house; I'll see you out front. Look forward to meeting you Ms. Quinn; goodbye." Deanna never even got a chance to say thank you, he seems very direct, and she does have the interview.

Deanna's next call is to Collins, to let him know that she has the appointment tomorrow and sees if research has turned up anything on the mysterious Mr. Doyle.

Agnes picks up the phone and tells her to wait one minute while she patches through to Collins.

"Hey green pea what's new? Have you gotten anywhere with the interview yet?" He says with a hint of hope.

"As a matter of fact, I have, tomorrow at one o'clock I will be having lunch at the ranch with Doyle. I was wondering if research as had any luck digging up something for me to study before I go there." She asks him.

"Tomorrow," he stutters, "give me until the morning to come up with something, even if I have to keep them working all night long. You've done a great job; I mean that Gaynor, I knew I was right about you. I'll talk to you in the morning or possibly tonight, talk to you later, unbelievable job Gaynor, incredible job," he repeats to her and hangs up.

Feeling competent about herself gets Deanna out of her mood that Katy put her in, so good, in fact, she starts to think about what they could have for dinner to celebrate the new job and landing her first journalistic interview. Deanna knows her son Jonah will be happy for her at least. She'll call and order Chinese, and they all enjoy that.

Deanna thanks God Katy is her only worry right now; and of course how to pay for Jonah's college next year. He feels confident that he'll win a scholarship for Honors. He's still toying with the idea of going to a college, where can he complete in the National College Rodeo. She knows he's pretty good, but she doesn't want him to throw away a chance at becoming a lawyer either.

Katy is coming down the walk now, and by her walk, she does not seem to be in a more pleasant mood than when they arrived "Hi Honey, how did it go, feeling better?"

"No, he is such a dick!"

"Katy, you know I don't like that kind of talk." Deanna says to her sharply.

"Yeah, I'm sorry, but I talk, he writes and just smiles with that stupid smile of his and then asks me more questions, and he never has any answers. I hate him; I don't see why I have to go to see him at all." She sounds depressed.

"Look Katy, I understand I really do, but when you took all those pills you took it out of our hands. Try to work with the doctor, and then we can get you out of therapy and work on us being a family again."

"Are you and Dad going to get back together, because that was when we were a **family**? Now we are all boarders living under the same roof and not talking, or we're fighting. You know there are times when I hate you for throwing my father out and ruining my life." Anger fills her words. Deanna has no answer, so she drives in silence; she'll order the food when they get home; the least said now the better.

They pull into the driveway, and she jumps out of the truck crying again, heading to go talk to her horse. Deanna is at her wits end as to what to do with her anymore.

"Hi Mom, how was your day." Jonah calls, that would be Deanna's son by her first marriage.

"It was great; I'll tell you after I order some Chinese food. We can sit down, and you can tell me how your day was, then I will fill you in on mine."

Watching Katy walk away, Deanna feels not quite as elated as she was before Katy came down from the doctor's office. Deanna's shoulder's slump as she walks in with Jonah, thinking how different they are. He's upbeat, happy and helpful while she is morose and unhappy most of the time. She thinks Katy feels responsible for the divorce.

Steve is her father and not Jonah's. She was too young to tell the truth, unlike Jonah. If Deanna told her the truth now she wouldn't believe her. She was always so close to her father, she prays to God, that he stops using Katy to get back at her, and she starts to get well.

"Well Mom what happen with the job interview, did you get it?" He asks her with hopefulness in his voice.

She looks up and smiles, "Yes, I did, and they gave me a very difficult assignment. My boss gave me a really tough one, trying to get an interview with a reclusive man at a new ranch just outside of the Village.

"Wow that's great, what are you going to be writing a story about, the ranch or the man?" Jonah sits down across the table and smiles up at her.

"No one from the magazine has been successful in getting an interview, guess what…I got one today and I have to be there tomorrow and have lunch with the owner. By the way, if the phone rings tonight it might be my work calling with some research stuff I asked for. Make sure you tell Katy in case I forget.

Why don't you call in an order of Chinese food, Katy always gets the same, and I will have spare ribs with pork fried rice? I'm going to change and feed the horses and put up some hay.

"OK Mom I'll call than come and help," Jonah calls after her as she heads up the stairs. "I love you Mom."

"Love you too; there are days when I don't know if I would make it without you." She blows him a kiss and goes up stairs to get into her ranch clothes.

Chapter 3

"In Search Of The Truth"

It's nine o'clock and Deanna is drinking her coffee when the phone rings, she flips the intercom button. "Hello Deanna here," she answers casually.

"Hello Deanna, This is Collins, I have some more stuff that our people dug up at the Hall of Records, but not much more than what we gave you the other day I'm afraid. When you talk to this guy, try to get some background on him and the real purpose of that ranch. His rehab certificate is for children in crisis, so at least it's not a bunch of drunks moving into the Village. Get back to me after your meeting with him. Oh by the way, do you want Tim to meet you out there as well?"

"No, let me talk to Doyle and make sure a photographer will be alright, and then we can set up a longer interview time and photo session later. It might scare him off if I show up with a cameraman at the first meeting. If he says "no" there won't be much of a story anyway."

"Alright you got the interview so go with it, but if it blows up Ellsworth is going to have a conniption fit and you and I might be looking for gainful employment, so keep that in mind. I'll send over by fax the stuff I have, what's the number?"

Deanna gives Collins the fax number, and he hangs up. Waiting for the fax, Deanna begins to wonder what to wear. She decides on a simple shirt top and jeans with paddock boots, after all she's going to a ranch and told him she owned a farm also.

After lunch, she'll ask him to show her around the place. Deanna wonders how old he is, his voice sounded not young, but definitely not as old as Haskell's. The limited bio she has of him does not indicate if he is married or single, maybe there is a Mrs. Doyle somewhere. The fax may illuminate something new on him and the purpose of the ranch.

Deanna goes downstairs and looks over the fax, just two pages not much in there mostly tax records and permits. Here's something interesting he's sponsored three Mexican Nationals for work visas and two Argentineans. She wonders why, unless he has some Spanish heritage he would bother to help get visas for South Americans with so many Hispanics looking for work in the county. Is there a connection, maybe something else for her to note down for the interview?

Deanna looks up in her Spanish Dictionary, to find out exactly what the name of his ranch means, she puts each word together and finds that in English it translates to mean "Ranch of the Angels." A strange name for a piece of property Deanna muses. More questions for her to ask him, she has to start writing these things down so she'll remember to ask about them.

Continuing to work for two additional hours on the topics that she wants to pursue today, Deanna must keep in mind that she wants a more in depth interview after working out an outline for the piece. She must remember to try keeping the more pointed ones for this one and save the others for possibly afterward in the week if he agrees to let her do the story.

It's almost twelve thirty, she checks herself in the mirror and thinks she'll get high marks, makeup is neat not too much, shirt is perky and the jeans look pretty good. The hair is her only concern; she thinks it will look good in a pony tail…… Yup, the country look, that looks much better she decides. Heading for her car she hesitates, thinking the truck would be better, more down to earth. Putting the tape recorder and notes in the truck, she takes inventory once more before starting out.

Arriving at the entrance to the access road to the ranch, she stops by the intercom and announces herself and the gate swings open. Coming to a Bougainvillea covered entrance gate she pulls the truck through and parks. Deanna sees a tall man standing in front of a Spanish style hacienda home. She notices his physical characteristics right away; he has blondish hair and broad shoulders that taper down to a narrow work hardened waist. He's wearing jeans and a shirt with pearl button down pockets and boots with run down heals. Deanna takes him for one of the cowboys who work at the ranch.

He walks up and opens the truck door, a smile on his face and the deepest blue eyes she's ever seen, warm and piercing. His age she would put somewhere in the mid forties, his looks are rugged but very handsome.

"Ms. Quinn, I'm Jamie Doyle, it's a pleasure to welcome you to my home, won't you, please come in." His voice, it's different than the other day on the phone it falls gently on her ear.

Deanna is taken off guard, she was expecting him to look quite different, and taking her by the arm Jamie escorts Deanna into the hacienda. The front entrances are double dark oak and hand carved, the foyer is cool and lightly lit with several areas extending from it.

"I asked Rosa to serve us lunch on the rear patio if you don't mind. The view of the lake is very tranquil, and the western breeze today is delightful, but we can also eat in the dining area under air if you prefer." He has an easy and comfortable manner. Deanna is impressed with his style.

"Wherever you would be more comfortable is fine with me Mr. Doyle." Deanna says to him in her most courteous manner. She can't help but admire the interior decorating as they proceed to the patio; it's Southwestern and very Spanish, with pictures of people Deanna assumes are his family.

"I was not sure as to what you might prefer so I left it up to Rosa; she felt you would like something light, and easy. I've found Rosa is usually right, so I never contradict her judgment." Deanna wonders who Rosa is, his wife perhaps.

Pulling out a chair and holding it for her, Deanna can't help but notice that his mannerisms are different than any man she's ever met, except for Roberto. Almost nineteenth century, his every movement is natural and his touch puts her at ease immediately.

"May I suggest a glass of wine if that would be alright, some fine Pinot Grigio perhaps? If not, I have many other excellent wines if you prefer."

"That would be wonderful; it will go marvelously with this setting. It's so gorgeous here and your home is beautiful. Who did your decorating; I have never seen anything like it?" She remarks, trying to make small conversation.

"Actually Rosa and Dyon are the masterminds of all this. I would have something more like a tack room if it were left to me" His smile reflects a sense of humor but with a lot of honesty. She decides to be very careful with this man, she likes him already and the magazine expects her stay objective.

"Ed told me that he knew you as a young girl and your family back in Virginia. Are they there now?"

"My mother is, my Dad and first husband passed away some years ago. I settled here with my second husband after we were married." A look crosses his face, than it's gone.

"Oh, you're married that must be a very full life? Running a farm and working for the magazine, plus taking care of a home must keep you very busy, do you have any children?"

She suddenly senses he is interviewing her instead of the other way around. Deanna realizes that if he's put on the defensive, than she may not get the interview the magazine was hoping for. So she answers his questions.

"It is, but I must confess something Mr. Doyle, My name is Gaynor, and I'm divorced. I allowed Mr. Haskell to assume that I still went by the name of Quinn in the hope that he would help me get this interview with you. It's very hard raising two children, a boy and a girl, running the farm and trying to work.

He stares at her for what seems like a long time, his hands clasped together under his chin. He's looking at her with those piercing eyes, as though he were looking deep into her. Deanna wonders if she has just shot herself in the foot.

"First, please call me Jamie as we will be working very closely on what I can assure you, will be an incredible story. Over the next couple of weeks, you will learn about this ranch, and me, and what we hope to accomplish here. It's one that can't be told nor seen in only a few days' times. Secondly, I promised Ed that I would help you, and he has been a devoted friend for a very long time.

Ah, I see that Rosa is bringing the wine and some lunch. Rosa this is Senora Deanna, I would appreciate if you and the vaqueros would answer any questions she may have, as I have decided to be interviewed for her magazine.

Deanna please allow me to introduce the woman who runs Rancho de Los Angeles"

"I am very pleased to meet you Senora, the Patron is very much like an errant child and needs a Mamacita[2]." She looks at him and scowls. Rosa is young, I would have thought the way he spoke of her that she would be much older. The lunch consists of a delicious looking salad some cheese and flat bread that look like a pita and a bowl of salsa.

"I hope you will like your lunch Senora Deanna, I thought if you were to take a tour of the Rancho with the Patron it might be better if you had nothing heavy sometimes he forgets that we are not all like him"

Jamie looks up and smiles affectionately and says "Thank You Mama" and he chuckles.

The lunch and the conversation are light and wonderful. She feels that they are connecting and coming to know each other better. Waiting

---

[2] mother

for an opportunity to ask if he has any children, she observes a wedding band, but it's on the wrong hand.

"By the way, is Mrs. Doyle as involved in the ranch as you are?" He looks at her with that searching look again, not answering right away, just looking. Seeing a pained look upon his face and his eyes change, sadness comes over them for only a moment, then change back as Jamie answers.

"She would have been very much involved, but sadly she passed away about three years ago, this was very much a part of her dream. In a way it has become somewhat like a memorial to her. We had talked about doing this for quite a number of years. I had to put it off when she became so ill, it took me awhile to start to dream again. I guess it was Dyon that got me back on track. You'll like her; she is very honest also, like you."

"Dyon, is she your daughter?"

"No she's my ward and my student. One of the things we hope to do here is providing a place where children in crisis can belong, a place where they feel safe and can learn to cope with their problems.

Dyon was involved in a car thief and was a tough street kid; no family except a gangster brother heading for God knows what. She was the first child the State placed here a little over a year ago. Now she's an accomplished equestrian, honor student and quite a young woman who is going to rock this world of ours."

"Do you have any other children here?"

"We now have a total of four students here all girls. Having Rosa living at the ranch is kind of like a mother, it has been better to accept girls. Next year we hope to bring in some boys and try that, but for this year the state has placed three girls in addition to Dyon"

"Do they live here at the ranch or are they dropped off for therapy?"

"Yes, as a matter of fact they do. T.J. stays here five days a week and visits her mother most weekends, and she's ten. Tia and Marianna have their own rooms, unfortunately they have no visits and very little parental time and then only under proper supervision."

"Could you explain how your program works? How do you handle their treatment, are they each required to have their own therapist?" She asks that because of Katy's required treatment.

"No we use equine therapy and a healthy home environment, instead of doctors and questions. Eduardo, that's Rosa's husband, picks them all up from school and brings them home for their chores, homework and riding lessons. One of the things that we use, are horses and all these girls have one thing in common, they love horses. It calms them down being around the big animals. They all are given their own animal to take care of it gives them a sense of responsibility." Jamie explains.

"What kind of equestrian training are they doing?" Deanna moves the recorder over toward him. "Do you mind?"

"No, not at all," He replies.

"Today you can plug recorders into laptops, and they will print the conversation to the hard drive." She comments to him.

He nods his head, "They are training for Hunters and Jumpers; in fact, we hope to be ready for this month's Horse Show in Wellington." He beams and his eye's light with a fire and his smile is infectious even as he speaks of them.

"What kind of problems do these girls have, emotional or mental?"

Jamie stiffens before he answers, "Can we hold off on the problems for awhile until you meet them, I don't want to embarrass them with people getting the wrong idea. I am aware of the concern that many of the blue bloods are having and the rumors are flying faster than winter geese. That's why I said it was going to take you more than a few days to write this story, because I am using you to further their cause. Any of the motives that are in the back of your mind about me or the reason I bought this place will be made known to you. I hope that I will be able to prove to you that there is no fraud going on or schemes either, fair enough" he sits back and waits for her to respond.

"You are direct I'll give you that, You intrigue me Jamie, but I will promise this, I will hold nothing back, if I find something going on that's not right I will print it."

He smiles and asks if she would like to see the ranch and the girl's rooms.

"Yes I would, thank you." He surprises her with a natural ease of manners not seen too often in twentieth century American men, like getting up and pulling out her chair for her.

"We can begin at the barns if you like, we raise Corriente[3] cattle and train Hunter and Jumper horses here at the ranch. Mostly, the vaqueros take care of the cattle. I train the horses with some help from Dyon. She has a gentle hand with them and will make a fine trainer someday if that is what she wants to pursue." His comments again hold that sense of pride, when he talks about them.

"Corriente, aren't they the ones used in Bull Fighting?" She asks him not quite sure if she's correct.

"Yes, they are known for their courage, but here we use them for meat cattle, and they were bred to with stand high heat and the type of grass that grows in Florida, I prefer them to Argentine Brangus[4] because they have horns."

Walking into the barn with him, Deanna notices a gorgeous black horse with his head hanging out of a stall, he seems to be watching them and is starting to prance in his stall and toss his head.

"Ah, I see my problem child is not going to let us escape without some attention," Jamie indicates the black. He walks over to him and starts talking to him and rubbing his neck which the horse seems to enjoy immediately.

"This is Storm, he is a big baby even though is he's sixteen, if I don't give him some attention when he sees me, he'll kick the door down. I guess I've spoiled him."

"He looks to be gaited."

"Yes, he's a Tennessee Walker, one of the old type blood lines. They were big and powerful, and as you can see high spirited as well. Storm

---

3 Large Spanish cattle used primarily in Bull Fighting, know for their courage

4 Cross breed Angus to Braham for hot weather climates, big meat producers

and I have done some miles together. Being a gaited horse he has helped make doing those miles much smoother on me at the end of the day.

"Do you use him here at the ranch then? I didn't know they were a good cattle horse."

"No not that much, I have a very savvy Quarter Horse for working on the cattle, which I ride here. Storm is my choice for long distance endurance races that I still compete in," Jamie explains.

"You're what they called a Long Rider?"

"Haven't heard that expression in a long time, where did you learn that, not in Virginia I'll bet?"

"In fact, I did, it was from my Dad, and he used to compete in one hundred mile races before he passed away."

"I would have liked to have met him; he sounds like my kind of man."

"You amaze me more and more Jamie, I mean you are not your typical equestrian from Wellington. You almost seem to belong to another century, at least from another time and place." Jamie just gives her a strange kind of a look and walks over to the big black horse.

He pets his horse and smiles at her in a manner which indicates that she might be right. "Are modern men that boring or unusual to you, or is it maybe that you have not met too many men that think from both sides of their brain," again he chuckles and flashes a knowing smile.

She suddenly thinks to herself, he may be right she certainly has never met anyone like him before except maybe her father a little. Maybe that's what draws her to him in this inexplicable way. The easy way he moves, so comfortable in his own skin, confident about himself, and what he's about. There is something about the way he makes people feel around him that she can't quite put her finger on, a power he seems to possess. Watching him as he strolls past the stalls naming the other horses and seeing how they react to him. A love and respect one does not see all the time and she see's that it's returned.

Suddenly, she becomes very faint and dizzy; he catches her in his arms. "Deanna is something wrong, come sit over here in the shade for a while, are you feeling ok? Ruben, please bring us something cool to drink, por favor[5]." A young man nods and runs off to the hacienda. "

"It was just coming from the dark of the stable to the radiant daylight and the heat. It kind of threw me for a minute I'm fine really." She tries to reassure him that she is alright.

"You have some beautiful horses and they all seem to love you very much. I see that you devote much of your time to them." Deanna sees he is still very concerned about her. She reassures Jamie once again that she's fine and asks him to continue to tell her about the Rancho.

Jamie sits down next to her and answers her question. "I try very much to get into their heads during the training periods, it's a method that works well for me, and it calms them down so that I may help them overcome their fears. Here comes Rubin with those drinks now." As Rubin sets the drinks down on a small table under a huge fichus tree Jamie places his hand on Rubin's arm, pausing him.

"Rubin this is Senora Deanna, she is a guest at the Rancho, I would appreciate if you might show her around if I am not here, or while I'm giving the lessons to the girls. She is to have full access to any part of the Rancho, comprende[6]." Rubin nods his head and gives her a big smile and goes back to work on some tack that he was cleaning when they walked up.

"Rubin is one of my vaqueros, he can't speak, because of an accident of being thrown from a horse, but his good nature and winning smile speak volumes for him.

Hopefully, Eduardo and Esteban will be back before you have to leave, as I would love for you to meet them today. If not it is my wish that you will want to come back again soon. I know, why don't you to come for dinner sometime and please bring your children as well, Rosa loves to cook for quests, and you would also get a chance to see the girls in our everyday routines? They would feel more comfortable talking to you under those circumstances, I'm sure."

---

5 Thank you

6 comprehend

"I would love to come back, and yes I could bring my son and daughter if you really would like them to come." She tells him honestly. "May I ask you for a favor?"

"Of course if it's within my power"

"The next time I come, I would like to meet everyone and watch by myself, talking to the people here at the ranch without a tour, you know to just be a fly on the wall so to speak, I think it would be more objective about the story, if you wouldn't mind."

"Not at all, in fact, I will give you a pass card of your own so you may come anytime you wish. Would that work for you? You'll always be welcome; I know Rosa would love to have the company with another woman. If you are feeling OK now, maybe we could go down by the paddocks.

Let me introduce Dyon to you, I see she's coming down from the house to work with her gelding before lessons. I want you two to meet; she was my first student as I told you." He stands and holds her chair as she rises and offers her his arm. She looks to where he's indicated and sees a young woman walking toward them with long black hair down to the middle of her back wearing a pink polo and tan riding pants and black boots.

"Hola Jefe[7]", She calls out, a wide smile on her face. Deanna notices that she's strikingly beautiful with an aristocratic bearing, like a princess, with composure and a natural grace similar to Jamie's. There's music in her voice and her eyes are dark and sparkling.

She runs to him and gives him a big hug. Deanna can see she did this on purpose as he blushes and says to her, "Dyon, I want you to meet Deanna Gaynor, she's writing a story about the Rancho and us, so please don't give her the wrong idea and behave yourself."

"I am very pleased to meet you, I don't really know why I did that, please forgive me." Dyon says with a smile on her face and a saucy look in her eye.

"Dyon are you going to work D.C. before lessons?" Jamie asks her.

---

7 Hello boss

"Yes Jefe[8], he's in the west paddock. Wait until you see what he will do for me now." She runs off toward D.C.'s paddock

"She normally does not give me hugs like that it must have been for your benefit, but I don't know why she would do that." Jamie attempts to explain her behavior.

"Because she's becoming a woman, and she loves you." She somehow feels obligated to explain that to him.

"She is just a kid and like my own daughter." He says naively.

"Even Daughters become jealous of losing your attention when another woman enters the picture. Especially if they love you, and she does, you can see it in her eyes." She observes him to see his reaction

"Thank you for bringing that to my attention, I guess I'll have to try to remember that. Soon she will be dating and off to college, and I may have to share her with someone else," Deanna senses a note of sadness in his tone. "Let's go and watch her train her horse if you don't mind."

"No that will be fine Jamie." She takes his arm as he offers it to her; contemplating if there is more here than meets the eye.

Walking with him, Deanna feels now is the time. "Jamie you have a wonderful place here, well organized and peaceful. I look forward to coming back and spending more time, I really have to talk to my publisher and convince him into making the story a feature for the Holiday Edition. There is more here than just two columns as you said, that is if you don't mind?"

"You're the writer Deanna; I trust your judgment, that's why I said it would take more than a few days." She's taken by surprise at his comment, because he has only just met her. He seems to have more confidence in her than she has herself.

Deanna notices that two exercise rings look to be brand new. "I see you are making some improvements very nice."

"We have just finished our new riding rings so that our students will have the feel of what to expect at Little Wood and Horseman's this season."

---

8 Bossman

"Then you are expecting to have them compete this year at the regular schedule at Horseman's?"

"Yes the girls are ready, this month we will show. We will have four in Hunters including Pita, Rosa's daughter and Dyon will be in Jumpers. It will be their first show, and they're very excited, in fact, everyone here at the ranch is. My vaqueros are probably the most excited; they are very protective of all of them and offer hints all the time."

"When you use the word vaquero you mean cowboy or ranch hand don't you?"

"Yes, they are Hispanic and think of themselves as the vaquero which has a deeper meaning than just hired hands, it is a way of life for them, some vaqueros spend their whole life on the same ranch as do their children. It's a matter of pride and being part of the success of the ranch.

The men that work at this ranch have worked cattle all their lives as well as horses, this is the only life they have lived or known, and I am proud to have them. We are like a family here, I hope they will marry and raise their own families on this land as well.

You know Eduardo and Rosa were the first ones to come and settle here at the ranch, he's my Segundo, which is the foreman or second in command, and I have already told you Rosa runs my household. They also have a little girl, Pita, whom you will meet later. I spoil her as well, she is one of the points of lights that we have here."

Pride radiates from him as he talks of those who work and live here, something that she's never seen or heard before. It's as if he truly believes in this way of life, which is so different from the Wellington she knows.

Jamie watches as Deanna jots down notes, himself taking mental notes like the way the light plays off her hair the contour of her checks. The way her smile plays well with a twinkle in her Irish eyes. She's a woman with a sensual figure that stirs a man with thoughts of desire. She has a way of making conversation that makes you enjoy talking to her. She makes him feel in a way that's comfortable, as though he has known her for a long time; he even enjoys the touch of her hand. How similar she is,..... to what was once.

"Dyon's with her gelding out there now," he points to the next paddock.

Deanna looks at where he is pointing and sees a magnificent palomino with a flaxen mane and tail and white socks. Dyon is working with him without a lounge line just using verbal commands, as he goes from walks to trots and switching to canters, she notices that he never misses a beat. The transitions are smooth and when she reverses him the lead changes are perfect.

"He is part Quarter horse with Draft and Andalusia, which gives him power and speed, he's also gaited for looks, he loves her to death. When she rides him, they are like one entity, not just a horse and rider."

"He moves beautifully, and I see that he could be a champion, but can he jump?"

"He Jumps 3' 9" right now and finds his spot naturally. She's not jumping him today, but you'll see her soon, and you'll see what I mean."

"Did she start him or did you?" Deanna asks him.

"No I started him, but one day when I was working on him, he saw her. It was love at first sight like a puppy dog, he's followed her ever since."

Deanna glances at her watch and notices the time, "Jamie, I have to go pick up my daughter, and it's getting late. Please thank Rosa for me for a wonderful lunch and thank you for the tour as well. I look forward to coming back and meeting the other girls."

"Deanna here is that card I promised, just swipe it and the gate will open." Jamie takes hold of her hand and presses the card into it.

"How would you and your children like to come out at lesson time say on Friday? I have an idea, why don't you all stay for dinner as our guests? We start at four o'clock, and then you can see the girls at training and at home, besides how they are with just the horses. Please say you will, I would consider it as a great favor. I promise you will not be disappointed."

Deanna wants to come back now more than ever if only to learn all she can of this fascinating individual and the people of this ranch. It's like going back in time so gracious and gentle. She knows that this is a feature story, now she'll have to sell it to Ellsworth and Collins. Why with a photo layout it could be huge maybe something the syndicated press might pick up on.

Jamie still has hold of her hand as he waits for her answer. "Yes Jamie I'll ask the children, I can't promise for them, but yes I'll accept your invitation and will see you Friday. Oh, will it be alright if I bring a photographer with me to take some color shots for the story?"

"Of course, the more the merrier, he'll be welcome to stay for dinner. Please call me about the children so I may let Rosa know how many to expect, even though she makes enough to feed armies.

There will be a friend of ours here also, Father Scanlon, he runs a mission in Loxahatchee for migrants. He comes for dinner every Friday. I hope you don't mind he won't be very religious more like an old grandfather. The girls love him so, as does Rosa, she dotes on him when he's here."

"No of course not that may add another side to the story."

He walks Deanna to her truck and kisses her hand, "Until Friday, I await the pleasure of meeting your son and daughter as well as your company. I must call Ed and thank him for sending you to me."

He smiles and waves as Deanna heads the truck down the drive to the gate. Looking in the mirror she sees he's still standing there waving as she comes to the bend in the drive making it impossible to see him anymore.

On the drive to pick up Katy, she reflects on the day's events and is beginning feels something special about the story. She's having thoughts about this mysterious man; he is almost too good to be true. Having been burned by Steve, she's not going to be taken in so easy by a man again. She will reserve her thoughts and remain objective, for the time being.

Chapter 4

"The Feature"

Deanna worked on the outline; proof reading it over and over until the early hours of the morning, knowing in her heart that this was not a two column piece, but an incredible feature story either about a super con man with a tremendous twist or a larger than real life unique person. She's just not sure which one it is yet.

Jamie is using what appears to be a unique form of therapy, and she must have more time to get to know all the players and see what his program is. She wants to observe him using his technique for these children, and how it helps them. Talking to a child therapist to try getting a take on that side of it won't hurt either.

Satisfied with what she has already, and feeling confident that she can sell it to Ellsworth and Collins in the morning, Deanna decides to turn in and get a couple of hours sleep.

He has a strange effect on people one senses,____ that is the right word, an undercurrent that works on people's emotions. Deanna can't help wondering that there's something hidden within this story. This man, something is driving him, and it's more than a pledge to his dead wife. Lying there in the dark, thinking of him, she finally drifts off to sleep.

The alarm is going off like a brass band and Deanna wakes up to the morning sun streaming into the room, time to get up and feed and water the horses and get the kids off to school. Jonah is already up when she goes down stairs.

"Sorry we weren't here when you got home. I told Katy to call you, Steve picked her up, said he wanted to take her out for dinner. More of his brainwashing I'm afraid, she was talking about going to live with him last night. I tried to tell her he just wants to hurt you, but you know how stubborn she gets even when she knows the truth." He looks at her and shrugs his shoulders.

"I heard you late last night working on the computer, so I fed and watered everyone this morning. How did your interview go?" He brings her a cup of coffee and gives Deanna a kiss. She still can't believe how much he has grown up this past year; he is going to become a wonderful man.

"The interview went great; in fact, we have been invited to dinner Friday night at his ranch. I think you and Katy will enjoy it very much. He has a girl there that's his ward, kind of like a foster child. I think you will like her, and she's very pretty as well."

"Before you accept for all of us don't you think you should ask us if we want to go? Maybe I have made plans, did you even think of that Mother," says Katy in an angry voice from behind her mother.

"As a matter of fact, I was going to ask you, but now I'm going to tell you that you are going, and I don't care what plans you've made. It's time young lady that you start to remember who is the parent and who is the child. And if you think that you are going to get away with any of your father's bullshit with me, forget it and that goes for him too.

You are not going to live with him and as of now you will see him on his visitation time only. If he picks you up again without my permission, I will put him in jail. Do you understand me…**Do you?!!!**" Deanna screams at her?

Katy does not know how to respond to her mother, she's never spoken to her like that in her life. Looking down she says, "Yes."

"**Yes what**," Her mother says to her very pointedly, Deanna's fists are clenched with her finger nails digging into her palms, she's so mad.

"Yes Mother," she stands and stares at her mother with her mouth open.

"Now sit down and eat your breakfast, I'm going to get dressed, and I don't want any more attitudes from you young lady, have I made myself clear."

Answering meekly Katy says, "Yes Mother."

Turning on her heel Deanna stomps up the stairs so angry she could scream, not as much at Katy, but at that son of a bitch, father of hers. One of these days he will run into someone he can't intimidate. Deanna can only hope she will be there to see it.

Down stairs Jonah tries to reason with his sister. "You know Katy you brought that on yourself, you were out of line. I always take your part, and you know it, but Mom is right this time. All she's trying to do is keep this place and make us happy. The divorce was not her fault, nor ours, it was your father's, don't look at me with that face. I know because I caught him with another woman.

Mom never wanted you to know because of the way you feel about him, but now it's time you did. You have been beating her up and yourself all this time when it's him, you should be angry at. I'm sorry I never told you, but Mom made me promise. You're old enough to know now, she wouldn't tell you because she loves you that much and so do I."

Katy does not know what to say, but she knows her big brother has always looked out for her, and she knows they never lie to each other. It's just such a shock after all this time and blaming her mother to find out it was him all the time.

"Jonah I'm sorry I have been such a bitch to her, and look what I've done to myself as well." Katy starts to cry.

"Well, now you know and maybe it will help you with some of the issues that you have been dealing with, either way we will deal with all this as we always have together as a family, Ok? Don't let Mom know that you know or your father, because we all can be weak and fall down. All it just proved was that their marriage was not strong enough to survive. Lots of people get divorced you know that. Just remember we are a family, You, Mom and Me.

Don't let him turn you against anyone anymore, just open your eyes and think more with your head than your heart." Jonah walks over and puts his arms around her "I will always be your big brother and be here for you. Now go get yourself ready and wipe your eyes." He turns to go out when suddenly he faces his sister and says to her, "I believe you're stronger than you know." He tells her this as a way to reassure her.

Katy looks up at him and nods her head, "I'll be ok, I love you, and I'm glad you're my big brother," and she gives him a hug and goes up to get dressed. Jonah hears his mom coming down the stairs and pours her another cup of coffee.

"Mom, don't worry about Katy, I spoke to her, and she's ok with this morning. Just let it pass and concentrate on your new job. Katy and I will be fine and yes, we will go with you tomorrow for dinner. Tell me about this man, and the pretty girl." He plops into a chair, a huge smile on his face waiting for her to answer.

"Well he's a charming person very accomplished and his home is right out of something from 19th century California, I mean the way it looks and the way the interior and exterior are designed. Even the barns are of Spanish architecture. There are white fences and adobe walls, large fichus trees and bougainvilleas everywhere, and lots of flowers.

He's a horseman, I feel it more than I know it, and he does more than just train them. I think he is the real thing when it comes to riding them too. His people, at least the ones that I met, are all Spanish and treat him like a Don of old Mexico, they even call him Patron.

He told me to call him Jamie from the first time we met. What I mean is, he's not snobbish or aristocratic himself, it's just the way his people that work for him have of showing respect. You and Katy will have to understand that when you go out there, it is like nothing you've ever experienced." thoughts of Jamie are in Deanna's mind as she explains all this to Jonah.

"Do you like him, I mean as a person or do you still think that he is up to something underhanded and trying to make a killing on a land deal. He's holding up the horse estate thing that they're trying to get passed the zoning dept you know." Jonah sits back with a very adult expression on his face.

"How do you know about the zoning dept?" She is somewhat amazed that an eighteen year old would know anything about it.

"Everyone is talking about it at school, I guess it's a topic of conversation at just about every dinner table in Wellington and many people are planning on investing in Southwest Properties when they go public. Even I know that ranch is the gateway to that development, and he holds the key." He sits back with a smug look on his face. He is going to make one hell of an attorney.

"Well Mr. Knows It All, don't be saying anything when we go out to the ranch. That is part of what I am trying to find out by doing this interview.

Mr. Ellsworth, he's the publisher of Pro Horseman, and he is very suspicious of the principles of SWP, and that's why he wants the story on Jamie and the ranch just to make sure that they are not conspiring together. They could all be crooks, and we have to be careful."

Jonah looks at her and says "Mom give me more credit than that. I'm not just a kid anymore. I understand perfectly and if I can help you, I will you know that," he smiles and gives her a big hug.

She's so lucky to have him, he is very much like his father, kind and intelligent it's a shame, he never got a chance to know him.

Hearing Katy coming down the stairs, she wonders what kind of mood she is going to be in after the episode earlier.

"Ok, I'm ready I don't feel much like breakfast if you don't mind, I will get something at school. Mom I'm sorry about before I was wrong, are we alright now?" Katy gives her a hug and a kiss something that she has not done in a long time.

"Sure baby I was going to say the same thing to you. I love you very much." Deanna says holding back the tears.

"Well if we're alright, I am going to get the car," interjects Jonah "Let's get going Katy, or we'll be late. Mom I'll drop off today and I can pick Katy up to, there's no practice until next Tuesday, the coach has some stuff to do and the season is over except for the Christmas Tournaments. Let's get a move on Katy; I'll take you to Mickey D's, Ok," he says over his shoulder as he runs out the door?

"Mom I'm glad I have a big brother." She says with a smile.

"Me too Sweetie, me too, and I'm glad I have you. Love you, have a great day, see you tonight."

At the door, she turns and runs back and gives her mother a big kiss, then turns and runs out the door. Sometimes her children never cease to amaze her.

Deanna suddenly realizes that she has to call the magazine and talk to Collins. This story is too good to waste with just two columns. She has to influence them with not what she has found out, but his whole lifestyle not to mention the ranch, the rehab plus his sensitivity with people and horses. The man is a story all by himself, regardless of any of the other ingredients thrown in.

Knowing horses as she does, they are extremely intuitive not to know people who aren't sincere; he has a touch and understanding that told her he may be the real deal. His rehabilitation techniques are certainly different and until Deanna can check them with a qualified therapist she can't say that they don't work. He's invited her to come and observe him at any time, either he thinks her stupid and inadequate, or he has nothing to hide.

She has noticed that Jamie has a love and a concern for the land that a developer wouldn't, just the way he talks about it and the cattle and quality of the range. She finds it hard to believe that this is some land scam, if it is then Jamie deserves an academy award as a great actor, which he might just be.

Dialing into the office Deanna waits for Agnes to pick up, "Hi Agnes, how are you, this is Deanna Gaynor, is Mr. Collins busy? He wanted me to call in today with the results of my interview yesterday."

"Please hold I will see if he can speak to you."

How she hates listening to elevator music when they put you on hold it always seems like it is the longest time before they come back on and the music sucks.

There is a click in the receiver, "Gaynor, I have been waiting for your call, what took you so long, I've been here since seven this morning." He growls. "What have you got, good news I hope, when can I see some copy?" He fires questions at her machine gun fashion.

"Well Mr. Collins, I was coming in this morning to talk to you about that if you have the time. There are some things that came to light that we may need to evaluate before we rush to print, and it would take too long to go over on the phone. I can be there in about an hour if that would be alright with you." Deanna holds her breath and waits for him to hit the roof, he's so impatient already.

"Are you telling me that you didn't get anything yesterday at all?"….. She imagines his anger rising in his face to the color purple on the other end of the phone.

"I did, but it's more complicated than we first assumed, and I wanted to go over it with you and get your opinion before I proceed further along sir," Deanna lies to him, but it's working, he's thinking over what she just said.

"Ok, see you in one hour, Ellsworth is breathing down my neck, which means his wife is all over him about it, understand?" Collins hangs up the without even saying goodbye.

Well, she'd better go get ready if she's to be there in one hour. Deanna's not sure how to approach Collins, but she'd better come up with something pretty quick. What would be the best way to start off, maybe by telling him that this story could be one of the greatest stories the magazine's run in long stretch, and she needs more time?

Deanna pulls into the office lot and parks in visitors parking and heads for the front entrance. Upon entering the building she notices a well dressed large man crossing in front of her. It's Ellsworth the publisher she recognizes him from his picture hanging as you exit the elevator on the second floor offices of the magazine. She takes the initiative and speaks to him.

"Mr. Ellsworth, I'm Deanna Gaynor and I've been assigned to the Doyle story. I was just going up to Mr. Collins office to lay out some very interesting facts that we were not aware of. I've uncovered a whole new slant for this story. I was wondering if you might sit in and listen to my proposal. Your years of experience as a newspaper man would be invaluable with what I've put together so far. I need some old blood hound sense of sleuthing, not that you are; ah, you know what I mean." She smiles with her most innocent look at him. She's thrown out the bait, now to see if he bites and takes it.

"Well it has been a few years, since I've been asked to use that kind of instinct. That look on your face, I've seen before, and it won a Pulitzer Prize in journalism. Ok, have me paged when you get in with Tom, and we'll sit and see what you've got." The door opens for her floor, and she gets out turning to smile at him and wave rather sheepishly.

Turning toward the editor's office Deanna spies the formative Agnes guarding his gate like a faithful dog. She can't help but think of her in that manner, what with her hair in a bun, glasses, and business suit. She's so prim and proper Deanna wonders if she ever makes mistakes or even passes gas. Oh well, she's only doing her job.

"Hi Agnes, Collins wanted to see me, as soon as I got here. I just left Mr. Ellsworth and he said for you to page him as soon Mr. Collins can see me. He wants to sit in on this meeting." Deanna tells her with all the authority she can muster.

"Mr. Collins never mentioned anything to me about it, maybe I should check with him first." She seems to be unsure what she should do, but finally she waves her in and picks up the phone. Deanna sees that she is hitting the penthouse line. So far, so good now to prep Collins for the big boss coming in, and make it look like it was his idea, just so he can save face.

"Mr. Collins I ran into Mr. Ellsworth coming up in the elevator, and we were talking about the story. I told him that you wanted his advice, from the side of an old newspaper man about the new developments on the story. He's coming down right away," trying to show him that it came from Ellsworth.

"Why would you do that without talking to me first?" Collins's face is getting red and his voice is rising.

"Mr. Collins, just like you told me on the phone, both of our jobs might be on the line here, just let me do the talking and maybe you will have the best thing you have ever published or you can berate me in front of the boss and still save face. How about it, just go along with me on this? I promise you, I won't let you down and you will go up some in his eyes, Ok?"

They hear Agnes greet Mr. Ellsworth, "Good morning Mr. Ellsworth, please go right in they're expecting you." Agnes states loud enough for us to hear, good girl, she thinks to herself.

"Mr. Ellsworth, Good morning sir, I was just telling Gaynor here to wait until you arrived before filling us both in on what she's got."

Waiting for him to take a seat, she opens her brief case and takes out the tape recorder and the outline that she prepared last night.

"Mr. Ellsworth, Mr. Collins did a pretty good job of finding out all he could on Doyle and his holdings. We have uncovered a connection between him and an ex U.S. Senator, who happens to be a powerful financier. This man happens to come from the same area of the country that I did and sat on the board of the college that I graduated from. Using that as a spring board to get to Mr. Doyle, I called him and sure enough I got the interview. Mr. Doyle could not, for some reason, refuse a request from Senator Edward Haskell; I went there yesterday and was quite impressed with the ranch and the man.

He wants me to do an in-depth story on him and the ranch along with the children that he is giving therapy to as well. There are no drunks or drug addicts on his ranch. The children the State has placed in his care are children in crisis. I watched this man work with horses and met with some of the people that work for him and from what I could see; he seems to be the genuine article.

I can't help but sense that there is more here to this than just a two column story. I think it could turn out to be either a great human interest story or one of the greatest frauds to hit this county ever. I feel based on a gut feeling that this would be your Christmas Feature, and I would like to pursue it in that way.

It's a way of life that they have out there and something about him that I think hides a deeper story, a secret, The Secret of Rancho de Los Angeles. Even the name inspires a sense of mystery. Let me have a month to collect all the data and see what we have. He has given me full access to his home and the training sessions. He also wants me to follow him at the upcoming horse show that he plans on entering his students in competition.

He's trained all the horses himself, and they look magnificent if I do say so. It is not about drunks and drug addicts, but children in crisis and how he reaches into their troubled minds and souls to recover them. It's about him, if you met him, you would see what I saw. He is the kind of person that walks into a room with one hundred people, and every eye would turn to look at him without him saying a word. He commands a presence that few people ever achieve."

Deanna sits down realizing she made the whole presentation without ever referring to her notes or maybe even taking a breath. Now she waits for one of them to say something, and the silence is pressing down on her. She had not expected to be so wordy, and she didn't even plan on saying what came out of her mouth. She still can't get over not referring once to the outline. Now to await the sentence, it's kind of fish or cut bait.

Ellsworth, who hasn't said a word since sitting down, stands up and faces her and says. "Ms. Gaynor I have a feeling like I used to when one of my reporters came to me with a hunch for a scoop, I think you have that same fire in your belly that most writers don't seem to have anymore.

I'm inclined to go with you on this thing and see what you come up with. I want facts and results do you understand me," looking directly at her over his glasses.

"Yes sir, that's why we need the extra time, Mr. Collins was saying the same thing just before you came in." Deanna can't believe it worked, and she has the go ahead to run with her story.

"Tom was this the way you saw this?" Ellsworth looks at Collins.

"Yes sir, I just felt like we did in the old days, when we used to dig out stories. I was hoping you might feel the same way as I did when Deanna outlined this to me, felt you should have a go at this before we signed off on it though, what with the pressure on you from certain circle's sir," Collins jumps right on track, like "I knew you were right all along," letting Ellsworth think he thought it was a great idea all along.

"Keep up the good work here Gaynor, I'm going to keep my eye on you, don't let me down." He winks and smiles, then gets up and leaves the office.

Collins clears his throat before saying anything to her, "Deanna you almost had me choking when you sat down, but I have to admit you made a great case for the feature, now you will have to deliver it, and it has to be as good as you say." Collins is mopping his forehead with his handkerchief trying to look relieved.

"I think it will be huge no matter what I discover, Human Interest or The Great Florida Land Grab in Plain Sight Deal. Either way it shouts of a tremendous article. I will need Tim tomorrow; we have been invited to the ranch for dinner with all the students and some other guests, along with a picture interview and a tour of the ranch. Jamie gave me permission to interview the people that work for him without him present if I like.

I have a pass card, so I may enter the ranch grounds, whenever I like unannounced. I'm starting on this tomorrow, and I need you to find me a top notch child therapist, so we can have a reference of his methods against conventional therapy to see he's actually helping these kids that the State has placed in his care.

We also need a full background check on him as well, go back say twenty five years if you can. Like I said there has to be some connection between him and the whole Spanish theme of the ranch and everything he does. He does not seem to have any Spanish heritage at all. He's big, blond, with blue eyes. I would put his age at mid to upper forties. I'm going to work on Haskell next week he seems more than just a friend.

Oh, by the way, see what you can come up with on a Father Scanlon some priest that runs a mission in Loxahatchee will you. Fax over whatever you can get to me ASAP," she starts packing up her stuff to head out.

"Ok I'll get on it right away, some of the stuff is going to be tough to get, but we will put all the tools we have at our disposal for you. Where will you be this afternoon?"

"I'm going home and plan on going to a dinner party and spend some time with my family, something I think rubbed off on me from him yesterday, I'll explain in a few days. Would you have Tim call me on my cell phone," Collins nods at her as she gets up to leave?

Deanna walks out of his office with a new feeling about herself; she's made a good presentation and sold the idea, achieving what she set out to do.

Passing by Agnes, Deanna remembers to ask her about the parking space, and could she please take care of in a couple of days.

"Yes Ms. Gaynor I will call maintenance right away, congratulations on your getting the feature. Mr. Ellsworth has already instructed layout to be prepared for full color and hold the set up until you submit your completed piece. By the way, Ms. Gaynor you were fantastic in there, it's going to be nice working with you.

Have a nice time at the party and could you maybe get Tim to make an extra shot of this mystery man for me? I would like to see what he looks like. You made a mental picture of him that sounds dreamy." Agnes whispers to her as she beams a smile and winks, looks like Deanna passed her test.

"Thanks Agnes, that means a lot to me. I will get you one, don't worry, we will go to lunch next week, and I will keep you up to date. Ok?" She smiles and Agnes smiles back reassuring her that she has secured a place at the magazine.

"See you after the weekend and have a good one Agnes." Deanna turns and walks a little taller than when she came in.

chapter 5

"An Angel To The Rescue"

Deanna's mind is spinning as she drives home from the meeting with her Publisher and Editor; she has a feeling like she just hit a grand slam in the World Series. She can't believe that she is going to write a feature story for a Fortune Five Hundred magazine. Steve won't be so smug with himself from here on she's in command of her destiny now, and loving it."

The events in the last two days still have her not believing her success. A feature story, Katy's turnaround this morning and dinner tomorrow night with one of the most interesting people she's ever met. On top of all that getting paid, how great is that?

Deanna pulls into the driveway and sees her ex-husband's car. Parking she proceeds up the driveway waiting for him to exit his car. She's almost up to it now when Steve suddenly throws open his door and gets out of his car, dramatically.

"I want to talk to you, what do you mean telling Katy she can't see me except on visitation days? Listen you bitch, I'll grind you into the dirt if you try pulling that shit with me. She's my daughter and I'll see her, whenever I want, do you understand me!" He is screaming at her as usual, and steps up raising his hand as if to strike her.

Deanna steps back and puts her arm up defensively, when out of nowhere a large dog comes up and stands between her and him. Growling deep within its throat, snarling, its belly close to the ground, ears laid back tight against its head. With jaws dripping from saliva the beast slowly starts backing him up.

With the animal advancing on him, Steve turns white at the sight of the big dog; he slowly step by step backs toward his car. The animal stops just a foot away from him, giving him time to jump into the automobile as shouts at her.

"This is not over you'll see I'll have you in court so quick, you'll see, you'll be sorry Bitch." He shouts at her tearing down the driveway with the brute after him.

Steve burns rubber down the street and the dog comes trotting up the driveway with almost a smile on its face. Deanna is quite naturally frightened and is rooted to the spot watching as the animal approaches. Coming up to her it sits and seems to be at ease with its tongue hanging out the side of the mouth and panting. Deanna notices that it's a female American Bulldog, and she looks like she's been without some decent groceries for a while. With some hesitation she reaches down to pet her and for some reason she can't explain can tell she's a good dog.

"How would you like to have something to eat it's the least I can do for what you just did." She licks Deanna's hand and wags her tail.

Turning she follows her into the house, as though she lived there all of her life. Deanna watches her go over to the side of the cabinet and sits down to await the meal Deanna promised her. Getting a bowl of water for her first she then proceeds to go through the fridge and see what's in there in the way of left over's for her to eat. She doesn't want to make her sick by giving her too much rich stuff, not knowing when the last time she ate was. The dog wolfs down the food and then comes over and lies down at Deanna's feet and looks up at her with soft brown eyes.

"Where did you come from and what's your name? You sure put the fear of God into that bastard. You look as though you need a home at least for awhile, would you like to stay here until we find your owner?... What should I call you?"... She sits and stares at her for a few minutes thinking of some names to give her.

"I know, how about Angel, you certainly were my guardian angel before. He would have hit me if it hadn't been for you, Angel it is."

The dog sits up at the second mention of her new name and licks her hand and face. Deanna doesn't know what it is about her, but she trusts her as much as any animal she's ever known. She knew just what to do with Steve, she didn't bite him, but she gave him all the signs that if he tried to hit her, she would have ripped him apart.

Didn't she wish for him to run up against someone that he couldn't intimidate? Was it just yesterday or today? Well, she got her wish.

"Angel I hope we don't find your owner and by the look of the condition you're in, I think it has been a while since you saw her or him. Your feet look like you have been doing some miles; I'll put some cream on them later, after I change, Ok?" Wagging her tail, she goes and lies down on an old rug by the door that leads to the garage.

Going up stairs thinking to herself, she has one more blessing to be thankful for, a new friend. She goes in and turns on the shower and takes off her clothes, turning, she sees her reflection in the mirror and a thought quickly crosses her mind. She wonders what kind of woman does Jamie prefer young ones, mature ones, blonds, red heads, brunettes or what.

In her mind, she suddenly sees him standing in the driveway waving to her until she was out of sight. Looking at herself in the mirror, turning one way than the next, Deanna take an inventory from her breasts, which have always been large, but she can still pass the pencil test, then the butt, and finally the abdomen not bad, but she could work out a little just to tighten everything a little, she thinks to herself. Funny she hasn't looked or thought of herself in a competitive way for a long time, years in fact, well that is about to change, as is her life. Everyone is about to see a whole new person, and she hopes it will be a better one. Her mind spinning with the events of the day she steps into the shower.

Drying off Deanna can't wait until the kids get home, so she can tell them the great news and introduce them to Angel.

The dog is sleeping when she comes downstairs so Deanna, tip toes into the kitchen. She should call the vet and make an appointment for her right away, just to make sure she's healthy. Dialing the number she waits for them to pick up.

"Hello, this is Deanna Gaynor I was wondering if you had an opening tomorrow morning. I just got a dog and I wondering if Dr. Paterson could see her.... No, I have no history on her at all; she will need shots and maybe a worming... It's hard to tell maybe four or five looking at her teeth.... She looks like an American Bulldog possible full blooded.... Oh that would be wonderful...Yes she seems very gentle, but under nourished...Yes I will. Thank you, see you at ten Bye." Deanna hangs up the phone and turns toward Angel.

"Well it's off to the vet in the morning girl." She gets up and pads over and sits down next to Deanna, who pets her behind the ears which she seems to enjoy very much.

"Wait until Jonah and Katy see you. They've both have been after me to get a dog for years now, and it looks like you're it." Deanna thinks she'd better tell them how she got her because she knows Steve will tell Katy that the dog was sick'd on him or that the dog is vicious, not that he was going to hit her and the dog just came to her defense. "Here they come now Angel," hearing them at the back door.

"Hi Mom," Jonah comes over to kiss me and Angel gets in between him and Deanna barking,

"Easy girl," she says to her. Angel stops right away and sits down next to her.

"Mom what the hell is that, will it bite me?" Jonah's a little shaken up, but places himself between the dog and Katy. Katy is standing behind him pale, fear in her face, not moving.

"No, she'll be alright, I didn't expect you to burst in like that, and you took us by surprise that's all. She just showed up today out of nowhere, and I'm glad she did." Deanna feels an explanation is in order to try to alleviate the anxiety in the both of them.

"Katy your father was waiting for me when I got home and was furious about the visitation thing; I guess you spoke to him today. Well, he was screaming at me and went to hit me, when out of nowhere the dog ran up and started to growl at him and backed him into his car, forcing him to leave. He was not happy and I expect he will try and do something about the dog. She really is a very nice dog, just come over to her so she can sniff and get to know you."

Jonah starts to talk to her and Deanna tells her it's Ok. Angel starts wagging her tail and starts to lick his hand, and then she jumps up on him putting her paws on his shoulders licking his face.

Next Angel goes over to Katy and lies down and rolls over on her back, tail wagging the whole time.

"I think she wants you to rub her stomach Katy, try it, she's ok."

Katy reaches down and rubs her tummy and Angel loves it, now they are all friends. The kids are playing with her and running from room to room.

Jonah stops on his way through, and asks me, "Are we going to keep her, she is beautiful isn't she? Look how smart she is, I bet she'll fetch to."

"Can she sleep with me, can she please." Katy pleads.

"I think we will let her decide where she feels the most comfortable tonight; I'm taking her to the vet in the morning, then we will decide later after you get home from school."

"How did you know her name, did she have a collar on or what." Katy asks.

"No I brought her in and fed her, she was starving, and I was talking to her trying to think of something to call her, when I thought that she was like a guardian angel. I just called her Angel, and she responded like it was her name always."

Jonah steps over to her and puts his arm around her neck. "Mom maybe that was her name before, she seems really to like it and when you call her, she comes right away. I guess it's a great name for her, she looks like an Angel don't you think? Hey, I hope she's housed broken. I'm going to take her out and see if she has to go. I'll feed and water the horses. Come on Katy, why don't you help then we can play with her before dinner? Come Angel." Jonah opens the door and Angel and Katy go outside, the dog walking with them side by side.

Deanna has good feelings about the dog and Katy didn't try once to defend her father how odd. Their lives seem to be taking some spectacular turns, she just can't believe it, and maybe this is a sign of good luck for them.

chapter 6

"Angel and the Doctor"

It's Friday and looks like it will be a gorgeous day out, dry and in the eighties. Nothing on the fax yet and Tim hasn't called to set up a time to go out to the ranch. Angel slept on the old rug last night and went out with Jonah first thing this morning, he says she goes all the way out to the far pasture and does her business and immediately returns to his side. Deanna watched from the kitchen window, and she never leaves his side even when he's working. Somebody seems to have put a lot of time and training into her. She can't believe that she was roaming for so long; her pads on her feet have blisters on them from walking it seems.

The Kids want to stay home and go to the vet's office with her, and she doesn't have the heart to say no. So she has decided to make it a family day, first the vet, then the pet store to pick up a few things for Angel. By the time they get home it will be time to go out to the ranch for the interviews and dinner. Deanna decides to call Tim and asks him to meet her at the office around two o'clock so they can head out to the ranch. He says he can meet her at the house instead and then leave from there. Deanna mentions that he's invited for dinner also; she suggests bringing something nice, just in case they dress for dinner. He says that won't be a problem and hangs up.

Telling Angel to come they head for the car, she tags along and Jonah opens the door and tells her to get in. She looks at Deanna and she tells her its ok, with that she jumps in and moves over next to the window like she had done this all of her life. Deanna brought a lead line and puts on an old collar Jonah found in the tack room, just in case they need it.

On the way to the vet's office the three of them are having fun something Deanna realizes they haven't done in a long time. Pulling up in front of the vet's office and parking they exit laughing at how Angel seems excited about going to the Vet, gripping the leash and pulling on it. Jonah opens the door for them and Angel walks right along into the office and sits down next to Katy, as if she had been there hundreds of times, she is patient and gentle even with other dogs present.

The receptionist calls Deanna's name and they all file in to see the Doctor. "Hello, Dr. Paterson this is Angel," Katy says introducing him to the dog.

"Well hello Angel, we need to look you over, do you think that will be alright with you?" He asks her as though she were a human being, petting her getting to know her a little before he starts the exam.

Deanna tells him how she got her, and he thinks it would be best to assume that she needs all of her shots and gives them to her strait away.

"Give me a minute and I will check to see if she has worms if she does, we will take care of that too. She is a well mannered dog, how is she at home, house broken?" He remarks as he inserts the probe.

Katy announces even before Deanna can answer. "She's wonderful doctor, we only have to tell her something once, and she gets it right away. I have never seen anything like it in my life. She was heaven sent, I think, she has brought so much joy to us already."

"Well other than being a little under weight and foot sore, she's in good health. So enjoy her, she also has no chip embedded under her skin. See you in about six months; kids have a nice holiday and Deanna you as well." He turns and goes into another room as they go to pay the cashier, then off to the pet store to get some things for Angel.

Arriving at the pets store they take Angel into the store to see which toys she might like and get dog food for her. Katy takes her over to the toy section while Jonah and Deanna get the food and some biscuits. They can hear Angel barking and Katy laughing, as Deanna remembers her doing so long ago. Turning the corner of an aisle, they spy Katy, sitting on the floor with Angel next to her selecting toys out of a large pile on the floor. Angel seems to like three of them and carries them to the counter. Deanna takes them from her and the cashier rings them up along with the food, as Angel patiently looks on. Leaving the store they walk toward the car happy and content, all of them normal for the first time in ages.

Arriving home Deanna tells the kids to pack something that would be suitable for dinner. Angel is busy with her new toys, and she sets up bowls for her food and water, with this accomplished Deanna goes on upstairs to change and get ready for what might prove to be the most important day of her life. Katy comes in and asks if she should wear her riding clothes, and she tells her yes, and to bring her good shoes, but to wear her riding boots out there.

There's a knock on the door and Angel barks and positions herself right behind the kitchen door. Looking out, Deanna sees a young man standing with what looks like camera equipment, Deanna assumes its Tim. She hurries downstairs and tells Angel its ok, and she lies down, but never takes her eyes off the door.

"Hi, I'm Tim," he announces timidly. Opening the door he smiles and says, "Is it OK to come in?"

"Hi I'm Deanna and that's Angel. Your right on time we're almost ready."

"Is the dog ok, it won't eat me will it, sounded like it was coming through the door at me?" He appears a little shaken.

"No you'll be ok, she understands who's a friend and who's not, she's just protective," she yells up to the kids to hurry that they have to leave. They bound down the stairs into the kitchen, almost colliding into Tim, Deanna introduces them him.

"Hello", Tim says, and shakes Jonah's hand and nods at Katy.

Deanna tells Angel to stay, and she returns to the old rug in the corner. Going out the door Deanna turns and remarks to the dog, "Watch the house while we're gone." Angel lifts her head as if in recognition, barks at her, then puts her head down.

"Do you want to go in my car Tim, or would you prefer to follow us there?" I ask Tim.

"It would be better if I follow you, I have all my stuff in my car, and you never know what I might need." Heading to his car he calls out, "Jonah, want to come with me."

"Do you mind Mom?" Jonah asks me.

"No that would be fine we have to go to Flying Cow Road, you know where that is in case we get separated."

Katy and Deanna get into her car and pull out of the driveway and head toward Route 80. "This is pretty important to you isn't it Mom," Katy asks.

"Yes it is, probably the most important thing in our lives right now. I have a chance to prove that I can make it on my own and be able to keep the farm and our horses. So I would say that is pretty high on the priority list, but you and Jonah are the most important people in my life, I hope you know that. I know we have been having our difficulties, but you will be fine, and we will make it, you and I." Deanna wants her to know that she loves her and will always be there for her.

"Jonah told me about my Dad, and what he did, I didn't know, and I never knew that he ever hit you, I'm so sorry." She has tears in her eyes.

"Jonah loves you and me, guess you had to know sometime I was just trying to protect you from it; I never meant to deceive you." She reaches over and grabs her hand and squeezes it.

Coming up to where the turn off is, they make a u-turn and head for the ranch, Tim is right behind them. Pulling up to the gate, she takes the card out that Jamie gave her and swipes it, the gate swings open, and they drive in heading for the main house. Deanna sees Rubin and he indicates where they should park. He approaches and takes her hand warmly in his, shaking it gently. He then does the same with Katy as she introduces him to her. He greets Tim and Jonah by shaking their hands as well, Deanna explains to them that Rubin can't speak, that he is a vaquero on the ranch. Rubin smiles at them, and then begins pointing toward a small house that's detached from the hacienda, and leads them toward it.

Rosa greets them at the door. "Senora you come, that it is good, and I see that you have brought your family with you. This is your Senor?"

"No Tim is one of our photographers from the magazine and this is my son Jonah and my daughter Katy. Everyone, this is Rosa, she's in command here according to our host Mr. Doyle."

"Come I have made some refreshment, then you may go down to the riding areas as they are working some of the horses before the girls get here from the school." Rosa tells them as she invites them in.

"Thank you Rosa that would be nice I could use some of your fabulous coffee. How about you Tim, Rosa makes the best I have ever had?" He nods his head; Jonah and Katy each grab a donut and some juice looking anxious to go to the barns. After having some small conversation with Rosa, Deanna notices that Tim and the kids are getting antsy to go to the barn. She tells them to go ahead without her as she would like to spend some time with Rosa, if she doesn't mind.

Deanna explains to Rosa that there are many questions about the ranch and Jamie that she thinks it would be better answered from her point of view.

Rosa looks at her thoughtfully before answering, "As you wish Senora, in my country the women often get together over chocolate or coffee and discuss the important things of the village or the rancho. It is good that you come, for you bring a life that has been missing here like the rain brings new life to the land."

Deanna wonders what she meant by that, maybe she chose the wrong words and meant to say something else. She fills coffee for the both of them and sits down across from her.

"Would you like the cream and sugar Senora?"

"Both would be fine Rosa and please call me Deanna, I want for us to be friends."

"Si, I can do that Senora Deanna, it would be nice to have a new friend, sometimes it gets lonely here because I am the only woman right now, and the vaqueros are still looking for the wife. I think I will have to find them some, so I can have company." She laughs and sits down again. "What is it that you wish to ask of me?"

"Why don't you tell me how you came to be here at the ranch? I wish to learn about all of you, so I can write the real story. I think you can help me, Will you do that?" Rosa takes a drink from her coffee cup and sits back in the chair

"I will tell you how we came here, but I can tell you little of the Patron before us. My Eduardo came here five years ago to try and earn enough money so that we could have a better life, but he was offered only low paying work and sometime the people would not pay him, and because he was afraid of being sent back, they got away with it. So he started to collect the cans from the side of the road to sell to the trash man to earn money. Sometimes he ate very little because he would send us all the money he earned.

On one of these days the Patron saw him and asks him if he wished work, Eduardo says, "Si, what kind of work?" Patron tells him that he wished to have him do the yard work and work with the horses. Eduardo, say's to him "I will work for you if you pay me." Patron he said, "I'll pay you for the work you do for me." Eduardo says he will start the next day because he has to sell his cans. Patron, he agrees to pick him up at the same place early in the morning.

Patron he is there waiting for Eduardo the next day and takes him to his old farm and Eduardo, he never leaves. The Patron he needs someone to do the work because his Senora was very ill. Patron would hire no one to take care of her, and he would not leave her until she goes with God. The Senora wanted Eduardo to send for Pita and me. By the time Patron got visas she was not with him anymore. Patron and Senor Haskell they buried her together.

The Last Celtic Angel

Eduardo says he was very sad and cried mucho; he spoke to no one, until Eduardo thought he would go loco. One day he told Eduardo to come to the house to see him, when he came, he thought the Patron was going to tell him to leave. The Patron he handed Eduardo the permission to bring us to the United States. When I come here, he asked me to take care of the house, I say yes, and we have been with him since." She explains with tears in her eyes.

"How long was that before you came to the ranch?"

She takes a minute to contemplate, "It was six months I think, he asks me would I keep his house, and be the Duena[9] for the girls. I say yes, very quickly, I was proud to do this for him. He asks Eduardo to be his Segundo also." Deanna can tell she's telling her something that is very emotional for her.

"He is like a father to my Pita, and she adores him, as do all of us, even old Tanner loves the Patron. He is a good man Senora; he never asks of us something that he would not do himself. He is for these children a rock upon which they may stand, I believe he would give his life for any of us." I sense that she is devoted to him, like Rubin.

"Rosa I know that Jamie got four visas for people, I assume that two of them were for Pita, and you were the other two for Esteban and Rubin?"

"Si, they were Gauchos[10] in Argentina, and in my country, they are called Vaqueros[11]. They came to work for the polo team, to ride and train the horses. When they got here from their country the Anglo, who owned the team told them they would be the groom not riders. One day he told Rubin to work out a new horse that he had purchased, the horse was wild and when Rubin said first they must work with him, the man ordered him to ride the crazy horse, his pride made him do it. The Diablo horse went crazy with Rubin in the saddle, he tried to ride him down and

---

9 Chaperone

10 Argentine cowboy

11 Mexican cowboy

get control, but he could not. The horse was too strong and threw Rubin and when he landed, he bites off his tongue.

The man refused to take him to the hospital and ordered him off the property without even paying him, Esteban took him away. They were treated very badly and not paid what was promised and when they went back to the head man he laughed at them and told them to go away, or he would have them arrested. Rubin and Esteban did not know where to go. They were told to go to the Mission of the Virgin, when they get there the Padre he called the Patron.

When the Patron heard of this, he came and took Rubin to the hospital to see if anything could be done, but it was too late he would never speak again. They said he was very angry, the Patron went to see this man and try to reason with him for the men's sake, but the man, he was rude to him and ordered him away.

Eduardo said that the Patron was terrible to behold and shook the man like a dog when the man he try to bully the Patron. The Patron he say to him "I am all the things that men fear in the dark. **You** will do the right thing **now!**"

Eduardo says he looked into Patron's eyes and believes what he says, so did the fat man. He also tells the pig, if he ever hears of him mistreating his men or horses again he will come back and break him. The man he give him money and he give the crazy horse called Storm too, now the horse loves Patron muy mucho[12].

He has given us a future, he treats my Eduardo like a brother, and he is sending him to learn Ranch Management and Pita thinks of him as a Grand Papa. He spoils her so, but she listens to him always. The Patron has given us a future as well as Rubin and Esteban.

They are men again and walk with pride, because the Patron has allowed them to be men not servants. You must understand we come here not looking for handouts, but to earn the right to stay.

The Patron has given us that chance when no one else cared. He

---

12 Very much

pays more and gives us the roof over our heads. He opens bank accounts for us and Estaban and Rubin, all the vaqueros are given a share of the rancho, which is ours to own. Each will own fifty acres when we become citizens." Rosa states as she goes and pours more coffee.

"We have become a family because we have no one else. All my people call him Malo El Hombre[13], He is how you say like a guardian for those who cannot speak or protect themselves from being taken advantage of. Many of my people pray for him, they light candles in his name." She states with pride.

"He then made me Mama to all. My friends in my old village still do not believe that God sent us a savior. Senor Jamie has done all this and asks nothing of us except to help him in his quest.

Did you know that the Patron supports the mission for migrant's run by the old priest who was a drunkard and lost his way? Many good things he has done, but wants no one to know.

You must excuse me now I must start the dinner. I will join you on the veranda." She begins gathering the necessary ingredients for supper, and Deanna walks out to the covered veranda where there is a cool breeze blowing out of the west.

Concentrating on a bird that singing Deanna suddenly she becomes aware of music coming from the main house, sweet music and a strong voice singing what sounds like a love song. Not recognizing the tune or the artist singing the ballad, she listens closely, trying to get a clue as to the person singing. Rosa comes back and looks at her smiling.

"Rosa the music and that song is someone singing up at the house or is that a tape or record, I can't seem to place the melody or the lyrics"

"Senora that is the Patron, Don Diego is playing the piano. It has been a long time since we have heard him play and sing. He used to write and play music once upon a time."

"Don Diego, do you mean Jamie, he's a musician and sings as well?"

"Si, Diego is James in Spanish," Says Rosa. Deanna is thinking,

---

13 A very tough or bad man

more parts of the puzzle, like the Gordian Knot, it has no beginning nor visible end.

"Si Senora, he has a beautiful voice and can play wonderfully as you can hear. All the children must learn piano, as well as me. He is very stern about this, when we have the fiesta we hope we can get him to sing for us. I think you will have to come for the fiesta it is a sumamente grande momento[14]. I think Patron will look for you to come." She smiles mischievously.

As they listen to the song, Deanna realizes that it is a song about love and keeping faith to that love. Rosa and her stand listening to the sweet melody not saying anything to each other, when it ends, she asks Rosa,

"He must have loved her very much to write such a song."

'Si, he loved her more than I could imagine, I only wish that Eduardo could love me so. It is God's gift to give of one's self for another like that. Tanner he says the sun shined from their eyes when they gazed upon each other. Old Tanner says they were the only people that loved from the first and forever, he also says that Missy will be waiting at Heaven's Gate for him. Sometimes that silly old grouch, he says the craziest things, but he knew them the longest."

"Rosa who is Tanner, for both you and Jamie has mentioned him a few times, does he work here or just a friend?"

He is just Tanner; he has been with the Patron since he was a young man I think. You will meet him tonight at the dinner he is out with the vaquero's now. Rosa turns and goes into the kitchen.

Rosa leaves Deanna to her thoughts, standing there listening to him playing his music. She thinks to herself could he ever love anyone again with the same sense of intensity that's represented in that song, she wonders? Suddenly, Deanna feels she has to leave and get out of there.

Rosa calls to her, "You will find there are many sides to the Patron, and he is a very good man. I tell you this only so you know what kind of man he is; it is not for your story, but for you Senora. His acts of goodness

---

[14] Extreme great time

are not things he wants made known, why I do not know. The old Padre of the mission has known him long as has Tanner, maybe it is to them you should go." She offers as an explanation to me.

"Is that Father Scanlon, who will be at dinner tonight?"

"Si, he comes every Friday night and brings T. J.'s Mammacita[15], Eduardo says he has been to Friday dinner since before the Senora passed."

"Thank you Rosa, you've been wonderful and given me insight into the man and his purpose" Deanna turns to leave once more.

"Senora Deanna please, mi casa is su casa, as to the man, the more you see only shows how much more there is. To the purpose even we do not know the real purpose or why he feels the way he does about this Rancho or its people. All I ask is that you write from your heart and with the truth. Patron says we are to trust you, we are not as trusting as him, but he believes that you will do the honorable thing. I pray he is correct, there are many that live in the village that wishes him to fail. I trust you, because he does Senora." Rosa walks up to her and gazes into her eyes and takes hold of Deanna's hands in hers. "Go with God Senora," she whispers to her

She contemplates about that as she strolls to the arenas, she wishes research would dig up a background on him, where did he go to school, how he acquired his wealth? What social circles has he been associated with in the past before coming to Florida, all questions she needs to find out in order to finish this story. She sees Tim coming from the barn area and waits for him in front of the house.

"Oh Tim, I was looking for you. I thought you were gone, did you get some pictures?"

"Yea I got about three hundred so far. You know the house and barns, some cowboy working cattle on the other side of the lake and old blacksmith guy out back who is not so friendly.

Oh yea, I took some of Jonah and that Dyon girl working out a big

---

15 mother

horse, along with a guy I assume is Doyle. I think I have enough for today. I'll have them ready for you on Monday.

"That sounds like a plan; I should have a pretty tight outline by Monday. Could you make me some copies of the one's with Katy and Jonah, please?" Suddenly remembering Agnes, "Oh, and some of Jamie too. I promised some to Agnes."

"Sure no problem the magazine pays for all the pictures anyway." He smiles and laughs. "Have a nice weekend." And Tim turns toward his car.

"Tim, don't you want to stay for dinner you haven't met Jamie yet?"

"No thank you, I really like to meet all my subjects through my camera, if you know what I mean. I have a hot date tonight with one of the new girls in research. Besides I don't think you need anymore men around tonight." Tim chuckles as he heads for his car.

I like Tim; he knows his business and goes right to it. I can't wait to see some of the shots he's taken, and how they will play into the story.

As Deanna walks from Rosa's home toward the barns, she can't help thinking how clean and neat it is. Her kitchen is warm; it radiates love as does she. How wonderful the way she sees things, there are so many corners to this story, what is the real story here?

Down by the barn Deanna sees Jonah by the paddock fence watching Dyon work out a jumper, as Jamie stands in the center calmly talking her through a series of jumps and transitions. He uses a steady and reassuring voice that seems to calm both horse and rider. Dyon sits a horse with a natural style and grace. She has perfect equitation as well. She's a natural rider, Deanna being an equestrian knows it is something that she was born with.

Jamie is speaking quietly to her as she puts the horse on the correct lead. "Softly, softly now, that's it, approach the center, find his spot and lean up and over. Stay even with the plane of his neck, not too far now, good girl, excellent. Stretch up when just before you land, look to the next jump, no, with just your head….. Good use your leg to guide him to the jump, squeeze____, perfect. That's the way we will build power and speed, you'll see no one will top you at the show if you just keep working like that. Ok, walk him out and cool him down." Walking from the ring Jamie calls back to her, "Dyon I'll need your help with the girls today if you don't mind."

Turning to Jonah he says, "Maybe Jonah will help you with D.C?" Jonah literally jumps at the chance.

"Yes sir, I would love to help, if Dyon wouldn't mind," Jonah blurts out awkwardly.

Deanna notices that Jonah is enthralled watching Dyon ride, he seems smitten with her, and she can't blame him, she looks like a movie star on or off the horse. Her son she realizes is becoming a young man now and will have to accept.

Jamie turns to leave the arena when he spies Deanna. Walking up with a smile, he reaches out and takes her hand holding it, but not squeezing.

"I was wondering if I was going to see you before we had dinner. You look lovely, is everyone co-operating for you?" He inquires in a casual manner.

Deanna feels she has to apologize to him. "I'm sorry I should have come and said hello to you first, but I've been with Rosa talking and having coffee at her cottage. She's a treasure you must be very glad to have her with you."

"Oh yes, I wouldn't know what I would have done without her. What she lacks in years she makes up for in love." He replies with that easy smile of his as he shows genuine respect. "She and Eduardo have been my right and left hands here; I really wouldn't have been able to accomplish what I have without them."

Listening to him praise them, she can't help wondering about him. He is kind and sensitive, but strength emanates from him, strength that would back up a bear if necessary. His talents seem endless, education, art, music, athletic ability, all combined with a grace and natural handsomeness, he appears too good to be true.

Jamie takes her arm and guides Deanna gently to the Hunter ring.

"I've asked Katy if she would not mind riding one of my horses that needs to be worked. That is, if it's alright with you? He's very gentle but has not been ridden in a while since Pita got her new pony," He explains to her.

"Well it could be a problem; you see she has this problem with severe panic attacks when she becomes frightened or angry. It's a result of my divorce from her father. She's in therapy now twice a week and Dr. Winman, that's her therapist, he thinks she's not ready. He's not had any success in trying to help her," Deanna warns him.

Jamie seems to think about it for a minute before he answers her. "I understand, actually Katy told me all about it while you were up with Rosa. I think she will be perfectly fine, we'll be taking it easy. I'll be in the ring with her the whole time. That seemed to make Katy feel at ease knowing that, and she expressed a desire to try. She and Finnegan have been having quite a discussion about this for forty minutes. Katy is doing it right, working with him on the ground before she claims aboard. Why don't you let her try and see how she handles it?

I told her Tia has the same problem, and we have overcome a lot of hers. The two of them actually have been hanging out together which for Tia are something short of a milestone. She does not take to new people readily, but the two of them seem to have hit it off wonderfully. Sometimes just talking about something with someone who has walked in your shoes aids in recovery, knowing you're not the only one. So if it's ok with you, I'll tell her it's a go." He stands in front of her waiting for her answer.

Deanna nods, too afraid to speak, he has her disarmed, and he seems not fazed by what he's learned. She senses it will be ok, there's that word again, sense.

"She will be more at ease and enjoy herself if she's participating rather than as a spectator. All I ask is that you let me take charge, no matter what happens. Leave everything to me, can you do that?" He asks with his brows furrowed together.

Deanna's worried, she's seen her when the panic takes place, he hasn't, and she's not sure he can cope with her when it does, but he seems so confident.

"Alright, but please be careful Jamie, her therapist says she may not be ready yet, he thinks she needs more time. It's not that I don't have confidence in you, I'm sure you're good, it's just ___ she's mine." Deanna confides in him.

"I totally understand, I will be very slow and gentle with her, and I'll be with her the whole time. Just sit back and try to look calm, let me handle the lesson, she'll be fine."

With that he calls the girls to bring their horses over to the gate. "I want Marianna to go first, followed by Katy, Tia, T. J. and Pita you will be last, Ok?"

All of them do five times each way at the walk around the arena warming up the horses. "Alright, now walk over the poles a few times, then go to the center of the ring and stand...... Keep a space between yourselves, that's excellent, very good.

Marianna I want you to trot to the first jump than pick up the canter and do two, three, five, and six stopping straight ahead before the fence. Go ahead ___ heels down that's it, toes up, center of the cross rails two point ___ good pick up the cantor and two point ___ stretch up.... Beautiful that's it ___ and stop. Perfect, you do just like that at the show this month, and you will pin for sure. Now pat him on the neck, let him know he did a good job, that's it.

Katy your next honey, Let me check your girth and reins, before you start." Jamie walks up to Katy and places his hand over hers and leads her to the first jump. "Ok your tack is fine I just wanted to talk to you before you start" he squeezes her hand a little. "Look at me, you can do this, focus and listen to my voice, I will be right with you the whole time. You understand, just listen to my voice and only my voice, Ok?"

Katy looks down at him, and he gently releases her hand. "Yes Uncle Jamie, I will" she feels a new confidence flowing into her.

"Ok Katy, start at the walk than take it up to a trot."

Wallace Jan Ecklof

Jamie turns and goes back to the center of the ring. Katy walks off and just before the jumps, she picks up the trot.

Suddenly, Katy loses one of her stirrups and Deanna sees the panic on her face knowing what is to come next. Before she can react, she hears Jamie's voice calling out to Katy.

"Katy, just relax, sit and find the stirrup, use your right rein and gently turn him, ___ find your stirrup, just listen to my voice, ___ you're alright, you have great balance, that's it. ___ Good now turn him back and trot to the jump, ___fantastic. Two point and sit up, heels down, toes up, look to the next jump, perfect, I'm right here" Jamie keeps walking toward her as he talks her through this.

"You can do this, you're in control, feel the control, go back and finish your line." He turns and announces to all of them, "Now that ladies, is how you recover from that situation, thank you Katy, I'm very proud of you. You handled that like a pro."

He looks at Katy and winks, almost like it was all planned. "Very good that was all you had to do, use your seat, that's what it's for." She finishes all of her jumps perfectly and when she finishes, she is smiling from ear to ear.

"Ok, you two walk out your horses and Dyon will finish the rest of the class. Deanna has seen him using a therapy that is unconventional yet effective, Katy has what she did not, a sense of confidence that she didn't have before.

Katy is so excited she can hardly contain herself, "Mother did you see me, I did it, I recovered all by myself, I jumped almost a perfect line. Oh Mother I can't go back to Miss Rose, I hate her, and she is a lousy teacher. I don't care if she is Daddy's friend, I just can't, why can't I take lessons here?

You said that all his students are children in crisis, and **I am** a child in crisis. Mother, please ask Uncle Jamie, you don't know how it felt when he came over and touched me. I felt like he empowered me with courage.

When he talks, you can hear him in your head, now I know what

Tia meant when she said he has a magic that he uses. I didn't panic not once, I was scared, but when I heard him talking to me, I felt I could do it, and I did."…. Mother, I don't feel different here like at school or at Miss Rose's barn, there I feel like everyone is looking at me waiting for me to have a fit or something." The look on her face, it's the first time in almost two years that she's seeing her, like the daughter she used to have. Looking for guidance and giving her the feeling like she can make everything alright again.

Deanna doesn't know what to say to her, she's here to write a story and maybe expose a land swindle. She can't have her in the middle and Deanna's not sure how she feels about Jamie herself.

"Let's get dressed for dinner, and we'll talk about this when we get home. Ok. We need to hurry up and finish with this horse than we can go get cleaned up. Come on now, no more discussions on the subject for the rest of the night. I promise I will think about it."

She walks the horse out and cools him down and Marianna and her head over to the staging area to remove the tack.

As Katy is brushing the horse, Jamie comes by, "You were very good out there Katy and I wanted to thank you for giving Finnegan a workout. You really helped us today you must come back some other time with your Mom and brother. You know we're having a big trail ride to the old quarry on Sunday; it's about a ten mile trip out and back. We would love for you all to join us.

How about it Mom," Katy asks, "Can we all come?"

Jonah is looking at her with a big grin, knowing she has just been set up. "How can I refuse a ride to the quarry? Would it be alright if we brought our own horses," She says a little sarcastically?

"No, as a matter of fact, that would be great, I think we would have been short on a couple of horses if you don't, we can discuss it after dinner tonight. Well, I have to go to the house and see to the dinner preparations, I am sure that Rosa will have me going to the store or something before I can get dressed." He comments to Deanna before turning to walk toward the house.

Watching him go, she can't help but admire him for the ease in which he manages everything around himself.

"Mother maybe you can ask him over this weekend, and I can get another lesson from him, do you think I could?" Deanna hardly heard what Katy was saying, she was so preoccupied with watching him.

"Hum... Maybe we can ___ we'll see honey, come on now finish up we have to get ready for dinner." Deanna casually answers her, watching Jamie walk away. There is so much about him that she finds familiar, but Deanna can't seem to put her finger on it. This place, it is almost as if she had been here and done this before.

chapter 7

"An Evening of Surprises"

Upon entering the house they see that the whole place is a buzz with activity. Rosa is setting a large table in the formal dining room and there are three young women that she's issuing instructions to in Spanish. Looking up she sees us and comes over.

Rosa says, "Senora's, come, I will show you to your rooms where you may refresh yourselves and dress for dinner."

Going up a winding set of stairs she leads the way down a long carpeted hall that has many doors, to one that she indicates is the one Deanna is to use. Opening the door she finds a spacious suite with a formal sitting room leading to an incredible bedroom. Off the bedroom through French doors there's a balcony with a magnificent view of the ranch that is breathtaking. It faces the east, so one can watch the sun rise.

"Senorita Katy is across from you, while Senor Jonah will be in the one next to you. I will show him his, when he comes up from the lessons. I have taken the liberty while you were down with the lessons to lay out some clothes; maybe you like to try them on? I was not sure if you have the dinner clothes with you. Tia thinks the Senorita Katy might like to share something of hers for tonight."

Katy jumps at the chance to look at what Tia sent for her to wear. "Senorita your room is across from this one let me show you, por favor." Going out and opening the door to the room opposite of mine she shows Katy to her room.

Running into the room Rosa has opened for her Deanna hears her squeal; she runs to investigate and sees Katy holding a dress. "Mother isn't it beautiful, I love it, we're the same size, and it will fit perfectly." She exclaims, holding it up against her and dancing about the room.

Deanna nods and smiles, seeing Katy happier than she's seen her in such a long time. She closes Katy's door and returns to her room. Looking at the dresses that are laid out on the bed, she's wondering which one to try on, or should she tell Rosa no thank you, and just wear what she brought. Rosa comes back to her room as Deanna holds up one of the dresses.

"Your pardon, Senora, forgive me please, I mean no offence that your clothes are not lovely. I just thought you might like to try something a little different, a little Spanish for tonight. If you do not, it will not offend me or the Patron. I will leave you to dress now; dinner will be in two hours. Drinks will be on the veranda when you are ready."

"Wait Rosa, I love the dresses, and I hope they will fit. Thank you for trying to make us feel welcome. They're so beautiful, are they yours?"

"No Senora Deanna, they were just here, I must go and see that the girls do not make the big mistakes. Con permiso[16] Senora." Rosa leaves and closes the door.

Deanna looks at the dresses more closely; they are of knee length and brightly colored with scoop necks. The texture and quality are magnificent, as if they were made for her. She tries on the yellow one with the bodice of white lace it's perfect, except, she'll have to wear it without a bra as the straps would show. Deanna's not sure that she feels comfortable with that though, turning back to the others, she notices a tube top underneath the last one. Rosa has thought of everything. Deanna puts it on and it's perfect, putting the dress back on it fits like a

---

16 With permission

dream, making her feel pretty and sexy at the same time. The door opens and Katy rushes in.

"Look mother isn't it beautiful, Wow, you look great I have never seen you look so attractive, the colors are perfect for you, don't you love it here, and it's like going on vacation… Everyone is so nice and this house and everything is like a dream castle, don't you think? Can I go find Tia, I want to thank her and show her how I look?" She is so excited. How can her mother say no? "Alright but just to show her then come right back."

"Ok Mother I will."

Deanna sits down at the vanity and questions begin to pop into her mind. Thinking about the dresses, where did they come from, maybe they were his late wife's? She's curious; she'll have to wait to ask Rosa as it would be in bad taste to bring it up to him. There is a knock on the door.

"Come in." The door opens and Deanna sees that it is a very pretty young woman that Rosa was talking with, when they came in downstairs.

"Perdona[17] Senora, Rosa sends me to do your hair, me permite[18]?" and she takes over finishing her hair, "My name is Theresa."

"I am pleased to meet you Theresa; do you work here at the Rancho?"

"Only sometime, I hope to live here all the time with my Esteban when we take our vows."

"You must tell me sometime when we have more time when that will be; I have not met Esteban yet."

"The Senora will meet him tonight, at the dinner, Friday is La Familia." Theresa explains as she finishes the braid, Deanna sees that she is quite expert in doing hair.

"The Senora has beautiful hair, it is thick and shines like copper in the sun, I make you pretty for the Patron. No?" Theresa smiles and

---

17 Excuse me

18 Permit me

announces that it is finished; she looks in the mirror and the one that Theresa is holding behind her and has never seen it done better.

"Thank you Theresa, it's gorgeous, and I love it." She smiles and Deanna can see that she's is very pretty, Esteban is a lucky Caballero[19] to have her.

"Don Diego awaits his guests on the veranda whenever you are ready Senora. I will leave you now." Theresa closes the door behind her.

Deanna sits looking into the mirror, all these people can't be wrong about what kind of person he is. She saw him today with Katy; he did in one lesson what Rose has been unable to do in a year. Katy says she felt something; maybe it was what Deanna felt the first time he took her hand. A sense of trust and a feeling of well being that came over her, as if she had known him before.

Walking down the hall, Deanna can hear laughter coming from the great room. Walking into the room she notices a red faced older man with white hair talking with Jamie, it must be Father Scanlon that she's heard so much about. They're standing in front of French doors leading to the veranda.

Jamie is dressed in dark slacks and a white shirt; his broad shoulders taper down to a narrow waist, his hair is of medium length almost touching his collar. Father Scanlon puts his hand on his arm and motions in her direction as he turns and looks at Deanna just staring, the sound level drops to silence. She looks to see if she forgot something with the way he's looking at her, suddenly he smiles and walks toward Deanna the older man in tow.

"Father I would like you to meet another of our guests tonight for dinner, this is the remarkable woman that I have been talking to you about, she is doing a story on us here, and about the ranch." Jamie takes her hand in his and says as if no one else were in the room, "You look absolutely stunning."

"Father this is Deanna Quinn Gaynor, Deanna may I introduce my

---

19 Gentleman

The Last Celtic Angel

good friend Father Tom Scanlon." Father Scanlon takes Deanna's hand and smiles warmly.

"Tis a pleasure to meet you darling, he has spoken of you, now I can see why. You've a bit of the old sod in you, a fair Colleen from the Emerald Isle. Tis my pleasure to meet you Deanna," he takes Deanna's hand and shakes gently.

"Father I've heard about you and your Mission, I hope you will give me an interview as I understand you're part of the story as well." Waiting for him to answer she notices a look between him and Jamie.

Jamie nods, as if giving him permission. Father Scanlon looks relieved.

"Of course any time you wish except for this evening, tonight I concentrate on one of Rosa's wonderful meals, but let me introduce you to Irene. She's T.J.'s mother and a bit shy, but a lovely lass none the less. Come with me, she's out looking at the lake. Will you excuse us Jamie?"

As Father Scanlon escorts Deanna to the patio, she hears Jonah call out to her. "Hey Mom," he crosses the patio with Dyon and gives her a kiss, "You look incredible isn't she beautiful Dyon? I never saw that dress before Mom, is it new?"

"No honey, actually Rosa brought it to me; she thought I might like it. She said it was one that was here, I guess someone left it, is that right Dyon?"

She smiles and states that she and Jamie purchased it and some others yesterday.

"Then it is you, I have to thank for having such good taste."

She answers Deanna curtly. "No Senora, Jefe[20] actually selected that one, I chose the size only."

"Thank you, it's a perfect fit." Deanna thanks her honestly.

So it was Jamie, who selected it, he has a feel for fashion as well. Deanna senses a little coolness from Dyon and she decides to move along with Father Scanlon to meet T.J.'s Mom.

---

20 Boss or Headman

The old priest walks her up to a small diminutive woman. "Irene I would like to introduce you to Deanna, she is writing a story on the ranch and the girls." Irene looks a little frighten and apprehensive.

"Just about how they are training and going to the show, nothing for you to worry about. Irene is my housekeeper at the mission you know." Father Scanlon explains to Deanna.

"Like Rosa takes care of things here, she sees to all the parishioners' needs, like housing and washing, making sure they get to the doctors and such. Don't know what I would do without her really. I'm not very good at domestic things, more into saving souls so to speak, it's easier." He chuckles and Irene smiles weakly, but still appears withdrawn.

"Well Irene, I will let you watch the swans a while longer and come and get you when dinner is ready, alright?" She nods and goes back to watch the swans, a faraway look in her eyes.

"I'm sorry about that; she becomes very agitated if she thinks that people are going to find out what happened to them." He explains.

Deanna sees a chance to ask some questions that she has been waiting for the right opportunity. "What did happen, I haven't heard anything about any of the children except a little about Tia. Do you know Father?" She tries to press him for some answers.

"I am afraid Jamie is the one to tell you that, especially since they are all minors, but I'm sure he will, he has asked us all to be as helpful to you as possible." Deanna can see she's not going to get the answers she needs from the old man.

Deanna asks Father Scanlon if he has seen her daughter Katy anywhere, he tells her that he thinks they are all in the game room downstairs. Jonah walks up and she asks him also. He tells his mother, they are downstairs, finding the stairs was no problem as Father Scanlon shows her the way.

"Thank you Father." Deanna tells him.

Deanna descends the stairs to the game room, it's incredible, and filled with video games and pool tables and a large plasma screen TV is on the wall. It looks like a movie theater; on the far end is a large fire place. She spots Katy sitting at an old fashioned soda fountain sipping a soft drink and talking with Marianna.

"Hi Mother," She calls out as she sees her. "Isn't this the greatest ever, how cool is this whole setup." She's laughing and smiling more than Deanna has seen her in two years. She is almost like her old self except for her eyes, the sparkle has yet not returned.

"What a great room, you all must love it and be very happy here," Deanna comments to the girls.

Marianna quickly answers "This is a place right out of a fairy tale. Uncle Jamie wants all of us to be happy and feel as though this is our home, always. He thinks that by making it fun and comfortable, we will want to stay at home more than any other place… That's why we have all this, so we don't feel like we have to go hang out at an arcade. If we want to invite friends they'll want to come to the rancho and hang with us. I hope to be adopted here someday, that's what I pray for." She sighs longingly.

"Do you live here all the time Marianna?" Posing a question that might shed some light on the girl's situation and help her understand what does go on at The Ranch of Angels

"I am here most of the time, unless I have to go to a supervised visit with my Father. Most of the time I get sick when they tell me I have to go, that way I don't have to go too often." She smiles, a knowing smile.

"Do you have your own room or share with one of the other girls."

"No Senora I have my own room in the main house as we all do. Dyon is like our big sister if Uncle Jamie is not here, plus there is Rosa."

"Why doesn't T. J. live with her mother, I just met her, and she seems very nice." Trying to figure out what the story is with that arrangement.

"T. J. needs special care and her Mama is very sick, so she stays here with Uncle Jamie all the time. We are like family, all sisters surrounded by Aunts and Uncles. You could not want a better home or be with nicer people than here, everyone cares, even Old Tanner.

Katy would be very happy training with us, if Uncle Jamie can fit her in. I know she would not live here like us, but she would have friends and would feel safe when she is here." Marianna sounds much older than her years.

Tia runs up to us. "There goes the dinner bell we'd better hurry. Father Scanlon will want to say the Benediction before the meal." Tia takes Deanna's arm and herds her toward the stairs.

They all hurry up stairs to the dining room and Jamie greets them at the archway. "I was ready to send out the troops to look for you. Allow me to escort you to your seat. As our guest of honor you will sit next to me, with Jonah next to Dyon and Katy will be between Tia and Marianna if that's alright."

When everyone is seated, Father Scanlon stands and starts to give the Benediction.

"Holy Father we beseech thee to shine your holy grace upon those gathered here. We give thee thanks for the bounty in our lives, as we enjoy the fruits of our labors. We also wish to thank you Lord for bringing to us three new friends to join in our rejoicing of your name. Bless this house and all who reside here with your Love and Compassion, in Jesus name we ask this. Blessed be his name now and forever, Amen." He makes the sign of the cross, as do those so inclined.

Jamie stands up and looks in his guests direction, "Deanna, Jonah and Katy allow me to introduce the rest of our family. Will all of those that have not met our guests please stand, from right to left. This tall young man is Esteban and next to him is Theresa his fiancée, Marta and Gila are next, they are Rosa's cousins and work at the mission with Father Scanlon, I believe you all met Rubin and Irene, T. J.'s Mother. That very stern faced fellow is Eduardo, Rosa'a husband and ranch manager. Where's Tanner? Oh, here comes our Mr. Tanner now. Tanner you're late I suppose you have the same excuse again?" Jamie has a smile on his face, but still tries to look stern.

"I will be on time when that old bible thumper stops asking the almighty to do the same things all the time; I've heard it all already." He answers gruffly and sits down next to Irene, who smiles at him as he takes her hand in his, and he returns her smile.

"You are looking prettier every time I see you Ms. Irene, yes siree, a right smart looking lady you are." He winks and Irene beams. It is the first time Deanna has seen her smile; she seems at ease with him there.

"Well I guess you will always be late Rufus Tanner, because I will say the Benediction the same way. I will pray for your soul anyway and for him to improve your disposition." The elderly priest says to him good naturedly.

"Well you have been a saying it that a way for all the years I've known you. I suspect you should know it already, you are just an old croaker."

"This Deanna is Tanner; he is my oldest friend, also the blacksmith and resident vet here at Rancho de Los Angeles. We go back a long time he and I, and age has not improved his temper or disposition at all. Tanner, say hello to my guests. This is Deanna Gaynor, her son Jonah and her lovely daughter Katy." Tanner stands and shakes her hand and Jonah's; he turns and smiles at Katy.

"Pleased to meet you all, Ms. Katy you make sure anything you need doing for your horse you come sees old Tanner, and I fix it up for you." He softens his tone when he speaks to her and flashes a huge toothless grin.

With introductions over Rosa and the other girls get up and go out only to return with a large tureen of soup along with plates piled high with delicious smelling food. Salad is passed out in addition to hot bread, Jamie stands and takes Deanna's bowl and ladles soup for her, then the same with Katy and Jonah, as she tries to protest.

"Please as my guests let me serve you first."

It's a typical family dinner with people having conversations and enjoying each other's company. Jamie asks the girls about their day at school and what they did, the vaqueros make ranch reports and Father Scanlon brings all up to date on the mission, current births and new arrivals.

Rosa's daughter Pita finishes first and gets up and sits on Jamie's lap against her Mother's protest. "Pita you know better than that, Don Diego has not finished his meal you must not bother him, you know this," she says with exasperation in her voice.

"Jefe, is it alright if I sit with you?" Pita asks Jamie, putting her hand on his face.

"You are going to get me in big trouble with your Mamacita little one, but I am finished now so it will be ok. And he winks at Rosa. Pita takes both her hands and places them on either side of his face looking into his eyes.

"Jefe, will you sing for us later I heard you singing today Por favor?" All the other girls chime in with Pita; they know he refuses her little.

"Please Uncle Jamie play for us. Please, Please," they all ask in a chorus.

"Alright I know when I have been outmaneuvered. Yes I will, but only after you have helped with the dishes and cleaned the kitchen." They all clap and giggle, Jamie turns to Deanna and whispers, "I'm sorry, but you will have to suffer through this."

"I heard you singing today, and I look forward to hearing you play once more." She says to him honestly.

"Well you all asked for it." And he laughs. "Rosa may we take dessert in the great room tonight?"

"Si Patron I will bring in coffee in a moment, go sit, let us clear the table." She states like a majordomo commanding the troops.

"Come my friends let's retire to the other room," Jamie stands and pulls out Deanna's chair and offers her his arm. Linking her arm in his they stroll toward the great room. Katy goes with the girls and Jonah asks permission to help also, Deanna thinks he wants to spend time with Dyon. Tanner and Irene have each found a comfortable chair along with Father Scanlon, while the men go outside for a smoke.

Jamie takes Deanna over in front of floor to ceiling windows and asks her to stay right there. Walking over to the wall by the fireplace he flicks a switch, walking back to her, he asks Deanna to look out the window. She's overwhelmed by what she sees; the lake has been transformed into a light show. A fountain in the center with many pulsating colored lights appears and the shore line is a blaze of color.

"Jamie it's magnificent I have never seen anything more beautiful." Deanna gasps unable to say anything more; the beauty of it takes her breath away.

"Deanna the only thing lovelier than what you see out there tonight is you. When you entered the room before dinner you looked like a vision from a dream, the dress, and your hair everything about you. Beauty entered my home tonight I hope it comes many times again," he takes her hand and kisses it.

She feels herself blushing and is saved from further embarrassment by the men returning inside from having their smoke.

"Come sit down enjoy your dessert, Rosa makes the most perfect pastries you'll love them." Jamie tells them.

He guides her to a chair by the fireplace that someone has started, a cheery blaze that reflects from the hearth and adds warmth and color to the room.

Jamie sits down and asks Eduardo "How are the bulls in the north pasture, when do you think the breeding will begin?"

"Patron the bulls are starting to fight now, so I had Rubin and Esteban move the younger ones that show no signs of bravery to the west fields, Midas is still the king, he will be first to the cows. They will be ready to put to him next week, I watch him to know when the season begins, and He knows when the time is right." Eduardo states as if he were talking about a person.

Jamie turns to Deanna and says, "Midas is the bull that Eduardo raised on my old place from a calf. He is very proud of him, and he should, he is huge and extremely virile."

Rosa and all the girls come in with plates of pasties and hot chocolate and coffee, placing them on the buffet table against the wall they all begin to serve themselves.

"Rosa these are wonderful you must give me the recipe, I would love to make these for the holidays," as Deanna put some more on her plate, the coffee smells rich and strong like the people that live here.

"Si Senora Deanna I will tell you, but you must write it down, my English is not so good on paper." She admits a little shamefully.

"Not a problem we can do it together I will write, and you talk and that will make it faster." Rosa smiles at her for making it sound perfectly normal.

"Si Senora, muchas gracias[21]." She is pleased with Deanna's answer.

Jamie steps over to Jonah. "Jonah, I was just speaking with Eduardo, and he tells me our cows will be ready to be bred starting next weekend, and I think we will need some more help moving them to the breeding pastures. Would you be interested in some part time work on weekends starting next Saturday? You would be working with the vaqueros moving the cows."

"Jefe, you said I would be working with the cows along with the vaqueros," Dyon says to him, her whole attitude now bristling.

"You know how I feel about you doing that kind of work Dyon, a young lady should be learning other pursuits." He shoots right back at her.

"I am as good a vaquero as Esteban or Rubin, it is only you and Eduardo that I can't outride Jefe," Dyon pouts.

"Ok, you will work with Jonah, if he would like the job, and it's all right with you Deanna." He relents to Dyon.

"I would love it that's my dream to work as a cowboy. It would be alright wouldn't it Mother?" He looks to his mother with a light in his eyes, Deanna feels trapped and nods her head yes.

"It's settled next weekend you start, you may stay Friday night if you wish so you can get an early start on Saturday agreed?" Jamie walks over and shakes Jonah's hand.

"Yes sir" he beams and looks at Dyon, she's smiling also.

Pita runs in, an almost bowls Jamie over jumping on him, shouting

---

21 Many thanks

"Jefe you promised that you would play for us, now Por favor." She cries and gives him a hug and kiss.

Father Scanlon laughs, "She knows how to play a room, don't you think?" Winking to Deanna

Jamie goes over to the piano and sits down and warms the keys up by playing the scales.

"Give me a minute and I will be ready. Alright what do you want to hear?" He asks Pita, she giggles and tells him, "Play a love song, Jefe." And she snuggles along side of him on the piano seat."

"Pita, you are hopeless romantic," chuckles Jamie.

Marianna and Tia chime in as well "Play us a love song Uncle Jamie."

He begins to play a song that Deanna immediately recognizes as a Josh Tatum's song, "You are more than a memory."

She listens to him play and to sing the lyrics, his voice is soft and sweet, he is an accomplished musician and vocalist. Pita adores him snuggling as close as she can to him and Dyon never takes her eyes from him, she sees Deanna looking at her and averts her eyes, Jamie finishes and they all clap.

"Eduardo where is your guitar come, we will play Melaguena[22] for our guests." Eduardo picks up a guitar from the corner of the room, and they begin to play a duet. Eduardo is a great guitar player himself, together they sound good enough to be on stage, when they finish everyone claps and cheers. Next they play songs the girls can all sing along too.

When Jamie finishes with the girls he asks Dyon to come sing with him an old song. "Put your head on my shoulder," together they are remarkable and Dyon has a wonderful voice, rich and vibrant. Watching them all interact one can see that this is a family, with love filling the room.

Father Scanlon moves over on the couch and whispers to Deanna. "She could be a professional if she chose; she's that good, wait until you

---

22 Famous guitar song

hear her at Christmas time. She will bring tears to your eyes, her voice is angelically sweet." He confides to her.

"Father I think she's in love with him." Deanna whispers to him as she watches the way she looks at Jamie.

Father Scanlon says "No, not in the way you think, she is protective of him because she does not want to see him hurt again, she loves him with all her heart, not as a woman, not in the way you think my dear. Dyon sees him as a person who stands tall, and she is proud of him as he is of her, but not in a carnal way, she is truly his daughter of the heart. He was the only person that cared for her ever. Remember each of them have a story, first hear the story than judge them." He pats her hand after that gentle chastisement, he than smiles and winks.

"I'm sorry Father you of course are right, but when will I hear the stories." She tries again to get him to open up to her.

He whispers to her. "When Jamie shares them with you, what Jamie wants, are the results of his program here to be known, not having their past paraded before the public." Deanna feels a little ashamed, and she must try to think objectively.

Jamie and Dyon finish their song and stand for a round of ovations. Deanna watches the faces of those in the room noticing how each seems to be at ease how much they seem like any natural family. Watching her daughter chatting, laughing much like any thirteen year old would be.

"Excuse me please." Deanna stammers and feels the need to get some fresh air and runs outside.

Standing there looking at the lake Deanna starts to cry, suddenly feeling hands on her shoulders then turning her around. Its Jamie, he puts his arms around her and holds her gently as she weeps not even knowing why.

"Let it out, we can stay here until you feel you have no more tears. I understand, you've had a life spinning week, so much is new, you'll see, everything will work out for you. You don't have to be afraid anymore." He whispers into her hair, as he holds her close.

Feeling the hardness of his body, she feels safe, like when her father was near. He releases her from his embrace. Deanna steps back and wipes the tears with a handkerchief that he had handed her.

"I will be alright now it's been as you said, a whirlwind week and my ex is giving me a lot of trouble. Seeing all of you in there and how much you care for each other just made me sad, comparing my own life." Deanna apologizes to him.

"You will not have a reason to be sad any longer, you have purpose and people that love you, here you will always have a friend and sanctuary, should you have need of it. Shall we go back in?" Jamie suggests and takes her hand.

"We really have to be getting home we have a new member of the family that has been alone all day." Deanna says to him.

"Really who is this new family member?" Jamie asks.

"She's a dog that appeared out of nowhere on my property, at the same time my ex husband was about to get very ugly. She just came out of nowhere, she's so sweet and very protective of me and the kids; I'm going to keep her, unless someone claims her."

"So a Guardian Angel has found you, I look forward to meeting this new found friend.

"Let me walk you to your car." He asks. They go in and she tells the kids it's time to leave, they say their goodbyes as Jamie and Deanna walk out to the car.

"We are having a trail ride on Sunday out to the old gravel pits, many of the kids from around here will be coming I was hoping you and your children will join us." He looks into her eyes and asks, "You'll come Sunday won't you?" He asks still holding her hand.

"Yes we will be here, what time are you planning on heading out."

"If you could be here around nine we can be heading out by ten and back by one so the kids can enjoy a swim in the pool before the barbecue. I forgot to tell you, Rosa says we are having a barbecue to celebrate the breeding season. You will stay for the party of course. Please."

She can't refuse the look in his eyes as he asks her again. "Yes, we'll come, you seem to be a man of many talents, and it will give me a chance to return this lovely dress you picked out."

"The dress is yours to keep; it was my pleasure, a gift to remind you of us."

"Thank you." She murmurs "I do love it; I just don't know how you knew I would like it."

"I don't really know, we were at the store, and Dyon wanted something new. I saw it and I felt it would be perfect for you. I normally don't buy personal gifts for people; this was one of those rare occasions." He just seems so naturally candid that she believes him.

"Jamie thank you for a wonderful day and for what you did with Katy, she's like a different person here. You have no idea how much seeing her happy and smiling meant to me today. It really makes me feel like a terrible parent, when a stranger can do for her what I can't." Deanna stands on the tips of her toes and kisses him on the cheek.

He whispers into her ear so only she can hear, "Hasta le vista, Lindo Senora.

"What does that mean?"

"Until we meet again, Lovely Lady," he replies with that same aura of honesty that she's felt since they first met.

Chapter 8

"Rehab for Losers"

Awakening to a glorious sunrise, Deanna lies in bed listening to the birds singing and watching the morning's sun's rays creep into her bedroom. Lying there with thoughts of fantasy, and knights in shining armor, she drifts between conscious and semi-consciousness. Nothing could be better than to dream that everything is going to be alright, even if only for a few moments.

Rubbing the sleep from her eyes, she turns over and sees Angel sitting next to the bed looking and waiting for her to get up. She was waiting patiently on the old rug when they got home last night and after Jonah took her out she came upstairs with her. She really is a remarkable animal in that she seems to sense things within them and has such a look of wisdom in her eyes. Deanna tells her she's not getting up right away and the dog lies down with a sigh. Angel hears Jonah getting up and going into the shower, and she gets up and pads softly out into the hall and down the stairs to wait for him.

Jonah and Katy had a tough time falling sleep last night; they both could not stop talking about what a wonderful time they had yesterday. All they could talk about was Jamie this and Dyon that, and the trail ride on Sunday.

She will have to talk to Steve, as much as she hates the thought of it, about the possibility of switching Katie from Rambling Winds Stables, out to the Rancho for lessons. He will argue with her because he won't be in control like he is now. It really depends on whether Jamie will agree to accept her. She will talk to Jamie on Sunday after the trail ride to see if there is a chance of her becoming one of his students, then she'll speak with Steve.

She wants to be a part of the program so much. She was telling them last night after they got home how different it is, the way Jamie speaks to each student, and the commitment that the girls feel toward what they are doing. Mostly, she said it was the way they care about each other in and out of the ring that made her feel welcome. That she did not feel different from the other students. She and Tia bonded like they were sisters. Katy made a comment that all the people at the ranch talk to you not at you, like at Miss Rose's barn or at school.

Jonah is so excited about his new job starting next Saturday and sleeping over Friday night. It has been a dream of his, since he was little, to be a cowboy. Now he'll get the opportunity to experience the reality of it for awhile. He certainly is attracted to Dyon, Deanna thinks he is experiencing first love. Jamie seemed to sense the same thing, but is not too worried about it affecting their relationship.

This assignment has so many angles and portals to it, both professionally and personally. She wonders if letting her family become involved is a good idea or should she leave them out of it. The problem is the traps are already set and some have sprung, for the kids and her also. Now Deanna has only his word that he wants her to write about the truth, as she finds it.

"Mother, are you awake, do you want me to pour your coffee now?" Jonah calls up to her.

"Yes I'll be right down," Deanna calls down to him before heading for the kitchen; she meets Katy on the landing.

"Good morning," Katy says to her mother with a happy voice and a smile on her face.

"Is this a new person that has moved in since yesterday morning?" Deanna asks her good naturedly.

"Yes it is Mother, and I would like to get to school a little earlier on Monday if Jonah can drop me. Tia and Marianna are going to meet me at my locker, so we can hang out for a while before the first class." She bubbles at her and bounces off to see Angel, who is waiting by the table for them as they come to breakfast.

The back door opens and Jonah comes in from feeding and watering, wearing a huge smile and gives his mother a hug.

"Mother if things work out well with my new job, and they can use me over the summer I would like to stay here this summer instead of going to Virginia and staying there with Grandma. You know I still have to make sure I can do the work, and they want me. It's just something to think about or maybe I'll get a job here for the summer. What do you think?" And he sits down digging into his breakfast.

"I think it's too soon to think about any of this. I think you should get at least one day's work behind you, before you think about disappointing your Grandmother. I was thinking of talking to you about going up this year anyway." Deanna answers him honestly.

Jonah would you mind taking Katy to school earlier on Monday, she wants to meet her new friends before the first class.

"No, not at all, in fact, I was thinking about going in early myself." He answers rather quickly.

"Meeting Dyon Monday morning are we?" Katy smiles and giggles, as Jonah gives a stern look at his little sister than smiles.

"Mother didn't you think she's beautiful, I mean not just pretty but really beautiful? I mean not like the other girls at school, she's so nice, I really like her a lot." Jonah looks off out the window as he eats his breakfast not wanting to have his mother see the expression on his face.

"Yes I do, and they all seem to be very nice." She answers trying to sound objective.

Katy almost chokes on her food trying to get the next word in.

"Mother did you know that T.J. does not speak at all? There was some kind of accident, and it left her without her voice and very scared all the time. Uncle Jamie says she is going to talk again when she's ready. Pita and T.J. home school at the ranch, Uncle Jamie has a special teacher for them. Mother I think your story is going to be so extreme, because it's the most interesting place in the world."

Katy is talking so much that neither Jonah nor herself can even answer a question. Katy rapid fires into something else and this is only after spending one day out there.

"What did you think of the entertainment last night, Uncle Jamie could be a rock star, he plays so well, and he has a great voice. I loved the song and the sing along afterwards was such incredible fun, I think he and Dyon should be on stage, I never ever had so much fun in my life. The dinner, even doing the dishes was fun, and everyone talks to one another. Rosa's cousins are funny too, you know they hope to marry Rubin and Esteban and live forever at the ranch. They said it is so much better than living in the village they grew up in." Stuffing her breakfast into her mouth and raving on about last night, her excitement seems boundless.

Before she can answer, Jonah says, "Mother, I want to check on my saddle at the Tack and Saddle Shop. I hope they have fixed the fender or put a new one on. I won't have a saddle to ride on if it is not fixed for tomorrow."

She forgot he broke the fender last week, Deanna hands them the keys to the truck. "Sure go ahead, I have to do some work on the story, and I could use some peace and quiet."

"Oh look at the time, come on Jonah. Bye Mother, I love you, see you later." Katy kisses her and runs out the door with Angel barking at her all the way to the truck.

"Be careful driving," Deanna says and gives Jonah a kiss before he leaves.

"I don't think I will get a word in with her all the way to the Mall, but everything she said is true. She was in my room until very late last night. I have not seen her this excited about anything in a very long time." He turns to leave as they hear the horn blaring. "See what I mean," he laughs and heads out the door.

"Bye bye, you better run she's getting impatient," she laughs and so does he.

"I will see you later, drive carefully and have a good day." She calls after them from the back patio as they start down the driveway.

Going back into the house with Angel, Deanna sits and thinks about all that Katy said. She has not had fun and enjoyed herself that much in a very long time. It was a moment to remember, not watching TV not listening to the stereo or playing on a computer. Just simple family fun, enjoying each other as a family was wonderful to observe. Jamie and his extended family enjoy each other more than anyone she's ever known.

The phone rings and she answers it, "Hello, Yes Mr. Collins we were there most of the day yesterday. I am starting the story today; in fact, I have enough for the opening I think. I will still need additional intel, I hope you will be able to get some more on his background....Yes I understand, Yes I'm going to try and fill in some of the gaps...... Your kidding, how many acres? With that much land he will isolate the whole green zone west to Big Sugar..... That will bring a lot pressure from the developers, I'm sure........ What did your contacts say?... Alright please let me know as soon as you find out...... I have the impression that he will be running cattle on that new land...... Yes sir, I'll get it over to you just as soon as I finish it. As a matter of fact, we're invited to go on Sunday....... I will try to pin him down. I think this will be the story of the year...... Good bye Sir, I'll certainly be very careful." Deanna is in shock as she hangs up the phone.

Rancho de Los Angeles has just acquired all the Delaplane Estate west and south of the ranch. Southwest Properties will be out on the equestrian mini estates with no access to the Green Zone. She thinks Jamie has just declared war on the most powerful group in the southeast. The pressure on him will be huge and the rumors will fly even more now that so much is at stake. Deanna wonders if he knows just how many enemies he has made for himself and his little family.

Deanna must reach out to Roberto and see what his contacts think of this new move by Jamie. She wonders did he act alone or is there a group of investors backing him in order to squeeze out Southwest Properties. Deanna thinks the lines will be drawn now with so many residents of the Village investing in Williams and Cerbon's Southwest Properties Group and very little support for Jamie.

Deanna's wondering why Jamie didn't mention that he was buying that place. The Magazine's investigators never even mentioned it was for sale? It's the lead in for the story now though, because of its impact on the community itself. That land has some of the best soil in the county and everyone knows it. It will grow anything; it was for years the largest nursery in South Florida. If Jamie is planning on putting cattle on it or horses it will be the best graze this side of Ocala. It's conceivably the most valuable track of land in all of Palm Beach County.

Picking up the phone she tries Roberto, dialing his cell number knowing that he's an early riser. It's just possible his people may have something very interesting for her to use in the story. As Jamie was not forthcoming about the land sale, she thinks as the phones rings.

"Hola[23], Roberto here, how may I help you?"

"Roberto its Deanna, how are you...Very good thank you…. Katy? She had her very first time yesterday jumping without a panic attack…. No, not at Rose's, she took a lesson from the owner of the ranch that I'm doing the story on….Yes, that's him, yes… I really don't know, but I can tell you this, there is something special about him and the way he trains, he makes everyone feel at ease. By the way, did you hear more from your friends, about him or some background on the rancho?... Oh yes that would be wonderful…… today at eleven thirty?…… Great I'll be there……… Yes. I just found out he bought the Delaplane Nursery, the whole thing….. Around twenty thousand acres… You're right they

---

23 Hello

will not be happy about it at all, that's one of the things I wanted to talk to you about. I will see you later…Thanks, bye." Roberto tells her he has some info on Jamie that may be of assistance to her. Deanna will have to do her barn chores and get dressed quickly if she's to meet him at the café on time…….

Turning out Katy's gelding, she watches him cavorting around the pasture like a young colt. She loves these moments with them, seeing them run the way they were intended, free and unencumbered with such beauty and strength.

Walking slowly back toward the house, Deanna becomes suddenly on alert when Angel starts to growl deep within her throat. Deanna looks around for the source of her agitation, but doesn't see anything. Deanna continues toward the house very apprehensive. Angel is still growling putting herself between Deanna and the patio. A man steps out away from the house startling Deanna for a moment, it's Steve.

He holds up his hands and yells, "Tell your mutt to calm down, I'm only here to have a talk with you." He tells her with a note of fear in his voice. This is something she's not used to, coming from him, fear.

"What do you want to talk about, because if it is a continuance of our conversation of the other day, forget about it and just leave?" Deanna tells him flatly. Angel is still growling in addition to crouching down, her ears are laid back against her head.

Still holding up his hands he blurts out, "It's about your new friend Doyle, we have to talk. Can we go inside?"

"No, you can talk to me out here, what about this new friend." Deanna just stares at him with loathing and wonders what she ever saw in him to begin with.

"I just met the man, and I'm doing a story on him and the ranch. I doubt if I would have any influence over him." Deanna states coolly, motioning for him to sit under the covered porch area.

"I just thought you might like to know that he is in for a lot of problems, starting in a couple of days. Anyone taking his part could be in danger themselves, you know."

"Is that a threat or are you just trying to scare me into doing something for you? I think you better be a little more specific about what you mean." Feeling angry at him, and she's not quite sure why.

"I'm sure you have heard from your magazine about the Delaplane deal. There are people who are very angry right now and calmer heads may not prevail. Someone may get hurt seriously maybe even fatally." His manner is threatening, almost evil, in fact.

"What exactly do you think I could do about it that might help your friends?" She asks him trying to draw him out to be more specific.

"Try to talk to him about negotiating with the right people, I'm sure they will offer him a substantial profit, plus provide an alternative site for his Rehab for Losers." He says sarcastically and then laughs.

"I have no influence at all with Jamie and as to his losers; I was going to tell you that I am considering enrolling Katy in his training program. Instead of with that no talent friend of yours, and I will pay for it myself." She shoots the words back at him, not knowing why. Maybe it was his remark about losers.

His face contorts with anger, and he starts to rise from the chair, his face working, but no sound comes from his mouth. Before he can utter a word, Angel's on her feet instantly with her fangs bared and snarling.

He mutters, "You've been warned." And he starts to back up toward the end of the patio, then down toward the driveway and gate. Angel is moving slowly with him step by step all the way to his car. She never takes her eyes off him. Steve has a terrified look as he dives through his window, one step ahead of Angel.

Watching him drive away, Deanna has a feeling, and is a little afraid. She's suspected for a long time that Steve was involved with this southwest deal. Now she's positive of it, and he sounded desperate. He has always been so sure of himself and the powerful people he knew. For him to come to her and try to enlist her help, he must be scared of something. She'd better hurry and take a shower and get dressed to meet Roberto.

Why is it, she always thinks more clearly in the shower as the hot water cascades over her? Deanna suddenly realized that when Steve was threatening Jamie. She rose to his defense mentally without any hesitation. This whole land thing throws a different light on the story and maybe even on herself. Now it's not just about troubled kids and a stranger in their midst. She wants to believe that the land is for building a dream out there for Jamie and his family. Not a land development scam, but look at Steve, she's been wrong before.

After getting dressed, she heads downstairs and sees that Angel is waiting for her at the bottom. Deanna pats her on the head and tells her to watch the house as she heads for the back door. She's nervous and runs to it barking; as Deanna opens it, she darts out and runs down the driveway calling to her doesn't do any good, she doesn't come back. Walking around to the car she sees that she is standing by the door, looking at her as if to say, "I'm going with you today."

"Ok girl, maybe you deserve to go." Deanna opens the door and Angel jumps in and sits down. Pulling out of the driveway she heads for the café on the other side of town. Deanna wonders if she should tell Roberto about the veiled threat from Steve. Alternatively, maybe she should wait and see if he tells her what he has overheard from the talk around the barn area first. She looks down at Angel, with her head in her lap like she has been with her for ever. Deanna can tell she hates Steve, and wonders why. Deanna wishes she had her when they first met she might have warned her about what a horse's ass he really is. She knows he would never have hit her with Angel around.

Pulling into the café's lot Deanna looks for Roberto's truck. There it is, he must be inside already. Parking the car and putting down the windows, Deanna tells Angel to stay and the dog lies down.

Walking inside, Deanna asks the hostess where Roberto is. She tells her he is waiting on the rear veranda having his espresso. Thanking her, she walks outside to meet him.

"Hola Roberto," Deanna walks rapidly to his table. He sees her and rises from his chair to greet her. Taking her hand in his he kisses it.

"Senora my friend, you look lovelier every time I see you. You brighten this heart of mine each time I see you with eternal hope." Offering Deanna a chair and waiting until she sits down, before resuming his chair. "Would you like some coffee?" Roberto asks as he sits down.

"Yes that would be wonderful."

Roberto hand motions the waitress to their table and orders some coffee for her." We have much to discuss today you and I, about this man you have become involved with."

She tries to say that she's not involved with him, but he stops her with a hand gesture like fathers sometimes do with a child he was trying to get a point across to.

"Say no more to me, let me tell you what the talk is first. My people say he is a Malo Hombre[24] when crossed, that he is afraid of nothing. He is a man with a mission, the land thing is very important to his plans for the rancho. He is bringing in many heads of cattle and is hiring vaqueros for the ranch as we speak from among my people. If I were him, I would be very careful, he is standing in the way of some who would make millions, but will lose it all if he does not sell to them.

"How do you know this Roberto?"

"Anglo's are very stupid at times. They have a tendency to think because we do not speak the language well, we do not understand what they say. They do not notice we are there when they are talking. This man El Tigre[25], which is what my people call your Senor Doyle, he has many friends among my people, so they listen. He will soon find out, how many come to his aid should he have need of them. They also speak of the woman with fire in her hair that he smiles on, so I think you have an interest to know, yes?" Roberto smiles at her a sly smile.

"Senora I have not met with him yet, but I will tell you that the one's who know him, they believe he is a fighter as well as a saint. A very

---

24 Tough man

25 The tiger

explosive combination to have and his man Eduardo is a well respected man himself. I heard he can be a dangerous man also when pushed. I think these Anglo's may not want to tangle with the Tiger." Roberto finishes and orders two more espresso's for them.

They spend the rest of the hour talking about Katy and her first lesson, Roberto listens and when she's done he says. "This El Tigre, he sounds like a man I will have to meet, a man who has been touched and now shares with others are a rare thing today."

Deanna looks at the time and tells him she has to go, Roberto nods and walks Deanna to her car. As they approach, they see Angel has gotten out and is waiting by the side of the truck. Angel gets up and walks to Deanna and looks at Roberto with her tail wagging. How does she know that he is a friend, she just seems to sense it?

"I see you have a new member in the family." He reaches down to pet her, and she smiles at him and licks his hand.

"She adopted us a few days ago we love her."

"What's her name?" Roberto asks as he fondles her ears.

"We called her Angel and it must have been her name before, she responded to it immediately.

"She's a fine animal and will be good for you and the family; she knows who she can trust and who she cannot. Listen to her, she is special for you, I sense something about her. She found you for a purpose Senora." He takes her hand and kisses it, and heads for his truck. Roberto stops and turns to her. "I will be seeing you soon I think, Adios my friend."

These people that Roberto knows may be right about Jamie. She senses that as gentle as he seems, it may only mask a man when pushed will push back. Deanna sees a determination in him that few people have, a will of steel. She only hopes that Steve was just trying to scare and impress her. Neither Jamie Doyle nor the men who work for him seem to be the type to frighten easily……

She gets home around one o'clock and goes to the study to work on the story, Angel comes with her and lies down at Deanna's feet. Opening the outline on the computer, she starts by inputting all the data she has amassed so far. She begins using speech writer software to begin telling the story. Her opening for the piece will be about the land purchase and the importance of it. Then she thinks about working in the angle about the ranch and children in crisis in rehab next. Deanna's thought process stalls with a moment of writer's block when she realizes that she needs to talk with Ed Haskell and Father Scanlon about Jamie and his past, Deanna needs much more.

She calls the old priest first at the Mission's office number.

"Mission of the Virgin, how may I help you." Answers a woman's pleasant voice it sounds like Irene, T. J.'s mom.

"Hello Irene, this is Deanna Gaynor, I met you last night at dinner. I'm doing the article on the ranch. I was wondering if Father Scanlon was very busy."

"Hello Ms. Gaynor, I must put you on hold while I see if Father is busy, please wait." The line goes silent while she finds the priest.

Father Scanlon gets on the line and asks her in a cheery voice. "Hello, so nice to hear from you, what can I do for you Ms. Gaynor?"

"I was wondering if I might come to the mission and speak with you. I need a little background and Rosa said you have known Jamie the longest, and Tanner, Who quite honestly intimates me a little."

"Yes, Tanner can be a might disagreeable at times, but he's quite harmless. I would be delighted to meet with you any time. Did you have a specific time or day in mind?" He asks her.

"I was wondering if I could today, if it won't bother you too much or inconvenience you."

"No not at all, its three thirty now, say about four then."

"That would be wonderful; I can be there by four."

He proceeds to give her directions from Wellington to the Mission in Loxahatchee. Deanna hangs up and tells Angel to come it's time to go. They are out of the house like a shot.

Arriving at the Mission, Deanna sees Father Tom standing out front with many small children, who seem to be enjoying the old priest.

"Hello" he calls out to her and walks out to meet her as she exits from the car. Father Tom halts dead in his tracks with his eyes as big as half dollars.

"Are you alright Father?" He looks as though he has seen a ghost.

"Yes, I'm fine…it was just seeing your dog that startled me that's all… fine, a fine looking animal." He stammers to her, never taking his eyes from Angel.

"She won't hurt anyone Father she is very gentle with people. I was at home the other day, and she just appeared out of nowhere needing a place to live and something to eat. . We just kind of adopted her; if it will make you feel better I can ask her to stay in the car."

The old priest says, "No, No, she'll be fine I'm sure, shall we get where it is shady. I wish we had some place that's air conditioned, but I try not to bother our benefactor that much with what we need. He's been very generous, and I have sinus infections from too much air anyway." He offers in the way of an apology.

The old priest pauses and thinks to himself, *"The dog looks like the one Mary had when she passed; no one saw it after that." He wipes his forehead looking at the dog, "Could it be that Mary's hound has returned after all this time."*

"That would be fine Father, I'll try not to take up too much of your time." They sit down under a huge tree out back of the office and Irene comes out with a tray of drinks for them.

"Irene, how nice to see you again,"

"Thank you Ms. Gaynor a pleasure to see you as well, will you require me for anything else Father?"

"No Irene thank you, please call me for the Evening Mass, you know how I lose track of time." He remarks with a hint of laughter in his voice and a twinkle in his eye.

"Yes, Father I will." Saying goodbye she turns and leaves them alone.

"Father, when I arrived with Angel you seemed to have seen her before, do you know who might have owned her."

"She reminded me of an animal I knew some years past, that was all; she is the same kind of dog. Now what is it that I can be helping you with?" He changes the subject.

"Well Father, I understand that you have known Jamie longer than anyone else except maybe Tanner. What I need is some background on Jamie. How he came to be here and how he acquired his wealth and why he is trying to help these children." She sits waiting for him to answer.

"I can fill in some of the gaps for you, but as to whether you will want to use it in this story is another thing entirely. I will have to give you some background on myself, you may find a little shocking. You will need it to know how I met with Jamie." He sits back and takes a drink of his lemonade.

"I was posted to a small parish in southern California, and I was very lonely and began to drink in excess of my ability to hold my liquor. So much so, that I was neglecting my flock and remiss in my duties. I began stealing from the church to support my alcoholic needs. I was found out and dismissed from my post, stripped of my robes and thrown out of the order for the good of the church. I wandered for a few years winding up in a small Mexican village. It was there that I met with him. He was a lost soul searching for redemption and helping out a small mission run by some nuns, to poor to even have a priest.

I was in bad shape, sick, wanting to die, when he found me searching for food in the trash. He helped heal me in my body, and mind. He asked me if I could try to help the nuns run the mission, mainly because of my background. I told him I would try, but could make no promises. We set up a food kitchen which he worked tirelessly on himself. He worked day after day with little or no help from any of the rich landowners trying to cause a change.

I was sober for almost six months and Jamie had been absent from the mission for a while. When he finally arrived back, he had with him a young woman who was in an extremely rough way. He said she needed me; she was an addict and an alcoholic who had fallen on bad times.

Doing things to try to get by that you may not have thought was a good thing. She was thin and did not think much of herself anymore. Little by little she came around; I knew it was because of him that she was trying. When she went into withdrawal it was him that stayed with her, and held her until that terrible time was passed.

She recovered, gained weight and worked at his side to help the poor people of that village. Jamie helped her regain her self respect, and she helped him with whatever it was that was troubling him. The both of them helped me stay sober. In time the church closed the mission and some of the old nuns passed away, the others were relocated.

We tried to run it on our own, but it was difficult. He was working and using all of his money to try to keep it going. It was at this time that he came to me and asked me if I would marry Mary and him. I told him I was not empowered to do that any longer. He said to me that in God's eyes, I was the only one who could join them together. I agreed and performed the ceremony; it was at this time that Mary told him she had contacted her Father. She told him where she was, and that she had plans to marry.

That week two men arrived and came to the mission asking for Mary. Jamie asked them what they wanted, and they said they were there to take her back to her Father. They were huge men obliviously chosen because of their capability to persuade him, and that it would be best if he left them to their business. I don't know what Jamie told them, but they left without Mary and in a hurry as well. Jamie told me he had to take Mary back home to try to heal whatever was between her and her Father, even if it meant giving her up. They left the following week to come back to Florida and meet with her father. When next I heard from him, it was to come here because I had work to do, and he needed me. I came and I started this mission."

The old man closes his eyes to blink tears away; Deanna feels he has told her much of the truth as he begins to drink some of his neglected lemonade. Another thought crosses her mind, and she asks him, "Father, then Jamie was not wealthy when he came here?"

"Oh, yes he was, he just didn't know it. That occurred after they were here for awhile; Ed assumed that Jamie was a fortune hunter out to take his daughter for her inheritance. So he had Jamie investigated by friends of his in the FBI, they discovered that Jamie had written and recorded some songs before he had dropped out of site years before, as a result he was a wealthy person in his own right. He had literally dropped out of life and no one could locate him. Neither his agent nor the music companies, so his money was deposited to a bank under the copy right laws and just accumulated.

In a short time Jamie convinced Mary's father that he truly was in love with her and wanted to make her happy for the rest of her life. Her father believed him and gave his blessing so a family was healed and what was broken was becoming fixed."

"Father did they ever have children." Deanna asks not really knowing why, but she had to ask.

"They wanted children and tried and tried, but no children came forth. The problem was Mary, because of the drugs she had consumed and the life she was forced to live, it had left her barren. She was unable to conceive children, so the one thing they both sought was denied them. For Mary's father, the joy of being a grandparent to his only daughter's child was never going to happen. Some years went by and they were happy together, and with the help of his father-in-law, he turned his fortune into what he has today.

"Father Tom, how did Mary die?"

"Mary was sick for many years she had cancer you see, that was why they never adopted children, when Mary passed, he grieved so much I thought we would lose him as well. One day he called me and said he had bought the ranch and was going to set it up for children in crisis. You see Jamie always had a power to reach the troubled, and he said now was the time to use that power."

Deanna moves closer to the old man and asks him. "Did Jamie ever tell you why he was at that mission or what caused him to give up his career in music?"

He has an instant flash back; he remembers Jamie's confession.......

Jamie and he were sitting outside the mission. Jamie was very contemplative and Tom asked him, if there was anything he wanted to say to him. He said "Yes, that he carried a dark spot on his soul"

"I don't believe that, what could you have done to so stain your soul to make you believe such a thing?"

"I've killed Tom, some not by my hand, but by my actions, and one I took his life with my own hand out of vengeance."

"Go on my son, something like this needs to be unburdened, not locked up inside, is it like a confession you would be wanting"

"Yes Tom, I was punished for the others, but the one act of murder that I was never punished for is the one that I'm afraid I will never be at peace, ever. To some they would say it was justice, to the law of man and God, I will never receive penitence. I'm not sure you may want to hear this and still want to be my friend."

"I shall always be your friend, for you have done what I was unable to do myself, you saved my life.

"It happened when I was released from prison, I heard from my friend Rufus that my baby sister had been raped and my mother had passed. The authorities arrested him, but he was released because my mother and sister were considered white trash. Fiona had conceived and she died in childbirth. The child welfare contacted the father who rejected the child, forcing the State to place her in foster care.

I hunted him down and he admitted to me what he had done, and he wanted to make a fight of it instead of turning himself in. I lost it and broke his neck, Rufus was with me and told me to get out, and he would get rid of him.

Not only did I loose my soul, I allowed him to injure his own for my sake.".........

"Yes he did, but it was told to me as a confession even though I was no longer a priest, the confessional was still scared to me, and you will have to try to get him to tell you that part of his life." Deanna senses it's better to drop the subject and move on.

"Father Tom, is his father-in-law still alive and living in Florida?"

"Yes he is, I'm sorry I thought you knew. Ed Haskell was Mary's father," he answers her with a look of surprise.

This was a shock to Deanna; she never would have made the connection, thinking they were just friends not related. She now sees where a powerful friend came in, to block any background checks. Ed Haskell is one of the richest men in America. She should have made the connection when Father Tom said her father had him investigated by the FBI.

"Father, was Jamie a missionary of some kind or, what when you first met him." Deanna asks him, because she's still confused as to why Jamie would go to some out of the way place in Mexico

"No, he was just trying to heal his soul and wound up in a tiny out of the way back water village, a sanctuary for lost souls so to speak." Irene comes up as he finishes speaking and reminds him that he must get ready for Mass. His parishioners are starting to arrive.

"Yes of course Irene, I will be ready in just a minute, would you care to stay and celebrate the Mass with us Deanna." He asks her, with that kindly Bells of Saint Mary's smile of his.

"I would love to Father, but I must get going, the children don't know I'm here, and I wanted to be home for dinner. May I come some other time for the Mass?"

"You will be more than welcome any time my Dear." He walks Deanna to her car and bids her goodbye.

Now she has some real background to work with, but needs some more information to finish her story. He must have had something that he was running away from when he met Father Tom and Mary. What could send a man like him to try and hide from the world and from a life that he was successful at? Deanna decides to put research to work on the music thing Monday morning, unless she can get it from him on Sunday.

As she turns into the driveway of the house Deanna sees that Jonah is home. She parks the car and opens the door, Angel runs out to greet Jonah as he comes from the barn not looking pleased.

"What's wrong with you, your face is dragging on the ground. What's happened?" Concerned that something may have happened with Katy.

"I just came from the saddle shop, and they didn't have my saddle fixed, what will I use tomorrow, bareback?" He says dejectedly she knows that he wanted to impress not only Jamie, but Dyon as well.

"Well you have your old English saddle you could use that." She mentions to him trying to be helpful. He looks forlornly at her and slumps his shoulders, she knows how much he hates riding in that saddle.

"Look I am sure that Jamie will have one that you could borrow, so bring the Corbett in case he doesn't." Jonah nods his head, but still looks down.

Deciding to change the subject she asks, "How did you guys make out at the Mall?"

"Good, Katy got herself a new outfit that looks great, but says she is going to use one of Tia's outfits for the barbecue, I got a new shirt. We started dinner for you." She gives him a kiss while wrapping her arm around his shoulder in a best friend gesture, and they go inside.

Chapter 9

"Sunday Morning"

The alarm goes off its still dark out, but the birds are singing and Angel is sitting looking at Deanna with a funning kind of expression on her face.

"Today we are going to leave very early, but you will have to stay home and watch the house and barns. Ok." She seems to nod and jumps on the bed licking her face than jumps down and goes and barks at Jonah's door. After three barks, Deanna hears a very sleepy voice.

"I'm already awake Angel, give me a minute." He tells her through the door in a very groggy voice. Next she goes to Katy's room, and sits by the door scratching, but not loud, but enough so that Katy open's the door and greets her.

"I was up already, but thank you for being so quiet Angel," and they both head down the hall toward the stairs.

Deanna is amazed at how she knows what each of them needs and how much she reacts to her new family. Deanna can't get over how their lives have changed as has Angel's in so short a span of time. She heads downstairs to get a cup of coffee.

"Good morning Mother, are you excited, this is like an adventure or going on vacation for the first time isn't it?" Katy says as she pours her mother's coffee.

"Yes it is in a way, we've never done this before, all of us I mean. I'm excited myself, I feel like a kid again. Is Jonah down yet?"

"Yes he went out already to hook up the trailer to the truck, he said to tell you to enjoy your coffee, and he would see to the tack." Katy is gulping down her cereal so fast Deanna feels compelled to say something.

"Slow down or you'll choke." Deanna can't remember her being so enthusiastic about breakfast.

"I'm going to go get Legion ready; I braided his mane last night, so he'll look pretty for today. I want him to make a good impression. I think I will have the biggest horse there, unless some of the new riders bring one that's bigger. How many people do you think will be going on the ride with us Mother?"

"I don't know Jamie said some of the neighbors were coming over and their children, maybe you know some from school." She says to her as she heads for the door.

Katy opens the back door, "Come on Angel let's go get ready." Angel is on her feet in a heartbeat and padding out the door right behind her.

As Deanna watches her run out the door, she wonders where that girl is, that was fighting with her just the other day. Katy's anger toward her mother seems to have totally left her; she is like the little girl she was before the divorce. It is such a coincidence that getting this new job and meeting Jamie has not only changed their lives financially, but on a personal basis also.

She sits and pours herself another cup of coffee and thoughts of Father Tom's conversation of yesterday come back to her. What kind of man was Jamie so long ago and what happened in his life for him to go to an obscure place outside of the country.

Suddenly, she has a flash back to her own childhood. Remembering a young woman with red hair on a white jumper smiling at her and saying she would be alright, that next time she would do much better. It was Ed

Haskell's daughter Mary. She was bright and so beautiful all the boys wanted to be with her.

Her Mother had been killed in a riding accident while out with her Dad on a Fox Hunt in Virginia. Here they are so many years later, and it seems to have come full circle, how odd and then Jamie marries her. Deanna thinks she will have to rummage through the old albums. She thinks there's a picture of her and Mary taken that day at the barn when she was so kind to her. Deanna was upset because she didn't pin and thought her Father would be mad at her. Deanna used to follow Mary around after that.

Here she is thirty years later doing a story on her husband and possibly, her Dad. Deanna still can't believe his wife was someone that was like a sister to her when she was not much younger than Katy. Her Father was her riding instructor for many years, she was one of his favorite students, and he genuinely loved her, Deanna wonders did Ed get her that appointment with Jamie remembering that connection.

She listens and hears Angel barking and Jonah and Katy are laughing, she had better go and get dressed, or they will be getting angry at her for making them late, Deanna can't recollect the last time she saw the both of them this excited.......

"Patron, how many shall we anticipate for the ride today?" Eduardo asks Jamie.

"Set up for thirty about half will be bringing their own horses so have fifteen of our saddle horses ready. Take some hay with you to the pits along with the refreshments when you go to set up. Oh, and take a load of towels just in case someone falls in like the last time." Eduardo looks at Jamie laughing, remembering Pita, she was the one that fell in the water, last time they were there.

Jamie's mind is full of thoughts today; the Delaplane deal is a great thing for the ranch. They will be able to run over a thousand head now and still have room for the horses on his ranch. Mary would have been pleased to see their dream starting to come to fruition.

"Excuse me Patron; the pretty Senora will be riding today as well?" Esteban asks.

"Yes I think she's still coming." Deanna's face comes instantly to his mind, what is it about her that he senses are so familiar? It's not that she just reminds him of Mary....

"Patron, then shall I make the stalls ready for her, No?"

"Oh yes, she will be bringing her own horses make room in the main barn. Please do me a favor Esteban, take Storm out and groom him until he shines, I want him to look his very best today."

"Si Patron, I will make him shine like the new peso. The one with the fire in her hair will be pleased to see you on such a fine horse." Esteban winks at him and hurries off before Jamie can correct him. Esteban mentioning Deanna causes him to think of her again.

She's quite attractive and he senses a very warm woman, one that would make any man proud to have at his side. He was very impressed with her ever since their first meeting. He must be careful not to think of her too often, she is a woman that could cloud your thoughts, and divert you from your purpose. It can't seem like he is manipulating the story either, he needs her to be objective in writing it. There will be enough people that will want to see him dead soon enough. They need all the good press they can get or everything will go up in smoke. There is too much at stake to lose now because he could not control his passions.

" Eduardo would you have Jake saddled up for me, I'm going to get some coffee from Rosa and ride over to Fiona's Acre for a little while before our guests arrive?"

"Si Patron, will you return here or meet us at the quarry?"

I won't be that long, I should return before they get here. If I'm not back, please entertain them for me, until I come. I know you will make them comfortable." Eduardo nods his head and heads for the barn, Jamie strolls to Rosa's house and knocks on the door.

"Hola Patron," Rosa opens the door for him.

"I came over because I smelled your coffee Mamacita." He kids her good naturedly.

"You are like the little boy, you are going for a ride early and want something to keep you company, No?" Rosa states as she smiles at him.

"You know me too well Little Mama, I want to let her know about some of the new changes since last I was there. Just bringing her up to date, I need a little guidance right now. I think better there, we are facing some tough times ahead." She pours him a cup of coffee and makes one to go.

"Please wait Patron," and she walks out to the patio and returns with a bouquet of flowers. "I thought you might be going today so I made them ready for the Senora. You tell her we are all here for you, that you do not fight alone." Rosa states defiantly.

He thinks to himself, the person who takes her on would be in for a world of hurt. He thanks God for her; he would have been lost without her and Eduardo. Jamie strolls over and gives her a kiss on the forehead and a big hug.

"I will be back soon." And he finishes his coffee and picks up the cup she made for him and the flowers and heads over to the barn.

Eduardo has Jake ready; the big horse seems to know where they are going and is impatient to be on their way. He starts to prance while Jamie mounts. He doesn't need to give him direction, he knows the way so Jamie just gives the horse his head. He sets off at his walking trot, eating up ground in that easy way he has that Mary loved so much…..

Jamie sees the little oasis of oak trees with the big fichus tree coming into view, ducking under the limbs, he gets down and ground ties Jake. The pond is crystal clear and the ducks come out to greet him.

"Hello Mary, another Sunday, sorry to be late, but we're having guests over today for a trail ride. We are going out to one of your favorite places, the old quarry. I have a lot to tell you… First you would be very proud of Dyon, she's doing wonderfully in school, and she met a young man that is quite taken with her. He's tall, good looking, and college bound. She likes him to, I can tell, His name is Jonah, he looks at her the way I used to look at you. She's the daughter we never had, and she gets more beautiful each an everyday.

The girls are all doing well, T.J. still hasn't spoken yet, but I believe I'm close now to making a break through with her, she is opening up.

Irene is doing as well as can be expected with Tom out at the Mission. He has a full house, but still won't let me put in air conditioning, he claims that a little discomfort is good for the soul.

The land sale went through so our dream is much closer to fulfillment; we will start cutting it up in sections as soon as the new hands arrive… Eduardo has hired the best around, all men who know how to work and fight if necessary. They'll have no backup in them, like him. I am expecting some trouble over it, but nothing I can't handle.

By the way…there is a young woman that's doing a story about the ranch, and myself, your Dad sent her to me. I think you might have known her in Virginia, her name was Deanna Quinn. She's been on my mind; nothing serious just wanted you to know. I promised you that I would try after you left… I was planning to ask her and her family over for the holidays if they don't have other plans. She also has a daughter that's in crisis; she tried to commit suicide and suffers from panic attacks and rage. Tia told me she was going to ask her mother if she could take lessons with us. She rides but has a problem with control, I gave her a lesson the other day, and she did well, we'll see.

Well Mary, its time for me to head back now and see that everything is in readiness for tonight's big fiesta. Rosa has everything worked out to a T, you and she would have been a great team. I was just sorry you never got a chance to meet her." Jamie turns toward Jake a tear in his eye and another running down his cheek. Wiping them away he mounts the old horse. "Let's go home Jake, I know you miss her too, don't you big fella. This will be your pasture soon, once we divide the land up, you can spend all your time here with her." Jake turns toward home and to the barn.

Chapter 10

"The Trail Ride"

"Patron, we have big trouble Patron! Patron!," Rosa exclaims dashing up to Jamie as he rides in front of the barn. Getting down he throws Jake's reins to Rubin, and hurriedly goes to his housekeeper to see what could have put her in such a state.

"What is it that takes you out of your kitchen in such a hurry," Jamie asks trying to calm her down.

"The caterers say they cannot do your party tonight." Tears flowing down her face, "I have failed you Patron, and I am ashamed."

He puts his arms around her and tells her. "You never fail me, we will think of something else… I know call the butcher have him deliver a whole steer. We can cook it over a roasting pit turning it slowly. We have Marta and Gila to make salads and beans. You know Esteban's friend, the one that owns the pork place, call him and have all the pulled pork he can get for us. We will use your barbecue sauce and slow simmer them, south western style. We can order all the liquor from Shanahan's and tell him I require two bartenders. We will arrange a Grande Fiesta[26], we can string lights all over the veranda in addition to candles everywhere. Don't worry Little Mama it's gonna be fine." Jamie heartens her, actually

---

26 Grand party

getting excited over what was a routine formal kind of party that he was dreading, to a happy and comfortable kind, they should have thought of this first.

"Patron what about the musica who will play for your guests, this is a muy importante[27] fiesta for you." She's wringing her hands and staring at him for an answer.

"Raul, Esteban's cousin has a small band doesn't he? I'm sure he wouldn't want to pass up an opportunity to play before such an audience as this. If need be, I'll play for them, you worry too much, everything will be fine. We will greet our guests in an old Hidalgo manner. Even I will dress the role and put on my Don's costume with the gold embroidery and the girls can wear the outfits you bought them for the Spanish cavalcade in Miami. We will all appear like Spanish royalty, and you shall be the queen." Jamie smiles and walks with her back toward the house his arm around her shoulders.

As they approach Rosa's side entrance, she looks up at him radiating with pride and says. "Si Patron we will make a party that will be spoken about for a long time, something these Anglos have never witnessed. I shall make them proud to go to the fiesta at the home of Don Diego."

Her tears have changed to smiles; she is catching the exhilaration of the coming event as well. Jamie knows she feels more confident doing things as she would in her country. Poor Eduardo, she will badger him to death today, he'll wish he was with them on the trail ride. He'd better go and apprise him that she'll be in frenzy until she sees that everything is going fluidly.

Jamie sees his Segundo and calls out to him, "Eduardo, you my friend must face Rosa's wrath today as she makes everything go well, I'm sorry to stick you with this."

"Patron, I have already heard. It is not misfortune for me, you know she is La Madona[28] for you and the Senorita's; she would do no less for

---

27 Very important

28 The mother

me or Pita. All will be well you have made her extremely happy, I will take care of everything Don Diego." He smiles and walks away confident in the knowledge that his Patron and friend relied on him.

Jamie takes a moment to reflect about the title Eduardo has just used, knowing it means James, It is such a formal title and Eduardo and Rosa use it so seldom, it's a way of respect he has come to understand. They both are sticklers for utilizing the proper title; still he's not used to it, even after all these years.

Jamie looks at his watch and decides he'd better go and get dressed it is almost eight thirty they can expect some of the kids to start arriving soon. The neighbor's children that live around the ranch enjoy visiting for any occasion.

"Tanner, keep your eyes peeled for kids coming in on horseback." Jamie calls to him as he rounds the bunkhouse, eating a donut and drinking his coffee.

"What you think this is my first fandango; that I don't know what I'm doing? You go get yourself dandied up, and leave the real cowboy stuff to me. Don't be telling me my business again, you hear me, and take that smirk off your face too!" He shouts at him and stomps off; Jamie knows his old friend will know what to do.

It's funny he really appears to dislike grownups, but the kids adore him. The patience he lacks with adults, he gives to kids, and they love him. He is one of the best friends Jamie has ever had. He and Mary always had a special closeness too, Jamie reflects.

Jamie goes into the house to take another shower after his morning ride and dress for the trail. He finishes up and feeling refreshed, he proceeds downstairs and bumps into Father Tom, who has just arrived.

"Jamie my boy I got here as soon as Rosa called and I brought over some of my parishioners to help with tonight's festivities as well. They're enthusiastic that they can help." Tom is as excited like a school kid, and red faced and puffing.

"Did you run all the way," Jamie kids him. "All kidding aside Tom, thank you so much, this was a spur of the moment idea, but I know many of those invited will come out of curiosity, some out of obligation, but I think the timing is right for us after acquiring the Delaplane Estate. I'm hoping to smooth out quite a few feathers tonight as well." Jamie confides in his old confidante.

"I think the idea of a fiesta is absolutely outstanding, much better than a formal gathering. By the way, your lady friend was out to see me yesterday and asked about your past. I told her how we met and Mary, and all that happened from San Rafael to here. I've still no clue what it is that you hope to accomplish, what with her digging into your past and all. When she asked me more about it, I told her the truth, the confessional holds me silent, but what if she finds out all of the past?"

"Tom, it's alright, I want her to know the truth. Don't ask me why, but I know that she will do the right thing with it. Don't ask me how I know, I just do. She's a very special person, and I believe we've all been guided here for a specific reason that only time will unveil. So we play the cards we've been dealt old friend, you and I still have much to do yet and miles yet to go." Jamie smiles and puts his arm around Tom's shoulder.

"That we do son that we do." Toms says to him in that lilting Irish accent that Jamie has come to love so much.

"I think Rosa still has hot coffee and some fresh donuts in the kitchen, why don't you have some? You will give the Benediction tonight before we all eat, won't you?" Tom says it would be his pleasure and strolls out to the kitchen to spend some time with Rosa.

Jamie's cell phone rings and its Tanner, "You better get out here right quick we're in for a long night. It's Dyon's mare she's going into labor." Jamie tells him they will be there immediately and hangs up. He notes that when he wants, Tanner speaks perfect English.

He finds Dyon out by the paddocks with the other girls and motions for her to come with him.

"What is it Jefe?" Dyon excuses herself from what she's doing and runs over to him.

"Come with me, Tanner just called me and said Penny is going into labor." Placing his hand on her arm, he restrains her from sprinting toward the barn.

"Stay calm she's in the best hands that she could be in with Tanner. He knows more about bringing in foals than any person alive, and you know how he is about people interfering with him about the care of his horses. We are only going over to check on her and see what he says." She looks at him with fear in her eyes, but nods her head in agreement. When they get to Penny's stall the mare is standing and appears very nervous and sweating.

"How is she Tanner, she looks terrible, what's wrong with her?" Dyon cries out putting her arms around Penny's neck.

"You let her go now, let Old Tanner be about his business, she is just a little uncomfortable right now, and she ain't going to drop nothing for a while yet. Maybe she will give birth late tonight, but that baby ain't dropped yet, but it is sure enough coming. I will be with her the whole time, you know that Missy, I'm gonna take good care of her, and you go do what you got to do for this fandango. Let me be about my work, bringing this here young'n into the world…. Don't you be coming down here all the time either? I'll call you when you have to be here. Jamie and I, we have done this a few times, I'll call the saw bones when I think we need him too. Now you go get them kids ready, because I got to stay here." He looks right into Dyon's face waiting for her to answer.

"Yes Tanner, I will do as you say, please call me if you think she needs me," she answers him with tears welling up in her eyes.

"Now don't you be getting your eyes all puffy, you got to look pretty for your guest's?"

"I love you," she wipes her eyes and gives him a big hug and kiss. With that, she runs back to her chores getting the children and mounts all ready.

"Wish she wouldn't do that, makes me feel funny." He grumbles and looks away, so Jamie won't see the smile on his face and the sparkle in his eyes. "You are old fraud; you love her as much as I do. Call me if any changes happen" Jamie says to him and returns to the house.

"There you go again telling me how I feel and how to do my job. Go take care of your elbow rubbing," he says gruffly. Jamie just smiles and goes back to arrange for their guests, knowing the mare is in the best possible hands……

The neighborhood kids are starting to ride in and tying up in the front corral.

"Hi, I'm glad you all could make it, are you ready for some fun today?" Jamie quizzes them.

"You bet Uncle Jamie were ready." One of the boys around thirteen answers him.

"Our folks will be over tonight, is it true that you are throwing a big party, and we are all invited?" Another youngster called Mark asks.

"Yep, we sure are and yes you are invited to our very first fiesta, you guys will have your party in the game room, and I know how you hate that place." Jamie says jokingly as a chorus of denials erupts from them all.

"Rosa has some donuts for you guys over in the kitchen and the girls are down at the staging area. We still have some more folks coming so we'll be leaving in about an hour." They all rush off knowing Rosa makes the best donuts, Mary would have loved to see this, happy kids having a great time, doing wonderful things.

He finds himself thinking, he should have called to see if Deanna was coming, maybe she ran into a problem and can't make it, or she changed her mind after talking with Father Tom.

"Is something wrong Patron?" Asks Eduardo as he comes to his side.

"No, my friend I was just watching the drive, you didn't hear from Ms. Gaynor today did you?" Jamie tries to sound not so interested.

"Patron if the one that lights such a fire were to have called me, I would surely have told you. She will be here this I know, her Nino has the eyes for our Senorita Dyon, and they will come." Jamie looks at him sheepishly and nods. Suddenly, he sees her truck coming up the drive pulling her horse trailer.

"Eduardo, do we have any extra hands to help unload the Senora's horses?" Eduardo turns and looks at him with that big grin of his.

"Si Patron, you and I will be the hands." He laughs and directs Deanna where to park the truck.

"Hello, I was beginning to think you had forgotten about today, it's good to see you all." Turning to Jonah, he asks, "Jonah how are you," and shakes Jonah's hand.

"I'm fine Sir, thank you for inviting us; we all have been very excited about today." Jamie likes this young man, he's honest and straight forward like his mother.

"Katy are you all set, I hope so, and we have some great things planned for today and tonight. Tia told me to tell you as soon as you arrived, to go down to the barn and meet her." Jamie tells her.

"Mother may I? She asks Deanna.

"Yes, we'll get your horse off, go and see what Tia wants" Katy whoops and runs toward the stable.

Jamie turns to Deanna taking her hand and giving it a tiny squeeze, while he gives her a kiss on the cheek.

"I hope you don't feel I was too forward, but here we welcome all our guests with warmth and friendship, I wasn't ignoring you just saving you until last." He smiles still holding on to her hand.

"Not at all I would have given you a kiss had you not done so first." She blushes at his smile.

"Come, let us give you a hand getting your horses off the trailer, and then you can introduce them to us." Jamie says changing the subject.

"Hello Eduardo, how are you," Deanna greets Jamie's top hand as he moves inside the trailer.

"I'm fine Senora now that you are here; Don Diego was worried that you would not come." He winks at Jamie as he passes.

"Maybe I should fire you as Segundo[29], and make you a groom." Jamie quips at him.

Deanna can't help but notice a real sense of camaraderie between

---

29 RanchForman

the two of them that goes far beyond an employer and employee relationship.

"As the Patron wishes, but it would not change that you stood and watched." Eduardo chuckles leading off Katy's horse Legion, next Jamie leads off Buck, Jonah's horse. Last to come off is Misty, Deanna's Hanoverian mare.

"These horses are fantastic, you are to be complimented on what excellent shape they're in, and you must run a fine farm." Deanna swells with pride that he thinks the horses are in such good shape, praise from someone like him is really gratifying.

"We will take them to the staging area and tack them up. Did you wish to lunge them first, before we head out?" He inquires.

"No they will be alright, Legion is the only one that might be a problem, but he should be alright with the others, he doesn't trail ride much."

"Excuse me Mr. Doyle; I was wondering if you might have a Western saddle that I might borrow. Mine broke a fender last week and the saddle shop did not have a chance to repair it as yet." Jonah asks.

"First, let's drop the Mr. you may call me Jamie, or Uncle Jamie that's what all the kids call me or any of the other names that my people call me here. No one calls me Mr. around the ranch, as to the saddle, no problem. Why don't you accompany me to the tack room, you may select any one that you like? Excuse us Deanna, Eduardo will see to your horses while Jonah picks out a saddle."

Jamie takes Jonah to a tack room; he unlocks it for the first time in a long time. Turning on the light switch Jamie hears Jonah gasp, "Oh my God, this looks like a saddle shop, look at all these beautiful saddles and things."

"Where did you get so many, do you sell saddles here as well?"

"No, I don't sell any, in a past life I once competed, I won these as prizes. I think I should have some that will fit you, what do you ride in seventeen or eighteen?"

"Seventeen will be just fine."

"Here we are, these five should fit you, pick which ever you like, the breast collars and headstalls are with them. We should have a bit in the tack room for your horse, or we can swap out yours to the new headstall."

He goes over and looks them over. "This says it's for **"All Around Cowboy, Calgary Rodeo 1974."** You won the Calgary[30]?" he looks at Jamie with a look of excitement on his face as his hand caresses the hand tooled saddle.

"Yes but let's keep it our secret, as I said that was another life. Remember I told you, I barreled raced once." He looks at the saddles undecided.

"I can't go on a trail ride with your show saddle this is brand new, I might ___damage it." He stammers not taking his hands off the fine leather.

"Nonsense, I can only use one saddle at a time beside I am a little bigger now, and I ride a eighteen inch, you would be doing me a favor and use it." Jamie snaps up the breast collar and headstall and heads for the door.

"You coming, come on grab that one if you like it. Let's go, we're burning daylight."

"Yes sir," And he grabs the saddle throwing it over his shoulder and follows Jamie out the door.

"Mother, look at the saddle that Uncle Jamie is letting me use, he won it at Calgary, isn't it beautiful." Even as he says it he looks at Jamie knowing that he said it would be a secret between them. "I'm sorry sir."

"It's Ok, Jonah; she would have seen the plaque anyway. By the way, it's yours to keep if you like it, consider it a bonus for taking the job here. Saddle up and go."

"Yes sir, I mean Jefe, thank you again."

Jamie likes the word Jefe coming from him, only Dyon and Pita call him that. Deanna pulls Jamie to the side and says very quietly, "I think you have won my son and daughter over. I have never seen them so

---

30 One of the largest rodeos in North America

excited, but really that saddle is too much to give him. I can't have him accept it."

"A gift given from the heart has only the value that one puts on someone's honor. His eyes told me it was the right one; you would diminish him by not letting him accept it. You are right though, I should have asked you first, so I ask your indulgence and let me make it up to you this evening."

"Tonight, what do you mean I thought you were just having a small barbecue tonight?" Deanna asks him.

"Yes we are, but I thought that as you and a few others would be coming, I might as well use it to celebrate my birthday and anniversary of the Rancho. I have taken the liberty of inviting some other guests for tonight, along with Mr. Ellsworth and his wife, I hope you don't mind."

Deanna's a little upset because she would have liked to have gotten him something as a birthday gift or at least a card. Now she's not sure that they have brought the right clothes.

"I thought it was going to be an informal type of thing I didn't bring anything for a formal dinner." Deanna says rather tersely.

"You will have time to go home if you wish or Rosa has many fine things that I'm sure you would fit into. Besides anything that you wear you will look beautiful, of that I'm certain." And he squeezes her hand, "Shall we join the others, I believe all the children have arrived. You and I will be the chaperons; their parents will be here tonight for the fiesta."

Walking over to the staging area Deanna sees at least thirty young people all talking and laughing around saddled horses. Dyon comes over to Jamie and tells him all is ready.

"Yes, would you and Jonah mind taking point, while Deanna and I ride drag, keep them heading out the north end through the Willows and down the creek." She nods her head looking at Deanna intently,

"Si Jefe, you are going to eat a lot of dust, is that what you wish?" She imitates the speech of the vaqueros.

"Yes it will give me some time with the Senora, and we will ride far enough back so the dust will settle." Jamie answers her smiling.

She turns and gives the order to mount up assigning positions to each rider and instructions to maintain distance. "There will be no galloping or heading out on your own, wait for my signal for a run." She is used to being obeyed Deanna can see that, she uses much of Jamie's style in the delivery.

"She is quite a young woman, isn't she?" Deanna comments to him, remembering what Rosa said about her being protective of Jamie.

"Yes I'm very proud of her, you have no idea what she was like a while ago, she was hurt and angry, an outcast rebelling against everything, following in her adopted family's footsteps. Now she has the confidence and ability to create her own destiny. She is going to be a huge success. The one thing she never lost was her pride; she just had to know that someone cared; now the world is going to be hers." Jamie says with his head held high.

Deanna sees a pride in him about Dyon that shows he genuinely loves her and wants the best for her. Riding along I ask him about Ed Haskell, and how he is connected to the ranch.

"You already know that Ed was my father-in-law from Tom. Ed is not connected here except through the connection that we both shared, his daughter Mary, whom I understand you knew long ago. He is like a grandfather to the girls as I am a father figure, Rosa is a mother, and the men are as uncles. Ed loves Dyon, as if she were his own grand daughter, Mary and I were unable to have children, so he was never given the opportunity to enjoy that, now he can. And he does a wonderful job at it too." He answers her in such a manner that she believes what he tells her and that Ed Haskell is not a partner in a land development scam.

"I heard yesterday you purchased the Delaplane place. Are you going to develop it for housing or what?" She almost accuses him.

"You have a right, I supposed to be suspicious, what with so many trying to find a way to develop the Green Zone[31], but I'm not one of them. I bought it because I want to build a ranch, one that will raise fine cattle and provide a way of life for my people. It was a dream that Mary

---
31 Agricultural area not zoned for housing

and I had to raise kids and horses here. To help those that were not as fortunate as we were, it's with my money plus her inheritance that we can make this possible. Nothing sinister about it, I hope to make you believe that Deanna, I really mean that."

He reaches over and takes her hand in his. She doesn't try to take her hand away as she looks at the beautiful country there about to ride through, feeling like she never has before. He has nice hands, strong but not overpowering. He also rides like no one she's ever seen, with an ease about him that is sure and determined. He has an affinity of oneness with the horse and his surroundings.

"We are getting close now to the quarry." Suddenly he's alert; as if searching for a source of something out of place. Dyon is riding back toward them, a posture of concern about her. Deanna senses something is wrong without knowing why.

"Jefe, the trail from this side seems to have washed away a little, do you still wish to travel down this way or should we go around?"

"You're the one riding point. What do you think?"

"I think it will be alright, but I am going down first and then Jonah can send the others down, but one at a time, he's good in the saddle, I trust him to take care of the rest of them at the top." Dyon waits for him to answer, testing to see if he will have the trust in her judgment.

"It's your call, take them down."

Jamie looks at her and tells her it will be alright.

Dyon heads down the slope toward the old rock quarry with D.C. taking it slowly and keeping his hind quarters low. She gets to the bottom and signals Jonah to send the next rider down, as each reaches the bottom; he lets the next one go down.

It finally comes to Katy's turn, and she's nervous as is Legion, he has never faced anything like this before. He starts down and about thirty feet down; he starts to shake his head and refuses to go any further. Deanna can hear Katy's voice, she is starting to panic. Before Deanna can react to the situation, Jamie is off, going over the edge without a hesitation. He reaches Katy's side as Legion start to plunge and rear.

Jamie places Storm on the outside edge, gently pushing Legion away from edge and steep drop-off. In a calm voice he reaches over to Katy and touches her arm.

"Katy, I'm here, relax, he's just scared. He needs you to give him confidence, that's all, just relax and talk to him. Sit still and relax your hand you are putting too much pressure on his mouth."

Storm is trying to keep his footing; he's so close to the edge from Deanna's vantage point it appears as though they both may plunge off. Deanna's heart is in her throat, as all of them down below watch a very dangerous situation on the quarry face, the trail down is narrow and filled with loose shell rock.

"That's it, ease up him on the neck, that's my girl ___ good ___ you got him now, just put a little leg on him to move him forward ___ I'm right here with you."

Deanna gasps as Storm loses some footing and seems ready to plunge over the lip of the trail. Jamie seems not to notice, intent on Katy and Legion. He sits his horse with ease as if unaware of the danger he's in.

Katy seems to have Legion under control and is moving forward down toward Dyon, who is sitting at the foot of the trail calmly watching Jamie take charge. Katy reaches the bottom and turns to look up at her and waves. Now Jamie proceeds down the trail, both he and Storm, none the worse for wear.

The rest of the kids all take their horses down, when the last one reaches the bottom Jamie holds up his hand, looking up at Jonah and Deanna. He rides Storm up the path as though he was a mountain goat.

"Are you two alright to go down, the rest of the kids had mountain horses or trail ponies so this is not a problem for them, but I am not sure of Buck or Misty."

"I will be fine Jefe, Buck and I do this kind of terrain all the time. Mother, do you think Misty will be all right?" He asks Deanna, concern on his face.

"We can take the long way around and come in on the quarry road if you prefer" Jamie tells her.

"No, I will be fine Misty is not spooky at all. Just lead the way and I will be right behind you." The three of them descend to the bottom.

Reaching the bottom all the kids cheer and head over to some tents they see has been put up for refreshments.

"Ok everyone, why don't you take your horses over there by the picket line and remove their headstalls. Make sure to halter them to the tie line, and remember to loosen your girths." Jamie walks over to check on the horses.

Suddenly Katy comes running up to her mother. "Mother did you see me, I didn't really panic, I was scared, but Jamie was right there with me, talking me through it. Mother I know you will think this is insane, but when he touched me all my fear left me, it was there, and then it was gone. I just listened and everything was alright. Mother he's magnificent, did you see him on the ledge, he didn't flinch once, Storm was splendid also, don't you think….. Today was the greatest day of my life." She is just bubbling within herself.

"I was so frightened until I saw Jamie reach your side, you were incredible, and you know you rode him down not Jamie." Her mother says to her in all sincerity.

"Yes I did, didn't I?" She announces proudly.

Tia and Marianna come over patting her on the back and telling her they are so proud of her, they run off to get some drinks as little Pita tags along behind.

"Pita, don't you fall in like last time or this time I will leave you there." Jamie calls after them as they rush to the water's edge and pitch some stones in the water.

Walking over to Deanna, Jamie asks, "Would you like to take a walk over where there's some shade?"

"Yes, to be candid my knees are still a little weak, that was quite a scare that you both gave me. I thought you were about to plunge off the outer side at any minute." Deanna confides to him quietly, so as not to let the children know just how scared she was.

"Katy was ok, Legion just spooked a little, but I think she did fantastic under the circumstances and so did you." Jamie says as he looks into her eyes.

Feeling suddenly faint she collapses into his arms. "Deanna, are you alright?" He asks.

Deanna's shaking like a leaf as he holds her in his arms. She feels his lean hard body pressing against hers and Deanna wraps her arms around him and places her head on his chest. She feels safe in his arms. He releases her from the embrace and takes her face in his hands.

Her head is swimming; her breathing is heavy, it's almost like the incident at the barn that first day. He tilts her head up and looks at her with those deep blue eyes of his. Without saying anything; he traces his finger tips down the sides of her face and cups Deanna's chin gently, kissing her on the lips. A kiss like she's never had, light not pressing, but with warmth that lights a fire within her, his lips linger on hers, until she's almost breathless and trembling. Their lips part and he kisses her gently on each of her eye lids, Deanna places her head on his chest again. She can feel the beating of his heart, or is it her own? They stand without saying anything until Deanna resumes breathing normally; she gently pushes back from him.

Jamie apologizes, "I'm sorry that was unfair of me to take advantage of your momentary weakness, it just seemed like the natural thing to do." He admits in that honest way he has.

"It's alright, I rather enjoyed it, I guess it was the moment, we're both grown adults and know that things like this happen sometimes. I assume that it was quite spontaneous, but I would be lying if.... I said, I... I didn't enjoy it," She stutters, feeling the heat emanating from her face.

"Your kiss will linger with me long after the moment of flame is extinguished." He says to her in a courtier's manor and smiles.

At that moment Jonah comes up to them, and bashfully announces that Dyon asked him to come and see if they're ready to get moving back.

"I think we're ready to ride back now, how about you Deanna?" He asks her holding out his hand to give Deanna a hand up from the rock she's sitting on.

"I think I've rested enough, are we going up and out or what?" She asks Jamie with false bravado.

"Tell Dyon I think we should use the service road to head back and use the cut off later." Jamie suggests to Jonah.

"Yes sir, oh, by the way, Jefe, thank you for helping Katy, I couldn't react soon enough, and I would not have known what to do, even if I'd been able to get to her in time." Jonah hangs his head.

"Don't you be silly, your job was to stay with the rest at the top, and you did. You didn't panic that's what counts, neither of you did, I'm proud of both of you, in fact, all of you." He pats Jonah on the back as we head toward the rest of the kids. Jamie said just the right thing; he praised Jonah when he was feeling ashamed, now he's filled with pride.

Saddling up they head out, with Jamie and Deanna riding drag far enough behind to let the dust settle. They ride in silence not talking, Jamie occasionally pointing out something of interest. Deanna rides with her own thoughts; he's a strange man and has a peculiar effect on all around him, his kiss and touch, which she can still feel left a sense of passion barbaric and wild. Deanna's never been affected by a man's kiss before that put her in such an aroused state before. It's unsettling to say the least, not having been with a man since Steve got caught with his tramp secretary, and her not having had the interest in anyone seriously. Jamie, he may not have been with a woman since his wife passed away. That would explain why they felt the way they did or at least the way she did and what happened.

Deanna musts meet with Ed Haskell and get his slant before she can start to finish this piece. She also wants to write in the results of the show and how it affects each of the girls, but it is certainly adding up to everything she felt it would and more. She just wonders how the Southwest Group is going to take the land purchase, and what they might do about it. Deanna doesn't think she should close out the story yet, and she'll tell Mr. Ellsworth about it tonight. Deanna still can't believe Jamie planned this big party and didn't say one word to her about it at all.

Seeing the ranch just ahead they turn into the lane toward the main barns and staging area. A man is there by the gate, and he is waving, it's Tim the magazine's photographer, and he's taking pictures of all of them. Deanna stops by the gate to talk with him, telling Jamie she'll meet them at the barn.

"Tim what are you doing here today, I thought you told me you never work on Sunday except at the National Horse Show."

"Ellsworth called me this morning and told me to get my ass over today and plan on staying late, or I was fired, and he didn't sound like he was all that happy with you either. What's going on anyway it looks like they are planning a wedding here or something?"

"Jamie didn't tell me about it until we got here, and I didn't have time to call you or anything. I was going to, as soon as we got back; I was hoping that you would still be home. I'm glad Ellsworth got you; it's a birthday party for Jamie and the anniversary for the rancho. Did you find out how many guests are invited yet?"

"Rosa said about two hundred, Ellsworth said all the right people have been invited, the president of the show grounds, politicians, a U.S. Senator, it looks like the who's, who of Palm Beach. So I am taking lots of pictures, did you know they are roasting two whole cows for this thing. And they have an army of people here, everyone's busy decorating, cooking, this is big. I think you might have blown this one baby, Ellsworth was livid." Tim tells her.

"Ok, just keep taking shots of everything we will figure out next week what we are going to use. I'm going over to the main house and try to see what I'm going to wear to this thing. I may have to borrow your car and head home to get something to wear, did you bring something nice."

"Yea, a tie and a corduroy jacket," and he laughs.

chapter 11

"The Medallion"

Rosa greets Deanna as she approaches the main house looking for Katy and Jonah. "Hola Senora Deanna, did you enjoy the ride? The Patron he asks me to show you something for the fiesta, I have many things that he has bought me, but I have no time to wear such beautiful things. Come I show you, sometime the men they forget that women like to fuss and pick the right things, is that not so? Come to mi casa[32] and you look, if you do not see anything that you like, then he gave me the keys to his car, and you go."

She takes Deanna by the arm, how can she say no to her, Deanna is afraid now that she will insult Rosa's taste? She wouldn't want to hurt her feelings for the world.

"Rosa your home looks new was it here when Jamie bought the rancho?"

"No Senora, Don Diego he says that I should have my own house for me and Eduardo and Pita, so he had the house built, he and Eduardo do much of the work themselves, I would not have so fine a house in my country, I will be glad I will be a citizen here in United States." She answers proudly.

---

32 My house

Going into her home she leads Deanna to a room with many closets. Opening the door to one that has so many dresses it looks like a boutique.

"See I tell you many have never been worn." She takes out several scoop necks Spanish style ones that have a handmade look about them with fine stitching and colored Spanish lace.

"This is beautiful Rosa it has such detail, but they are a little revealing I mean they are low cut." Deanna says examining one that she would love to try on.

"Nonsense you have a good body, men would love to hold and dance with a Senora that has such breasts." She says unashamed, "You must remember we are not so modest about our sensuality as Anglo women. Sometimes they are for to show not all, but just enough to catch a Senor." She smiles and winks....

Taking off her clothes and standing in front of the mirror, she remembers his kiss this afternoon and how he felt holding her against his body. She puts on the camisole and pulls the strings tight; her breasts become firm under the light weight material. Pulling the dress over her head, Deanna then adjusts it on her shoulders so that the camisole is just under the bodice of the dress. The length is just below her knees, and it sways with her as she walks. Looking into the mirror, Deanna doesn't recognize the person she sees. She is sexy and loves the dress; it fits as though it were made for her.

Coming out of the dressing room, Rosa is standing there looking at her smiling and says, "You are too beautiful, you need to try on nothing else, and it fits as if it were made for you. What size zapata[33] do you wear?"

"I wear seven and one half, why? Don't tell you have shoes for me also? Deanna says laughing.

"Si Senora look, still in boxes come try these on. She holds up a pair of gold sandals that lace up the leg to the calf. They fit perfectly; Deanna tells her she should open a boutique and make a million dollars.

---

33 shoes

The Last Celtic Angel

"Then who would look after Don Diego if I became a lady of business." They both laugh and Deanna tells her how much she loves the dress and would be honored if she could borrow it.

"Do not be silly, it is yours Senora, it fits you much better than I. It is my gift to you, you have made the Patron smile again, and he is alive once more. Come I must show you to your room, it is time for you to take the siesta and then the bath, and I will come and fix your hair so you will be the most beautiful woman at the fiesta tonight. Rosa replied smiling as she winds her way back toward the kitchen.

Deanna follows Rosa to the main house carrying the clothes she's just tried on as though she were one of the children. Rosa, although young has a commanding presence and Deanna knows not to try and argue with her.

"You will use the same one you had last time and the Senorita Katy will be across the hall. I have taken the liberty to place bath oils and shampoos in the bath for you, I hope you like the scent." She opens the door and Deanna smells roses, looking around the room she sees there is at least a dozen in a vase on the bed by the table, all yellow.

"What beautiful roses how did you know I love yellow roses." Deanna exclaims as she walks over to smell them.

"Don Diego ordered them this morning, along with the table flowers for the fiesta, he says to Eduardo make sure you get yellow for the Senora."

"How could he have known that they are my favorite flowers?" There it is again, that feeling of him knowing things about her, sets off a little bell inside Deanna's head.

"Sometimes he knows these things about us, we have wondered many times, but he knows, I ask him one day, and he says."

"I don't know I just do." He shrugs his shoulders and says no more. It is enough that he's right and that you like them, no?" Rosa questions her.

"I will leave you to your thoughts, I will return by five o'clock to help you and the Senorita to get ready." Rosa turns to leave.

Excuse me Rosa, is Theresa here tonight and could she possibly do my hair?" Suddenly realizing she may have hurt Rosa's feelings.

"Theresa… she did your hair last time. Yes, she will be here, I will have her come; she is much better than I. She was so proud that you love the way she did it, you made her feel wonderful…

Don't look so Senora, I am not offended, Theresa, she does my hair also." She smiles at her and closes the door, Deanna has never seen such intuitive skills, and these people notice everything at least Rosa does.

Deanna takes off her clothes and fills the bathtub; there are different bath oils on the vanity. She chooses one that's called Nature's Pearls, it's soft and sensual to the touch, the water is hot, and she eases into it. Oh, it feels great, warm and the oils go all over her body. Deanna runs her hands down her abdomen and over her legs. Lying back in the tub she rubs her hands over her breasts then up and around her neck keeping her hair up out of the water. Theresa will shampoo it when she comes; she prefers to do it that way.

For now Deanna enjoys just lying there and lets her thoughts stray to the events of the day. Jamie was very straight forward about what he intends to do with the land and Deanna wants so very much to believe him. She would like to have a relationship after the story is completed, and she knows the kids do too. Jonah thinks the world of him. Not since his Grandfather, Tom's Dad has he been this excited about a man in his life, not even his teachers or coaches. Katy hasn't had one outburst of anger since meeting him, they have not fought once. Deanna wants so much to keep him as a friend once the smoke clears. He reminds her of her Father in many ways. He's strong, confident and sure of himself, but he also stirs feelings in her that she doesn't quite know how to handle.

Deanna suddenly thinks of his kiss and how it made her feel. She wanted him to kiss her, and she wanted him to touch her as well. Deanna was not weak with fear, it was the nearness of his body and his kiss, and she could feel his power at that moment. He must have made Mary very happy, Deanna is sure he is a wonderful lover. His hands were so tender and loving; his touch gentle. She still feels him caressing her face lifting her to his lips. Deanna has goose bumps all over her even in the hot water…

The water is starting to get cold, and she's a little sleepy, so draining the tub, she steps out grabbing a large fluffy terry towel that's luxurious. Drying off she wraps up with it and goes into the bedroom. Deanna lies down and closes her eyes when suddenly there is a knock on the door,

"Mother, are you awake?" she hears Katy's small voice.

"Yes honey, come in." She opens the door and pokes her head in.

"Do you mind if Tia comes in with me, we have something to talk to you about?

"No, come in, hi Tia, How are you? Why aren't you two getting ready for the party?" They both sit down on the edge of the bed and Deanna can tell something is up.

"We were just discussing me training here with Uncle Jamie, Mother, after today, how could you not agree that this is where I belong? I can't think of ever training with anyone else again. Please you have to ask him. Tia please, won't you tell my mother what you told me?" Tia looks uncomfortable and ill at ease almost as if she wanted to be somewhere else

"Tia if you don't want to tell me, it's ok I can see you're not comfortable." She waits for her to speak.

"Senora, I do not know where to begin only Rosa and Uncle Jamie and now Katy knows why I am in this place. I would not want for my story to be in the magazine, I would be too ashamed for people to know." She says with tears in her eyes, Deanna's heart goes out to her because she can see she's in pain with the telling.

"I was sent here because I was abused by the men of my family… I was made to work at the streets for money, they arrested me for selling myself, but because I was only thirteen I was not sent to jail___" Tia stops talking and looks away before she continues. "My father and brother were sent to prison and my ____ my mother, she killed herself….." She again takes a moment to collect her thoughts. "Uncle Jamie got them to put me here because he thought he could help me. I was so angry and ashamed I tried to commit suicide____ I would hurt myself and others if they tried to stop me. My rage was such they thought I would spend my life in an institution for the insane. You, __ you see, I too had rage and panic attacks like Katy." Deanna sits and listens horrified as Tia takes another minute to collect.

"When I came here I was scared and very angry at everyone, especially men. Uncle Jamie came; he sat beside me and placed his hand on mine. My first reaction was to tear my hand from his, but I couldn't move. I felt something when he touched me, something I had never felt before, ____ safe. He then spoke softly to me and asked me to trust him. I said, "Why should I trust you?" He said he would be able to help me if I would only just for the time it would take to walk with him out to the barn.

He led me to the barn, I didn't know why I followed him there, but I did. He said for me to go and let my horse pick me. I had always liked horses and used to draw pictures of them when I was in the home that they sent me to, after I was removed from my home. I walked down the isle of the barn and looked at all the horses until one of them noticed me and came to the front of his stall. It was a horse called Tom Tom, he nuzzled me and let me pet his neck. Uncle Jamie said that he had picked me to look after him. He had a big scar on his neck and when I ask him how the horse had gotten the scar. He told me the people that had him before had burned him and were mean to him. Uncle Jamie had to help him to be normal, and learn to trust again like me. He asked me if I could love him, because he was too busy to take care of him. If I wanted to, he would be my horse. I looked into his eyes and saw his pain. He was my first friend here, we took care of each other and Uncle Jamie looked after us both and helped put away my anger.

I seldom have panic attacks now, it is only when I feel threatened, or I am reminded of the past. Uncle Jamie says that will pass in time and that I am to concentrate on here, and my future. I also wish to become his ward, we all do, but if that can't happen, he's told me he will arrange for me to finish my schooling here until I am an adult. I will always have a home at the rancho and that's important to all of us. We know there may be more students coming here in the future, but that will not change that we're family."

Deanna thanks Tia for sharing what must have been very painful, and hugs her. Telling her she will keep the promise she made her. "I know how hard it must have been to share that with me," Deanna tells her.

Tia looks at Deanna and says, "I did it because Katy is my friend, and I want to help her. If you really knew how much he has done for each of us than you would want her to come here as much as she wants to. It's not just him; it's this place, the people, the whole program. It is about a love that protects us and strengthens our spirit for what we will face outside of here." She's passionate about how she feels not only for him, but for everything. Deanna puts her arms around Tia and so does Katy; they both have much to think about.

There is a knock on the door. "Senora are you alright I heard crying." It's Marta.

"No, we're alright Marta, just having a family tear session, thank you."

"Si Senora I will send Theresa up if you are ready."

"A few minutes more please Marta," Deanna calls out to her.

"Si Senora, I will leave the Senorita's towels in her room."

"Well you two better get dressed for the party. Katy, Theresa will be here to do my hair, do you want her to fix yours as well." Katy nods her head still wiping tears from her eyes.

Turning to Tia she says to her, "I want to thank you for all you have done for Katy, I pledge I'll do what I can." Tia gives Deanna a smile and a kiss before they both leave to get ready.

She looks at the clock and sees that it is almost five o'clock, getting up and putting on the robe that somebody has thoughtfully placed within reach of the bed she looks at herself in the mirror and wishes she had brought some other jewelry with her.

"Senora may we come in," Rosa calls from the hall.

"Yes, please do its open. Hello Theresa, I'm so glad you're here; you did my hair sensational last time. I know you will prepare it beautifully for the party."

"Senora you are too kind, I will do my best for you." She tells Deanna with a swell of pride in her voice.

"Rosa the only thing I wish was that I had time to go home and get some nicer jewelry to wear with your beautiful things. What I brought with me was for the plain outfit that I was going to wear, before I knew it was to be a big party." Deanna laments to her looking at the beautiful dress she gave her.

"I will be right back, do not worry La Dona." And Rosa rushes from the room.

"Don Diego una momento por favor[34]." Rosa calls to Jamie as she comes down the stairs and rushes up to him.

"The Senora is sad, she has not the jewelry to wear with the dress she has picked out, you should have told her about the big fiesta. I thought maybe she might wear something of the Senora Mary's for tonight?" She looks at him with reproach, her eyes are scolding him, it's his fault that Deanna came unprepared, and she's correct.

"Of course she may wear whatever she chooses to, go get the case, she may select and you too Little Mama. Don't think I don't know how you maneuver me at times," He says with a smile on his face.

"Si Patron, I will hurry and get the case." Rosa hurries to the master bedroom to retrieve it. Upon getting it, she runs down the hall, bursting into Deanna's room, all out of breath.

"Senora, I have something for you to look at." Rosa announces as she runs into the room out of breath and beaming. She opens a jewelry box; it's filled with gorgeous earrings, pendants, bracelets and rings. They are all so beautiful; Deanna is at a loss for words momentarily.

"They are all very beautiful, but I could not wear your jewelry too." Deanna tells her fingering a pair of large loop earrings.

"No, Senora they were the Senora Mary's. The Patron says for you to

---

34 One moment please

pick anything you wish to wear if you don't mind. She would have wanted you to, if she were here."

Deanna's not sure that she would want to wear things that were hers, and she says so to Rosa.

"Please you would do her a great honor to wear something of hers on his birthday and the anniversary of the dream they shared together. You would honor all of us. I understand she was your friend, from long ago too. Please Senora just try some on." Rosa holds out the case for her.

Deanna takes out a set of large gold loop earrings and a gold medallion with simple rope chain and a beautiful bracelet in red gold. The medallion is stamped with huge sunburst with a man holding a child in his arms in front of the sunburst, "I think these will do, what you think?" Deanna asks them as she puts on the earrings and medallion. Theresa says they are perfect. Deanna turns toward Rosa and she's is looking at the medallion with tears in her eyes.

"What is it Rosa, why are you crying?" Deanna asks her.

"It is because you look so beautiful, and you have found and wear Don Diego's lost medallion." Deanna looks at it again in the mirror and says to her,

"I will pick something else then."

"No, no, Senora it is meant for you to wear it, Madre Dios[35] for it has been lost to him for a long time now. You must wear it, this is a sign." And Rosa and Theresa both make the sign of the cross.

"I will leave you now, Donna Deanna."

Rosa says to Theresa, "You must do magic tonight, my cousin, pausing at the case, she selects a petite tiara and hands it to Theresa.

"Set this in her hair, so that it radiates the light." And Rosa leaves the room. Teresa washes Deanna's hair and begins to comb and dry it when Katy comes into the room with a towel around her head.

"Mother when you are ready will you come and help me finish dressing." Of course she tells her.

---

35 Mother of God

"Where have you been," Deanna asks her.

"I was downstairs and we went out to the barn to see Old Tanner, we were telling him how nice the house looks with all the decorations and lights everywhere, he says that is nothing, wait until Christmas. He is so funny and kind to us, he is helping a horse give birth tonight you know."

Deanna thinks of Tanner and the last thing she would call him is funny, but Jamie did say he is wonderful to the kids; it's adults he doesn't like or seems not to get along with.

"Katy, you go get ready for Theresa to do your hair, and I will be, in as soon as I finish dressing." Her mother says to her.

"Ok Mother, your hair looks great, I love it." And Katy heads to her room.

"Senora please put on your dress, and I will finish and put the tiara in place, por favor." Theresa instructs me.

Deanna pulls the dress over her head with the help of Theresa, and she finishes the final touches on her hair before setting the tiara in place with pins that you can't see. She's very professional and should be a hairstylist, and Deanna tells her so.

"Si Senora, the Patron is going to set up a shop for me as soon as my license comes. You make me happy with your praise, now I must go and fix the Senorita's hair so that you all make the Patron proud of his women." She gathers her things and goes to Katy's room. It's odd they all seem to think of her as his woman.

Deanna finishes putting on the sandals and perfume, checking her make up one last time to make sure that it is just right. As she looks in the mirror, Deanna realizes that she has not taken this long to prepare herself since college. Looking into the mirror Deanna's seeing a whole new person, she loves this makeover from a country girl in jeans and shirt to a princess going to her first ball. There have been a lot of changes in her in just one week also. It's almost too good to be true, so many wonderful things in a short a period of time, if someone had told her this happened to them, she would not have believed them, and thought they were exaggerating a bit. Deanna can't wait to tell her Mother, suddenly realizing that she has not spoken to her all week.

Deanna goes and knocks on Katy's door, and she says,

"Come in I'm decent." Katy turns around as Theresa is finishing her hair in a bun.

"Mother you look so different, I love it. You look like a queen with a crown. Where did you get the jewelry, it's so beautiful?" She asks her eyes large and full of questions.

"They belonged to Jamie's wife Mary, and he has graciously lent them to me to wear tonight." Deanna tells her and moves up close, so she may admire the medallion.

"I have never seen you wear earrings like those before, you should wear them like that all the time, and that medallion is so gorgeous, don't you agree Theresa?" Theresa smiles and says,

"Tonight, you will all look like story book princesses, you and your Mama will be the most beautiful, like Cinderella in the story, only no pumpkins and no rats. Can you imagine Rosa chasing the rats?" They all laugh at the thought of Rosa running after rats.

"We must go Little One to see to your friend, they wish to wear the hair the same, Senora. Tonight they all want to be proper Senoritas." Katy gets up and turns around for Deanna to see she is wearing a full skirted dress in the Spanish tradition, colorful, with her shoulders bare with an elastic bodice instead of a drawstring like hers; she is lovely looking, very grown up. Deanna thinks to herself.

"Tia gave this to me; we are all wearing the same type of dresses, all of us including Pita. Tia says to wait and see Dyon that she will look fantastic. She is so pretty, don't you think Mother?"

Theresa tells her they must go, time is getting short. Deanna thanks her again for all her help as Theresa and Katy leave.

Coming out of Katy's room she almost bumps into Jamie, he has a look on his face that she can't quite fathom, but it lasts only a moment than he composes himself.

"Deanna I came to escort you down to the cocktail party, if you don't mind, excuse my lack of manners, but you took me by surprise coming out of Katy's room. You look like a vision; you took my breath away for a moment. I've just been reminded just how beautiful a woman can be. I hope that you will save some dances for me this evening, I only wish that you were all mine, and I did not have to share you for this night." He bows gallantly and takes her arm in his.

"Thank you for your compliments and the loan of Mary's jewelry, I hope it does not cause you any discomfort." He turns and again looks into her eyes when he speaks to her, something she's come to expect from him.

"Not at all, it they look lovely on you; she would have wanted you to wear them also. His gaze leaves her eyes and falls upon her neck. His hand involuntarily touches his own, in a searching manner looking for something that is no longer there.

"I see you found what was lost; I never thought to look for it there." Deanna goes to remove it thinking he wants it back.

He puts his hands on hers and says. "It's perfect where it is, please allow me to give it to you as a gift." Jamie fingers it and she feels the touch of his hand against her neck, and it's warm and makes her tremble.

"I can't accept it, this is too valuable." Deanna tries to protest.

He holds up his finger to her lips. "It's my birthday and here at Rancho de Los Angeles, we celebrate not with the receiving of gifts but in the giving of them, so you must accept. This way you will remember me always." He takes her hand and kisses it; his lips are warm, sending sensations up and down her arm.

"I welcome your gift with all my heart, but you must tell me what it represents." As they reach the landing overlooking the great room.

"It represents an Irish King called Nuada, who searches and finds those of his kind that were lost, bringing them back to the people of Tuatha De Danann[36]." He says quietly.

"I have never seen anything like it before. Do you mind me asking

---

36 Ancient tribe of Iberia thought to have conquered Ireland Means Family of the Goddess Danu

where you got it from?" She sees a faraway look in his eyes before he answers her.

"It's very old, from The Children of Danu of Irish Celtic myths. I received it a long time ago from a very special person. It can't be purchased it's a one of a kind, and it may only be given to one with a good heart. Shall we go down now and relax with a drink before our guests arrive?" Jamie takes her arm and turns toward the stairs.

Before they start down the stairs, Jonah and the girls come from the patio and look up at them and clap and cheer, all yelling Happy Birthdays to Jamie. Deanna looks in awe at the transformation of his home; there are lights twinkling everywhere, and the scent of flowers fills the air. Bouquets of roses are on tables and sidebars around the foyer, the great room is a collage of color from so many flowers.

"It wasn't me, its Rosa she's amazing, I don't know how she does it, but the government might use her talents for getting things done right, her and Eduardo. This is all their doing, together with the army of friends she transported here today. They love a fiesta it's virtually like a religion with her people, all about detail and protocol." He elucidates to her as they reach the bottom of the stair case.

Jonah comes up to Deanna and gently puts his arms around her. "Mother I have never seen you look more attractive, I'll have to get a photo of you." Before she can answer she hears a familiar voice.

"Won't be necessary you have a professional photographer here this evening." Turning, she sees Tim standing off to the side.

"I will make sure that we have enough pictures of this event and your Mom will be in many of them, I promise." Deanna had forgotten Tim was here.

"Jamie may I present Tim Manning, he works at the magazine and will be doing all the photos for the story." I introduce him and Jamie shakes his hand.

"Glad to have you aboard Tim, I hope you have a good time tonight as well."

"Thank you Mr. Doyle, you have one heck of a place here." He shakes Jamie's hand.

"Please call me Jamie, we're all friends here." Jamie tells him as he pumps Tim's hand.

Taking their drinks they go out to the veranda to watch the sunset, it is absolutely gorgeous,

"With a sunset like that it will be a warm sunny day tomorrow." Jamie comments.

Deanna looks at it and sees the golden amber and purple colors of the setting sun, thinking what a wonderful day today has been.

"Jamie I am almost finished with the story except for a couple of more interviews, I wanted to talk to you about Katy, I was wondering if you might fit her into your training program and help her with her riding. I'll pay whatever the fee is." He's silent a couple of minutes before he answers me.

"Can I think about it for a few days before I give you an answer, it may have some complications?" He asks her.

"Of course I did not mean to put you on the spot or anything like that, we can discuss it next week before the Horseman's Show or after, whenever you prefer." Deanna tries to ease out of it because it seems to have placed him in an awkward position.

"Tia and Marianna have both come to me concerning Katy, it's just I have to give it some consideration and of course whether I have to time to take on another student right now. I will give you an answer this week I promise.

Right now I have something I wish to ask you, would you do me the honor of standing on line and helping me receive my guests, many of whom I have never met before, and you may have." He asks her with an imploring look in his eyes.

He is looking again into her eyes; she sometimes thinks he never looks at her body. She has rather large breasts and men have always been attracted to her because of them, but his eyes never stray from her face. Is he not attracted to her physically, she wonders?

"Yes I would be honored, thank you, but don't you think Dyon should be or Rosa." She questions him as she doesn't want to alienate her by thinking Deanna's trying to push her away.

"No, Dyon's not of age and Rosa, she would never allow herself to, she would consider it incorrect to have my housekeeper on the receiving line for my guests. She's very old fashioned even though she's like my family, she would never consent." He replies still holding her hand.

We sit and watch the setting sun as the lights are turned on, in and around the lake and the veranda, turning it into a wonderland right out of Disney World, all the men and women who are working as servers are dressed in traditional Spanish dress as is Jamie. Jamie's is an ebony suit with gold embroidery on the front of the jacket and the sides of the pant legs with flared bottoms over black Spanish styled boots. His coat has been made for him fitting perfectly, not gaudy, with a lace shirt and black string tie. He is a picture of an old California Don, dignified and handsome. The women are in long dresses of many colors similar to mine just not as fancy, the men are dressed in tight fitting trousers with ruffled shirts under fitted jackets. I watch him going about the room making last minute checks with Rosa and Eduardo, dressed as he is, he moves like a matador. Jonah slides next to her, and whispers in Deanna's ear quietly.

"Mother, have you ever seen anything like this in your life, you should see the food and outside it's decorated everywhere like it is in here. Even the barns and stalls have been cleaned and well lit; grooms have been working on the horses, since we got back. I love this lifestyle don't you, he is going to blow all these fancy pants away tonight, this will be the talk of the village you wait and see." He states to his mother proudly.

"You really like him don't you; I mean not just the money and how fancy it is? I mean him." Jonah looks at Jamie before he answers her.

"Mother I don't know what it is about him, but I trust him more than any person outside of you in my whole life. I can't explain why, it's like I've known him all my life, I feel comfortable being around him, don't you?" Jonah is looking at her waiting for an answer.

Taking a long moment before acknowledging him, finally taking a deep breath, she says to him, "I like him very much, but I have to stay objective at least until I finish the story, you understand that don't you?" he nods his head.

"Have you seen Dyon yet the girls told me she is wearing something very special tonight and wants to surprise Jefe. I can't wait to see her; she really is the most wonderful girl I've ever met." He states with stars in his eyes, Deanna sees that first love has smitten him hard.

Jamie comes up to them and asks Jonah how everything looks, "Fine sir, I have never been to such a grand social do in all my life." He admits awkwardly.

"Well, can I tell you both something, neither have I, this is my first go at this; your mother probably has much more experience than I have. I'm hoping she will get me through it without too many blunders." He laughs and looks at Deanna.

"You are kidding me aren't you?" Deanna asks.

"No, this is my first try at the high society, and I would appreciate all the help you can give me. You after all, were the reason I threw this fandango."

"What do you mean I'm the reason?" Deanna is astonished, that he would make a declaration like that.

"I thought about why your editor and publisher wanted to do this story and why they sent you. They wanted to know what I'm doing here, and I figured it wouldn't hurt if they got to know us and get a look at the Ranch. Plus if you needed more time for the story Ellsworth would be more willing to give it to you, if I could convince him and his wife that we are not the monsters we're being made out to be. It's like killing a bunch of birds, with one stone so to speak."

"So you were using me to get good press?" She asks him, her Irish is getting up and Jonah backs away thinking that Deanna might explode.

"No, not at all, I knew after I met you that you would do an honest story about what you found here, but I'm not uninformed as to what is being circulated around about me, and my girls or motives. Ellsworth's wife is in the forefront trying to get me to sell out, now with the Delaplane thing; they will be applying more pressure. I needed more time and so did you, am I right?" He disarms her with his reasoning, Deanna has been thinking the same thing, it's just she thought she was doing the manipulating, but it appears, he can also.

"Please, sometimes I have a tendency to act without always consulting, and it can be annoying. Just be patient with me, I promised I would never lie to you remember."

Deanna calms down and says to him. "Well in the future Mr. Doyle, I would appreciate if you talked to me first before you make any more life changing decisions on my behalf." He laughs and crosses his heart; she can't stay mad at him any longer.

"I swear to you, I will be more forth coming where you are concerned Senora," he chuckles.

Eduardo approaches Jamie and whispers in his ear. "Don Diego, your guests are coming up to the gate now. Would you like to welcome them outside or at the door and should I have Raul start to play the musica?"

"Yes Eduardo, have him play, just keep it soft for now, we'll heat it up later. I'll greet them outside and have the fans on, to keep any bugs out of the house.

"I will have the men park the automobiles in the east paddock." He tells Jamie, and turns to Deanna.

"Senora, you grace us tonight, you are a picture of beauty. Thank you for making my Rosa so happy also. It is good that you are here… You will excuse me now, La Dona." He bows and departs before she can thank him for his compliment.

"What did he mean by La Dona?"

"It means My Lady and old Mexican term; Eduardo comes from an old fashioned line of Spanish gentlemen." Jamie interprets to her.

"Jamie, Eduardo is not dressed for the party is he not coming?" Deanna asks him a little confused.

"No, he wants to handle security tonight with his new vaqueros, he after all is the Segundo[37]. He worries too much, but he feels it's his job, and I let him handle it in his own way." Before she can ask why he whisks her to the big double doors at the front entrance that have been opened as the first guests begin to arrive.

---

37 Ranch foreman

chapter 12

"The Grande Fiesta"

The guests are beginning to drive up and the line is long, the valets are getting them out of their cars. Each guest has an invitation that is checked by security and shown to the receiving line which has formed at the front entrance. Jamie is as gracious as any Fortune Five Hundred CEO at a corporate stockholders meeting. Smiling and shaking hands in his warm and genuine style, he is winning many over. When Deanna sees someone she recognizes, she whispers in Jamie's ear.

Deanna sees Mr. Ellsworth and his wife are next; both are looking at her with surprise, as she introduces them to Jamie.

"Mr. Ellsworth my pleasure sir, I have been a fan of yours for years, both of your newspaper articles and your wonderful magazine. No, don't tell me this must be you're exceptional Melody that I've heard so much about. Mrs. Ellsworth, you must let me help you with the fine projects that you chair in this county?"

Mrs. Ellsworth is flattered that he would be aware of her charities. "Of course you must come to one of our events; I will have my personal secretary contact you." Melody says after recovering from his flattery.

"Mr. Ellsworth I would very much love to talk with you later I hope you will give me some of your time." Jamie asks Mr. Ellsworth. He has disarmed the old bear and Ellsworth doesn't know it and Mrs. Ellsworth is enchanted with him Deanna can tell.

Jamie's handling the reception line beautifully and Deanna is familiar with half of the names he has invited. She helps him with many of the Equestrian elites; they are some of the most prominent in South Florida society. Looking up Deanna see's Roberto is next in line, and is elated that he's been invited.

Roberto steps up to him, "Senor, allow me to introduce myself. I am Roberto Diaz; it is an honor to meet with you and thank you for your gracious invitation."

"Senor Diaz you are known to me by reputation, as many of the people that work here at the ranch speak highly of the Great Diaz of the Columbian Equestrian Team. You must allow me to come and watch you at the next show; I understand you have the best jumper of the year." Jamie seems completely versed as to Roberto's reputation.

"To friendship my friend," Jamie takes his wrist in a camaraderie clasp.

"To friendship my Celtic friend I see we have much in common." Roberto looks toward Deanna and he takes her hand, kissing it in his usual style and charm. "Senora Deanna, as always your beauty takes my breath away, I am your servant." She can't help blushing, as Jamie looks at her smiling with a little envy.

Finally, after about an hour all the guests have filed through the receiving line. Rosa and her team have made all comfortable inside with refreshments and appetizers. Raul's small band is a wonderful background to the whole affair as music fills the air from the veranda.

"I think that went well don't you, I can't thank you enough for all the help and your support. I was as nervous as a cat in a room full of rocking chairs." Jamie whispers into Deanna's ear,

She hadn't noticed, but he must have taken hold of her hand sometime during the reception process. He let's go of it, and she realizes that her palm is sweating, as his is also. They both take a deep breath, as they prepare for their entrance to the great room.

"You were wonderful, and you did everything perfectly. I think most of them are under the assumption that we're an item," Deanna whispers to him.

"Well it's time for the big show so let's not disappoint them." He whispers back.

The two of them enter the great room with Deanna on Jamie's arm. He leads her to a table that all the other tables radiate from. He pulls out a chair while she sits down. Jamie excuses himself and strolls up to the piano picking up the microphone.

"Ladies and Gentleman, Friends and Neighbors, I bid you welcome to Rancho de Los Angeles. Tonight we wish to have you celebrate two occasions, one is the anniversary of the Rancho and the second is my birthday." There is a round of applause from everyone, Jamie looks over and smiles at us.

"I wished you to be here so that many of you, whom we have not had the pleasure of meeting, might get to know us and see that we wish only to be good neighbors and be a part of this beautiful community. You are also welcome to tour the grounds and barns this evening if you wish.

Now I would like to present to you my students and members of my extended family." He motions with his hand and Dyon looking like a Starlet stands and collects each of the girls including Pita. They approach the piano to stand next to him.

"Ladies and Gentleman, if you would permit me may I present to you, my Angels. Starting from left to right, let me introduce my ward Dyon Thompson, next is Tia Rivera, Marianna Davidson, T. J. O'Neil and Pita Sanchez. Wait we are missing one more. Katy Gaynor please come up here will you." Katy is in shock and Jonah helps her to her feet.

Deanna says to her, "Go." She walks up to take her place at the end of the line, they are all smiling at her, and she has tears in her eyes.

These young ladies are my students, and your future equestrians, but all are a part of this home, my family and my life." Everyone claps and the girls all give curtsies.

Jamie gives the toast. "Now shall we all enjoy music, some great food, and good friends? Please be welcome to Rancho de Los Angeles." The guests all give them a round of applause.

Jamie and the girls come back to the table; Deanna is at a loss as to what to say to him. He's made Katy happier than he would ever know. She's bubbling with joy, with tears glistening in her eyes like stars in the sky.

"I could not introduce them and have her sitting there with pain in her heart; I looked at her and knew what I had to do. She's welcome here and I wanted her and you to know." She looks into his eyes and knows he's telling her the truth.

She excuses herself and goes out to the veranda, unable to hold back the tears.

Jamie follows her out and places his hands on her shoulders, turning her toward him.

"Are you angry at me again?"

She turns and kisses him on the mouth, long and hard. After many seconds, their lips part, breathlessly she whispers to him.

"No I'm not mad at you, how could I be? I think you may be the answer to my daughter's emotional stability and to the turning of our lives, I don't know who, or what you are. I just know that we're happy, and you've made that possible, my fear is what effect that'll have on us all."

He puts his arms around her and tells her, "There will be nothing that you have to fear from me. Whatever you learn will not change who and what I am. Now you will have to go fix your pretty face, you owe me a dance." Jamie still has his arms around her, and she feels all will be well.

Deanna and Jamie end their brief interlude and return to the great room amid great festivity and gaiety. Couples are dancing, and the girls have taken their guests to the game room. Jonah and Dyon are dancing and Deanna can see that they both are attracted to each other.

Jamie turns toward Deanna and says, "I believe this dance is mine, Ms. Gaynor." and he takes her in his arms, and they join the others on the dance floor. The song ends, he holds her in his arms, not wanting to let her go, until he notices that she's blushing, and they are the only ones left on the floor.

Holding Deanna's chair as she sits, he bends over and expresses to her. "I have to circulate among the guests and try to get to know them, but please save me some dances."

Melody Ellsworth watches Jamie as he circulates among the many guests at the party. John is discussing county policy with the Deputy Mayor of Palm Beach. She believes that she was misled about everything she was told about what was going on in this place. When John returns to her side, she says to him. "John maybe I was mistaken about this man, he appears to be such a personable individual and this home is magnificent, he appears to have class and breeding. Those girls all look to be wonderful, and Ms. Gaynor appears very attracted to him as well. They do make a glorious couple don't you think? Have you read any of her story yet?"

"No Mel, I haven't, but I intend to go over it this week, if fact I'm intending to speak to him myself sometime this evening if I can. I feel the same thing that Deanna did though, there's a story here, and I'm just not sure what it is. I know this honey; Williams and Cerbone at Southwest Properties will try to do whatever it takes, to harm this man. He stands between them and too much money. I don't think his ideals will protect him if they decide to get nasty." He ponders just how ugly.

"John, I sense he's a good man, and I also believe that our Ms. Gaynor may be falling in love with him, unless I miss my guess." She looks at her husband and smiles.

"She may need our help too," Melody Ellsworth states to her husband.

He takes her hand and says to her. "That's why I love you Melody Ellsworth; you always see the right side."

She hugs and kisses this big tough man that she cherishes so much. She remembers with pride, once he too stood alone against the odds to affect change.

"I want to read it when she's finished, before it goes to print. After all, you wouldn't be doing this story if I hadn't pressed you so much." She expresses to him with a knowing smile.

Jamie approaches John Ellsworth's table, "Hello Mr. and Mrs. Ellsworth, I hope you're enjoying yourselves, is the food to your liking?"

"It's superb this is the first time we've had beef barbequed like this, I mean over open hot coals. Is this how it's done in Mexico?" Melody inquires.

"It's prepared like this throughout the Southwest and Mexico. I have to be honest with you, the caterer pulled out this morning and Rosa my housekeeper threw this together for us this evening. I would be truly lost without her." Jamie confides to her.

"She has done a wonderful job, everything is so lovely, I would never have known that it was not cratered, could I borrow her for one of my parties?" Melody asks sincerely.

"You may ask, but the decision would be up to her. She's a very independent person." Jamie answers her good naturedly.

"Mr. Ellsworth, I would like to take this moment to thank you for sending Deanna over to see me. She's an extremely good reporter; I've enjoyed her company very much and look forward to the completion of her story. It was very fortunate that you had her on staff, and she knew Ed Haskell. I wouldn't have done it otherwise; sometimes things work as though by divine providence, don't you think? We ought to have lunch together soon, I would love to hear some of your exploit's as a top crime reporter." Jamie asks him.

"Mr. Doyle I would love to, my secretary will call you, and we can set up a date." Ellsworth answers and shakes his hand knowing that trying to get him into a private conversation tonight is out of the question.

Turning to Mrs. Ellsworth Jamie says, "Everyone raves about you so much, I would love to help with some of your charities." He takes Melody's hand and kisses it in a sincere bow, "We must all get together over lunch soon so you can decide how I can be of service." Jamie sincerely smiles at her as he releases her hand.

"If you will excuse me, I have to make the rounds to some of my other guests. Please enjoy our hospitality and feel free to wander the grounds if you'd like."

Deanna takes a moment to check on Katy and the other girls by going to the recreation room. Katy sees her Mom and runs up to Deanna, "Mother, I still can't believe it, he's accepted me to be one of his students. I'm so happy and all the kids are congratulating me as well. You know a lot of them that are here live in Loxahatchee, and stop by just to hang out. They think Uncle Jamie is the coolest person in the world."

Deanna asks her. "How did they come to know him, I have been wondering about that all day?"

Most of the boys want to be rodeo riders and Uncle Jamie assists them, he also takes them over to the Posse Grounds if their parents can't make it. They all think he's just wonderful, some, I think some have crushes on Dyon and some of the other girls. Uncle Jamie or Tanner always supervises all the trail rides and lesson just to make sure there are no other problems."

"I'm ecstatic you like it so much Katy. Why don't we to talk to Dr. Winman on Tuesday and see what he thinks about you cutting down on the number of visits you have to make to see him? Would you like that?" Deanna waits as Katy almost explodes.

"Mother I would love under no circumstances to have to go to his office ever again, but if we could get the number of visit down, that's a start. Oh, by the way, the girls were asking me if I will be showing at Horseman's this month, will I?"

"That is up to your new trainer, if Jamie says it's ok, I'll pay for it. I'll handle your father about Rose also, so don't you worry about it."

Katy puts her arms around Deanna and gives her a squeeze and smothers her with kisses. Mother you are the best; I have to get back to the others."

Deanna can't believe how good she feels about everything, her daughter, the job, the article it's like a fairy tale come true. Two weeks ago, she was financially without funds, didn't know how she was going to save her family and the farm. Now here she is helping to entertain some of the elite and famous for Palm Beach County.

Mr. Ellsworth comes up behind her and taps her on the shoulder. "Deanna may I speak with you for a few moments."

"Of course Mr. Ellsworth, let's go out on the back patio it will be a little quieter there." She leads the way through the crowd and out the French doors.

"Deanna, how is the piece coming."

"Very well, I think I'll have the rough draft finished and on Mr. Collins desk by Tuesday. I have only the horse show to add to the end, and I was waiting for the background check on Jamie before finalizing it."

"That's what I wanted to talk to you about. We have come up with nothing other than the last twenty years here in Florida. Before that he never existed, that means he's either a spook from a government agency or a criminal in the witness protection program. If he is the latter I don't think he would have pictures taken or speak with you."

"That will raise even more questions if I can't fill in some more background on him, he did tell me that he would not lie to me so maybe if I just ask him I'll get the story." Deanna comments pensively, her emotions are in a real crisis.

"I'm pulling some favors in Washington to see if we can come up with something there. Keep working on it, even if we have to put it off until the January issue as a lead into the National Horse Show. There is something familiar about him; I just can't place what it is. He reminds me of someone from a long time ago, but he was just a cowboy, I can't remember what it was for the life of me. It will come back to me, I'm sure."

"Ok, I'll finish what I have so far, and then we'll sit and go over it and put it on a story board." She tells him.

"Deanna, just some advice, please keep objective about this whole thing. He's won over Melody already, and that was in only a few moments. I wouldn't want to see you get hurt or anything like that." He says to her, reaching over to take one of her hands in his seeing the inner conflict in her eyes.

"I'll be extremely careful, he is charming and very sweet, but I will be professional until the end. After that I hope to keep a relationship with him as friends, regardless of the outcome of the story."

"Alright, just giving some fatherly advice, not trying to sound like your boss. We are a family at the Magazine, I hope you know that. You will have some great assignments after this young lady." He smiles at her and squeezes her hand and goes back inside.

Standing there with a west wind blowing on her face, she watches as the light show on the lake is dancing to the music inside. It's a wonderful place here, serene and pastoral, so out of place in the present day world. Deanna wonders if she can just stay objective until the piece is done and will he still want to see her after it's written?

She thinks about what John has told her about Jamie. John's right he couldn't be a criminal, but some kind of spy? Why is there no history on him? Father Scanlon knows, but won't tell. The only person that might know, is Ed Haskell, she must talk with him. He will be back right after this month's Horse Show; she'll talk to him then.

For the time being, she decides to enjoy the rest of the night and wait until more information comes in about him before making a permanent decision about him. Katy has to be her first concern right now no matter what he was once. Deanna has seen what he has accomplished with her, and it's short of being miraculous.

chapter 13

"The Gift of Life"

Jamie and Deanna are dancing and enjoying the end to the fiesta, most of the guests have already left. Jamie's made a great hit with most of them. His mannerisms and grace are what won them over. The party has been a huge success and will be an incredible assistance to his cause for the ranch.

Suddenly, Jamie's phone rings, "Yes Tanner is it time?" He asks. "I'll be right there… Yes, you know she will, I'll get her…. Give me five minutes."

Jamie turns to Deanna and tells her, "I have to go to the barn, Penny, Dyon's mare is giving birth, and it looks like it breached. Tanner will need my help; I'll make my apologies to our guests. Could you see to the remaining guests for me?" He turns and starts to walk away when suddenly he turns and says, "Thank You ____ for everything."

Surprised at his remark she answers, "For what?"

"For just being here, I hope someday to tell you how much it has meant to me."

"Go, I will take care of everything here and meet you out by the barn in a little while." Deanna tells him.

Jamie steps up to Raul asking him for the microphone, "Ladies and

Gentleman may I have your attention, please excuse me. I need your indulgence for just a moment. I must leave you and attend a mare that's giving birth, but I'll leave you in Deanna Gaynor's capable hands. Please feel free to enjoy what's left of the evening. I'll see each of you again very soon, I bid you good night and thank you so much for coming this evening." He turns and goes to find Dyon.

Deanna circulates among those guests that still remain. She finds they are very sympathetic to the situation and ask her to let them know the outcome as they are equestrian people as well. Soon the remaining guests make their goodbyes, and she then makes her way to the barn.

Deanna finds Jamie and Tanner in the stall with a very agitated mare that is kicking and biting at them both.

"Jamie I'm telling you, we got to give her something to calm her down, she gonna strangle that baby inside her if we don't!" Tanner exclaims.

"Tanner, please step out and leave her to me, I'll get her to calm down." Jamie says trying to sooth the mare.

"You are crazy boy, she is wild with pain, and she'll kill you for sure. I'm a calling the Doc."

Have Dyon go call, I will need you here as soon as I can get her to calm down!"

"Dyon you go and call him and tell him we need him now, you hear me!" He yells to Dyon, who's been standing white faced and terrified.

"Easy girl I won't hurt you, you know me, just let me touch you, and you'll feel better." She is starting to stand spread legged and sweating, Jamie steps up to her and places his hands on her neck, much like he did with Legion out on the gully wall. She calms down and he gently strokes down her back communicating to her all the time. She seems to sense that he is trying to help her with the pain and begins to calm herself.

"Tanner, hold her head, I'm going to try and turn the foal we can't wait for the vet any longer." Jamie moves to the rear of the mare, the most hazardous place for him to be. If she starts to kick, he will have nowhere to get away from those flailing hoofs that could cut him to pieces in such a confined area.

Reaching his arm into her, he starts to turn the foal getting the head in the position to drop, the mare is starting to fidget and the foal is kicking. You can see her sides jump every time it does, Penny's in intense pain. Jamie has his arm inserted into her now and has a hold of the baby.

"I've got a hold of it, and its turning, just a bit more, and I think we'll make it." With that Penny lashes out with her hind leg catching Jamie in the lower stomach and knocking him down.

Getting to his feet he motions for us to stay back. "I'm alright, hold her head, I almost got it that time, just one more time, and we'll make it." He instructs Tanner.

I notice that he is bleeding on his side just below the belt, and it seems to be quite a lot, I am about to say something when He cries out "Here it comes!" The baby emerges sack and all. Jamie is unable to get out of the way and the foal drops on him including the afterbirth.

Jamie sits back with the foal on his lap and removes the birth sack. Penny turns and starts to lick them both. He looks up at them and begins to laugh, lightening the intenseness of the recent situation.

"I'll bet she thinks I came out with the baby." We all laugh and breathe a sigh of relief as the moment of danger is past. Dyon comes up crying, saying she couldn't get the vet. She sees Jamie and the foal on the floor of the stall, and she throws her arms around them both.

Jamie takes a towel from Tanner and wipes himself down; he notices the blood and tries to cover it with the towel.

"Let me look at that," Deanna tells him, trying to pull his shirt up and undo his pants to get a better look at the injury.

"**No**," he tells her curtly. "I'll be alright, it is just an old injury that opened up, I will have it fixed up right away I know what to do." He turns and walks away toward the house before she can say anything.

Deanna doesn't understand what he's trying to hide. However, he did not what her to see his wound. Is he ashamed of it or what? She's watched him do what no Vet would have without the aid of tranquilizers; he did it with the touch of his hands. Where did he learn to care for animals like that? He seems to have a type of comforting healing touch.

"Tanner, he's hurt and bleeding pretty badly, we should take him to the hospital or at least put a bandage on it." Deanna begs Tanner to go after him.

"Missy he will take care of it, he always does, this isn't the first time he busted it open. Someday maybe it will heal, when the Good Lord thinks he has suffered enough I guess. Don't you be pressing him on it though; he'll be fine you'll see?" Tanner immediately diverts the conversation to Dyon.

"Tanner look it's a colt, and he's a red palomino with flaxen mane and tail." Dyon exclaims as Jonah looks on completely dumbfounded and unable to say a word about what he has just witnessed.

"Yes darling, you got yourself a fine looking colt. Whatcha gonna call it?" Tanner asks her.

"I'll call him Magic, that's your name little one." Dyon coo's at him as Penny looks on maternally protective, but patient of her humans touching and making a fuss over the precious baby.

"I think that's a good name as it took all my magic to get him out." Jamie laughs walking down the aisle to the stall, cleaned up and wearing a new shirt without any signs of blood.

"Are you ok, you gave me quite a fright with all that blood, you could have been killed do you realize that?" Deanna's yelling at him, mainly from a sense of relief seeing that he's alright.

"I'm fine; she just tagged me on an old scar and busted it open. I fixed it already and it stopped bleeding, just looked worse than it was really. Well let's take a look at our new family member, his legs are straight and eyes look clear, How about his breathing Tanner?"

"There you go again telling me my business. You think this was the first baby I ever helped drop, he's as clear as new fallen snow. Look he loves her already even before his Mama." Tanner smiles down at Dyon pretending to be cross with all of them. Deanna senses that the old man is relieved that the birth is past.

Jamie steps over to her and speaks to her in a whisper, "How about a dance before you have to head home. I think I have some music that would go very nice right about now." And he takes her by the hand and heads toward the rear patio of the house.

"I think you were a huge success tonight. The guests expressed to me how very impressed they were with you and every aspect of the ranch. You should be very proud of yourself."

"I was very proud of everyone here tonight, I felt good with you standing by my side Deanna. It seemed kind of natural, the two of us greeting everyone and entertaining if you don't mind me saying so."

"Jamie, there are things that you and I have to talk about before I can finish the story. They are about your past, and what you did before coming to Florida. I will have to know that before I can think of us being anything more than friends."

"I will tell you everything before you go to print, but first the Horse Show. Second I have to take Dyon up to Virginia to look at a college that's offered her a scholarship. When I return, I will answer all your questions.

I'm asking you to trust me, just for a little while longer. You won't be disappointed, I promise you. All I can tell you now is that your faith and trust will be tested and more than one future will depend on its outcome.

"Jamie why can't you tell me now is it that bad."

"Please don't press me right now, I can't explain, but I will. For the time being please don't take this the wrong way, but until I am no longer Katy's trainer what has been happening between us must be put on hold, as it wouldn't look right. I hope you understand."

"Yes your right of course, I must still try to stay objective, but we could still be friends couldn't we?

"Of course we will remain friends, good friends." Jamie reassures her.

Deanna wants to trust him, but down deep she is afraid to give that much trust to anyone.

"I will give it a little more time for Katy's sake and for the other's. Jamie if I find out that you have deceived me, or anyone else I will blow the lid off of it for sure," She warns him.

"Fair enough," he tells her with confidence in his voice, and turns to get her a drink.

"Here's your drink and the music is on, remember you owe me a dance, we never finished the one from before." He takes her in his arms, and she's torn three ways between being a woman, a mother and her job. To which one does she owe her first loyalty? Deanna wants to believe him in the worst way, but still can't shake this feeling of doom that seems to surround him at times.

It's the mystique that surrounds him, Deanna is almost afraid to learn what the past is, what it hides or reveals. Will she still feel the same way about him as she does now? Is this what John was warning her about? Is she still being objective? What does she do about Jonah and Katy? The web is tightening in ever closer circles, to what end, she wonders? Questions, all she keeps coming up with are more questions with no answers.

She closes her eyes and feels the rhythm of the music and the comfort of his arms. The moon is bright and the stars are twinkling, as his hand moves gently through her hair, she listens to the whisper of the wind letting herself succumb to the moment .

Chapter 14

"The Horse Show"

The show is today and Katy is so excited she can't keep it in any longer about the Horse Show. She's up before five o'clock rattling around the kitchen and making noise so everyone will get up. They have practiced for two weeks now and Jamie thinks she's ready to compete. Deanna only hopes she does as well as Jamie thinks she will.

She wishes she had more confidence in Katy, but having seen how she is when she panics, Deanna is apprehensive. She also has not spoken to Steve as yet; he still thinks she will be riding under his friend Rose's barn colors. Deanna will have to speak to him at the show grounds, but is not looking forward to it. She only hopes he doesn't make a scene or anything that will upset Katy.

"Mother, are you awake." She hears Katy call to her from the hall.

"Yes honey, how could I not be, what with the racquet you've been making in the kitchen?" She opens the door and runs in and jumps on her bed.

"I will be great today, I mean I will be ok and everything, Uncle Jamie says not to worry about pinning or anything just making a good ride. I love the way he trains us, it's not all about winning. He claims the important thing is that we have fun and do our best, but he always says "look good". It is about equitation, is that what your Dad used to say to you," She asks her mother?

"Yes your grandfather was a stickler for that too; he said more ribbons are won with good equitation and a smile than talent alone. He used to have me ride for an hour posting and walking just to improve my seat. He was a great trainer too, Jamie reminds me of him very much." The more time she spends around him, the more she sees her father in him. They don't look so much alike in physical appearances, just some of the mannerisms. In size and their first impressions, they are very similar. Dad was dark haired with brown eyes, but he gazed into you like Jamie does. They say a woman is always drawn to a man because he reminds her of her father.

"Are you all set, I mean your clothes and trunk are ready to load into the truck?" She asks Katy just to check.

"Yes Mother, we packed it four times, I'm so happy for tons of reasons, I may not have to go back to that wacko doctor anymore, and not having had an attack in three weeks. I also have real friends, and we aren't fighting any more. All these things happened because you got the job, and we met Uncle Jamie. Oh, by the way, what did Daddy say when you told him I wasn't training anymore at Rose's?"

"Honey, I haven't told him yet, but I will when he gets to the show grounds. I don't want you to worry about him. I will take care of all the details, and if he has anything to say, I will take the heat for you. Just concentrate on what you have to do, nothing else. He won't make a scene at the show, too many people around; you know how he is about doing anything in public. It will be alright Mr. Ellsworth's lawyer said I can do it because I have the right." She tries to build Katy's confidence as well as her own.

"Why don't you go down and start the coffee and wake your brother, while I take a shower and get dressed."

"Alright, I have to take Angel out anyway she is sitting by the back door waiting for me. Are we going to take her with us today?" She almost pleads with Deanna applying that "please" look she has.

"I don't think so there are too many people and could be other dogs, and we wouldn't want to create a scene if she got out of hand, besides she hates your father, remember."

"I forgot, ok I will play with her for a while until you come down stairs and Jonah comes out to do the barn chores. Legion looked very comfortable last night at the show grounds didn't he? I never thought I would be doing this, I still can't believe it." And she jumps up off the bed and runs down stairs banging on Jonah's door as she passes.

"Wake up sleepy head it's time to get going." She yells for him.

"Ok, Ok, I'm up, any more yells out of you, and I'll throw you in the manure pile." Jonah answers good naturedly.

Katy has waited also an hour and she is getting impatient finally calling up to Deanna from downstairs that the coffee is ready, and they have to hurry, she wants to meet the girls at the breakfast shack before they have to get ready and Pita is showing at eight o'clock in cross rails.

Deanna is pulling up her jeans when she hears Katy telling her to hurry up. "I'm almost ready, be there in five minutes, she yells down.

Coming down to the kitchen they are waiting for her by the table, Jonah is dressed in jeans and wearing a pearl button down western shirt with western boots and cowboy hat. Katy looks every bit the equestrian in her riding pants, shirt and jacket. Deanna is proud of both, but she kids him about looking like a country western singer instead of an English gentleman.

"Mother I am more relaxed dressed like this, besides, I'm sure Jefe will be wearing something just like this, I would be willing to bet on it. Don't you think Katy?" He queries his sister hoping for support.

"I don't know, he said he would be dressed the way he should be, that's all I know. Can we get going now, please?" she heads out the door to the truck, yelling over her shoulder, "Jonah put my trunk in the truck already Mother."

Locking arms Jonah and Deanna stroll out to the truck, and Katy is in it already. "Well what do you think Honey, is she ready or not?" Deanna asks him.

Smiling at her, he says, "I think we are all ready, how about you, anything happening between you and Jamie, or is it still objective fencing." Holding up his hands laughingly he ads, "Don't bother to answer me or tell me that it's none of my business. You would be right if you did, just asking that's all." Before she can answer he jumps behind the wheel of the truck and yells, "Alright, let's get going, we're burning daylight."

Something Jamie would say, Jonah is beginning to sound like him more and more now that he is working with him, and she's not sure how to feel about that yet either.

It all comes down too not knowing all the facts yet about him, Deanna feels she has to be cautious about how close she gets to him. There is something about him that draws her toward him, and she can't put her finger on it, just when Deanna thinks she knows what it is, it slips away, like trying to hold water in your hands.

They pull into the show grounds and check in with the guard at the gatehouse, he tells them where to park the truck to unload the trunk and saddles. Jonah pulls off all the tack and puts it outside of Legion's stall. Deanna notices all the other girls are absent their tack is unloaded and standing by each horses stall, which means they should be at the breakfast shack. Deanna looks at Katy and tells her to go on ahead, and they'll meet her as soon as they're finished unloading. She runs off faster than she has ever seen her run.

Jonah comes up after parking the truck. "Jamie's truck is here so he must have left for the canteen already, why don't you go over to breakfast, and I'll get Legion ready. If Dyon is there please tell her I'm over here taking care of the tack. Maybe she can meet me here, if not call me on my cell phone, ok." And he goes about unpacking Katy's trunk and getting her tack ready.

"I'll help you with that if you want, then we both can go over together." She says to him, but he gives her a look that says he would rather do it by himself. Puzzled Deanna agrees and sets off for the shack.

Deanna sees Jamie and Eduardo sitting with the girls and they all seem to be talking, and having fun. She remembers back when she was showing, the morning of the show was the most fun. Before they started to compete, her father would order breakfast for everyone and talk about how they would do, and to remember that it was all about having a good time, enjoying the horses and their friends, just like they seem to be doing now.

"Good morning everyone, I see you are all set for today, you all look great." She says to all of them, but she meant it more for Jamie's sake. He looks so handsome in his riding boots and pants wearing a yellow polo.

"Hi, good morning, sit over here by me," Jamie says as he slides over to make room for her to sit next to him.

"We were just saying how beautiful the day is going to be and the grounds are really first rate. See how they're getting ready for the National Show. I was just telling the girls that this is one of the most beautiful and expertly done places in the country for an outdoor event. New York is an indoor arena so it is a different type of setting. This must remind you of the show grounds up in Virginia, I have never been there, but they say they are spectacular." Jamie explains bringing her up to date on their conversation.

"Yes Virginia has some wonderful arenas, but I think here has the most spacious with all the different rings going on all at once. How's the coffee?"

"Not as good as Rosa's but we will have to make do until she gets here. Eduardo tells me she's coming with food for us and lots of hot coffee; she's going to set up back by the stalls, kind of like a party. She had Esteban and Rubin loading chairs and tables and should be here in the next fifteen minutes or so. There was no arguing with her when she sets her mind, right Eduardo." Jamie remarks to his Segundo.

"Si Patron, she is very set in her ways, and she says no one shall go hungry today, besides the senoritas need a place to rest and have their friends come. I am only Segundo not the boss," and they all laugh.

"Dyon, Jonah is waiting for you over by the stalls, he is unpacking the tack and getting Legion ready, I think he wanted you to go over if you

The Last Celtic Angel

wanted to." She hints to Dyon, she nods and excuses herself and walks off toward the barns.

"I think they have more than a passing attraction for each other, she was just asking Katy if he was here." Jamie tells her quietly.

The girls excuse themselves to go over to look at Ring One where Pita will compete. Deanna waits until they all leave to ask him if he was alright about Dyon and Jonah.

"I am fine with it, Jonah is great and Dyon is a good girl, besides, they're almost eighteen. If I tried, or you to interfere, they would rebel against it. I think they will handle it very well, they have two good examples to follow about controlling one's passions, wouldn't you say?" He smiles with that funning smile of his, as if he's joking, but not joking.

Changing the subject Deanna asks, "How is Jonah doing at the ranch he talks about nothing else since he started there? It's about Jefe this and Jefe that, he's suffering from some hero worship, you know."

"I try to pair him up with Eduardo and Esteban, whenever I can. He wants to learn rodeo, and he is pretty good too. I promised him I would teach him, if it's alright with you. I know you want him to go to a good college in the fall, but he's going to do it anyway. Maybe if he has the right instruction, he can get it out of his system this summer and be done with it, so he can concentrate better."

"Are you trying to talk me into it for him, it sounds like a set up to me? I want him to go to college, so he can make something out of himself. Have a career and be able to earn a good living, is that so wrong of me to want that for him?" Suddenly Deanna senses she may have insulted him and tries to make up for it. "I mean that some people can't all be All around Cowboys and be successful."

"It's ok; you're right most cowboys just wind up broken up and broke. I would want the same thing for him myself, but you have to remember that he is a proud young man, and he will have to try. I'll work on him to temper his enthusiasm and convince him that education is the most important thing for his future. You didn't hurt my feelings by the way, I was pretty good, but I didn't handle it well at all and would never encourage him to follow in my footsteps." He takes her hand and holds it reassuringly,

"He'll go to college you'll see. I promise you he will."

"Uncle Jamie it's seven thirty we have to get Pita ready they are calling for warm up." Tia runs by and shouts as they all head back to the barn.

"I have to go and give her some warm-up. Dyon will have her pony ready, by the time she gets there. We might as well head over to the ring now if that's ok with you."

"I told Tim I would meet him here at eight, I want some shots of the girls and the show for the article, I will meet you over there." She gives him a kiss and wishes him good luck. He turns and starts to walk away then turns to look at her, touching his face where she kissed him with his hand and smiles.

"Thanks, it's been awhile since a pretty girl kissed me and wished me that before a show, it sounds and feels kind of nice. Watch out for Tom and Irene, he's bringing her for the show. T. J. was so excited that she will be here to watch her, maybe you could just stand by just in case… Please, you know another mother for support besides Rosa." Deanna senses this is something he needs her to do.

"No problem I will be happy to stay with her, and I hope she won't mind. She wasn't too sure of me when I met her at the ranch or at the mission." She explains to him as he rushes off to Ring One.

Pita comes walking by on her pony smiling that big smile of hers. "Lots of luck today Pita, I will be rooting for you." Deanna yells to Rosa's little girl.

"Thank you Senora, I just hope I can get through this before I have to pee again." She laughs and grins at her with that mischievous look she has.

"You better not Little One, or I will make your seat very hot for you, behave yourself and make us proud." She hears Rosa from behind her.

"Hola Senora, we will have a fine day, Si? I have brought much food and cakes for all, you will eat with us today no? Rosa asks Deanna.

She is beautiful today; she and Eduardo both are dressed to

complement each other. Both proud and beaming for the child that everyone seems to share.

"Senora even old Tanner has come to watch his girls, he will be at the fence pretending how miserable he is, but he is like the old hen." She laughs with a hearty laugh as does Eduardo.

They are here as a family all of them, the vaquero's and their girlfriends to lend their support and love. She feels as though that she too is part of this family, they're so proud and they bring so much emotion with them. All held together by one man and a dream, he dreams their dreams and helps make them come true. Her thoughts are interrupted by a tap on the shoulder.

"Hello Deanna, I made it, where are they starting, I want to set up so I get the right light?" Tim asks.

"I'm sorry; I was spending some time day dreaming I'm afraid, they will be starting at Ring One. Pita is doing cross rails; they're warming up now, so we'd better get started over there."

"I'll just take lots of pictures, and we can put it together later this week if you like. I like to get as many candid shots and action shots as possible, then I can get posed shots to finish out the layout. Is that's ok with you?"

"Tim, I write and you take pictures, I trust your judgment better than mine. I'm here to just be a spectator, I will write about this day later, so have at it and I'll see you later. Oh, by the way, Rosa has set up at the barn for us to have food and refreshments, don't go and buy anything, ok." Deanna sees Father Tom and Irene coming up the path toward the ring.

"Hello, I see you made it, can I walk with you two up to the stands. Irene you look wonderful, are you excited about T. J. being in her first show? Katy has not been able to sit still for three days." Oop's, she realizes that Irene does not live with T. J. and Deanna feels she may have made another blunder with her.

"Thank you for the compliment. Yes, she has been very excited; Father has taken me over a few times this week, so I could help her with her clothes and things. She uses sign language you know so we can talk. I pray to God that he will restore her speech one day, just so I can hear her voice once more before……"

"Now you know she is going to speak again, hasn't Jamie told you that, she will very soon, you believe in him don't you girl?" Father Tom interjects himself into the conversation cutting Irene off before she could finish whatever, she was about to say.

"How are you Deanna, you look like a picture, just like you was at the Irish Sweepstakes? Oh, look there, the girls coming over on their horses to watch Pita, sort of fitting, don't you think. He's done wonders with them in such a short time too." Father Tom rattles off in that Irish lilt of his. "I see Rosa had chairs set up for us, that girl is a wonder she thinks of everything."

We take our seats and watch eight girls ride in about thirty minutes, each one has done very well and completed the course, all have made it without any refusals. Pita's name and number are called, and they watch as Jamie walks with her to the gate. She's smiling and looking everywhere, except where she is supposed to be looking. Rosa is getting angry at her and keeps poking Eduardo in his ribs, telling him it is his fault that she does not pay more attention. He nods and takes the blame on his shoulders with a smile.

Jamie sternly tells the little girl. "Pita you must pay attention now and stop being the goose. Make your circle and take the right line, do it at the walk than move to the trot after the first jump then let him canter. I will be watching you and just remember all that I have told you, keep going over it in your head, ok?"

They call out her number, and she enters the Ring. Jamie watches her and she can hear him talking to her even though Katy can't hear him at all, going over each jump with her, as though she were standing next to him.

Pita makes a perfect round, smiling at the judges all the time her equitation is wonderful, shoulders back, hands relaxed, her pony performs with precision and poise. She makes her circle and heads for the gate, smiling and starts to talk before she leaves the ring. Hopefully, the judge didn't hear her as she says, "I aced it Jefe."

As she leaves the ring, we wait for the numbers to be read. First Place is awarded to a girl of about nine on a small welsh pony, second is given to the first girl who rode, third is awarded to Pita and the spectators stand erupts with applause. Jamie sweeps her from the saddle and hugs her and kisses her cheeks.

"You made us very proud of you Little One, now you must repeat for the second ride and try to do as well. You may have a chance at Grand if you can place high enough. Just do what you did the first time only in reverse going the other way." He tells her.

Rosa and Eduardo come over to congratulate her and give her more hugs and kisses. "You made your Papa proud, you ride like me" Eduardo says to her.

"Yes Papa, but I don't look like you, I'm prettier." Everyone within hearing of her turns and starts to laugh; she is such a funny little person.

"I will do better the next time I was just a little scared, and I have to pee." She announces much to Rosa's embarrassment.

"Come quickly with me. I told you not to drink so much." Rosa scolds her as they rush for the Porta Potty. We all laugh so hard there are tears coming down our faces.

They are calling the numbers again and Pita comes running. Jamie picks her up and puts her in the saddle. She gets in line to take her last ride for the final position of her class. We wait as she enters the Ring and traverses the opposite direction riding perfectly toward the first jump. She makes it but chips on the second one finishing with a frown because she knows that one mistake could cost her a high pin. Jamie greets her as she exits the ring, and she has tears in her eyes.

"Why are you crying, you did well, many riders chip once or twice going around? There's no need for you to cry or be upset, I'm proud of you. Remember it's about having fun. Did you have fun," he asks as he helps her down?

"Yes Jefe, more fun than anything, but I wanted to win for you to prove that you are the best trainer and have the best barn." She sobs in his arms.

"Baby girl, I won the minute you entered the ring and rode. You just made me the biggest winner of all by wanting it for me instead of yourself. My winning is watching you have fun and doing what you love to do." He hugs her and she smiles as he tickles her and makes her laugh.

They are announcing the winners of the Cross Rails Class. Grand is given to the girl who placed second in the first round, Reserve Grand goes to Pita, and she is jumping up and down and hugging everyone including her pony.

"I did it, look everyone, I did it!" She yells holding up her ribbon.

Jamie strides up to Deanna and smiles. "That was a close one, now we're on to the Walk Trot Hunter for T. J. Walking over to the WTH ring. T.J. is so small and looks scared getting upon her pony, Jamie is standing next to her speaking to her quietly, "You will be all right you'll see. Do you still want to do this?" She nods her head yes. "Good girl now all you have to do is concentrate and remember all the things we've gone over, I will be right here by the gate. If you feel funny doing this just head your pony toward the gate and come out, ok." Jamie has a worried look that Deanna has never seen before, as he turns from her toward the Ring.

T. J. enters the ring and makes her circle before starting her course; she seems to be riding well and makes the first leg of the course with ease. Approaching the second she seems to be hunching over a little and she sees her shoulders start to tremble. Deanna edges over to be near where Jamie is standing, and she hears him talking to her, as though she were standing next to him again. She looks back at T.J., and she is sitting with her back straight and eyes front, as though she could perceive his instructions from across the arena. He never stops talking her through the course, and she appears to hear him, maybe what Katy said about them hearing him in their heads is true. T. J. is trembling as she exits the Ring. Jamie rushes up to greet her, a huge smile brightens his face as he takes her in his arms, and she's crying and shaking all over. He holds her and tells her how wonderful she was. Irene comes running up to congratulate her as well.

T. J. turns at the sound of her mother's voice and puts her arms around her. Suddenly, she turns to Jamie and looks at him and stammers, "Th__Thank__y__you Jefe."

Stunned by these words we see both Irene and Jamie both have tears well up in their eyes as the little girl's face brightens with a glow that would melt even the hardest of hearts.

Father Tom breaks the tension by giving a short prayer of thanks and we all start to talk at once. Tim is taking pictures of this moment; I only hope he captured the emotion of what just took place. The announcer gives out the standings and T. J. has placed fifth, and she's ecstatic.

Tanner ambles over and presents to her a silver horse pin, and even he has tears in his eyes, as she hugs him and accepts his gift by saying, "Thank you."

"See there ain't anything you can't do once you set your mind to it. My babies are all winners; I told you so didn't I?" He rambles on about how he knew she could do it, as Irene embraces him; the smile on his face is huge.

"He smiled on her today and granted her wish. This day is truly the first step back for her toward the road to recovery, and I only hope she will handle the next trial as well." Jamie mutters not so much for her to hear, but to himself.

"What was that you said," Deanna asks him after hearing him mumble.

"Oh it was nothing, just that she has more roads to travel. Now she has the time to do it in, or something like that. I think it was part of an old Irish poem I heard once. Come let's get ready for Katy, she's up next in Low Hunters," Jamie had her skip cross rails and enter in the slightly more difficult class. "I need to warm her up." He calls Katy to come over to the practice ring and start warming up for her class.

Watching them, she can't help but wonder the way he gets results from these kids and the good that he's doing. Why is it, she is always looking for the other shoe to drop? Is it because not having the answers to questions that keep bugging her, nagging at her every time she starts to get comfortable with him? Was he always like he is now, or is this just something that developed since Mary passed?

Those were real tears in his eyes when J.T. spoke to him, he tried to hide them by stepping back and letting her mother and all the rest show their love. There seems to be a power in him not just talent and ability, a way to heal and communicate that transcends education and training, something unnatural.

Watching him now with Katy and the way she responds to his training, is beyond anything that anyone would have believed possible just a few short weeks ago. She prays that there will be no skeletons that pop up in his closet, something that might cast a shadow over people that care so much for him. The one's who believe that he's who, and what he appears to be.

Turning back toward the spectator's section Deanna sees Steve storming over to her, with an angry face and his nostrils flaring.

"Deanna, I need to talk to you right now, I just spoke to Rose, and she tells me that Katy has not been over to her barn for training for weeks, and that she is not registered as her trainer here today either. You better have a good excuse for this bullshit, or I'll make you wish that you were never born, I'll crucify you." He threatens her and carrying on like she's never seen him, posturing for battle in public is very unlike him.

"Steve how nice of you to make it today I am sure Katy will be thrilled that you came." She tries to be as pleasant as possible, so he won't make a scene.

"You bitch, I warned you what would happen if you interfered with me again, didn't I? Where's Katy, she's leaving right now, and you're paying for all the lessons she missed?" He demands, getting right into Deanna's face.

Katy is watching from the practice arena and sees her father storm up to her mother. Having learned from Jonah what he is capable of, she's afraid for her, and it shows on her face.

Katy turns to Jamie and says, "Oh my God, that's my father, and he's angry at my Mother, for taking me out of Rose's program and letting me train with you. What am I going to do Uncle Jamie?" Katy is starting to go into a panic attack, her color is draining from her face and her hands are starting to shake.

"I'll take care of this, you just walk Legion, so he won't get nervous, and everything will be alright. Go on, I'll talk to him, it'll be ok." Jamie reassures her and she quiets down a little.

Walking over unnoticed by either Deanna or her ex-husband, Jamie excuses himself and intercedes. "Excuse me, is there a problem here? You must be Mr. Gaynor, how are you? I'm James Doyle your daughter's new trainer." Before Steve can speak, Jamie cuts him down. "You know your voice has carried out to the ring where I am warming up a horse and rider. I would appreciate if you would either take this somewhere else or kindly be quiet." Steve turns toward Jamie with hatred glaring from his eyes.

"That was not a request Mr. Gaynor, it's an order. Let me point out to you that as custodial parent, Deanna has the right to engage anyone that she sees fit to train her Daughter. That sir happens to be me. If you interfere with that training you will be in violation of Equine law in Palm Beach County. As a member of the Florida Bar you must be aware of that. That's the first thing, the second is I will take it very badly, and you don't want me to do that." Jamie gets up to Steve's nose and Deanna's afraid that Steve will try to hit him.

"Listen you son-of-a-bitch, I'll slap you silly if you get in my way." With that said Steve tries to punch Jamie, but suddenly finds his wrist in a vise like grip that's twisting him to his knees in submission.

Jamie whispers to him as he falls to his knees. "The mistake you just made is that you thought this is my first time at the rodeo, it isn't. I'll break your arm if you ever try that again, with me or Deanna. Go home Mr. Gaynor I don't wish to see you ever again. I'll spare you the embarrassment of a beating you justly deserve, but only for your daughter's sake. I won't be so forgiving next time, **Go away!**" Having given him evidence to his exact intentions, Jamie releases him as Steve grovels in the dust. Steve slowly gets to his feet, and she sees the same fear in his eyes as the day Angel chased him to his car.

Jamie then takes Deanna's arm and escorts her to a seat in the spectator's box. "I'm sorry, but there seemed no other way around that situation, I hope you'll not think too badly of me. I could not have him upset Katy or threaten you much more." He apologizes to her then says, "I have to get out to Katy now and try to get her mind ready for this class, excuse me."

Jamie strides off to the ring with everyone just staring after him not saying a word. She can hear whispers saying they never saw anything like that in their lives. How quick he was and how easily he put Steve on his knees. Mostly, it was the look in his eyes that they focused on. Jamie's eyes went from an azure color to cold ice blue in the blink of an eye. His look put a chill in the otherwise tropical air, and that whispered threat, rasped against their nerves, a sense of fear they all felt. The fear that Steve felt was what they experienced. A few began talking to her, saying how sorry they were, that. Steve was such a jerk. Some of the women actually were titillated by how Jamie just took command and took down an obvious bully. One or two knew who Jamie is; all were impressed.

She now knows there's no backup in him at all, if it comes to a fight, he will fight for what he believes or feels he must protect.

The judges are calling off the list of riders and Katy is scheduled to ride second. Her color has not come back yet, and Deanna knows that Katy's still worked up by her Father's behavior. She's afraid on how it will affect her ride, will she blow up and suffer embarrassment in front of all these people, Deanna trembles at that thought. She closes her eyes and prays, "Please, don't let her lose it out there, it will destroy her."

Jamie is talking to her and tries to get her ready by keeping her focused on the girl that is riding in front of her. Pointing out what she has to concentrate on.

"Katy you have to listen to me, you're going to be fine, sometimes adults make fools of themselves, and it has nothing to do with you. Your job today is to take Legion out there and show everyone how good he and you really are. Just think about all the things I have told you, and that you know. You'll be just fine.

Anytime you start to get into trouble, you will hear me talking you through it. I will be right here if you think of me, and you'll hear me." Jamie places his hand on hers and gives her hand a little squeeze, Katy tries to give him a smile, but manages only a weak one.

It's time for Katy to enter the ring, and she makes a tight circle, not a big one then heads for the first jump in line riding a little stiff. I look and Jamie is talking again as though she were right beside him, each stride he tells her how good she's doing. Taking the second jump a little long, but she recovers and goes on to the third. Katy looks up and sees Jamie as she crosses to the center heading back toward us. Katy nods her head, as if she hears his instructions and goes on to the rest of the jumps. She finishes a good round except for the start and the long jump. Exiting the Ring she comes to a halt in front of Jamie.

"Well how do you think you did?" He asks her holding Legions head as Katy pats his neck.

"I think I did well except for my entrance and the second jump, but, I could hear you as I rode around, every stride, I could hear your voice. Will it always be like that?" She asks, her voice cracking a little.

"Only for as long as you need to."

Deanna walks over after giving Katy and Jamie a few moments like her mother used to when she exited the ring. Her father as her trainer would always come over after she finished her class and discuss the ride with her for a few minutes.

Deanna now walks over and Jamie takes Legion out of the way and looses his girth. Katy runs over and gives her a big hug. "Mother I think I'm going to be fine, from this point on, thanks for hanging in there for me. I hope Uncle Jamie doesn't think I'm mad at him for what happened with Daddy. I saw it even though he tried to send me over to the other end of the ring. Daddy tried to hit him didn't he?"

"Yes Honey, I think he would have, but Jamie handled it like a gentleman and persuaded him to leave without causing anymore trouble. Everything will be alright from here on out." Deanna tries to explain to her, so she doesn't feel more embarrassed than she already does.

She looks down at the ground and whispers, that she wishes her father was more like Uncle Jamie. Deanna wishes he had been to, but you could also wish for pigs to fly.

The judges have finished tallying up the scores and Katy got a third, she is elated and all the girls are patting her on the back and already start planning for the spring shows. Dyon takes Katy's ribbon and pins it on Legion's headstall, and he seems to be very pleased with it also.

The rest of the girls did well in all their classes, and we go to celebrate with some of Rosa's wonderful food as the vaqueros take care of the horses, parading them around for all the others see.

"Why are they doing that, Rosa" Deanna asks.

"They are proud of the Senoritas and the horses, so they are showing off. It is a thing of pride for them and a way to show their Rancho to the others. It will make them jealous and cause some bad feeling, but they will get over it. The vaqueros take their jobs very seriously. They feel that they have won too.

They did do well, two Grand's, two Reserves and nothing more than fifth, it was a very good day. Dyon won all of her classes against many rated riders and very expensive horses. The Rancho did well and that will give them much pride.

"Do you not feel the pride as they do? Senorita Katy won more than just a ribbon today, no?" Rosa says.

"Yes Rosa, I have not felt this way, since I was a little girl riding for my Father, I feel like I belong." She says to her longingly, remembering back to when she was Katy's age, and what it felt like to be part of something that she loved.

"The Patron made a choice for you today and maybe a bad enemy as well. He as I once said to you, is the rock upon which we stand" Rosa reminds her.

Turning to look at the girls sitting, chatting and laughing with Eduardo playing his guitar and Jamie singing, she's reminded of a time in her own past. Deanna takes a moment to reflect before returning to the afternoon's holiday fare and party atmosphere. She can't help but want for this to go on forever, not just for her children, but herself as well.

Chapter 15

"A Mother's Secret"

"Hello Mom, how are you?" Deanna says to her, as soon as she picks up the phone.

"Deanna, is everything alright, the kids ok."

"Yes everyone is ok, sorry, I know I always call you after seven, but I needed some advice….. And I needed to talk to you; do you have a few minutes?" Deanna asks her.

"Of course I do. What's the problem; you're not getting back with Steve are you?"

"No, this is more like, letting me sound off to you and then seeing if I sound crazy or what. I have had the most incredible four weeks of my life.

"What are you prattling about?"

Before you say anything or ask me questions could you please just listen and let me talk, ok? The last time I spoke to you, I told you about the new job and the story that I was working on. Well, the gentleman that owns the ranch has become Katy's coach and therapist. He has done more for her in this short period of time than you could imagine.

You were on that Thanksgiving cruise with the church when Katy had her first show. She placed third, if you had seen the way he handled her, you would have thought it was a miracle, she rode perfectly on Legion. All the girls did wonderfully, and it was an electrifying weekend. You see all the girls except one he teaches, have some kind of crisis or emotional problem. He's so much like Daddy its unreal.

"You are beating around the bush, what's the problem, are you falling for this guy or what?" Her mother sounds like she's a little peevish with her.

"Mom, please let me get to what I want to talk to you about, can you do that just once, please?"

"Ok, go ahead. Is this going to be one of those Mother Daughters things again?" Her mother answers and asks her, a little petulant again.

"Well yes, remember Mary Haskell? She was Daddy's favorite student; her Mom was killed in that jumping incident during the fox hunt." Her mother is silent about what she has just said; it seems to be a long time.

"Hello Mom, are you there," She asks?

"Yes, um, I was just fixing the phone cord." Answering her, but sounding like a little distant.

"Jamie, that's Katy's trainer, that's his name, Jamie Doyle, you're not going to believe this, but he was married to her, and she passed away from cancer. I've had this feeling that he knows me, or we've met before, but I don't know where. He knows what I like, right down to the clothes that I would prefer, flowers, even the wine I like. I keep getting this feeling of Dejevue any time I am with him. He's tall, rather good looking, very gentle and patient. I know he's a man who if pushed will fight for what he believes in and is very devoted to his principles. He loves his family with a love that reminds me of Daddy, his friends would also die for him like Daddy's.

He and Steve got into it at the Show Grounds and Steve was getting really ugly. He even tried to hit Jamie, but instead, Jamie almost broke his arm, he never lost control, nor raised his voice. He told Steve that if he caused Katy or me anymore grief, then he would deal with him and sent him packing. I saw strength in him that I never thought I would see again. He seems to have a power that makes you feel safe, protected, it emanates from him. I have tried to stay objective about him for the story's sake. I am so confused about how I feel about him. He's kissed me a couple of times, but not since he became Katy's teacher and therapist. I think I'm falling in love with him, but I have this feeling that he hides a terrible secret.

The magazine research department could not find anything about him prior to twenty years ago. Mr. Ellsworth seems to think he may have been a government agent you know what they call a spook or is in the witness protection program. He's very wealthy, but you would never know it by meeting him or talking with him. He just possesses so many unnatural qualities that sometimes I think he will vanish if I blink my eyes.

Mother, I'm very confused as to how I feel about him. Do I keep on with the story or do I ask Ellsworth to assign someone else?"

Deanna's mother is listening to her go on about this mystery man, and how wonderful he is, but her mind stopped when she mentioned Mary. *That was so long ago, and then she disappeared after her mother was killed and Ed left right after that too. She never heard from either one again. Moina was her best friend, they grew up together in Virginia, and both went to college getting jobs as interns in Washington. That's how she met Robert. He was working for the Kennedy's, and Moina got the job working for Ed Haskell when he was in congress. My God, she can't tell her after all these years that Mary was not Ed's child; she was her father's first child. When Moina was killed that day neither Mary nor Robert were ever the same or her either. Now the past is coming back to haunt them again. Deanna is falling in love with her dead sister's husband. Does he know, is that why he knows so much about her, does she tell her and how?---------*

"Mother are you listening to me or not," Deanna asks her?

"Yes honey, what is it that you want from me, approval? I can't tell you what to do, I don't know the man."

"Well the problem is, he will not pursue how he feels about me while he is Katy's therapist. Do I wait for things to work out or drop it and move on, I'm not really sure how he feels about me? I have some men that are asking me out, what should I do?"

"Deanna I know nothing of this man, and you yourself think that he hides a terrible past. I think you should back away, let him help Katy if he is able and move on." She can't tell Deanna that she's scared to death because then she will ask her, why.

"Mother I have tried that, but it's very difficult, because I see him a couple of times a week with Katy and about this story. How do I control what I'm feeling, he seems able to sense what I'm feeling? I am getting angry with him because I'm feeling frustrated, and I seem drawn to him the more I see him."

"Honey I will talk to you another time, the church ladies just pulled up, and I have to go. Just try to keep your distance and by all means don't turn down any dating situation that may present its self. Say hello to Jonah and Katy for me, and I will talk to you for the holidays. I love you, Bye."

"Mother I still need to talk to you," but she's already hung up. Deanna was hoping that she would give her some insight as to what she should do about her feelings, but as usual she ducks the question and tells her to walk on the safe side. Just once Deanna would like her to tell her to take the plunge; she married Steve because she thought he was the right choice, being a successful attorney. Thinking about it now, she decides it was not a good idea to ask for her mother's advice. Her mother thought Steve was perfect and they all know how that turned out. She should have waited until she knew him better than she would have seen he was a piece of crap and an ego maniac he really was not to mention abusive.

Deanna always got along with Mary's mother better than my own. She seemed to understand what she was feeling and gave her good advice.

Deanna found the old albums the other day and was showing them to the kids. Moina was beautiful and she loved the horses so much, so did Mary. She had forgotten the times when she would take them shopping, even when Deanna was so young, and she had such patience with her, more than her own mother had at times.

Her Father was very fond of Moina and Mary, Deanna thinks back on it now, she wonders if he ever thought about her in a romantic way, and Mr. Haskell was much older than her at the time. Her thoughts and imagination are getting the better of her.

She says to herself, "Oh what am I thinking, that's silly my thoughts are getting crazy. My father was Mr. Straight Arrow of our community; no skeletons in his closet, my Mother would have been more likely to have had an affair than he would."

Thinking back to the show grounds she's still amazed at the way Jamie handled Steve, he was so confident in his ability. Deanna was quite scared when he lowered his voice and spoke to him, his voice was chilled, but without malice. It was like ice, cold and final. She sensed that Steve knew he was in trouble when he looked into Jamie's eyes; they weren't blue any longer, but silver, and hard.

There was no warmth there, but when he turned and spoke to her, they were back to normal. Those are the things that bother her about him, his ability to react and change so quickly. She had the feeling that if Steve had not backed down that Jamie would have seriously hurt him. There is a level of violence that lies beneath the surface that makes him a dangerous person. In that respect, he is much like the horse, he rides, power, speed, and courage waiting for the time when it's needed. It's his confidence and a sureness that seems to make everything turn out alright; it just frightens her at times and today was one of those times.

chapter 16

"Tanner's Loss"

It's eight o'clock and Deanna's getting ready to go to the office when the phone rings, "Hello Rosa, what is it, I can't understand you, please slow down…? When did it happen?___ How is she now?___ I will be right there; do you need me to pick you up? ___ Alright I'll see you there." Hanging the phone up, Deanna grabs her bag and runs out the door.

Katy is just coming out of the barn when she sees her mother and can tell by the look on her face that something's wrong.

"Mother, what is it? Katy calls out to her as she sees Deanna running for the car.

"Irene was rushed to the hospital, and is in serious condition. Rosa just called and said Irene wants to see me immediately. I don't have time to tell you more because I don't know myself." She yells to her, opening the car door.

"Wait I will go with you, T. J. might need me." She jumps in the other side of the car, her face is very white, but she's in control. She is going to her friend in spite of what it may cost her. Deanna knows she can't tell her to stay, these are the little breakthroughs that she needs, to overcome her own anxieties.

As they drive in silence to the hospital she wonders what could have happened to Irene that would have caused her to be rushed to the hospital. Was there an accident at the Mission, or is it her illness, that they made reference too? Katy is pensive and chewing her nails and holding back the tears. "It will be ok honey; she's in a good place, the best in the county. I'm proud of you for wanting to stand by your friend, she may need you."

"Mother what if her Mom doesn't make it, what will this do to her? She just started to talk again after so long. Her Mom has to make it for T's sake". She looks over at her and sees that she is praying something she has not done since she was very little, her hands folded and eyes closed. She has come a long way.

They pull up in front of the hospital and look for a parking space, finding one they run for the entrance and ask at the desk where Irene is. They said that they moved her to the intensive care, fourth floor. Deanna turns to go to the elevator when the security guard stops them and asks if they're family?

"Yes we are," Deanna says without hesitation, knowing in her heart, she believes it to be true.

Rushing to the elevator noticing that it is on the second floor, she hits the down button and the seconds seem like minutes and the elevator seems to be taking incisively long, to go from two to ground level. Finally, it shows one and the door opens, they jump in and Deanna presses four, and it slowly ascends. Getting to the fourth floor and exiting, they are greeted by the ever vigilante Eduardo. "Where is she, is Jamie here, where're T.J. and Rosa?" She fires questions at him in rapid succession.

"Senora they are waiting down the hall that way." He points toward the west wing. "The Patron is with her now, so is the Padre. Rosa has the little ones at the TV room. Only a miracle can save her now Senora. The Patron is worried for Tanner; he is just sitting there and will speak to no one." Eduardo turns and heads down the hall.

As she walks behind him, she feels a heavy weight upon her chest, wondering what she will say to them. She has never been in this situation before, and doesn't know if she can handle it. Rosa sees them from the lounge area and comes out and takes her hand, Deanna sees that she's been crying, the tears have stained her face.

"Senora, perdona mi[38], I did not know what to do. The Patron he is beside himself, we thought you might be able to reason with him, so that he may help her at the end. Eduardo says he was not even like this when his Senora passed. He has not shed a tear nor has he eaten since she was brought here. He will not leave her side, it's almost like, if he stays with her, he can save her. He needs you Senora, and she has asked for you. Please you must help us to help him. Tanner will need him at the end and right now he can help no one." Rosa pleads with her.

Deanna does not have the slightest clue what she's talking about. How could Jamie have prevented the illness and what's causing it? What could he do other than be here with her? These people think he has some powers to change and alter the future. Is he starting to believe it himself?

Suddenly, the big double doors that lead into intensive care open and a nurse walks out asking, "Is there a Mrs. Gaynor here." Deanna stands up and the nurse says to her to please come with her.

Upon entering the ward, she sees Jamie kneeling beside Irene's bed, his head bowed as if in prayer. He looks at her, but says nothing as she walks over to stand next to the bed. Irene opens her eyes and tries to smile at her. The exertion seems to bring on a coughing fit, and she has blood coming from the side of her mouth. Jamie reaches up and wipes it for her and strokes her brow, telling her to rest.

He looks at Deanna and his eyes no longer hold the deep blue shade that they always seem to have, instead they are dark and brooding. She sees anger in them, but Jamie's voice is soothing and his touch is gentle, standing there looking down on this very small woman as she is wracked with pain. She sees that his shirt has blood on it again; his wound seems to be bleeding once more.

Irene takes his hand and pushes it away, opening her eyes, she

---

38 Pardon me

whispers haltingly with great difficulty to Deanna, who has to bend to hear what she says. Jamie tells her not to try to speak, but she says she must.

"Ms. Deanna.... Thank you for....coming," Irene strains to speak. "I want to ask you....to....to do....something for me?" Coughing spasms cause Irene to choke on blood spatial. "Please help them look....after.... my....my....baby....they are all she has....Please, Please promise ....me," another coughing fit and more blood.

Deanna leans close so she can hear her, "I promise I will do all in my power to help her always, and love her as you have." Irene takes her hand and squeezes as tight as she can.

She whispers again very faintly now, "You must trust...in him and help...to make it come true.....He's trying....to....to take my pain.... it's... It's too late now....You must trust.... remember trust in him..." She seems to have become unconscious, Jamie calls for the nurse to come and help her. The charge nurse comes over and takes her pulse and tells us we have to go outside as she calls for the emergency team stat.

She takes Jamie by the hand, and he's reluctant to leave her, "Jamie let them try to help her, it's the only way." Deanna drags him outside, and he looks at Tanner and just nods his head. The old man buries his face in his hands and breaks down.

Father Scanlon is asked to go in, as is Tanner by the doctor, he says she has just moments more. Father Scanlon helps Tanner to his feet and guides him toward the doors, watching his hunched shoulders they feel his pain also. These people are bound together by love that Deanna has never seen. They feel this passing more than anyone would have believed. She's been drawn in also, for Deanna gave her word to a dying woman.

John's words are ringing in her ears "Do not become involved, stay objective, stay focused." How can she do that now?

Father Scanlon comes out and tells Jamie that Irene has passed, and that they have things to do. They all look at Jamie and he seems to have aged, no longer does he have that vitality and strength that they've come to expect from him, he now appears draw and weak, Raising to his feet, he thanks Deanna for coming and turns to leave. "Jamie let me come with you, let me help. Please you should not be alone right now." She begs him to listen to her.

"Deanna, you don't understand, now is when I have to be alone. I have things I have to work out by myself. I don't expect you to understand I don't quite understand myself, please try to help the others now and he walks away.

Turning to Tom Scanlon Deanna grabs his hand, "Father, I don't understand how he could leave them all here, and walk away as if he were the only one that matters, or is hurting." She asks Father Tom angrily.

"He is not walking away he is going to prepare for her resting place, she will be buried next to Mary, in this, we cannot intrude. He will do it by himself except for Tanner, who will be there already in case you have not noticed, for he is gone also."

"Father this is beginning to frighten me, it is like something out of, I don't know what. Please tell me what's happened here today." He nods his head and sits down next to her.

"For me to tell you that, I must first explain to you T.J.'s story I believe it's time you knew.

Tanner found Irene out by the quarry, and she was half dead. You see, T.J's. Father had taken his entire family out there, and beat her mother so bad that he thought he had killed her. Her brother apparently tried to stop him, and he shot him, and then tried to kill T.J. as well. Thinking he had, he turned the gun on himself, we found that out later. Irene dragged or walked three miles through some pretty rough country.

Tanner was out looking for a mare that was about to drop a foal, and he came upon Irene lying out in the saw grass. He carried her back in his arms to the ranch. It was nearly two hours before Irene was coherent enough to tell them what happened. She whispered that her babies were still out there, and that she had to find them. Tanner was with her when she spoke, and he told her he would find them and will bring them back.

The Sherriff's Dept. said they would have to wait until morning to mount a search party. It was storming that night when Jamie and Tanner rode out to find them. They looked for hours and hours, soaked to the skin, but neither would give up. Tanner heard a whimper in some scrub by the quarry, and it was T. J. Tanner told Jamie to take her back, and he would continue to look for the other child. He found him at daybreak; he carried the little boy back in his arms knowing that he was dead. You know Tanner never left her side for almost two weeks in the hospital, said he was responsible for her now as Jamie stayed with T. J. around the clock at the ranch.

Irene recovered, but they found that she was dying of cancer, that's what set her husband off, we supposed, the fact that he was going to lose her drove him over the edge. Jamie has done all he could for her since, the best care and the finest doctors just to give her more time.

She knew that she was dying and asked Jamie to care for T. J. at the ranch full time. She didn't want her to see her sick all the time. She sacrificed what precious time she had left, to give her daughter a chance on being normal. Irene didn't want T.J. to be reminded of that terrible night when her entire world crashed. Jamie agreed and I took Irene in at the mission.

He tried everything, treatments, drugs, herbs anything that might bring her relief. He promised her that she would hear her daughter speak again, and she did. He thought he could save her somehow, like he helps others in trouble or pain. This time maybe it just brought back that he couldn't save Mary either, I don't really know.

Now you know T.J.'s story, maybe you will comprehend what drives the man. You keep searching for the truth to his past, when it's the present that really matters. Since I've known him, he has done nothing but good for those around him. Even for those who knew him not, he's given what he had. The Medallion you wear was left him by one who gave up his own life, So that Jamie could learn the meaning of his life."

"Father I have to ask you about his wound, how long has he had it and why hasn't he had it taken care of properly, it's been weeks, and still it continues to bleed."

My dear Deanna, I wish I could, but even I don't know the mystery that surrounds his wound. There are certain things about Jamie that seem to transcend the realities of the present.

Out at the ranch two figures stand under the big fichus tree and begin to dig in the soft earth, each one wrapped in their own thoughts. One is digging with anger while the old one seems to take more thought with each shovel of dirt he removes.

"Tanner I'm sorry I couldn't do more for her, I tried so very hard." Jamie speaks out at last.

"I saw what you were trying to do boy, she knew too, wasn't only her you were trying to save it's still about them others. You can't do nothing about them, they are gone, and you got to stop, or it's gonna kill you for sure, it's those other babies what need you now.

When my time comes, you're gonna plant me here next to them? I ain't ever asked you for nothing before, you know that, but I'm asking you to do this for me… Some folks, they ain't gonna take kindly to a black man lying next to two white women. I don't know where else I would be happy, except next to them that I've loved best…"

"You promise now, right here with them as a witness." Tanner stands and looks at Jamie, waiting for him to answer.

"Tanner, this land, this place, was meant for all of those we have loved. We will all be here together, each and everyone one of us…"

The day of Irene's funeral was bright and warm, the birds were singing and the butterflies were plentiful. The casket was carried in a wagon laden with flowers as they walked to the plot of land known as Fiona's Acre. Arriving at the little cemetery plot, Jamie and the rest of the men lift the casket gently and lay it on planks across the open grave. The old fichus tree offers them shade as Father Scanlon starts his eulogy.

"Heavenly Father we beseech thee in Jesus name to accept our beloved sister Irene. She was a gentle soul who loved her Daughter and her friends with a genuine passion and honesty that we all came to love. Protect her with your love and make her welcome to your table. Give her the peace she so deserved in life, free of pain and suffering. May the Angels of the Lord gently come and carry her to your bosom. In Jesus' name, we ask thee O Lord, Amen."

Deanna watches as each of those present passes and places a single rose on the casket. Rosa holds T. J.'s hand as she places her ribbon on the casket and says "I love you," to her mother one last time.

The simple ceremony completed, Deanna notices that Jamie doesn't place anything on the casket. He stands alone, supporting Tanner, who appears frail for the first time, since she has met him. He bends over and places a small gold locket, upon the coffin. He falters as he tries to rise and Jamie catches him to help him stand erect. After the ceremony, everyone heads back toward the ranch, except for Jamie and Tanner. She turns to watch them lower the casket into the grave and begin to fill it with earth. Deanna knows the two of them won't return until they have seen to Irene's resting place.

Before Deanna leaves to head back to the house with the others she notices a small headstone at the other end of the little plot. She considers going over to see who else is buried there as she thought Mary was the only one. As she turns to go and look a strange feeling comes over her and a sudden chill. She feels strange being there and hurries to catch up with the others. It is almost like she felt a presence there, but not of this world. Maybe it was because Mary was there. Knowing how much Jamie loved her, and it being a private place for what he considers for his family. The chill and eerie feeling doesn't leave her until she leaves the burial ground and heads back toward the ranch.

Rosa has prepared a lunch for all of those who came to the funeral. There were almost a hundred people there, most from the mission and many from around the ranch who were neighbors and whose children have became friends with T. J. and the other girls. It is a somber day, one that many just sit and give solace where they can.

Jamie arrived later and was quiet, distracted and very distant. Deanna feels it's best to leave him by himself, reckoning each person handles grief in their own way. Jamie soon leaves without a word, riding out on Storm heading out west of the ranch. Something seemed to change that day between the two of them something she feels may never be the same again.

Jonah, Katy and Deanna left later that day for home each of them lost in their own thoughts……

Chapter 17

"The Impersonation"

Deanna sits and watches as Jonah cleans and oils his saddle, lovingly caressing it. Of all the things he owns, it's his prize possession, because Jamie gave it to him. Jonah respects him more than anyone he's ever known, and they are becoming closer all the time. Jamie has started working with him on his barrel racing, teaching him the tricks of the trade as far as rodeo competition and training Buck as well. She hopes that Jamie will remember his promise to her about Jonah going on to school next fall.

Katy too, is doing well under his training methods. She will be out of court ordered therapy soon because of him. She has noticed how much he cares for all these young people that surround him in his life, but she can't get rid of this feeling that there is something that he has still hidden from her, a secret that she's yet to discover.

Since Irene's passing, Deanna and Jamie's relationship had been strained. He's the same with Jonah and Katy, but there is now remoteness between her and him now that she feels.

"Mom I wonder how old Jamie was when he won this saddle at Calgary, he couldn't have been more than fourteen or fifteen, he must have been the youngest rider ever in National Rodeo Finals.

"I don't know, what does the plaque say again?"

"It reads, wait while I remove the polish, All Around Cowboy, Calgary Stampede 1974," Jonah replies to her.

"Your right, he couldn't have been that old, I wonder what the age is for that level of competition." Deanna begins to get a bad feeling about this, How could he have won something that he could not have been of age to qualify? Suddenly, she begins to put together all the pieces that have been bothering her.

"Jonah I have to go to the office, please feed and water everyone for me, and I will leave some money for you and Katy to have dinner. I may be late coming back I have some research that I have to look into."

"Sure Mom, is there anything wrong? I mean this is kind of sudden." He looks concerned.

"No I just want to tie up some loose ends before the story goes to press next week." She grabs a coat and her bag, running out the door and jumping into the car and then speeding off. Her heart is racing now; this could be what she's been afraid of all along.

Driving over to the office her heart is in her throat, this thing about Calgary could be a huge hurdle; Jamie has lied to her and deceived her children. She can't believe that he would create a story like that and let her believe that he is something he's not. Her own feelings for him are turning Deanna inside out, just when she was starting to believe that there might be someone out there for her that she could count on for the truth and grow old with.

She can't believe that he could have deceived her about doing something that he didn't. It just makes her wonder what else he may not have been truthful about, not only with her but all the people that think he's something he's not.

Deanna must get to Ellsworth and tell him what she suspects; he may have the means to find the truth. This is the first thing that precedes Jamie's history in Mexico all those years ago. Why didn't she see it before? So far, his past came up a zero no school, military, nothing, why didn't they check out the rodeo angle before now, and she should have checked about the song writing also? Deanna has to know the truth, the only person that could have the power to hide someone's past that much, has to have been Ed Haskell. He had the connections to bury or create an identity. Why would he need a new name or life, what's he hiding?

Deanna pulls into the parking lot of the magazine and rushes inside. "Is Mr. Ellsworth still here?" She demands of the security guard at the main desk.

"Yes Ms. Gaynor, he's in a meeting with production on the third floor. Do you want me to page him, is anything wrong?" He inquires of her.

"No I'll just go up and talk to him, if I happen to miss him, please tell him that I have to talk with him right away. It's very urgent." He nods and immediately buzzes her in.

Deanna waits for the elevator to come down from the upper floors, as she tries hard to compose herself before she meets with Ellsworth. The door opens and takes her to the third floor. Ellsworth is standing waiting for her as she steps out. "Deanna are you all right, Sam just called me and said you seemed distraught. What's wrong, are the kids ok?

"I'm Ok, I just need to talk to you about the story and something that came up today we need to check out!" She says, raising her voice as she steps out. "

"Come into my office and calm down, then you can tell me what's got you so upset, whatever it is we'll figure it out, just calm down and tell me all about it." He opens the door to his office and pushes the button on his intercom for his secretary.

"Yes Mr. Ellsworth," the intercom answers.

"Would you get me, a scotch and water and some white wine please?"

Then turning toward Deanna, he asks, "Now tell me what has you so worked up and why were you crying?"

"Mr. Ellsworth I believe that Jamie has been lying about certain facts in his past, what little there is of a past. He gave Jonah a saddle that he claimed to have won at the Calgary Stampede in Canada."

"Well what's wrong with that, I would think that is a very magnanimous thing to do." He says with a puzzled look on his face.

"No, you don't understand, he would've had to have been around fifteen years old. You can't be on the National Rodeo circuit at that age you had to be at least twenty one. Why would he lie about that? We need to find out who won that saddle and why he wants us to believe he did. Who do you know that might know who did personally? I guess I could have Googled it, but I panicked and came right over here, it just really shattered me. Have you gotten back that background check from Washington yet?"

Ellsworth appears to be thinking for a moment; suddenly he goes through his rolodex looking for something.

"There is one person who might be able to button that down, and he lives locally. His name is Jake Clayton; he lives out by the lake. He's the PRA past president and in his younger days he was a top contender on the national circuit, and he also sits on the board of the National Rodeo Museum. I have his number here somewhere." Thumbing through his rolodex, he says. "Got it, I'll write it down for you, if anyone will know the answers to your questions, he will. Let me ask this, do you want to have the answer or would you be better off letting this go? Your story is really done, we can run it with what you've got, and it's good. Are you sure it's about the truth, or that he might have deceived you personally? John asks her."

Ellsworth sits back waiting and watching for a reaction to this question from her, not sure himself which it will be.

"I won't kid you that I am not interested in him as a man, but I have already married one phony, I don't need another one. I have to think of my children as well and those other girls too. We need to have that background check, if someone buried his past there has to be a trail somewhere and a reason why. I need you to find that for me Mr. Ellsworth."

"Alright Deanna, I'll have the report by tomorrow, unless he's under a presidential seal. I'll find out all there is about him, I promise you that." He swears to me.

"I'll try to call this Clayton guy tonight and drive out there sometime tomorrow if he can see me. I will touch base with you after I speak with him. We may have to do a rewrite on the story if Jamie comes up a fraud... Mr. Ellsworth, thank you for being a great boss--- and a friend." Deanna says to him as he hands her a tissue.

"Melody and I hope that you find nothing that will change your story, but if what you think is true I hope you will be strong enough to handle it." He gets up and walks her to the door and pats her on the shoulder as she leaves his office.

Driving home Deanna feels terrible about this new development, she really believed he wouldn't lie to her. Why would he make up something like that? He didn't have to impress her or Jonah; it seems out of character for him, Jamie's so talented in so many ways. It just doesn't make sense, but if he's lied, she can't forgive that. What she needed from him most of all at this stage of her life was honesty, that was the most important factor of all.

Pulling into the driveway she notices the truck gone, Jonah must have taken Katy to dinner. She can't help but think what this will do to her, if Jamie is less than what she thinks he is.

Angel greets her at the door and she proceeds to her study to dial Jake Clayton.

"Hello Clayton here," Deanna hears a strong but deep voice with a western drawl to it.

"Hello Mr. Clayton, My name is Deanna Gaynor, I work for John Ellsworth. He's asked me to give you a call. It's about Rodeo Champions. He said if anyone would know the answers to what we need, it would be you."

"Old John said that, did he, and how is the ancient news hound anyway?"

"He's good would it be possible if I came out to see you sometime tomorrow if you have the time?"

"Sure thing Mame, I will be at the Grill tomorrow, just come out to Okeechobee City my place is right on the main drag, center of town. It's called Jake's Place you can't miss it."

"Thank you Mr. Clayton, see you tomorrow afternoon around twelve thirty."

"Looking forward to it Mame," Jake says and hangs up.

chapter 18

"Jake Clayton"

Parking her truck in the parking lot next to a saloon styled structure in the town of Okeechobee, the large sign stating "Jake's Place" tells her she's at the right location. The smell of ribs and country cooking pervades the air and walking in you can tell it is a special place. Proceeding over to the bar she asks for Jake, the bartender tells her to have a seat, and he'll get him for her.

Looking around the room there are hundreds of pictures on the walls of cowboys and cowgirls taken at rodeos in black and white and color. Over in the corner surrounded by a padded fence stands a mechanical bull. Up front is a large stage with instruments on it and a substantial dance floor. There is a sign behind the bar that reads "Lady's Night, Thursday, Drinks For Free" and Line Dancing Saturday Night.

"Howdy Mame, I'm Jake. You must be Miz Gaynor, pleasure to meet you." And he shakes her hand wearing a handsome smile.

He's a substantial man, but not fat, well over six feet tall and looks to be around three hundred pounds, with huge hands.

"Howdy yourself Mr. Clayton, you have a great place here real authentic."

"Just call me Jake everyone does, won't you follow me into my office?

Would you like something to eat or drink? Just let Slim there take your order."

"Some ice water would be great," she answers him.

"I'll get it Slim." Drawing Deanna a bottle of water from the cooler and handing it to her, he gestures for her to follow him to his office.

"Now what favor can I do my old friend John, seeing as he is living with the rich and socially accepted," he asks me with a huge smile.

Deanna asks him if it's alright to turn on her recorder, he nods. She then asks him her first question. "We were wondering if you knew who might have won the Nineteen Seventy Four Calgary Stampede for All around Cowboy."

"Let me see Seventy Four Stampede you said, yeah, I remember him alright, that was J.D. Thompson. He was top cowboy of the year. He won every event that whole year.

"Are you sure that was his name, did you know him personally?" She asks Jake.

"That boy was a story all by himself, knew him about ten years, we come from the same area of the country. I heard tell; he got himself killed down in California about a year after Wade Davis was killed by a bull. Why, is old John gonna do a western story for a change instead of his highfaluting high brow stuff?"

"As a matter of fact, your Mr. Thompson may very well figure into a story we're doing. Can you tell me all you know about him?"

"Sure thing, he came from the Texas Big Bend area originally, moved to Wyoming when he was around ten."

"Do you remember exactly what year that was Jake?"

"That would have been, let's see, about sixty one or sixty two. Clarksville, Wyoming was a sleepy little cattle town then, not much to brag on. He moved into a little place just outside of town, with his parents and baby sister. His Pa was a drinker and beat up on them pretty often, I remember my Ma talking with the parson about it and how it was a shame, what with them young'uns having to watch and all.

J. D. was a big kid even then. One day his Pa come home roaring drunk and started to hit his Ma, well he up and grabs the old man by the collar and throws him off the porch into the street. Standing there with his fists clenched up tight, waiting for him to try to come in again. The old man got up, fire in his eyes, and he came a boring in. Well, he walloped him upside his head, and his Pa went down like he was pole axed. It cracked his head, J.D. he got scared, and took off before the sheriff arrived, he never know'd that his old man was arrested and sent away. His Ma died shortly after that and I don't recollect what happened to his sister. I think there was some kind scandal; back then folks didn't talk about certain things. Any way I don't remember what it was. His sister went to one of those State run foster care places for unwed girls. He never showed for her funeral. It was a some years later that he was making a name for himself on the local rodeo circuit.

"What year was that Jake, do you recall," Deanna asks him?

"It was nineteen seventy two, I remember because my son was born that year, and I needed to make money and that boy beat the hell out of me in every event. I started to look for rodeos that he wouldn't enter, because he just couldn't be beat. I was doing pretty well and in a couple of years I was ranked third in the standings and my agent thought I should go to Calgary and try for the really big purses up there.

J. D. and Wade showed up to, along with an old rodeo clown that I can't recollect his name, but the three of them rode together. Wade always said J. D. thought the old clown was for luck, but the three was friends. Actually Wade was more like an older brother to him than a friend. Well Old J. D. cleaned our clocks up there, he won everything there was. He made a pile of money and a name for himself, it was some kind of party I'll tell you that. He would light up any place he walked into, handsome guy and could sing the birds right out of the trees.

"Was J.D. a singer and songwriter," I interrupt him to ask.

"Sure was, had himself a bunch of big hits, but the way he was living I knew it would wind up a bad end."

"A bad end, what do you mean by that Jake?" Deanna asks him to explain further.

"He was involved with a barrel racer by the name of Trinity Lopez prettiest little thing that ever was and spirited too. She used to get him all worked up and make him jealous by flirting with all the rodeo guys until he was battling with just about everyone. Of course it didn't help that they all thought he was drawing the easiest rides."

"You me like setups?"

"Yeah, that's what they was saying, but some of us knew he wasn't and the promoters weren't doping his animals either. You see he had this way with the bronc's and bulls, he always went over just before he was about to get on and talked to them and he would stroke them, I swore he could almost talk to them. He would then get up on them and they would like calm down and he'd have himself an almost perfect ride.

"Then he was very successful, but you said something about a bad end. What about that?"

"He and Wade were arguing all the time about his drinking and driving and using pills. The night before Wade got killed, they had them a showdown and J.D. told him he wasn't going to carry the old man anymore, and they got into it, right in the bar slugging it out until J. D. knocked Wade out and he and Trinity walked out.

The next day was the main event and Wade was waiting for him to show, but he didn't. They made the last call and when J.D. failed to answer the roll call for the bull he had drawn, Wade moved up in line for that bull that J.D. was supposed to ride.

It was a bad one that no one had ridden yet, and he liked to bust up riders after he threw them. Wade was too old and broken up for that bull and everyone knew it, but he wouldn't back down. His pride was hurt by what was said the night before. J. D. showed up right after Wade was being taken to the hospital, he was still drunk and so was Trinity.

Wade died on the way to the hospital and was buried a couple of days later with only some rodeo people there. The way I heard it was, J.D. didn't say anything to anyone that day. He just stood there and stared at his friend's casket being lowered to the ground. When that was done he put on his hat and walked off. I never saw him again after that.

I heard about a year later that he was involved in a bad accident down in California and some folks got killed including his wife Trinity and himself. She and he got married that night him and Wade fought, by a justice of the peace."

"Jake, would you recognize him if I showed you a picture?"

"Sure would, in fact, there are about a dozen of him hanging on the walls outside"

She takes out some of the pictures that Tim had taken of Jamie at the ranch and horse show. Handing them to Jake he looks at them.

"That's him, a little older maybe than the last time I saw him, but that's him or could be a relative. When were these taken Mame?" "Last month in Wellington, that man goes by name of James Doyle and owns a huge ranch and trains horses for the show ring," Deanna tells him.

"Mame this must be a relative or something, because he would be close to sixty now and that man there, ain't but in his mid forties. Maybe old J.D. had himself a son we never know'd about? Jake says with finality in his voice. Could I see the pictures you said you had, and would you know or remember some songs that this J.D. wrote and sang, just for reference?

"Sure enough Mame, you can take the pictures, they are only copies anyway, and I have some extra records here too you can have." He leads her out to a section of the club that holds hundreds of black and white photos from the sixties and seventies. He pulls down a half dozen and hands them to her. The resemblance is uncanny; staring back at her is a slightly younger looking face that she has come to know, only too well.

Jake walks Deanna to her truck, and they say goodbye. She thanks Jake for all of his help, he extracts a promise to send him a copy of the story and the answer to what is now a weird puzzle.

Driving back to West Palm, she hopes Ellsworth has been able to come up with something on Jamie's past. Deanna has so much to think of, the mystery surrounding them both now is becoming bazaar, something out of a Stephen King book.

It's crazy, how could they both be the same man, what happened

The Last Celtic Angel

to Thompson and why is someone like Haskell protecting Jamie? It just doesn't make sense; they seem to be two different types of people. One rough and ready, hard drinking and the other polished, composed everything he does so choreographed. She has to get to the bottom of it, wondering is this the secret to Rancho de Los Angeles?

Deanna decides to call Ellsworth on his cell phone.

Answering his phone he asks her, "How did you make out?"

"Jake was all you said he would be, he said the winner of the Seventy Four Calgary was J.D. Thompson. He said that this Thompson would be in his late fifties maybe sixty, does that sound like our Mr. Doyle. Did you get anything on his background?

"Not too good, have all the bio stuff on him. Doyle came back with not much more than we had, somebody hid him really well. My source says sealed by congressional seal, that means old man Haskell, you were right. You remember when I said he looked familiar, but I couldn't recall, well you just rattled my brain cells it was this rodeo rider that was sweeping the nation and then dropped out of sight back in the seventies. There has to be a connection maybe a younger brother. When will you get here?"

"Within the hour, do me a favor and call Haskell and set up an appointment for me to see him, I think I have to talk to him before Jamie gets back from Sweetbriar with Dyon. There is something very queer about this whole thing, and if I can just get a chink in the armor, I believe it will fall apart like a house of cards."

"Deanna, are you all right, I mean, well you know what I mean."

"Yes John, I have to see this through to its end, for all our sakes. Oh, check out these song titles for me. My Fears for You, Voices on My Mind and Fire, Jake said Thompson wrote and sang them; they were hits on the country charts in the early seventies. See what your people can come up with on J. D. Thompson, he had some kind of fatal traffic accident in California" He puts me on hold and then comes back and tells her.

"Agnes says you have an appointment with Haskell at his home on Hanover Drive the number is 13756 at eleven A.M. tomorrow. Good luck, I'll have this stuff by courier over to your house right now. You are sure you don't need me for anything?"

"No, I'll be alright, what else could happen to me, find out, I was adopted?" She tries to make light of the way her life has now taken a complete flip, from great to crap.

"You know what I mean, somebody who will be there in case you discover that a hero has feet of clay," concern in his voice.

"I certainly see why Melody loves you so much. You're a dinosaur John Ellsworth, when this is all done, I probably need those big shoulders of yours to cry on and tell me I'm going to be alright. I just wish I had taken your advice and stayed objective," as she holds her emotions in check.

chapteR 19

"The Secret"

An elderly white haired man answers the door and Deanna recognizes him. It's Ed Haskell; he looks much like he did when she was little just older. "Mr. Haskell, I'm Deanna." She addresses him formally and a little nervously.

"Hello, how are you, please come in. I must admit I was taken somewhat back a little when your secretary called asking for this meeting. She said it was very important that you speak with me." He says, as he shows her in. "Come, I was just about to have some coffee. Would you care for some or may I get you something else?

"Coffee would be fine, thank you."

Deanna, you have grown into a beautiful woman, and you still have red hair. So tell me a little about yourself before we jump ahead to what brought you here today." He sits back looking at Deanna and waits for her to answer.

"Well I have stayed into the horses and have a little farm west of here, and I have two children, which I'm sure Jamie has informed you of. Katy is training with him, and I have been widowed and divorced. There really isn't a lot to tell." She keeps it short and hints that she's sure that he has spoken to Jamie already, so knows her history.

"You seem to have either not had much in the way of happy times to relate, or you want to get right to the heart of what brought you here. I assume it's about the article that you're writing and not to go over old times, am I correct?"

He's direct and doesn't miss a whole lot in spite of his age. Deanna can see why he was successful in politics as well as business.

"Mr. Haskell, I need you to fill in some gaps on Jamie's past for me, and I have to ask you what might be some tough and embarrassing questions. Remembering the past relationship you had with my family, you don't know how sorry I am to have to ask what may be very difficult ones for you." Deanna explains to him.

He looks at her and sighs, "My son-in-law has spoken to me, and I'll try to answer your questions with as much honesty as I have. I hope that will satisfy you. He thinks you won't be content, until you know everything, is he correct Deanna?"

Deanna is so twisted inside that she almost breaks down. She needs to know the truth for herself. As far as the Magazine is concerned the story is really finished, but she's unable to walk away and leave it until she knows all the truth.

"Yes, I have to know all of it, for the story and for my self."

"Here comes your coffee, please fix it the way you like it, and I'll tell you what I know of Jamie." They both go to the buffet and fix their cups before going back to their seats.

"I will try not to go over what I think you know already. You have of course spoken to Tom Scanlon so you know all about that part of Jamie's life. The only thing I can fill in for you, would be what my people found out about him prior to his coming here, that Tom wouldn't be privy too.

When Mary called me and told me she had married him. I went crazy both from not hearing from her for many years and that she had involved herself with some bum. I was at my wits end with worry about her for so long, now to hear she had married some cowboy in Mexico, and was living God only knows what kind of life.

I sent two ex-C.I.A. guys that I knew who happened to be in private practice to get her and bring her back. They were two of the toughest men I'd ever known. Excellent in covert extractions and difficult people, I felt confident that they would do the job. When they came back and said that I shouldn't worry about her, and that they could not interfere with him. I couldn't believe my ears, what could he have done to these two to have changed them so much? They said that I was wrong about him, and that he would be contacting me soon? I fired the both of them, but they were changed men, which puzzled me, what could he have said or done to make such men as these cower? A father's sense went off imagining all kinds of things inside me.

My next course of action was to reach out to a friend of mine in the Justice Department and try to find out more about him. They said they would give it to friends at the F.B.I., but it would take some time. The official word was that with them in a foreign country, it would then be out of the question until they crossed the border.

Later that week my phone rang, and it was Jamie, he introduced himself and said he was bringing Mary to see me the following week and hung up.

Week later I received a visit from Jamie at my Office in Washington. He introduced himself to me and said he wanted to make an appointment to bring Mary to see me. I told him what I thought of him and the whole marriage sham and that I intended to have it annulled and have him put in jail if I could. He said he understood how I felt and that if he couldn't prove that he could make Mary happy then he would walk out of her life for good. I didn't know what to make of him, except that I felt something about him that made me want to believe that he was not just after my daughter's money, or mine.

They came to see me the following evening at my home. When I saw her she was so fragile looking, but she was joyful to see me, and dove into my arms crying and laughing at the same time. Jamie just stood there not saying a word, he accompanied us into the house and Mary was talking non-stop about all that had occurred to her since meeting Jamie and how marvelous he is.

She said that she was happier than she had ever been. Looking at her, I believed she was. She enjoyed the work that they were doing, helping others and trying to build this mission and how much good they were doing down in Mexico. She was not the spoiled rich girl anymore, but a sensitive young woman that had found purpose.

It was then that I knew, he would make her happier than I ever could. I suggested that they relocate, that they could continue doing the same work right in Palm Beach County, which they had started in Mexico. I thought with all the homeless and displaced people that we had there it might work.

Jamie knew that I was just trying to keep her close to me. Jamie suggested that they look into it, as the mission in Mexico was about to be closed by the church and the Nuns were already relocated somewhere else. I was not running for reelection and would be returning to Florida and to private enterprise. Mary was ecstatic about the prospect, so excited with it in fact, she just glowed when she glanced at him.

About a week had gone by since our reunion when my friends at the bureau got back to me on Jamie's background. He was quite wealthy from investments his agent had made for him some years before. It was from music he had written and was receiving huge royalties on. I also found out his real name.

Jamie was an ex-convict released two years before from a state prison in Texas. He had served five years and was paroled on good behavior, for five counts of vehicular manslaughter.

Jamie was involved in a car crash. His wife, a rodeo barrel racer and four migrant children died in that crash. He was drunk and hit a school bus loaded with kids on the way to a Sunday festival. Jamie himself was pinned in the wreck for almost an hour before they could get him out and was in a coma for four months. When he came out of it, he turned himself in and stood trial. The prosecutor wanted the maximum term, and he didn't try to fight it. He served every day of his sentence until early release on good behavior. When he came out, he just walked away and wasn't heard from again.

James Doyle was born that day; you see J. D. stood for James Doyle. Doyle was his mother's maiden name. They said Jamie was a changed person from the time he woke up in that hospital, not at all like the person had he been previously. He had gotten out of control and was drinking heavenly because of his friend and felt responsible for his death the night of the crash.

I was the one that had my people bury his past so as not to make it hard for them to get started, and for my Mary's sake. I didn't know whether she knew all I did, but it didn't matter she loved him with all her heart. I let them struggle for about a year before I told Jamie of his fortune. You know what he said to me, he said that was great news. They would be able to buy some land and give Father Tom a real mission of his own.

Jamie never knew that I had buried all the bad stuff and J. D. Thompson. From that time on I helped manage his money and make the necessary land transactions. He has never been one that showed off, just used it to make others more comfortable and to make Mary happy. He was wild once, but he's who he is now, not what he was once. Something happened to him that morning of the crash, something that has stayed with him every day since.

Tom Scanlon thinks that he was touched by God. Maybe he's right, J.D. Thompson died that day, not just in the spirit, he died in the operating room. They couldn't bring him back, the doctors were disconnecting everything from him, when suddenly he gasped and his heart started once more. The doctors couldn't explain it; they had never seen anything like that before.

I have said to you things that even he doesn't know, and for other reasons that I can't tell you, someone else will have to do that."

Deanna sits in overload trying to absorb what Ed has related to her, it must be true, because she could have it checked out in Texas now.

One nagging thing still has her puzzled, "Mr. Haskell, I'm not saying that you are not telling me the truth, but how can you explain that he's not aged in all these years. That he should be fifty nine not forty something, are you sure you investigated the same man?"

"Yes Deanna, I thought much as you, being a cautious man, I had his fingerprints checked. He is who he is; he just doesn't age in the same terms as we know somehow. He has not changed that much since I first met him. Time seems to be standing still for him somehow, as if waiting for him to fulfill his destiny before his life clock begins again." He smiles and gets up and puts his hand on her shoulder in an effort to comfort her.

"Deanna, there is someone that I think you need to talk to, please wait here while I go get her." Ed tells her, as he turns and walks to a door off the solarium, opening it, he calls softly, "I think she's ready for you now."

Deanna is looking toward the door as he opens it to allow whoever is on the other side to enter. Deanna can't help wondering who it might be, suddenly a woman walks into the room and Deanna gasps.

"Mother, what are you doing here? She jumps up from her chair in a total state of surprise. "I thought you were not coming for the holidays, why didn't you call me?"

Her mother comes over and gives her a kiss and a hug, that's different from any she's ever given her before.

"Deanna, I called Ed after I spoke with you last week. We both agreed I should come down as soon as possible due to recent events. Please don't start asking me a thousand questions I will explain everything to you. It was just well____ Ed wanted to talk to you first about your friend Jamie before we talk." She sits down and looks more uncomfortable than Deanna has ever seen her.

"Jennifer, I'll leave so you and Deanna may speak more candidly if that's alright with you. Before I leave may I get you both something a little stronger than tea or coffee?" He offers as he rings for the houseman.

"Yes Ed, I would like double vodka on the rocks and Ed please stay. What would you like, besides answers Deanna?"

"A Bloody Mary would taste good about now, please." Deanna is still a little shaken by the turn of events. Why would her Mother sneak down to confer with Ed and have something to say to her. It must be something bad that requires her to have a drink like double vodka.

"Honey, you know that Ed's wife Moina was my best friend, since we were kids. I won't boor you with all the details of how Ed and her met and married, but they were happy, and she loved him with all her heart. They wanted to have children so bad, that was all they could talk about. The years passed and nothing happened so they both went for testing and the doctors found that Ed was incapable of having children, but Moina could.

I had married your father by this time, and we lived not too far from each other. Ed and your Dad turned out to be great friends. Moina came to me one day to ask a huge favor, while we were out by the pond she told me what it was that was on her mind. I was sickened at first until she started to cry, and then I knew what I had to do. I asked your father to be a sperm donor for them, so she could conceive."

Deanna jumps out of her chair and confronts her mother, "What are you telling me, he slept with her to make a baby." Yelling at her not believing what she has just said, her Father would not do that, not for anyone.

"Deanna no, that's not what I'm saying, he donated sperm to a doctor and Miona was inseminated. Everyone thought that the child was Ed's, and we all agreed that was best, Mary was your sister." She has tears in her eyes and is trembling so much that Ed puts his arm around her.

Ed speaks to Deanna trying to calm her down, she feels like her world is coming apart. "Your Father was the best person I knew and was proud of the gift he gave us, so was Moina. Your Mother and Dad were the closest people I knew just like family. He remained Miona's best friend until the day she died. He never quite recovered from feeling it was his fault that the accident happened. The worst was yet to come for all of us; we never suspected any of it. This is something I should tell you, because it was because of me that we all drifted apart so long ago.

Mary was your Dad's prized student, and he was naturally proud of her because he knew she was his. When her mother was killed, she took it very badly and ran out to be with him. Going to your Dad she broke down and told him how much she loved him and always would, at first he didn't comprehend what she meant and tried to comfort her. You see, to her, he was her first love not knowing he was her Father.

When he realized what she was talking about, he handled it very badly, telling her how silly she was, and that she should get that nonsense out of her head. He hurt her so badly that she ran away that night, and we couldn't find her at all.

When he told me what happened, I was enraged with him and told him that I never wished anything to do with him again. I had just lost the two most precious individuals in my life.

Your Mom said he was never quite the same again after that. Mary had just disappeared, we didn't know where, back than young people could drop out and no one could find them, not even me.

You're very much like Mary, now more than ever. Even when you two were young, and she was so much older than you, people remarked how much you looked alike. Jennifer and Moina had the same coloring and green eyes, and your Dad and me, both of us being Irish, so no one ever made the connection to your Dad."

Deanna sits there dumbfounded not quite grasping what's just been told to her. She had come there expecting to obtain the truth about Jamie, now she has found out it's not just Jamie that has dark secerts. Mary was her sister, and she never knew it. She used to watch out for her all the time when she was little.

Deanna's fallen in love with her sister's husband, and he still loves her, she can tell. He's not ready for anyone yet, because he can't let her go. Not while she's around to remind him of her constantly. Deanna wonders is this reason he took to Jonah and Katy because her blood runs in them, and he could not have children with her?

"Deanna, are you alright?" Her mother asks her. "I'm so sorry, but you have to see there was no reason for you to know. Who would have thought that you would ever come in contact with Mary's husband, or anything that's happened? The fates have not been kind to any of us.

When you told me on the phone I almost died thinking you were getting involved with him, and I called Ed right away. He said he had just come back and did not think that it would have gotten to this stage, or that you would have been so persistent in finding the truth. I forgot how much like your Father you are. Please talk to me I can't stand seeing you so hurt." She pleads with Deanna.

"Mother, you have no idea how much I hurt, now or since Daddy died. You have never known nor have you ever listened. I finally find a man that stirs me as no other has done, I tried to use the caution that you so often preached I should use. Now I find out that I have fallen for my sister's husband, and he's still in love with her ghost. I feel you have deceived me with never telling me something like this. You have no idea how much I hurt, please don't come to the house just go home. I don't want to talk to you anymore not for a while at least." Deanna sees the hurt in her eyes, but she's hurting more.

Turning to Ed Haskell Deanna apologizes to him. "Mr. Haskell I'm sorry for you, it must have been very painful for you to have to relive all this again. I won't bother you anymore, the story will end the way it is. His secret does not have to be told, let someone else discover his past. I'm all done with it and him."

"Deanna, you may be all wrong about him. He loved Mary more than anyone I ever saw, but that does not mean he can't care for you or love you, just as much. Give him a chance to prove it to you. He won't break his principles about Katy and you, but when Katy doesn't need him anymore, and then there is that chance for the both of you. It's not what he's said to me about you that make me feel this, but the way he looks when he tells me about you.

The medallion you're wearing belonged to his family. It is directly descended from the Celtic kings Dagda and Nuada. He must set great store by you to have given you that, it's the only thing that ties him to his past and he never gave it to Mary, in fact the only time I saw him without it was when Mary died.

Please for all your sakes give him the time he needs to finish what he's started, then judge whether he can bury his dead and move on." Ed begs her to reconsider.

"Mr. Haskell, he can never bury his dead he carries them with him day to day, as he carries Mary with him. I believe that he has too many ghosts to let himself love once again. I see what his mission is now; he needs to forgive himself and to receive atonement and absolution, something I don't think he ever will. Your right Mother I shouldn't give up any offers or miss any opportunities. Thank you Mr. Haskell, but I think I have to leave now and call my editor and tell him the story is done." Deanna gets up to leave and her mother breaks down and begins to cry covering her face with her hands. "I will see myself out sir." Deanna tells Haskell and walks to the front door.

Ed Haskell watches her leave knowing he should try to stop her somehow, but he believes that he must try to comfort his old friend more. How will he tell Jamie that it all went so sour? The truth was not what she needed; the lie was of greater comfort. Deanna is more like Mary then she knows, storming out like this reminds him of her so many years before.

It is like history repeating itself, and she's hurting just as bad, except, there is no Jamie to save her and bring her back, not if she believes that Mary is still so much alive to him, and he's not sure if she's wrong. He loves him as the son he never had, but much of him is a mystery, and he's just not sure.

"I should have told her when Robert died; she had a right to know what caused him to go downhill as fast as he did. His heart was broken and I think Deanna always thought she was the cause of it. God please forgive me, Oh my God, oh my God." Jennifer cries and her body is wracked with sobs, as Ed tries to comfort her.

chapter 20

"The Story Goes to Press"

As Deanna heads back to the office, her mind still spins from the revelations of the morning. How could her Mother have been so callus about her having a sister, even if she couldn't tell her when she was just a kid? How about when her Father died or when she was in college? Didn't she think that she had a right to know? Deanna tries to compose herself before she calls Ellsworth.

"Hello Mr. Ellsworth, Deanna here, kill the background check I have all the information, nothing I learned is relevant to the story____ Yes I'm sure, I'll tell you everything when I get to the office, and I think you'll agree with me____ I'm alright thanks, it was quite an interview I'll tell you that____ He is really a great old man____ Alright for lunch____ I would love to see her again____ I'll go home to change and meet you both there____ Goodbye." Hanging up she knows that that he's the best boss and has become a great friend to her, now he wants her to go to lunch with him and his wife Melody and finish up the story.

Deanna pulls into her driveway as Jonah comes out of the barn, "Hey didn't think I was gonna see you before I left to go to work. We are moving all the new cattle unto the new property, and Jefe wanted me to ride the fence line and make sure all the wire is still up." He walks up to give her a kiss and see's her face. "Mother what is it, you've been crying. You didn't have another run in with Steve did you?" He gets that same worried look that his Father used to get.

"No, it was one of those women's moments, just starts, and sometimes it feels good to let it out. I'm alright now; I'm meeting with Mr. Ellsworth to wrap up the story this afternoon. Will you take Katy to the ranch for her lessons and bring her home?" She asks him trying to be nonchalant as possible, because he knows her so well already.

"Sure no problem, but I thought you wanted to watch how she's doing. You're not going to be long are you, you know she always hangs out with the others after practice, you could pick her up later after you finish with your boss?"

"I'm not sure that I want to be around the ranch so much anymore, Mr. Ellsworth said he was going to have another assignment for me." Deanna lies to him hoping he doesn't pick up on it.

"Mom, is there something going on between you and Jamie that I'm not aware of, I mean did you two have a fight or something? You two seem different somehow; you know you can always talk to me."

"No we didn't have a fight; it's just that I would rather be friends than trying to be a couple. He has a lot on his plate with the new property and trying to get the Crisis Program going. We have decided to put anything else on hold. He thinks that it would be inappropriate for he and I to be anything more than friends while he's Katy's trainer. We should keep it just like that until after we deal with Steve. If he thought there was any hanky panky going on it would make his argument stronger that I was not a fit parent for Katy." She tries to explain to him, so he will accept that she will be going out there less. How could Deanna explain what she learned this morning to him knowing how he feels about Jamie? She's really not quite sure how she's going to handle this whole thing from here on out herself.

"I understand, but the two of you seemed to be really getting on so well, I mean a kind of natural thing, as though the two of you had known each other forever. Sorry just my opinion, not trying to tell you what to do. By the way, have you spoken to Grandmother yet?"

"No not really, we had some words over something that came up, and we're having one of our feuds, she may skip Christmas this year again."

"When did you talk to her, today, could that be a reason why you were so upset?"

"Yes I spoke with her today and yes some of my reasons for being so upset were because of her, but it has nothing to do with you or Katy, it's just something between the two of us. I don't want you to interfere, or attempt to play peacemaker, ok. Please promise me Jonah." He looks at her face and nods his head. Deanna thinks he knows she means business this time.

"I have to go and change and get ready for the meeting with Ellsworth, so I will see the both of you later."

"Oh Mother, I will stay at the Ranch this weekend we have a lot of work to do, if Katy is invited, I will call you and let you know what we're doing. Rosa is getting all excited about the Horseman's Christmas Banquet and starting to make ready for the holidays."

Deanna knows he's trying to keep her involved with what's happening at the Ranch in the hope that she will change her mind.

Driving to the restaurant that Ellsworth has asked her to meet them at; Deanna can't help thinking about the moments she shared with Jamie. How tender he was and seemed to know what she was feeling. Is he that intuitive or is there really something to this legend business, Haskell said he died that night, and they couldn't revive him, and he lunged back to life as they unplugged the equipment? Was it his will to live, or could it have been something else? She shakes it off and pulls into the parking lot.

Entering the restaurant a hostess greets her and asks, "A table for one."

"No I'm meeting John Ellsworth, would you know if he's arrived yet."

"Yes Madam, if you would accompany me please." She leads the way to a table in the rear, where John and Melody are sitting talking. He gets up as soon as Deanna walks over to the table.

"I see you made it, have a seat we were just waiting for some drinks. What will you have, you look like a good stiff one is called for?"

Deanna says hello to Melody, "I think a Cosmos if that would be alright."

Melody looks at her and says, "How are you doing, and don't dare lie to me, your eyes are still puffy from crying, tell me what happened before you say one word to him." She demands, sounding more like a mother than the boss's wife.

Deanna tries not to cry again as she tells them about the meeting with Haskell, starting with her Mother first. Melody is shocked and reaches over and takes Deanna's hand trying to comfort her.

"You poor thing, that must have hurt to find out something like that, after all these years. You know I'm not trying to defend what they did, but I can see how they would have thought that it would have made very little sense to enlighten you at the time because of your age. After Mary ran away it wouldn't have occurred to them after so many years to inform you. Especially since Haskell moved away right after she disappeared, like they say, out of sight, out of the mind kind of mentality." Melody says to her in a comforting tone of voice.

"Mrs. Ellsworth you might be right, but my father was never the same after that, now that I look back on it. They should have told me, so I would understand what was bothering him. I thought it was because of something I did."

"Yes I can see that, but hindsight is what we all have, but seldom get a chance to use. Now tell us about what you learned about Jamie, and call me Mel, I am not your Boss's wife, just your friend, ok." Deanna nods and gives her a big hug, she's really wonderfully warm and genuine, and not the kind of spoiled person Collins led her to believe.

Deanna tells them all about Jamie's background, and that she feels that it would have no bearing on the story or him, and if they had this much trouble finding it out the average person would not know either.

Mel is saying it is the most terrific ending to a novel, but for a human interest story it would be better to let sleeping dogs lie.

Mr. Ellsworth agrees and says they should run with what they have. "I will have Tim bring over all the prints, and we will put it up on a story board on Monday."

Mel looks at her and asks, "Tell me how you're feeling right now, about him, not the story. You need to talk to somebody, and I am a good listener and so is John."

"I'm angry at my Mother, but I feel like he used me, I was really starting to feel deep emotions for him, and I believed in what he was trying to do." She has to stop for a moment to get control of myself.

"Was it because you felt he deceived you about the ranch, or what he was doing, or is it something else." Mel asks her.

"You didn't have relations with him did you?" John asks as he tries to be fatherly, something that does not quite fit him, but makes Deanna feel better as she laughs at him a little.

"John what kind of question is that to ask a woman, you didn't, did you," Mel looks at her and smiles.

"No I didn't, but it was the tender moments, his touch and the way he looked at me. It's just a combination of so many things that have happened to me over the last four weeks. His kiss was like none I had ever been given, a fire that burned, a gentleness that I could depend on. He spoke with his eyes, the way they looked right into you, and the way he was with my children, all the things that I could have looked for in a man. Why couldn't he have told me the truth, about Mary and even his age? He let me think that it was about something else, just to get good press for her dream.

He used me Mel; I was falling in love with him, and all the time it was about her. How do I compete with a dead woman, I just feel so burnt up, I thought when he stood up to Steve that he really cared about me, but it was just about Katy and her doing good?

They could not have children what if he knows about Mary being my sister, and he only wants to be near mine because they share the same blood? I never want to see him again."

"Come with me honey, you need to be somewhere more private, you have not gotten this out of you yet. John you meet us later, I'm taking her home with me." Melody gets up leaving John sitting there with a blank expression on his face. "Don't look like that, you never had a daughter so you don't know how it feels to be dumped or deceived, and you're not a woman." Melody and Deanna leave the restaurant and head for Deanna's car.

Mel asks to drive because she says she is terrible at giving directions Deanna agrees to give her the keys. The house is in a lovely section of the Village, a spacious brick colonial backed up by a lake with a circular driveway. Pulling in they park in front and go inside.

"Mel your home is spectacular everything is so warm and bright."

"Why don't we go in the kitchen, and I'll make some coffee, unless you want something stronger." Mel asks.

"No that will be fine I'm really not much of a drinker, it's just sometimes it dulls the pain. I mean I don't always reach for a drink if things go badly." She tries to explain to her.

"I know exactly what you mean I do that myself sometimes; I feel that we are going to be close if you don't mind me saying so. John and I never had children, and I was an only child and John had never been married. If I did have a sister, I would like her to be like you. I admire you, starting a new career, all you've been through. I always had everything, except what you have, children, a challenge, but maybe if I can be of help than it will be like I was sharing your experiences if you know what I mean.

I know that you're angry at your Mother, and maybe you have a right to be, I'm not going to try to tell you that you don't. The situation right now is what we're going to do about you and this man." Melody shocks her with that statement.

Melody is not much older than herself, but Deanna likes her and begins to confide things to her that up until now she has only questioned in her own mind. "Mel you don't understand he's in love with my dead sister, not just another woman, the person that I share the same gene pool with. He sees her in me, and he can't let go of her. Do I love him, yes I do, but I can't share him with a ghost? Besides there is too much about him that I still don't understand." Deanna admits to Melody what she's been unable to admit to herself.

"Honey what is there to understand, he is a good looking man that has lots of money, talent that puts him in a league of his own. Not to mention he seems to have found the fountain of youth. How do you know that he doesn't care for you?" Mel tries to reason with her.

They both sit there and drinking coffee contemplating the whole thing. Mel seems to be waiting for her to open up and tell her what she's thinking.

"If he cared for me, he would have confided to me and not used the excuse that we can't be more than friends while he's Katy's trainer, and she's in therapy. If he really cared for me, he would have let himself go and at least tried something more than some kisses and holding my hand. Don't you think?" She starts to cry and Melody starts to laugh.

"That sounds to me like you're mad because he was a gentleman, and didn't tear your clothes off. Did you ever think maybe he just doesn't want to admit that there is a huge age difference between you and him and that you wouldn't want him if you found out?" Mel has a knowing smile. "You know my John loved me to death and was afraid I would laugh at him because he was twenty years older than I was. He would send me notes and flowers, but when it came to the hot stuff he was scared to death. I would laugh at him, and he would get crazy and walk out. You know he was a lot like your Jamie, tough when he had to be, no quit in him either, but the gentlest man I ever met. Maybe you are being too hard on him.

What you need to do is start dating, and I know just the men to get the ball rolling, maybe if he sees that you are seeing some eligible men, he will get off his ass and tell you how he feels. Either way you'll have nothing to lose and the Banquet is coming up. We have tickets for it, leave everything to me. Just promise that you will let me help plan the wedding," Melody laughs and so does Deanna.

It sounds like a plan and what's the worst that can happen, Deanna meets some nice men and the best would be the way Mel thinks it might turn out?

"Mel I love the way you think, if he really cares and if he thinks he might lose me, and then jealousy might bring him around. There may be a way to clip an Angel's wings. Thanks so much for being here for me; I have no one that I could have told my true feelings to." Melody tells her to finish her coffee because they have work to do, and she goes and gets her address book.

"I kind of knew you felt more for him than you were letting on back at the restaurant, John might have bought all the anger bullshit, but you didn't fool me a bit. I knew you had fallen in love with him the night I saw you two at the party at his place. Promise you won't get angry if I say something to you."

"I promise, you can say anything to me, I won't get defensive. Deanna says to her.

"Well, when you two were dancing that night at the party, I watched the way he looked at you and there were real feelings in those eyes of his. Both of you were making love on the dance floor, I never saw two people more in touch with each other. I said so to John, you know what he said. "He looks at her the way I look at you." That was the nicest thing he'd said to me in years. I recognized that night that you were in trouble, but I didn't know how to help you."

They hear the door open and John comes into the kitchen. "Why is it, whenever I observe two women in a kitchen, I start getting very apprehensive? Mel what are you two up to and by what means can I help?" John commences to laugh and Mel runs over and throws her arms about the big man.

"You just did sweetheart, more than you know. Deanna now do you comprehend what I mean about men; you never truly know how they are genuinely reacting when they love you." She delivers him a big kiss, and he turns beat red and commences clearing his throat.

"Deanna is going to commence to date some extremely eligible bachelors. First off to observe how serious this Jamie is about her, second to recognize how she really feels about him." Mel says to him as she releases her arms from encircling his neck.

"John what about that attorney friend of yours, what's his name Axel something isn't it? You said you wanted her to go to see a lawyer anyway about her ex-husband."

"His name is Axelrod and he is one of the best. Tell you what Deanna I'll have my secretary call him on Monday and get you an appointment. Is that alright with you?"

"Well of course she'll go talk to him, and in the meantime I'll start seeing who is in town that will make a wonderful date for you. You know the Horseman's Ball is coming up in a couple of weeks and it wouldn't hurt to let the eligible and available men know you're free." Mel states and smile with the look like the cat that ate the canary.

She thanks them both for all their help and promises to meet with the lawyer at the first opportunity. Deanna will let Mel know about their plan after she talks with the old priest. She bids them goodbye and heads for home. As she is about to leave their house her phone rings, it's Jonah.

Katy has been invited to stay at the Ranch and Jonah is working the whole weekend. She tells him it's ok because she wants to talk to Tom Scanlon and needs a few days by herself to think things out.

Mel's plan sounds like a good one, and if he does not care for her, then she will at least have met some nice men. It can't hurt to have some dates in the wings anyway, she thinks as she drives home.

After finishing a light dinner, Deanna cuddles up on the sofa by the fireplace and decides to put on the songs Jake gave her that Jamie wrote and recorded. Fingering his medallion and listening to his voice, she falls asleep with Angel lying next to her.

Chapter 21

"The Mercenaries"

Deanna is unable to get together with Tom Scanlon until later in the week, so Melody's scheme will have to wait just a couple of days. Tom has been doing all the things that Irene was doing for him at the mission, since she passed.

Empowered by these past few days, and John Ellsworth's confidence, it has inspired her to stand up to her ex-husband Steve. The magazine's legal dept. has referred her to an attorney Kenneth Axelrod. He happens to be John's friend, maybe he can do something about Steve and the strangle hold he has on Deanna and her children, something that her lawyers were unable to do. Steve wasted very little time in serving her with papers trying to get custody of Katy in retaliation for the incidents at the show grounds and the house. She has an appointment this afternoon; the power of the press is amazing.

Driving over to the lawyer's office she can't help think about the situation with Jamie. She honestly feels he has intentionally misled her for his own gains and she is still furious with him. Pulling into the attorney's parking lot, she see's her ex-husband Steve coming out of the building so she ducks down on the front seat giving him time to get to his car and exit the lot before she enters the building.

Getting off the elevator she checks the directory for Axelrod' office, locating it Deanna decides to check her makeup and use the women's facility before she goes in to see him. Upon entering she stops by the mirror to check her makeup and can't help but hear what seem to be two men standing just outside the lavatories door engaged in a serious conversation.

"Listen we have to get him to sell out to us, or we'll be finished. That lawyer Gaynor says he knows some people that will ensure that the bastard will sell to us given the right pressure."

"Williams, I don't want to have any backlash from this stuff. I have a great deal at stake locally, and I can't afford to be involved with anything that hints of being illegal. Just handle it and get my results, but under no circumstances do I want it to touch me, do you understand me."

"I understand perfectly these guys are all Black-Op's Mercenaries, that's what he told me, they are used to jobs like this. If they get caught, they know it is their ass not ours, that's why they are so expensive, you buy their silence." The one called Williams says.

"Just make sure he sells out to us and makes no trouble, this guy gives me the willies. There is something about him that does not add up correctly. You're sure he will scare given the right incentives."

"These guys would scare the crap out of anyone, just by saying, "Hello." Imagine them coming out of the dark and telling you "do this or else," you would not have to tell me twice," William's states with a shudder in his voice.

"You're sure we can trust this Gaynor guy to handle everything, I don't like him at all, and he seems like a real piece of crap, all mouth and no backbone."

"He's being paid the right amount to ensure he will do his part, don't worry." Let's go have some lunch and drink to his success shall we." William's states sounding confident.

They board the elevator and head down, Deanna opens the door to the lavatory and makes sure they are gone before she leaves. She believes they must be referring to Jamie and the Rancho and are proceeding to hire a number of people to make things a little unpleasant for him. She dials Jamie's cell phone, but he is not picking up, so she leaves him a voice mail to phone her right away.

Walking down the hall her mind is full of what she's just learned; Deanna must call Ellsworth right after she meets with the lawyer. Finding his office she walks in and gives her name to the receptionist, and who tells her to have a seat, that Mr. Axelrod will see her presently. Deanna tries Jamie one more time, but still no answer. Her stomach and mind are racing, what if they are planning something diabolical or worst physical intimidation she's thinking. Jamie will not be intimidated, nor will Eduardo, they are two of a kind. Steven is up to something sneaky and the two he is working for sound, as if they could be gangsters.

"Ms. Gaynor, Mr. Axelrod will see you now," states his secretary.

Deanna picks up her folder as the secretary shows her into a conference room to see Axelrod.

"Ms. Gaynor, I'm Ken Axelrod it's a pleasure to meet you," as he extends his hand to her.

John said this morning that you might have trouble that I may be able to help you with. Why don't you tell me about it, and we'll see what, if anything I can do?"

He reminds her of Jamie. He's tall, good looking and sure of himself, she shakes his hand and sits down.

"Mr. Axelrod, I hope you will be able to, you see the problem is my ex husband's an attorney, and he thrashed me up pretty good in court. I'm not sure that what he accomplished was altogether kosher, if you know what I mean."

"I'm familiar with the term, why don't you just tell me from the beginning and let me decide what was and what was not kosher, Ok?" He sits back to listen to her story.

Deanna tells him all about the divorce, just staying with the facts. Then the situation with Katy, along with the court ordered doctor and therapy.

"Have you had her evaluated by your own doctors?" He asks her while he's taking notes.

"No, I didn't think I would be able to after the court ordered me to take her to his doctor."

"I think you may have misunderstood the court. The fact is, as the custodial parent you were probably ordered to take her to a qualified psychologist and therapist. You're the one that decides who she sees. I can petition the court so that you will be able to do that. How was she doing under this doctor, any improvements?"

"No, not really, I was assigned to do this article on a re-hab in Loxahatchee, it's about Children in Crisis, and she went with me and loves it there. The owner invited her to take a couple of lessons and Katy showed a complete turnaround. His method of therapy is not conventional, but produces positive results, so I have not taken her back to either the therapist or the training barn she was with previously, in weeks. She's improved more with him than she did in a year with this other doctor and trainer that my ex was forcing me to use as a therapy treatment."

"Well, we'll fix that right away; you send her where you think she'll get the most help and let me worry about the attorney part of it. I'm very good, you'll see, it will work out for the best.

John told me you are one of his bright and upcoming stars, and that I should keep my eye on you, also that you are very single. Don't get me wrong I won't mix business with anything else, but after I fix the problem, I would be very interested in taking you out to dinner, if that would be alright with you?"

"Well let's take care of the legal things first, and then we can see. Now can we discuss your fee, I would have to make payment arrangements if that would be alright?"

"John and I go back a long time, don't worry about the fee I will make it affordable for you, the important thing right now is to see that we get things under your control and not Steve Gaynor's.

I failed to mention before, but I'm familiar with Steve Gaynor, and I don't care for either him, or the people he represents. This may wind up being a community service pinning his ears back. I will call you or my secretary will notify you of any court appearance that may be required. I do have a number to reach you at, don't I?" He asks her.

"Yes I gave her my home and cell number. Thank you so much you don't know how much better I feel just talking to you, not to mention for my moral." Deanna gets up and shakes his hand.

"I'll call you in about a week, lots of luck with your story."

She walks out feeling so relieved, it finally seems she has a lawyer who is on her side and not overwhelmed by Steve. Saying goodbye to the secretary, she heads out into the hall just as the two men from earlier come out of the elevator still engaged in conversation. Putting her head down looking in her brief case for something as they pass, she heads for the elevator just as the door is about to close and jumps in.

Getting to her car the first thing she does is to call Jamie again with the same results as before. Hanging up she dials John, "Hello, Ellsworth here," Deanna breathes a sigh of relief, and then shouts into the phone as she enters her vehicle.

"Mr. Ellsworth this is Deanna, I need to talk to you right away it's about Jamie and the ranch, may I swing by and see you?" Sounding urgent she waits for his answer.

"Doyle you say, and then by all means, can you make it over here right away. Did you keep the appointment with Ken?"

"I just left his office, thanks, he's great. I'm on my way I should be there in fifteen minutes." She tells Ellsworth.

Rummaging in her purse to find her keys, Deanna has the feeling of being watched and looks around, but does not see anyone suspicious or at least none that she can see.

Driving from Ken's office to the magazine she tries remembering everything they said so she can relate it to John.

Entering the Magazine's downstairs lobby she spies Collins exiting the coffee shop.

The Last Celtic Angel

"Hey you, what's going on, I haven't heard from you in six days, you're still working on the story aren't you?" He asks her rather perturbed.

"Yes I am I'm on my way to Ellsworth's office if you care to sit in, he's had me checking in with him, I thought you knew."

"Hold on there and wait for me, I'm still the editor around here in case people have not noticed. I would appreciate if you touched base with me, so I don't look like a complete ass hole." He says to her very pissed off.

"Sorry, I have been so busy with this thing; I thought you had spoken to Mr. Ellsworth. I will keep you informed from this point on, we have to hurry. I called him and told him I would be there in fifteen minutes and that was twenty minutes ago." Deanna turns to go up to his office.

"Wait for me." Collins exclaims and takes two steps to catch up.

John's personal secretary looks up as they walk in, Deanna says, "Mr. Ellsworth is expecting me, the name's Gaynor."

"Yes Ms. Gaynor, he said for you to go in as soon as you came in, I guess you too Mr. Collins," she says with a smirk on her face.

As they enter his office, Ellsworth crosses the office and comes over and asks. "Deanna, I'm glad to see that you're alright, you sounded as though you might have been in some kind of trouble. What happened that caused you to call me in such a dither." He turns to Collins, "Sit down Collins for God's sake so she can tell me what happened. Ok, what happened to get you so worked up?" Ellsworth questions her.

"I went over to Ken Axelrod's office as you suggested, and as I was on my way to his office. I saw my ex-husband come out of one of the offices. Not wanting to encounter him, I waited until he left the lot I went in and stopped into the ladies' restroom. When I was about to exit the lavatory I heard two men talking very loud just outside the door so I waited to hear what they were saying as they mentioned my Ex. They were speaking about Steve setting up, I think he said Merc's, or something similar to that and getting someone to sell out to them or else. It sounded as though they were talking about Jamie and the ranch. One of them was called Williams the other was not called by name; he was short and looked to be Hispanic. I saw them when I was leaving Ken's before I called you and I recognized the one called Williams's voice. It sounded as though they mean for someone to have an accident or something."

Ellsworth thinks pensively then says, "It sounds as though it was Williams and Cerbon, and they will play dirty if it comes to that. They are as crooked as it comes, from what I've heard of them. They have offices on the same floor as Ken. Give me a minute to think here." He paces up and down in front of his desk.

Finally turning to Deanna, he says, "We should warn Jamie and his man Eduardo if that's what you think they meant. If anything was to happen, and we did nothing it would be the same, as if we did it ourselves. I will call some people that I know that can access which Mercenaries are available and in the country right now. Let's see if we can nip this thing in the bud before anyone gets hurt."

"I have been trying Jamie's cell for almost an hour, but he doesn't answer. I'm driving out to see him right now; I was so scared on my way over here." Her hands are still trembling she realizes.

"I'll call some friends in the sheriff's dept and let them know what we suspect." Ellsworth is a take charge kind of guy and must have been a force to reckon with in his younger days, she thinks to herself.

"You were sure that they didn't think you overheard them." He asks her

"No, I pretended that I dropped my folder while looking at the directory, and was busy trying to put all my papers back in. I kept my head and face turned toward the wall the whole time they were talking, walking from the elevator." Deanna suddenly feels scared again.

"Yes sir, this is turning into something none of us bargained for." Collins says, as he goes and picks up the phone to call security.

"Deanna I want you to check in with me as soon as you get out there, I want to know that you're alright. You understand me no more heroics on your part."

"Mr. Ellsworth I'll be fine, I think if they pull anything it's going to be from an intimidation stand point, not one that will bring down a lot of heat. Cerbon, the small one did not want for it to get messy and involve him. He was pretty adamant on that point, and he doesn't trust Steve. I'm going out there now and try to talk to Jamie; he's starting to bring in the extra cattle today for the new range. I'll keep my cell phone handy the whole time I'm out at the ranch Oh, these security guys, they' not in uniform or anything like those are they?" She points to the guards by elevator.

"No they will be dressed in ranch clothes, see to it will you Frank." He directs Collins. "Just to be on the safe side you go home and change into something else too." He points his finger at her like a stern father.

"Yes sir, Dad," She smiles at him, and he blushes, his bark is really worse than his bite.

Deanna drives to her house accompanied by two security people following close behind her. Concentrating on everything that's transpired today, she can't help but think about what kind of trouble Steve might bring to the ranch. Why hasn't Jamie picked up his phone or called her back yet she wonders as she tries him again?

When they get to the house she tells them she'll be just a minute while she changes into something more durable. She slips into jeans and polo, wondering should she take Angel with her or not? Grabbing her boots she heads for the stairs with Angel following behind me.

Roger and Marty are cautious and place their hands on the handles of their guns at the sight of her standing next to her on the landing. "Easy boys she's friendly, I'll tell her you're alright, just relax. It's Ok Angel, they're friends, let her smell you, and she'll be fine." Angel starts to wag her tail and looks for them to pet her. "Alright, I'm ready, maybe we should go in my truck, just in case they are out in the boonies, its four wheel drive." They quickly agree and they load into the Ford and head for the Ranch.

Pulling up to the gate, Deanna swipes her card and the bar rises, and they head up to the main house, when suddenly Esteban appears around the bend with a rifle in his hands, and he's pointing it right at her. She sticks her head out the window and yell's to him, "Esteban, it's me Deanna, what's happened?

"Senora, who is with you in the truck? Please get out with your hands in the air Senor's and make no moves to make me nervous." Esteban aims his rifle like he knows how to use it and on either side of the truck four more vaqueros appear all similarly armed. Angel is growling as Deanna tries to calm her down.

"Angel, it's alright they're friends. Deanna gets out and walks toward him trying to tell him these men are with her, asking him again what's happened. "Esteban, please tell me what's going on, is everyone alright?"

"There has been some trouble today Senora, two of our vaqueros have been shot and the Patron is out looking for those responsible now. You will come to the Hacienda with me, por favor. Your men must come with me also, for their own protection, it will be alright Senora. The Patron has told me to stand watch here at the rancho."

"Esteban what's happened, you're frightening me to death…. Jonah where is he, is he alright? --- The girls are they ok? Please tell me." She waits for him to speak, with fear in her voice waiting for him to answer.

"Senora, I will not tell you that there is no danger, for you would know I lie. The boy rides with the Patron and Eduardo, he would not stay, they are hunting, and they track two men.

Deanna is terrified at the thought of Jonah being in harms way as they drive to the main house. Pulling up in front, Deanna see's that Rosa is standing at the front door with Rubin, and he is armed as well. "Rosa what's happened here?" Deanna exclaims as she rushes up to her.

"Senora Deanna, There has been a shooting and some of our men have been injured," Rosa tries to explain to her.

"Who was hurt, where are they? Did you call the First Aid?" She asks as Katy and Tia come running from the house tears streaming down their faces.

"Mother they shot Tanner and murdered Dyon's colt, Mother, who would do such a thing? It was terrible, all the blood." She's crying almost hysterically, and holding on to Deanna, as is Tia.

"Come Senora, come into the house while we wait for the men to come, Rubin you and these men stay outside and watch for them and keep your eyes open for the perros[39] that have done this thing." Rosa commands them and Rubin and her body guards nod and takes up positions in front.

"Tanner is in the great room resting, along with one of the vaqueros he has lost much blood, he rode back to warn us and get the Patron. He is weak Senora, and he is old. I have been praying for him, we await the policia[40] and the doctors now."

Deanna looks and sees T.J. kneeling next to him holding his hand, a determined look in her eyes. Angel goes and stands by her; Rosa is holding onto Deanna crying, and shaking all over and is close to losing it.

Deanna places her arm about Rosa trying to comfort her "It will be alright I'm here now, and we'll get through this, Tanner will make it, he's a tough old codger."

Deanna is feeling guilty; her warning would have come too late. She now knows she should have come right away. Tanner and one other are gravely injured all because of greed. There is a knock on the door and Rubin brings in the emergency team and two Sheriff's deputies. They rush to Tanner's side and begin to work on him.

"Mame, could you tell me what happened here," The older of the two deputies asks Deanna ignoring Rosa completely.

"Officer, Rosa can tell you more than I, we just arrived here, but it seems that someone ambushed Tanner and another man and shot them both. The owner of this Ranch is out there tracking them now with his men." He calls it in and orders helicopters in the air and additional men for backup.

---

39 Dogs
40 Police

"Mame, do you know if the owner is armed as the other men I've seen around here." He asks Rosa and she nods.

"Yes, I'm very afraid for them, you must do something, and my son is out there with them. The men who did this are hired killers that have been employed by my ex husband and two other men by the name of Williams and Cerbon to force Mr. Doyle to sell his land to them." It runs out of Deanna before she can stop it from spilling out.

"How do you know this Mame, you just said that you didn't know much." He questions her.

"I overheard them today, it's a long story, but I was on my way here to warn them about this threat, never believing that they would have put their plan in motion this soon. I work for the Horseman's Magazine and Mr. John Ellsworth knows about it also."

"Mame, did they tell you directly that this was what they intended, or did you just overhear something and assumed what you told me."

"I overheard them talking outside of their office this afternoon. Why don't you just go arrest them now? I told you what I heard them say they were going to do?" Deanna is getting frustrated with him as he seems not to believe what she is saying to him.

One of the EMT officers walks up and breaks in," We have to transport the old guy right away the other one is dead, I'll fill you in later Mac, after we get him in the wagon and roll, I think I might need an escort, call it in will you."

"Mame, please have a seat in the other room and let the officers get your friend out to the truck." The EMT officer says to me.

"Wilson, call in the swat team for the shooters and let's see if we can get them before this local posse runs into them." The senior officer tells his subordinate.

"Senor if I may speak por favor. If the Patron or my husband catches them, they will not need your team. The Patron will hang them for sure if he catches them. If I were you, I would just stay out of the way." Rosa stands defiantly in front of him with her hands on her hips looking as though she would like to rip his head off.

"Mame, I hope for their sake, they don't run into those fellas or mess up the crime scene. Otherwise they might just get away with what they did here and your friends may be in a heap of trouble." He tells her, as though he were dismissing her.

"Senor if you are done, then you should leave here as I do not like you." Rosa turns and goes to Rubin and tells him to get the big truck ready to take her and the girls to the hospital to be with Tanner.

"Senora you will come to the hospital, or do you wait for your men?" She flatly states to me.

"I think I should wait here for them to get back, but I want to be with you at the hospital. What should I do Rosa? I'm so confused right now?"

"I must go because Tanner has no one, you must decide who you wait for, the Man or the Boy or both, If you stay, Esteban will stay with you, do what you think is right La Dona.[41]" Turning she leads the girls outside to the waiting SUV.

Deanna tells Katy to go with Rosa, and that she will stay and wait for Jamie and Jonah. Katy wants to stay with her, but she explains that she may be of more help to Rosa and the others. "Please Katy, I need to know that you're safe, and you will all need each other, now more than ever. So just go, I will be with you as soon as Jonah and the others get back."

Esteban comes and stands next to Deanna as they drive away. "Senora, the Patron will get these men, they are on foot, and he will run them down."

"Esteban, how do you know that?" She asks him hoping they get away so that the danger will be handled by someone other than the ones she loves and the other she has come to love.

"Tanner told us, after they shot him, he managed to get on his horse and ride. He passed a truck and cut the tires, so they are on foot, Patron has men that can track a snake over rock. So they will find them, besides the Patron, he knows every bit of the land they try to hide in. He also sends men to protect the fence lines to keep them

---

41 My Lady

heading into the Glades. He and Eduardo know how to hunt the beast; they will find them before the Federales[42]." He is seething with hate now, at those that have done this crazy and insane thing.

More sheriffs' deputies arrive and it looks like a military staging area, with vests, rifles and Humvees. An officious looking officer approaches her and asks her again what she overheard. Deanna explains for the second time what she overheard outside Axelrod's office. He then radios for a pick up order on Steve and the other two for questioning. "You're sure that's what you heard, about them doing something that would force him to sell." He asks her one more time.

Another deputy comes over and taps his shoulder, then whispers in his ear when the deputy is finished speaking with him the officer steps over to a command Humvee, and she sees him speaking on the radio. After a few moments, he returns to her and says, "Mame, the helicopters have just spotted a group of men on horseback a couple of miles west of here heading back toward us, they are shadowing them in. I'm sending out deputies to escort them in, I thought you would want to know." He is very considerate and tries to ease her anxieties.

"Thank you Captain, I appreciate it, I will be in the house preparing something. Would you or your men like something, coffee or cool drinks?"

"No Mame, we'll wait here until the rest of my men gets back, but I thank you, for your kindness." He answers gallantly, with as much southern charm as he can put into it.

"Esteban, I will be in the house, please call me when the Patron arrives. I want to be there when he gets here, so I can kill him myself."

Before Deanna can enter the house The Captain turns to her and says, "These Mex folks are a different breed, I'll tell you that, always polite, you just never know what they are really thinking," as he looks at Estaban who is smiling at her.

"Captain, they are very honest and straight forward, but their best quality is in loyalty to family and friends, something we Anglo's could

---

42 State Police Troops

The Last Celtic Angel

benefit from. Please avail yourselves of our hospitality." She turns and goes into the house her stomach is in knots, but she has learned one thing from Rancho de Los Angeles, be gracious and patient.

Esteban comes in and says they're approaching the west paddock area now, and all are accounted for. Deanna follows him outside to the barns, knowing that they will go there first and take care of the horses.

The sheriff's department has already sealed off the area to have them surrounded when they arrive. Calling for Jamie and his group to halt and place their hands on top of their heads, they move in, and disarm the vaqueros.

"Compenereos por favor, do as they ask, it's alright, just sit tight." Jamie dismounts from Storm and approaches the Captain, "Sir, you look to be in command here; I have the persons who attacked my men. They refused to surrender and shot at us, and we returned fire, killing one and capturing the other. They endangered both me, and my employees while on my property, we defended ourselves to protect our lives according to Fl. Law.

That one there had papers that implicate others in a plan to force me to sell. He claimed that the shootings were accidental, that they were out here to kill some horses and create an atmosphere of fear. Tanner and Miguel came on them in the act of killing the colt. They claim they were fired on first. Now if you don't need me anymore I must see to my wounded and my family, but as my men were not armed at the time I would disbelieve that allegation." Jamie gives him a complete report.

The captain is writing in his tablet for a few moments then tells Jamie, "Sir if you would please come to the station and make a formal statement after you leave the hospital, I would appreciate it. I have to tell you that you ran a huge risk in going after them by yourselves; you could have been injured or worst. I will also have to confiscate your weapons, so that I may run tests to see which gun fired the fatal bullet. Under the new State law, residents are allowed to use deadly force to protect their person and property. You would be advised that until our investigation is complete, you may wish to seek legal advice."

"Thank you Captain I can save you time, it was mine that fired the fatal shot, it has my initials on the stock, examine them by all means. My Segundo Eduardo Sanchez will show you where it happened if you need to look for more evidence." We didn't go out for vengeance sir; I went to protect my neighbors and my men. We knew these men were on foot and armed, we know this land better than you and there was no time to wait for you to get here." Jamie extends his hand and the Captain takes it.

"There will be more to this as you are aware of, please do not leave the county until our investigation is complete. Do most of your men speak English or will I need to get interpreters out here?" He asks Jamie.

"They understand English well enough."

Deanna has been held back by two sheriff's deputies from getting close while they question Jamie. She watches as the body of one of the gunmen is taken to the ambulance, while the second is cuffed and taken to a waiting patrol car. Jonah is standing ashen faced and looking after Buck, when they tell her she can go to him.

"Jonah, I was so worried about you, why did you go with them? How could you do something like that, I was worried out of my mind?"-----

She wraps her arms around him with tears streaming down her face, holding on to him so tight Jonah feels as though he will burst in his mother's embrace.

He stands tall as he gently holds her at arm's length and says, "Mother, I work with these men, and they are my friends. I would not be a man if I stayed here because I was afraid or needed your permission. Jefe needed me, and even though he told me to stay, it was my decision to follow them out after they left. Jefe didn't tell me I had to go. It was my choice, they were my friends too, that they cut down." Jonah proudly explains to his almost hysterical mother.

Deanna sees he left a boy and returned a man, one that she's proud of, as would his Father and Grandfather. She kisses him and holds on to him knowing that he has just made what men call, "A rite of passage".

Jamie walks over to them, and excuses himself, he speaks to her in a low voice, "Deanna, thank you for coming and waiting, Esteban has filled me in. Your son was a man today, and you should be very proud, he never flinched once, I was grateful to have him with me. I know you're angry at me for endangering him, for that I'm sorry, but it was by his own choice, one can't argue with that. I have to go to the hospital now and also make arrangements for Miguel. So if you will please excuse me.

Before he can turn to go, Deanna slaps him across the face as hard as she can; Jamie just looks at her and walks away.

"You're a bastard J. D. Thompson, she yells at him." He stops for a second and then walks on; everyone is looking at her, including the sheriff's men.

Deanna notices that Angel is not with her, looking around for her, she sees her following Jamie to his car just walking beside him.

"Angel, come here! Angel, come back now! She calls to her; the dog looks at Deanna and hesitates. Jamie says something to Angel, and she trots back to Deanna's side. Before she can think more of it Jonah takes her hand.

"Mother, what did you just call him? Why would you slap him like that, it wasn't his fault?" Jonah looks at her with puzzlement on his face.

"I will tell you later, but not now, he deserved to be slapped, he deserves more than that. Right now we need to go to the hospital, and be with your sister and the others. Oh shit, I forgot to call her," she reaches for her phone and dials Katy's number.

"Mother, is Jonah alright?" Katy asks her.

"Yes, he's fine they all are. We're on our way to the hospital now. I'll see you in a bit, how's he doing?" Deanna tells her.

"Please hurry Mother, Tanner's not doing well." Deanna hears her breakdown in tears.

"I will be right there, hold on honey." As she heads to the truck, Jonah's already there, and he's got the truck running with angel in the back.

chapter 22

"In Search of the Grail"

Driving to the hospital Jamie prays he's not too late, Tanner will understand why he had to go after them. He would not have tried to make it back to warn them otherwise, he's the closest thing Jamie ever had to a Father as well as being one of his best friends. Now he's in danger of dying for him too. First there was Wade, then Trinity, Mary and all the others. It seems that everyone he's close to; die tragically, now Tanner may be next.

So many have died because of him, is the reason he was saved and sent back, to cause more death? He's becoming weary, after the many years since his spiritual intervention. Not knowing why, that he's been driven relentlessly for so long. When will he find the peace he feels was promised, or is he destined to keep searching?

"Where am I, it looks like some kind of hospital, and they are operating on somebody?"

"It is a place of healing Kinsman, but it's not somebody they were trying to save, it's you.

You are dead nephew; you died as a result of your own foolishness, as did innocents. I have been sent to send you back once again. Only this time *you shall not be reincarnated, it has been decided that you will go back and finish the quest that began over two millennia ago and should you not, then we shall be lost.*

You're the redeemer, the chosen one, the last of our line. It's been left to you to set us free; you will complete our penitence as well as your own."

"If I'm dead, then who the hell are you and what are you talking about?"

"I'm Dian Cecht[43], your ancestor and son of Dagda[44], and you are the last Celtic Angel. I must send you back, to awaken in your own world; you will know…….you will know…..

With the thoughts of that evening racing through his mind, he almost misses the turn for the hospital. Driving across three lanes of traffic, Jamie eventually makes into the parking lot.

Walking toward the main entrance he sees some of the vaqueros standing guard at the entrance. "Hola Patron, have the perro's that have done this terrible thing been taken yet?" Eli asks respectfully as the vaquero's greet him with genuine concern on their faces

"Yes my friend, they have been taken and no one else was injured. Eduardo has you keeping watch I see, Bueno[45], Compadres[46]." He claps them on the back and proceeds into the admitting station; Eduardo is a cautious man, knowing these men will stand their post.

Jamie approaches the emergency room desk and asks, "Rufus Tanner, he was brought in a few hours ago…. Is he in emergency still, or in the operating room?" The nurse tells him Tanner's in surgery now, and the rest of the family is in the patient's lounge. "Thank you, which way is that"

"Down the hall to the left and then straight ahead, the entrance will be on the left as well Sir." Nodding he sets off to find the others and get an update on Tanner.

Walking into the lounge he sees Rosa and the man called Roberto

---

43 Great Irish healer of the Celtic tribe Tuatha De Danu
44 Irish King known as the "Good God" of the Tuatha De Danu over 2,000 years ago
45 Good
46 Companions

sitting by the window. As Jamie approaches, Roberto stands and greets him "Don Diego my condolences on your misfortune, I came as soon as I got word my friend. I have taken the liberty to have a number of friends go to your Rancho and assist with the security, in case others would attempt to do harm. I hope you are not offended my friend, as there was no way to contact you for your permission."

"Not at all Don Roberto," Jamie returns the title of respect. "The problem will be solved very shortly as Eduardo hunts the men responsible now. He left as soon as we got back to the Ranch, we captured one that killed Miguel, and he convinced the man to talk, before we brought him back and implicated those in the conspiracy. He feels responsible because he is Segundo, I'm sure you understand."

"Si Don Diego, I understand, and they are being watched as we speak to make sure they do not bolt, Cerbon is held at his home, and Williams is soon to be taken and left for the Federales. The pig of an attorney has run, but he will not be able to hide for long, I had promised the Senora Rosa and Senora Deanna to lend my influence to your cause."

Jamie thanks him and asks how he knew of Williams and Cerbon.

"You have many friends among my people Senor, the news did not reach me in time to avert the tragedy at the rancho, but we knew who was behind it and men were sent out. Do not fear they will be taken."

"My thanks, Don Roberto, if you would please excuse me I must speak to Rosa." Turning, Jamie seeks out Rosa to inquire of Tanner.

Finding her, he asks about Tanner. "He's very serious Patron, the bullet lies close to his heart, he was asking for you before they took him inside. T.J. has stood by his side the whole time showing great courage, as have all of them. Patron where is the Senora she did not come with you?"

"No, I'm afraid she's very angry at me right now, and the less people about around me the better, I have endangered too many that I care about. I don't want her to be involved more than she is already Rosa. We're at war now and until it ends, I must keep those I care about from harm's way. That means you and the children, no argument Little Mama.

"Si, Patron," she answers him with her head hung down, "But what of Senorita Dyon, she is to be home this week from the college, no? Where will she go?" She glances up at him with a hopeless look in her eyes.

Before Jamie can answer her, Deanna speaks from behind him.

"You all will come to my home and stay there until this calms down and sanity is restored, everyone except you Mr. Doyle. You have been deceitful enough and are not welcome." She proceeds over to Rosa and places her arms around her. "I won't hear no for an answer, Mi casa is su casa[47]. Remember when you told me that in your home." Deanna places her arms around Rosa and comforts her.

Jamie stands there and watches them as thoughts of the past, cross his mind. She's so much like Mary, only stronger. How can he tell her that all who seems to love him die? She knows now about his past, she screamed out his name back at the Ranch. If only she knew the truth, if she suspected that he's manipulated by spirits of his past ancestors, how fast would she run from him if she knew? It's better to keep the wall that has been thrown up now, and then have her physically or emotional hurt. He should have told her in the beginning, but she wouldn't have believed it. His side is beginning to hurt once more. Jamie excuses himself and walks off going toward the operating room to wait for word on how Tanner is doing.

Father Tom arrives and gives his solace to all there, and seeing Deanna alone by the window, he approaches her noticing how distraught she is.

"Deanna, it's good to see you. It's unfortunate that it's here instead of at the mission as we had planned," Tom speaks softly.

Deanna is trying to wrap her mind around the catastrophic events of the day as Tom sits down next to her. "Father Tom you don't know how much I wish that today never happened, that you and I just had our

---

47 My home is your home

luncheon later this week. I needed to talk to you as his friend, may I do that?"

"Of course my child, come with me to the chapel, there'll be privacy there." He takes her arm, and they walk down the hall. The old priest calls over his shoulder to the others that if he's needed, he will be in the chapel with Deanna.

Arriving at the chapel he opens the door peering inside to see if it's being used. Seeing that it's empty he turns to Deanna, and he asks her, "Now what is this that you are so fretful about? Here let's take a seat by the window, the sun will feel good."

"Alright Father, that would do nicely." They sit by the window next to a non denominational alter.

The sun's bright shafts are reflected from the golden cross, casting luminosity around Tom's white head as he begins.

"Jamie's past is the past, what occurred that day I can only speculate at, as I was not present and neither was any who knows him, except Tanner. He was as you see him now when I first met him, quiet and just trying to be of help.

When he made a sort of confession the first time, he told me a tale that at first I disbelieved and thought he was suffering from some mental disability. You see Jamie did believe that he did, in fact, die in the crash and saw himself laying on the operating table as the physicians worked on him. He claimed as he watched from above the table, gazing downward at his himself laying there. A light appeared next to him and from it a voice spoke.

"You mean he thought he perceived the voice of God," Deanna asks, disbelief and shock in her voice.

The old man tells her. "No, it was not the voice of God he heard, but a voice from his past."

"Did he say how he knew who this spirit was, or how he was related to him?" Deanna asks Tom a little disbelief in her voice,

"Yes he did, he said the voice was that of Dian Cecht, an ancestor and that Jamie was a direct descendent of old Celtic people known as The Children of Danu.

"It didn't matter to me whether I believed him or not, he believed it, so much that he changed his whole life.

He recovered and was released, except for the wound in his side that never quite heals; he has no other side effects from that terrible crash. He's worked very hard to bring life to those that would not have made it. Whether it's true or not, I don't know, but he believes it and feels he must finish the quest given him that day. I guess the best way to explain what I'm saying is, go, seek out the story of the Celtic Angel, and then you may know as much as I, what happened to him.

As to whether he still loves Mary. Yes, I know he will love her for all of his days, in a place in his heart that brought peace to him for a while. Whether he can ever love somebody again as he did her, I imagine not. I believe he'll love as intensely once again, but just in a distinctively different way.

You have to understand Mary was like a child, she needed his strengths and protection as much as his love. Right now he's wary that anyone he lets in his heart will come to hurt, and he can't accept that any longer. If you love him than you must be patient, wait for him to show his true feelings. He still has miles to go before he sees the end of his road." Father Tom explains to her with great patience.

"Tom, this is all pretty farfetched even for an Irishman. Coming back from the dead, speaking to spirits, supernatural things, you can't really believe all this? I can't accept it, I think his ego is so inflated that he believes his lies now." Deanna fires back at the old man.

"Deanna, you have seen him do many things, which you yourself can't explain in the normal sense. Couldn't it have happened, and he's one of the Angels that walk among us, as told by the ancients? Could he not be one, who was chosen, because of his own acts to come back and make restitution? Don't be so quick to judge him, unless you wish to judge yourself, whom has he hurt, what injustices has he done?

"He hurt me, he hurt me very bad Tom, he made me believe in him, then he shunned me, using me to further in own ends. I'm not able to get past that, I love him, dame his soul! I just can't get past the fact that he used me, and made a fool of me."

"If you believe that, I can't change your mind. I will say this, I don't believe either of you are quite done with each other as you would have me believe, but only time will tell. For the present, be at peace and let's concentrate on Tanner's plight right now. Unless there's something else you wished to know. I'll tell you this; I've broken my oath to tell you what I know. Only because I love you both, God be with you child." Getting up to head back to the others he asks. "Are you coming back with me?"

Thanking him, she says, "No, Tom, I just want to sit here for a minute to compose myself."

He nods and goes back to the others. Sitting in that chapel, thinking about what he's said to her, she wonders if some of it could be true. Can a person come back from the other side? Does God give us Angels to help and guide us? Can an Angel truly love in a mortal way? Again more questions, all Jamie creates are questions.

Tom heads back to wait with Rosa and Jamie. When he gets there Rosa tells him that Jamie is with Tanner in the ICU recovery room. Tom reflects back to a time when he and Tanner stood where he's standing now, as Jamie stood vigil with Mary.

"Is there a Father Scanlon here?"

Tom is brought back to the present upon hearing his name and says. "Yes, that's me self, is there any news of him?"

The ICU nurse tells him that Tanner is asking for him, and would he follow her. She shows him to a curtain shrouded area containing a gurney with Tanner lying upon it, and Jamie sitting next to it. Approaching, he notices Tanner's eyes open in recognition and his old friend speaks to him.

"Ah you're here Tom, I need you to do something for me. If I don't make this, I want you to tell this fool that he has to give up the past.____I've done told him that I will take his burden with me____so he doesn't have to tote it no more___he's paid back for all he's done___He just sits here a thinking as how I'm gonna be alright___ I told him that I spect he found that Grail, he was searching for, long ago.___Them Kids are all gonna be just fine, and My Missy, she knew that he was forgiven___she know'd for sometime that he won his forgiveness.___ Now. Now he has to live for them babies___and her. If I don't make it, I want none of your mumbo jumbo over me.___Just plant me with them that I loved,___You hear me." Tanner is asking Tom for something, the first and only time since they've known each other.

"Tanner, I will try my best, but God works through many, and if he accepts your offer than it will be so. I will always stand by his side as you have. He loves you as he would a Father, and it is as a Son that he stands by you now, as I stand as your Brother."

Tanner closes his eyes and seems to rest easier now, the charge nurse moves towards them and asks Tom to leave and Jamie to step outside as she checks his monitors. Toms proceeds back to the waiting room, but Jamie just stands to the side not really moving and by the look on his face, she knows better than to try to send him away. When she finishes, he steps closer to the bed and resumes his vigil over Tanner. She looks over at him and observes him kneel and bow his head, as if in prayer. She moves away to give him more privacy....

Jamie whispers as if speaking to someone or something, *"I've never asked anything of you, not even when you burdened me with this quest. I accepted it as a responsibility, as an act of contrition for the sins of my past and the past of the ancestors. I never asked you to save Mary, or that gentle woman who wanted nothing more than a good life for her child. I ask now for the life of this man, if I was given a power to heal then let it be now, and I will give you the rest of my days willingly.... Allow my strength to flow into him, heal him as you once healed me; don't take this man he's needed here."* He takes hold of Tanner's hand and his tears flow, he can't hold them back any longer.....

The charge nurse glances over and there seems to be a strong light coming from the small cubicle that Tanner is in. It appears to be much brighter than normal, and she walks over to investigate. As she approaches, the area goes back to semi-dark as it was before. Pulling aside the curtain she observes Jamie kneeling as before his forehead pressed against Tanner's hand.

"Sir, excuse me sir, are you alright?"

"What, I'm sorry, what did you say, I must have dozed off." Jamie stammers as if awakening from sleep.

Jamie drops his hand to feel for the familiar scar that has plagued him for so many years. His fingers tracing over the place that he's felt for years, but his fingers encounter only smooth flesh.

The ICU nurse quickly attends to Tanner as his color and breathing seem to have improved.

"How's my friend doing nurse, he seems to be resting much easier now?"

"Yes he does and his vital signs are almost normal I must get the doctor, please excuse me." And she rushes off and uses the phone on her desk.

"Doctor Thomas, your gunshot patient, he is showing all normal signs….Yes sir, his heart and pressure are normal…..Yes Sir, I checked it twice….I don't know, ten minutes ago I had to ask the priest to come in. He was in that bad of shape….No sir I have not been drinking,… Come down here and see for yourself!" She answers the doctor, annoyed that he would make such a remark to her. Hanging the phone up, she comes back over to Tanner, taking his pressure the old fashioned way with cup and gauge.

"How is he, does this mean he's going to make it?" Jamie asks.

"He's stable, for the moment, but I would say, yes, he's turned the corner and is stable now and his vital signs are strong, in fact, much stronger than they should be considering the severity of his wounds. I have asked the resident Dr. Thomas to come down and verify, but I think your friend is going to make it, if no other complications set in. It would appear your prayer was answered sir."

Jamie puts his head down for a moment and murmurs "Thank you Kinsman." then turns and takes the nurse's hand shaking it saying, "Thank you, Thank you." He leaves to tell those waiting that Tanner seems to have made a recovery.

With everyone sitting waiting for news of Tanner's condition, Jamie opens the doors to the I.C.U. recovery room and announces to them. "They think he'll make it, the nurse said his signs are good, he's not out of the woods yet, but at least he is on third base and heading for home." Rosa hurls herself into his arms breaking down, everyone else is jubilant as well. He looks at Deanna and she nods her head at him and then gets up and walks away. He now knows that there's no future there, her eyes were cold. The girls are swarming all over him, to the point that the staff comes over and tells them to quiet down.

chapter 23

"The Autograph"

Sitting finishing a letter to her mother, watching the sun rise, Deanna can't believe everything that's transpired. Mulling over the events of the last few weeks it all comes vividly back to her mind. She finds herself reflecting on the past six weeks of her life as she drinks a cup of coffee.

The sheriff's men found Cerbon at his home surrounded by Roberto's and Eduardo's men who prevented him from leaving as Roberto had said. He quickly gave them a confession implicating Williams and Steve; he thought he was making a deal for himself.

It's amazing how small people crumble when faced with the light of truth. These people had prestige, power and position; they could have made a difference in people lives for the better had they choose. Instead greed and avarice brought them down. Roberto said they went after the wrong man, and when Deanna asked him what he meant by that. He said, "A man alone is an easy target, but a man who is loved by many is not so easy."

She tells him that he was loved by many, and he said it was not him he was referring to. Deanna makes the connection and knows who he was talking about and her mind sweeps to thoughts of him.

Roberto told Deanna that he was going with Jamie to Argentina to take Miguel's body home for his family. They have become great friends, both men alike in so many ways, yet opposite in appearance and background. Take for instance Roberto, raised in wealth and coming from an old Spanish family, while Jamie is from a sturdy hardworking background. However, they're both equal, both caring and trying to effect change. Brothers in a confidence from the moment they encountered each other. She still finds it rather strange how Jamie binds people to him, how they embrace him and love him so.

Dyon has warmed to her now, and she's a wonderful girl more like a daughter than a friend. She and Jonah are very serious, and he's going to college starting right after summer as is she. They are together almost all the time it's not infatuation, you can tell it's real for them. They're in love even for one's so young; they are made for each other. Which presents a problem for her, how does she handle being around them and Jamie and not showing what she feels for him?

Yesterday when they arrived at the Ranch all the vaqueros were lined up in front as Eduardo greeted his family, he was dignified and very much the impatient father, fussing over the girls and holding Pita in his arms. He greeted Rosa with a huge hug and swept her off the ground as they all gathered around and welcomed them home. Dyon and Jonah walked off together, and she knows that somehow it won't be the same here as it was, only a few short weeks past. The twentieth century has invaded their little world and touched it in a way that will never be as it was just a short time ago. Eduardo thanked her for looking after his family and inquired when she will come again as a guest of the Patron.

Sensing that he's trying to put things back together as they were before. Deanna tells him she's was very busy at the magazine now that the story was done, but will try to find time to visit. Reminding him that he is to bring Rosa over to her house, whenever she wants to come, they will always be welcome. Eduardo takes her aside and tells her that she's not to feel guilty for what happened. It was God's will and she couldn't have prevented anything that happened that day. The warning would have come too late to have prevented it. Deanna thanks him, although still feeling it all might have been prevented if she had not kept the meeting with Ken.

Deanna walks out to the garden by the lake remembering the moments she shared with him there. Looking across the water her thoughts went back to the day before yesterday. Rosa and Deanna had talked about Jamie at length and Rosa said to give him time.

Deanna asked her if she thought he would ever love anyone else again as strong as he loved Mary, she had to admit that she didn't know. She said he's a man of passion, loyalty, and resolve, mentioning just some of his strengths. Never having seen him with any other woman, she couldn't really assess how he genuinely feels about her. Deanna tells Rosa what he said about being Katy's coach, and that he now could only be her friend and nothing more. That it sounded as though he were letting her down easy, not interested in Deanna as a woman. Rosa didn't know what to say to her and again said, "Wait and be patient."

Deanna also tells her that she would be starting to date again, and that she couldn't wait for a man who seemed not to care.

It's funny arriving home to an empty house except for Angel. Deanna realizes how much she missed them all, the chatter and confusion. Growing up and only child without having a lot of people around was what she missed out on the most. She feels that she was meant to be part of a large family.

She settles down to finish a letter to her Mother, bringing her up to date with what's transpired and to say how sorry she was for the way they parted when she came down. It was not right, the way she treated her that day, considering the fact that she left Virginia by herself for the first time since her father's death. It must have been very hard for her to do, that and to tell her something Deanna now realized was so painful.

The phone rings, and she answers, hearing Mel's voice. "Hi Mel, how's it with you?

"I'm good, how about you? What are you doing today?"

"Nothing, just a little lonely, everyone went back to the Ranch and the kids are staying there for a few days until Jamie gets back from Argentina."

"You poor thing, why don't you come over here for a while, we're having a pool party. I have invited some very attractive men over, just for you. You aren't going to disappoint me are you?"

"No, that may be just what I need to get me out of this funk, what time would you like me there?"

"Come over around one'ish we can talk for awhile before the other guests arrive."

"Is Ken Axelrod going to be there?"

"You like him don't you; I hear you have been out to dinner with him a few times." Mel inquires in an impish way.

"Yes I do, he's very nice. I'll see you later; I will need some time to get ready. Oh Mel, by the way, thanks." She's glad to have Mel as a friend. Mel giggles and says, "See you later, besides that's what friends are for."

Hanging up Deanna goes to clean up the kitchen before going up stairs to pick out something to wear. Feeling glad that Mel called, she is just what she needs to get her out of her blue mood, she's finding herself closed in and experiencing 'cabin fever' and needs to take her mind off of him.

Walking over to the closet she starts sliding hangers out of the way looking for something nice, something that's going to pop some eyes. Her eyes fall on the dress that Jamie gave her the first day they had dinner there. Taking it out and looking at it, she holds it up in front of herself as she twirls around in front of the mirror. She decides that it would be fitting to wear the dress he thought would look so good on her for someone else. Rummaging about for her old bathing suit, she tries it on to see if it still fits, but its old something new would be better. She decides to go to the mall before going over to Mel's and look for a new one that will knock their eyes out. She'll show him that she can find a lot more men that don't want to be just friends with her. Younger men that know what to do with a woman besides hold their hands.

Sitting at her dressing table looking in the mirror, she absent mindedly fingers the medallion that he gave her. She suddenly grabs it and tears the metal from her neck in a fit of anger and rage; she throws it across the room, expressing the first emotion since her outburst at the ranch when she slapped his face. Feeling better now she finishes dressing and goes down stairs to leave.

Noticing that Angel's not there, and calling her name, she hears her pad down the stairs toward her. "Angel what have you got there." Deanna notices she has something dangling from her mouth. She reaches for it and takes the object from her, holding it up to the light, she notices that it's Jamie's medallion.

"What are doing with this, I took it off because I don't what to wear it anymore," Deanna places it on the counter. Angel becomes agitated again and she begins to bark at Deanna and jumps up at the counter.

"Alright I'll take it with me if it will make you feel better." She takes it and puts it in her bag; Angel is still carrying on, pulling at the bag. She tells her to stop and lie down; Deanna closes the back door and heads to her car....

"I think we will have exactly what you're looking for. Would you mind if I went and selected some suits, that I believe will be just what you're looking for?" The salesgirl asks.

She then takes Deanna to a private dressing room and takes her measurements. She asks what type of suit she is considering and Deanna tells her one piece. The girl nods to her and she leaves her in the dressing room. She finds herself wondering what types of suits that she will select for her, when suddenly the girl comes back with an armful of suits.

"If you will try these on, I'm sure that you will find some that will look very attractive on you. I'll leave now, just call out if you wish any more assistance."

"Thank you so much, these are beautiful." She closes the door and departs.

Deanna notices that they are all one piece suits and picks up a black one with a turquoise stripe across the front. It's low cut in the back and crisscrossed in the front and comes up high on the hip. She puts it on and is amazed how it makes her look, as if they just made it for her. Cleavage in front and her butt is up at least an inch, she loves it. Taking it off she tries on some of the others and they all fit just as well. What a contrast coming to a place that measures instead of going off the rack. Deanna selects two of them, the black one that she tried on first and one other that she loves. The second is burgundy and green, her freckles won't show as much.

Deanna exits the dressing room with the two suits she's selected and tells the young lady that she wishes to purchase them. Smiling the salesgirl takes them from her and wraps them up.

"Will that be cash or charge Mame."

"Charge, I would like to say thank you for all of your assistance. It's been a marvelous experience; I believe I will shop here for my bathing suits from now on. What's your name if I might ask?"

"My name is Nicole Ms. Gaynor," she notices Deanna's name from her credit card. Oh my God, you're the woman who wrote the story in Horseman's Magazine. I recognize you from your picture at the top of the article?"

"Yes I am, did you enjoy it?"

"Enjoy it, I thought it was the best thing I've read in ages, I used to show for Applegate Farms when I was in Junior High. Everyone in my school is talking about it. They are already asking if there is going to be a follow-up. I have my copy right here would you please autograph it for me?"

"Well Nicole… Yes I will, you will be my first autograph and thanks for asking me."

She hands Deanna her copy, and she grabs a Primark from the desk and signs it feeling fantastic. Imagine someone asking her for her autograph, this day is looking up.

"Thank you again Nicole, you have made my day."

Strolling to the parking lot, Deanna feels so much better than she did when leaving the house, her phone rings, its Mel.

"Hi, I just got out of the mall; I bought two new bathing suits. What's going on, is the party still on," She asks Mel?

"Just checking to make sure that you're coming, John thought you might back out, and I told him I didn't think so. Are the suits gorgeous?"

"Wait until you see them, I bought them from that new swim suit place. They actually take your measurements and then bring you something that fits like it was made for you, I love it. Do you want me to pick up anything on my way over?"

"No, we have everything already, thanks. Just get a move on, so you can bring me up to date on what's been going on with you and Ken." She laughs and hangs up.

Arriving at their house Deanna parks in front and knocks on the door, John opens the door, giving her a big hello and a kiss on the cheek.

As they stroll through the house, he says to her, "I have been getting a number of very interesting calls about you. They want to know if I have you under contract and if not, can they talk to you."

"What did you tell them?"

"I said you were free to talk to anyone you like." He looks at her and winks.

Deanna stops suddenly and says to him, "You mean that don't you?"

"Yes I do, I said you had talent, and I would never stand in the way of any writer, if a good offer comes along." Looking into his face, she sees that he's sincere.

"Thank you John, you don't know how much what you just said means to me, but I think I will stay with you. I still have too much to learn and who could better to teach me than you."

"I was hoping you would feel that way, I can't tell you how much it means to me to hear you say it. Mel's in the kitchen waiting for you," he turns away, she thinks he's wiping a tear from his eye.

"Sure thing Grumpy, wait until you see my new bathing suit, I bought it just for you."

"Yea I'm sure you did what about the other ten guys she's invited here to meet you?" They both laugh and go into the kitchen.

Mel and Deanna sit down over a couple of Cosmo's and Deanna brings her up to date on what's been going on in her life since the hospital. She asks Deanna if Jamie has tried to contact her in any way.

"No, he's not even called me once since the day in the hospital. They brought home Tanner the other day, I was there, but Jamie was out making arrangements with Roberto to have Miguel's remains shipped home. Mel I'm not sure that your plan to make him jealous will work, I don't think he cares for me that way. Even when he was talking to Rosa about those he cared about he never mentioned me, just them."

"How do you know he doesn't, you slap his face, you tell him he is not welcome to your home, and pretty much tell him you hate him. It's not exactly what I would call putting out the welcome mat, if you ask me." Mel sits with a sarcastic look on her face, and Deanna knows she's right.

"I wanted to take it back, but he turned and walked away, he never looked back not once. He's the same with Jonah and Katy, it's me, and he doesn't want anything to do with."

"You are still carrying quite a thing about him, or you wouldn't be so angry. Let's give it some time and a couple of more dates, I'm sure the gossips will have you engaged pretty soon, especially since you two were the talk of the town just four weeks ago at the party and horse show. You know I heard that he punched your ex-husband out, because he said something nasty to you at the show grounds is that true?"

"That's not true, he stopped Steve from getting, unpleasant and grabbed his wrist, almost breaking it, but it was really because of Katy and how Steve was affecting her."

"Are you so sure of that, men usually defend our honor physically, before our children."

"Tell me; how it went the other night with Ken, you went to the Polo Club, right? Did you____ you know after, did he get to first base?" She looks at Deanna and giggles.

"No he did **not**, in fact, Ken was a perfect gentleman, he kissed me a few times and when I ask him to stop, he did."

"Why would you tell him that for God's sake? That's what you wanted, wasn't it, for him to have the hot's for you?"

'I did kind of, but when he kissed me, it was different, not like when Jamie kissed me. I didn't feel the same way."

"Hello, Look it's not supposed to be the same way each time," Mel laughs and takes a sip of her drink.

"No, that's not what I mean, when Jamie kissed me, I really felt something like I had never felt before. His kiss was hot, but not smothering, his touch made me tingle and when I looked into his eyes I would get lost in them emotionally. Really, Mel, when he kissed me, I could feel myself soaring high above everything, when he held me in his arms, I could feel the wind rushing by. No one has ever made me feel that way, safe and at the same time as if I was on an adventure. It's very hard to put into words, he just made me experience everything around me, and my senses were all on an edge, I could feel him, and everything around me."

"Honey if any man ever made me lose it like that I would never have let him go. Well, we have bigger fish to fry now. I have to get you an appropriate escort to the Horseman's Dinner next week. Maybe if he sees you there it will move him to do something about it or at least let you off the hook, so to speak."

John calls out to them that the guests are starting to arrive. Deanna starts to help Mel move some of the food outside to the covered porch, as John brings in the first guests to arrive; they are the neighbors from down the street. A nice couple, he's an investment banker, and she sells real estate. Upon hearing who Deanna is, they are all questions about the story and Jamie. She hopes they all are not going to be asking about him all day.

Deanna walks over to the bar and John introduces her to a man by the name of Mark, "Mark is with the Governor's office here in Palm

Beach, I was just explaining to him that you are one of the most talented writers we've ever had on staff."

"Really, Mark your job must be terribly exciting, meeting all those influential people." She says to him shaking his hand, hoping to get him to talk about his job and not about her.

"Not as exciting as your line of work, imagine being in on one of the hottest stories of the year. I understand your son was in on the capture of one of the criminals, and you yourself stayed there until they were captured. You must tell me all about it."

Mel comes over to rescue her from him, "Come on Deanna, why don't we change into our suits? There is no reason to waste this gorgeous day? If you will excuse us gentlemen, feel free to use any of the cabanas to change folks." Taking her by the arm, they go to the upstairs bedroom.

"Thanks, he was coming on very strong, don't you think?" They both laugh and go on upstairs.

"Get used to it, you have a thrilling tale you were involved with in comparison to their lives, you're a story book heroine, who saved the day and exposed the crooks." Mel smiles and winks at her.

Coming downstairs after putting on their bathing suits, they spy Roger and Ken who must have just arrived. "Hello boys, I see you were able to make the party." Mel says to them before they reach Deanna.

Ken is the first one to speak, "Deanna you look incredible, why you're a vision let me get you a drink." but he's too late Roger is at the bar and grabbing one from John.

"I've got one for you right here Deanna, please allow me, and you do look ravishing, is that a new suit? I will propose to you immediately, here and now. Please marry me and I will lay the world at your feet." Roger exclaims laughingly as he runs up to her with drink in hand.

"See what I told you, they may both be escorting you next week to the banquet." Mel whispers to her.

chapter 24

"A Letter Home"

"Miz Jenifer, Miz Jenifer, where are you? There is a letter here for you. Miz Jenifer, do you hear me?"

"Hanna, for god's sake what is all that yelling for? I'm right here in the setting room where I'm always at in the afternoon. You know that, I swear you are getting worst with every day you get older."

"It's a letter Miz Jenifer, where's your reading spectacles do you have them with you."

"No I don't, will you get them please and stop hollering, I'm not next door. Who's it from, you might as well tell me I know you know, or you wouldn't be making so much noise about it?" Jennifer Quinn answers her long time friend and companion as she turns down the volume on the TV.

"It's from Miz Deanna, and it looks like it a spinner too. You want me to open it for you?"

"I'm capable of opening my own mail thank you just the same. Did you bring me my glasses?"

"Here they are right where I said they'd be. I already ran it through the letter opener for you." Deanna's former nanny answers her, dancing from one foot to the other with excitement.

Taking the letter from her and setting her glasses in place she begins to open it. Turning to Hanna she says, "Well are you going to sit down or not? I'm not going to read this twice you know." Hanna sits in the chair opposite her as she begins to read it.

Dear Mom, and Auntie Hanna,

Jonah and Katy are well and send their love and regards. Jonah is working very closely with Jamie and true to his word Jamie is trying to convince him that college is the course for him to follow, not the rodeo circuit. He has told me he will attend college commencing in the fall.

Jonah respects him and they are closer than ever since the day Jonah rode out with him to catch the people on that horrible day. He idolizes Jamie and I believe he is a marvelous influence on him. I don't think you will recognize your grandson any longer, he's tall like Tom was and turning into a good and kind man.

Katy has done a complete three sixty with her problem, she's happy, content and very dedicated under his tutelage. An accomplished rider, she is completing on a whole different level. Her grades have gone from just passing to Honor's. I believe it's because of the friendship and the encouragement of the other girls. Jamie teaches them to support each other, and they are fantastic toward one another. She loves him and is devoted to the way of life that they live by. I asked her the other day how Jamie was doing, and she said he's well, just a little quiet, and he spends more time riding alone now on Storm, his big black Tennessee Walker. I asked her if he was still playing his music, and she sadly said no.

Jamie has been very distant with me, and I think he's not going to change. He loved Mary too greatly and with all that's happened, Rosa thinks that he's afraid to get close to anyone again. By the way, Rosa is his friend and housekeeper and his ranch manager's wife. She's become a very close friend as has Melody my employer's wife. They have been very supportive, and I have come to love them dearly.

I have been dating with the help of Mel, she knows all the eligible bachelors and is making sure that I meet as many as possible, plus the Magazine has me doing interviews with all the top equestrians from around the world. I am not necessarily looking forward to finding a husband right now, but I have some very nice men interested, one is an attorney and friend of John Ellsworth, my boss. He was going to represent me against Steve, but with his legal problems right now I don't need an attorney. So Ken has become a suitor instead. The other is from England here to complete in the National Horse Show, he's a Jumper and Trainer, very wealthy as well. I think his family is titled somehow, although he makes light of it.

I am doing well with my job and the story went national. I am being offered positions with some very large publishers, but I think I want to stay here, for the time being. The magazine has been great to me, and I feel comfortable even though John is still talking with some of the publishers about my future. By the way, John is my boss and has become my friend as well.

For me personally it has been rough, dealing with the past and trying to deal with the present. I am not going to say that I don't have feelings for Jamie; I would be lying if I did. He awoke in me something that I didn't know that I had, a desire and sense of belonging to someone again, a kinship like none that I'd ever known before.

Ken, that's the attorney, kisses me, and it's nice, but it does not light the passion as Jamie's did, nor does his touch. If anyone would have said to me that in just six weeks my life would have taken the turns it has, I would never have believed it. For now I am going to take your advice and walk on the safe side, which should make you very happy.

The National Horsemen's Banquet is coming on the twenty first, right before the holidays and all the girls have been invited to go. I am going, but not just as a parent, but for the Magazine as well. John has gotten my tickets and Ken may be my escort. I'm not sure how I'll handle things when I see Jamie. We have been avoiding each other ever since I slapped him at the ranch and told him he was not welcome to my home when we were at the hospital. I told him I hated him that day. I'm not sure if it was because I thought he was using me for his own ends, or because I felt guilty because of not getting the warning to him sooner about Steve. He only looked at me and turned away, never said a word, he just walked away.

Tanner has made a complete recovery and Jonah say's everything has returned to normal. Jamie took Miguel's body home for his family in Argentina, my friend Roberto went with him.

They have become great friends; Roberto thinks much of him as do all of his people. Roberto is convinced I should try to talk to him and not be so stubborn, but I told him that I don't want to be second in Jamie's' life. You see Jamie has countless people he has to put ahead of me, plus ghost's from his past. I just hope that we can be friends again, I miss that comfort he gave me, and I miss the Rancho. I had not realized how close I came to all those there.

I have to go now, I am sorry about not calling, but sometimes it's easier to put things in writing after an unpleasant experience than to try to talk about it. I love you and hope you will decide to come for the Holidays, as we miss you and the one thing I have learned from this whole thing is the wealth of family. Call me please, and forgive me for my anger and words when last we spoke.

Your Loving Daughter,

P.S. Hugs and kisses to you too Hanna, I know you're sitting next to her as she reads this. I love you too.

"Well are you gonna put aside all this foolishness and go, or are you gonna be pigheaded and let that girl make the biggest mistake of her life?" Hanna stands up in front of Jenifer, and she is showing her anger for the first time in all the years she has been with her.

"I'm not sure Hanna; do you think we should go?"

"Miz Jenifer I love that girl as much as you, and if you don't go than I will, she needs you now more than she ever has in her whole life. I ain't met this here man, but she sounds like she is in love with him something awful. From what you told me what Mr. Haskell said about him, she'd better not let him get away. You just remember one thing she was my baby too."

chapter 25

"Feliz Navidad"

Katy calls her mother and asks if she would run out her dress, so she could show the girls. Deanna was heading out that way anyway because Rosa had asked her if she could take her shopping for a dress to wear to the Banquet. Arriving at the house she has butterflies thinking about seeing Jamie for the first time since the Hospital. Dreading a meeting and hoping she would not just fall apart in front of him. Hitching up her pants and courage she walks up to Rosa's house and knocks on the door.

"Come in Senora Deanna," Rosa opens the door for her. "I will be ready in just a minute. I thank you for taking me to the stores; I have never needed such a fancy dress before. I need you to help me get the right thing to wear; I would not want to make all of you ashamed of me. You will know what I should wear, no?"

"Rosa it will be no problem, we'll make the day of it having some fun just us girls, I invited my friend Melody to go with us. You'll like her, she's my boss's wife, and she loves to shop."

Deanna looks at Rosa's house, and it's decorated for Christmas with colorful ribbons and flowers everywhere. "Your home is more beautiful than ever, I wish I could decorate like you, we have not even put up the tree yet."

"Thank you Senora, but first we must go to the main house so you can see what they have done there, everyone has helped the Patron decorate for Felice Navidad[48]. The girls had so much fun and the vaqueros all made something to hang. The tree is the biggest I have ever seen, they had to bring the ladder from the barn for the Angel. Katy was so happy, she cried last night from joy, and Jonah put his gifts under the tree for Dyon. Rubin has been working with him to make the saddle for her, it's beautiful. They put it in a big box, and he wrapped the whole thing himself." Deanna feels sad and left out, she turns to look out the window.

"I have made you sad, I am so sorry, you are my friend, and I wanted you to know what makes them happy. Do not be mad at me, but you should have been here also. The finest present you could give is to be with them, and have it is as it was, you know that."

"Rosa I'm not angry at of you, I'm raging at him for not being a man and telling me to stay. Instead he told me that he just wanted to be friends and nothing more. Has he called me once, no, he hasn't? I won't be a fool again for him nor will I worry about him anymore. You know I love all of you, but this is one thing he can't fix, it broke in too many pieces."

"Senora, as a woman I know what you feel, and I have told him so, but he is a man and men are many times ignorant in the ways of the heart. I just don't want you to be stupid with your heart."

"Is he here because if he is I'll wait for you in the car?" Deanna says to her emphatically.

He is not here, he left when I told him you were coming to pick me up, he said to say "Hello" and that he regrets he could not be present to greet you, but he and Eduardo had to see to the bulls." Rosa offers in a way of an apology.

"Sounds like bull crap to me, he just can't face me, he has courage to face killers, but he can't tell me how he feels. Why don't we go over and

---

48 Merry Christmas

look at the house, so I can give Katy her dress and see what they have done? I really do want to see it." Deanna's anger fades knowing she won't have to face him.

"Bueno, let's go now the girls are expecting us."

Walking together toward the main house she observes the changes around the Ranch and see's many new improvements since the last day she was there. The house has evergreen garlands all around it and some of the men are putting up lights. It looks like he bought out a nursery of poinsettias, everywhere you look, and there are many different shades and colors.

"Rosa the house looks gorgeous."

"Si, they are finishing up the outside today with the lights in all the bougainvilleas it will look like stars have come down from the sky. Patron is giving a big fiesta for the little ones from the mission and the neighbor's children. You are invited as well, you know."

Katy and Tia see her and come running, "Hey Mom, I didn't know you were here." Katy is ballistic to see her mother and hugs and gives her a kiss as does Tia.

"Hey how are you two doing, I have missed you guys, the house has been a little lonely since you came back here. I have your dress it's in the car, why don't you get it, Honey?"

"Ok, but don't go in the house without us, we want to show you what we've done. Wait right there." Rosa and Deanna stand and wait for them to return.

"They have missed you very much, and they wish to show you what you are missing. Please don't let them see how upset you are still." Rosa gently chides her.

"I won't, they're so excited, and I still can't believe she is the same girl that I brought out here just seven weeks ago."

"Tia is a different girl then she was also, only Marianna is the same for her the future is what it is," Rosa comments.

Before Deanna can ask her to explain the girls are back and pulling her into the house.

"Close your eyes, and don't open them until I tell you to, ok," Katy orders her mother. "Ok, you can open them now."

Deanna gasps not quite believing how beautiful and almost spiritual the whole scene is. "It's truly magnificent, you all decorated this by yourselves," Deanna asks?

"Yes Mother we all did, well kind of, everyone at the Rancho helped, and we saved something for you, look here."Katy shows her a box with many different ornaments and tells her mother to pick the ones she wishes to put on the tree in a section that's bare of decoration.

"This is your spot Mother; you must finish it before you can go shopping with Rosa, please Mother for my sake,"

Her mother reaches in and picks out a shepherd holding a lamb and places it on the tree, getting into it, Deanna rummages through the box until she has filled the space and steps back to admire her work.

"Now are you happy, I have finished my section, it is the most beautiful Christmas tree I've ever seen, in fact, the whole house is perfect, you all should be very proud."

"Mother, I want to be here for Christmas and so does Jonah, we want you to be with us as well. We all do, ask Rosa? Uncle Jamie wants you to spend Christmas here also, please think about it will you."

"Yes I will be here, how could I miss something like this with all of you." They both hug and kiss; Katy continues jabbering the whole time about all the presents.

"Mother look, there are presents here for you as well."

She walks over and looks; there is a small mound of gifts with her name on them. Deanna notices a few written in a different style, she wonders are any of them from him, and how can she spend the holiday in the same room with Jamie?

"We have got to go now, the mall is waiting for us Rosa, and I still have to pick up Mel, bye girls see you later. Katy, I'll bring back my camera, and you can take pictures of everything to send to your Grandmother, alright?"

Leaving the house Deanna observes all of the vaquero's standing along the driveway. The vaqueros tip their hats and smile at her and Rosa as they proceed down the driveway waving to them as they pass. Deanna had almost forgotten the warm feeling this place gives her.

"Mel this place doesn't sell formal dresses does it?" Deanna asks Mel. The store looks so small without any signage at all.

"This is the best kept secret in the Palm Beaches; they carry one of a kind dresses right from New York City, wait until you see. They have the latest stuff including shoes. Come on Rosa you're in for a treat," Mel states and bounces off happily.

Following her inside and true to her word the place is amazing. They have all the latest fashions. A smartly dressed sales girl comes over and asks if she can help them. Mel tells her they need three knock out dresses for the Banquet, and she starts by taking our measurements and selecting some of the most beautiful gowns for the three of them. They are all laughing and giggling like high school sophomores, but they're having fun.

Deanna along with Mel and Rosa finally select the ones they want and the sales girl tells them to come back in two days for a final fitting. Walking to the front counter to pay for the gowns, the cashier hands them their bills, it comes to over two thousand dollars, and Rosa almost feints.

"Senora Deanna, I cannot spend such money on just a dress, it would be a sin, I would be afraid I would damage it. What would Eduardo say? He would think me a foolish woman."

"Eduardo will think he is with the most beautiful princess in the world, and Jamie won't mind the bill, he can afford it." Deanna tells her thinking it would serve him right, maybe she should charge her purchases to him as well.

"He did tell me to pick whatever, I wanted, he gave me this card to use, see here it is."

"Well Honey, you just pick out whatever you want then, sometimes a man has to pay to have his women look good." Mel's laughing, as she looks at three hundred dollar handbags.

Deanna pulls Mel aside, and tells her she can't afford to spend this kind of money either.

"Deanna my friend, the Magazine is picking up your tab as per John, so don't you feel guilty. The magazine hit the highest circulation in its ten year history. That was all because of you and the best thing we have ever done. You are going to earn a bonus too."

"Really, you're not kidding me are you?"

"No, John called me just before you came to pick me up, he's on cloud nine. Collins is taking credit because he hired you, but that's ok he's not a bad editor."

Ladies shall we go to lunch and make the afternoon memorable." Mel takes both by they're arms, and strolls down the promenade toward some very upscale restaurants.

Coming to the entrance to one called Le Parisian, Rosa whispers to Deanna, "Senora Deanna, thank you for inviting me, I have never had so much fun, your friend, she's a good person, and she cares for you, I can tell."

Having lunch at the most expensive restaurant in the Village, Rosa is like a child in a candy store. Never hoping to have a shopping spree like they've had and neither has Deanna. Now to eat in one of the most eclectic places in Palm Beach is incredible. Mel said it will be a memory like no other, and she was right. They spend the rest of the afternoon laughing and just having girl fun. She really doesn't want it to end, but Deanna knows it must as the day winds down, and they head for the car.

Dropping Mel off at home Deanna says goodbye to her and heads to the ranch. She looks at her watch, it' now four o'clock and she has barn chores and Rosa has children to care for. On the drive back Deanna asks Rosa what she meant about Marianna. Her happy demeanor drops and she begins to speak haltingly.

"Senora it has been such a happy day can we not talk about this some other time."

"If it were you asking me, would you want me to put it off until some other time?"

"No...I just...it is that we are coming to terms with...the truth... Senora you must promise that you will say nothing, or I cannot tell you."

Deanna pulls the car over and looks at her, at first she has a million questions, but the look on her face tells her to give Rosa her promise. "I promise to say nothing, you have my word."

"Marianna's' problem is... she is dying, she has little time left. It is a brain tumor it is umm... how you say inoperable. The Patron has had the best people to take care of her."

"Oh my God, that was the last thing I was expecting, does she know? The night of the big party at the house a while back she was wishing Jamie could adopt her."

"She knows, she has always known, the other girls do not, except for Dyon.. Nor does she wish them to. She is very brave that one, the Patron tries not to favor her, but I know he cries for her. Remember as I told you, that the more you learned of the man the more there was. You have learned all the secrets, now knowing all of this; do you think he has done things for himself alone? Deanna you must never take off the medallion he gave you, it's his heart that you wear not just a metal. It is the place that holds his soul. You must never take it off, until you find a heart that is as pure as from whence it came. Promise me this as my friend, until you have found someone worthy of it."

Deanna has never seen her so distraught, "Rosa, you have my promise, but I love him more than you could know, but I can't share him with so many, nor can I compete with her. You don't know what it is like competing with something you can't fight against. I will keep my promise about Marianna too and I will be there to share Christmas with you all."

chapter 26

"The Banquet"

"Mom, wake up, we have to get ready… Mom did you hear me, it's time to get up." Katy is pounding on her door.

"Alright, alright, I'm awake, lighten up will you. Let me open my eyes." Looking over at the clock, Deanna sees it's seven o'clock. Putting her head back down on the pillow, she tries to get the cobwebs to go away.

"Mother we have so much to do today before we get to the ranch, hurry up, we're burning daylight.

Deanna knows today is going to be stressful enough, what with trying to get five girls, two women and a bunch of cowboys ready for one of the social events of the season.

Deanna will call Rosa when she gets downstairs and find out what time the girls have to be ready, so Theresa can get their hair done. She still doesn't think she'll be able to do all of them today. Mel is going to her also, since Jamie helped her open her hair salon and day spa. Getting up she goes and throws some water on her face and runs a brush through her hair before heading for the kitchen.

"Good morning daughter, don't even start until I have my first cup of coffee. We have to go take care of everybody before we think of going anywhere, and I have to call Rosa." Deanna emphasizes to her.

"Jonah did that all already he was up at six, so all we have to do is get ourselves ready and fly." Katy literally bounces up and down smiling smugly.

"You all had this planned pretty well didn't you? I suppose he's left for the ranch before the sun was up?" Her mother responds with a smile.

"Mother big brother has lots to do today too, he has to go pick up his tux, and get his haircut, besides taking Dyon for her dress, It wasn't ready yesterday as they promised. You know something Mother, I tried to call Grandma last night to tell her about the Banquet, but she didn't answer and neither did Hanna. You don't think anything is wrong do you?"

Deanna thinks to herself for a moment, it's odd that neither one of them didn't pick up the phone before she answers Katy. "They may have been out to a church function or shopping for Christmas. I will try them later today; I wish she would have let me get her a cell phone when I wanted to buy her one. One of them would have called if something was wrong or the pastor would." She tries to sound convincing, but something is nagging at her.

Deanna tells Katy, "We have tons of things to do, so go up and get ready first." She dials Rosa after Katy goes up stairs.

"Hi, it's me; we're getting ready and should be there in about forty five minute if that's ok. How about I pick up some bagels or something for everyone?"

She tells her that would be fine, and they're all ready. Mel is picking up their dresses from the shop. Deanna still can't believe how great they looked and Rosa's was the prettiest of all. She was so excited the other day it really made you feel like Christmas came early. Next she calls Mel and she answers the phone as if Deanna just woke her up.

"Hey sleepy head, did you forget we have to be at Theresa's at eleven today for a spa treatment all three of us?"

"No, I didn't forget," she says rather grumpy. "I'll be ready what time it is? My god it's only seven thirty, you woke me in the middle of the night."

"You wouldn't think that if you had a thirteen year old pounding on your door," She says laughing.

"These are the times when I'm glad we weren't blessed with children." She teases her. "I will see you at the spa, you're sure she can handle all of us?" She was so excited the other day it really made them feel like Christmas came early.

"Don't worry she is an artist with hair and Jamie spared no expense when he set up the Spa for her, it has all the modern stuff, and she has three other techs working for her. You'll be more than pleased I promise." Deanna replies.

"Ok, I'll see you in a little while; I have to run some errands for John this morning." Hanging the phone up, Deanna has a moment's thought about Jamie, if she'll see him at all today or just tonight at the banquet?

She hears Angel barking and looks to see what has her so upset. There's a florist truck out by the front gate, calling Angel into the house the man proceeds to bring up flowers along with what appears to be a corsage. They're beautiful, looking for a card and not finding one, Deanna turns her attention toward the wristlet. The wristlet corsage is of yellow roses trimmed with a crimped yellow and white ribbon with baby's breath. She asks the driver if knows who sent them, and he says he doesn't know, he just delivers them, that she should call the shop.

Going inside she dials the number of the florist and when they answer Deanna tells them who she is and inquires as to who sent the flowers. The man that answers the phone asks her to wait a minute while he looks it up. "Hello Miss, I'm the cashier, the person who took that order is not here, and it was paid for with cash. I'm afraid I won't be able to tell you that, only who they were for. The name for the delivery is Deanna Gaynor. Was there something wrong with the flowers?"

"No they're gorgeous, I was not anticipating them and there was no card, I was just wondering. They're really quite perfect, thank you so much." She says to him and hangs up the phone.

How would anyone know what colors to arrange that would match and compliment her dress except for Rosa or Mel, that's very strange. Maybe they're from Roger or Ken; she told them both that she would meet them there tonight? She had decided not to have Ken or Roger escort her tonight, as Mel had originally planned. They are both going to be at John and Mel's table, along with Collins and some of the staff editors from the magazine. Deanna's wondering if they could be from Jamie. He knows yellow is her favorite color, she wonders… maybe Rosa will know.

"Mother I'm ready and you haven't even started to dress yet. Hurry up will you, I just spoke to Tia, and they are waiting for us." Katy hollers at her from the top of the stairs.

"Where did these flowers come from? Wow, the corsage is gorgeous, am I going to get one to wear too?"

Deanna suddenly realizes that she forgot to order flowers for Katy or the other girls!

"Yes, you are I have to stop and order them this afternoon." She lie's to her and makes a mental note to do it.

Running up stairs Deanna jumps into the shower for a quick one, so as not to be late. She notices the time it's going on eight thirty, towel drying her hair, she jumps into her jeans and polo shirt. "Ok I'm ready to go, put some food out for Angel and check her water, I'll be right down." She yells down to Katy.

As they arrive at the ranch, Deanna again notices the many changes, starting with the driveway leading up to the house. It's planted with what looks like about a hundred evergreen trees all the way to the main house, and they're all decorated with lights and bows. You can feel Christmas in the air.

Parking the car in front of Rosa's house, Eduardo is the first to greet her. "Hola Senora, Rosa is in the kitchen, and I will tell the Senorita's you have come, I think you may want to use the SUV today. I have asked Jonah to clean it up for you. My Rosa will not tell about the dress she will wear tonight, is it magnifica[49]?" He asks her, hoping she will help him out.

"Eduardo you will have to wait, I'll tell you this, Rosa will look absolutely more beautiful than you have ever seen her." Deanna replies to him.

"You have made me a happy man Senora, I thank you." Eduardo bows graciously and kisses her hand.

Deanna has to ask, the suspense is killing her. "Eduardo is he here; I mean is he going down to see the girls before they go to the salon."

"I regret Senora; he left early this morning and will not be back until very late today. He received a call from someone he knew for many years and said he had to leave. I asked him what time to expect him, and he said he did not know." Eduardo has the look, as has more to tell, but doesn't want to.

"He will be at the dinner tonight won't he, he knows how important it is to these girls" Deanna asks him her anger rising with her voice.

"Si, I think he will be there Senora."

She goes in and Rosa is making coffee she almost forgets she brought the bagels, and sets them down with a bang.

"You are upset, what is wrong Deanna." Rosa asks, using her surname name for the first time, since she's met her.

"He is not here; I can't believe he is not around on this day of all days. Where could he have had to go to that would be more important than today?" Deanna fumes at the thought that he's not at the ranch "Is he just trying to avoid me, is he that much of a coward, or does he dislike me that much. I'm the one that has been offended. I'm the one that he used, Rosa; I'm going to kill him when I see him." Deanna stomps around angrily.

"Deanna, I don't know where he went, but you judge him without knowing, first find out who, then the why. She smiles and pours coffee for them both.

"You always take his part." Deanna pouts and she laughs.

"I am your friend too, I have scolded him many times to the point

---

49 magnificent

he avoids me now also. He is like the little boy, he must work out this problem, I say give him time. Come drink up, I will prepare the things you have brought so we may leave."

The morning goes well and Theresa's salon is the best, everything is a state of the art. Jamie spared no expense with anything, first they are given hot baths and then skin treatments, with Theresa fussing over them the whole time. Mel loves it and tells her that she will tell all of her friends, and that they must come there, insuring Theresa's success. Next we have pedicures and our nails done, the girls just love it. This is their first time in a spa along with Rosa. Finally, they are ready for our hair, Theresa oversees everything to make sure it's done exactly the way they what it and to her satisfaction. They are finally done with their makeovers. Each admires other, and Mel has to admit Theresa has done miracles.

"Theresa I can't thank you enough," as Deanna goes to pay her, She tells her to put her money away.

"You would insult me if you offered money, this is my gift to all of you, you have made all of us proud, and tonight they will all know the women of Rancho de Los Angeles. You will all make Don Diego proud." Deanna gives her a kiss and tells her, "thank you," as does Mel.

Going outside the shop Mel asks Deanna to help with the gowns she's struggling they are in boxes.

Remembering flowers she was supposed to order and asks Mel if she thinks she knows of a florist that could get all of the girls and Rosa corsages. Before Mel can answer, Rosa interrupts her. "That Senora has all been taken care of this morning. Jamie told me to order them."

Deanna asks her which florist she used, and she tells her the one in Loxahatchee. It's not the same one that brought hers to the house.

Saying goodbye to Mel they load up and head for the ranch. Deanna drops off everyone except Katy and asks Jonah when he will be home to change.

"Mother I will be changing here and driving Dyon and the girls to the Banquet tonight. Jefe called and said he's running late and would I stand in for him until he gets there."

"Alright, I'll see you there tonight I was rather looking forward to seeing you dressed before we got there, you know like your first prom or something." She's a little disappointed, but she sees he's proud that Jamie has asked him to stand in for him.

Deanna gives him a kiss and starts to go when she sees Tanner coming out of the house in a wheel chair, going over to him Deanna gives him a kiss which he fusses about and pretends to be grumpy.

"Tanner I was just coming over to see you before I left. How are you feeling?"

"Bored out of my mind, that's how I feel, they won't let me do anything, not even go down to the barns and look to my babies.

You're looking mighty fetching Missy, we have missed you something fierce around this here place, you got to stop being so stubborn the both of you. Dame fools, that are acting worse than children, aren't doing either of you any good. You two keep this up, I might have been better off dead."

"Now don't you talk that way, you are going to be right as rain and ready for the spring season, The girls need you, and you know it. You're just an old faker. Wait until you see them all dressed tonight for the dinner, you'll change your mind." She gives him another kiss and tells him she has to go get ready.

"Missy, I wish I was gonna be there tonight, you make sure you get me some photographs, you hear me." She tells him she will and wave's goodbye. Deanna thinks to herself what a sweetheart of man Tanner really is, realizing that she has come to love him in spite of all his garrulous ways.

Katy and Deanna head for home each wrapped in their own thoughts; Katy's very quiet and seems pensive. Deanna asks her what's on her mind by asking the same question she used to when she was very small, "A penny for your thoughts."

"Oh I was just thinking how different it would be now if you hadn't gotten that job, and we had never met Uncle Jamie and all the people at the ranch. I never told you, but I was trying to find a way to end everything, you know pills, even a gun, right before you made me go that day. I just wanted the pain to go away." Deanna is shocked at her words and for a minute doesn't know what to say to her, as Katy stares out the window.

"You don't feel that way now, do you? Because if you do, I want you to talk to somebody that will or can help you deal with those thoughts." Deanna is more scared of her answer than anything before in her life.

Katy turns toward her mother and says, "No, I'm fine now, I was just feeling sorry for myself and let my anger at you and Daddy fuel those feelings. I guess I've hit one of those maturity curves they talk about. I don't feel different anymore and people believe in me for the first time in my life, in a way that I feel. I know you have and Jonah, but now so do I. Uncle Jamie said that to me in the very beginning, he said all I had to do was believe in myself.

I find myself wishing I was his daughter, I don't ever want to lose that feeling of family that I have now. Am I making any sense to you, I mean, do you understand what I mean?"

Deanna finds that she can't answer her right away, pulling over to the side of the road, she puts her arms around Katy and hugs her letting her feel what she's feeling.

"Honey, I know exactly what you feel, and I wish it could be just that way you want forever. It's the way people love you that really matters, not how much they tell you."

They drive home not saying anything more, just holding each other's hand. Deanna knows that whatever he may be, Jamie saved Katy's life and her own also. The reality of it has just dropped the eight hundred pound gorilla into her life. She's determined to face him with it tonight after the Banquet, maybe Rosa is right, for now she can only hope.

Upon arriving home, she tries her Mother again, but all she gets is the answering machine, where could they be, she's starting to get really worried? What if they were in an accident? Deanna decides to call the

The Last Celtic Angel

pastor of her mother's church. Searching for her address book she finds it and hopes that was where she put his phone number, never really thinking that she would have to call him.

Thank god she finds it; dialing the number it rings and rings. Deanna is about to hang up, thinking that he doesn't have it on answering service, when she hears him pick up.

"Hello Reverend Small, this is Deanna Gaynor, I don't know if you remember me, I'm Jennifer Quinn's Daughter."

"Hello, yes I do how you are. Is your mother alright?" He asks with sudden concern in his voice.

"Well that's what I'm calling you about, I have been trying to get a hold of her since yesterday and there has been no answer at her house. I can't even get Hanna, it's very odd, and I'm worried." She tells him.

"I have not heard from her, since I saw her at last Sunday's service, she and Hanna seemed to be in good spirits. I'll drive over there right away and check on them if you like," Reverend Small offers.

"Yes Reverend, if you wouldn't mind I'm getting very worried. Please call me on my cell phone, or I can call you later if you would prefer." He asks her to wait while he gets something to write with.

He comes back on and Deanna gives him her cell number. He promises to call her, as soon as he gets back. He doesn't have a cell phone either.

"Thank you Reverend, I will await your call….Goodbye."

Deanna takes her dress up stairs and put's it on the bed, she strips down and starts to get her under things ready. Trying to tell herself that all is well in Virginia, She doesn't want to worry Katy. Deanna picks up the phone and calls Jamie's cell phone, but he doesn't answer, she just gets his voice mail. Deanna doesn't bother to leave him a message.

She looks at the clock and sees that it's almost six o'clock they have to be there between seven and seven thirty. Deanna starts to put on her make up and get dressed hoping this feeling of dread goes away. She looks at herself in the mirror and finds it hard to believe that it's her. Calling out to Katy to see if she needs anything, "No Mother, I'm fine be out in a minute." Telling her to meet her downstairs, she goes to let Angel out before they go. When suddenly she realizes that they had completely forgotten to feed and water the horses.

Deanna is startled by a knock on the back door and wonders who it could be and why Angel is not barking her head off. Turning on the back light she's relieved to see Esteban standing there.

Deanna opens the door quickly and asks, "Esteban is something wrong. What are you doing here?"

"Nothing is wrong Senora the Patron tells me this morning to come here tonight and take care of the horses for you. I knock before but no one answer so I go and do. The dog she comes and gets me, so I know you must be home." He smiles as he holds his hat in his hands.

"Thank you, do you want to come in, we are just getting ready to go to the Banquet; Katy will be down in a minute.

Esteban could do me a favor and take our picture if you wouldn't mind?" He nods She goes over and grabs her camera, stepping back into the kitchen Deanna shows him what to do.

Esteban looks at the camera and tells her he understands.

"Si Senora, you look like the princess."

Katy comes down and is surprised to see him. "Hola, Esteban what are you doing here?"

"He came to help with the stock, a good thing he did, we both forgot when we came home. Come on Katy stand over by the fireplace, Esteban is going to take our picture." Deanna tells her.

Pulling up to the country club, Deanna and Katy step out of the car and hand the valet the keys. "Well are you ready" She looks at Katy and squares her shoulders.

"Yep, let's go," she says, and they link arms and march up the stairs. Arriving at the front entrance Deanna shows their invitations to the head steward, and he directs them to the Banquet Room.

Upon entering the banquet area Deanna hands the Concierge their invitations, as he reads them, she looks around to see if Mel and John have arrived yet. The Concierge tells them which table to find them at and asks one of the ushers to escort Katy and Deanna to their tables.

"Mother, I want to sit with the rancho's table can't you ask him to sit me over there?"

"Sir, My daughter is supposed to be sitting at the Rancho de Los Angeles table, there must be a mistake, and could you check it out please."

He checks his seating arrangement and apologizes for his mistake; they follow him over to the table and Katy breaths much easier. "See you are right next to Tia and Dyon, they have not arrived as yet."

She notices that the table is set for nine with T. J. and Marianna on either side of Jamie. She was hoping he had put her name on the seating arrangement to sit at his table, but see's that he hasn't.

Deanna sees Mel and John coming in and over to greet them. "Hi, you two look incredible, John you do dress up nicely." Deanna compliments them both, as John gives her a huge smile.

Mel gives her a peck on the cheek as does John. "Deanna you look ravishing in that gown, the color and the flowers are perfect for you." John pays her one of his rare compliments.

Mel did John have flowers sent to the house for me today.

"No, he didn't, in actuality; I had to order my own because somebody forgot to." Mel says a little peeved. Deanna notices that John becomes beet red, looking at the floor, like some errant school boy. "Maybe Jamie sent them."

"I thought he might have also, but the flowers they ordered, came from a different florist in Loxahatchee. This came with a bunch of yellow roses also." Deanna explains to them.

"We'll see once Roger and Ken get here who sent them, no big mystery." Mel states dismissing the subject as she looks toward the banquet hall entrance.

Deanna looks up and sees Rosa shepherding everyone in, and she looks spectacular, so many eyes turn and stare at them. She looks regal and Eduardo looks just as grand in his tuxedo, next come Dyon and

Jonah, who make and an elegant couple, her hair is swept long falling to her waist. She is wearing a red gown, and she appears every inch a woman. She doesn't see Jamie with them and assumes he must be coming soon.

Getting up she walks over to greet them all and tells the girls how wonderful they all look. "Rosa you and Eduardo have made quite an impression you all look as though you stepped right out of a fashion magazine. Did you see all the flash bulbs going off as you came in? Is Jamie with you?" Deanna notices Rosa gives Eduardo a look of concern.

"He didn't make it back to the hacienda before we left, but Tanner says he will dispatch him as soon as he gets there. We haven't heard from him since he left this morning, and he was not answering his phone." Rosa says with concern on her face.

Deanna is just about to reply to her when her cell phone rings, taking it out of her purse, she sees it's Reverend Small. "Excuse me Rosa, I have to answer this. Hello Reverend what did you find out." She answers, concern showing in her voice.

He tells her that he went over to the house and no one was there, but some lights were left on, and the car was not in the garage. He then went to the next door neighbor to see if Mrs. Foster had seen them. She said they left sometime early this morning, and they had bags with them. Apologizing that he could not be of more help, but at least now she knows there was not an emergency.

"Thank you, Reverend Small, I just can't imagine where they might be off too, but it's a load off my mind to know. I'm sure they will contact me soon. Thank you again, sorry to have bothered you." Deanna says to him feeling silly for having been such an alarmist.

Turning back toward Rosa, Deanna is about to speak when she takes her by the arm and walks Deanna away from the table. "Senora, please, I do not want to upset the girls, but Eduardo thinks he may not be coming, I do not know why; please for their sake make no fuss about it." Rosa pleads with her.

"I understand they will be very disappointed if he doesn't show, I just don't understand why he would do something like this, and it's so out of character for him." Deanna is very confused, she feels as though a heavy weight has descended upon her.

Looking at Deanna, Rosa says, "I have said many prayers today for all our sakes, we will talk later." Rosa turns and heads back toward the girls and Eduardo.

Deanna starts back toward her table not quite comprehending what Rosa has just told her, when she sees a sight that makes her knees go weak. Standing next to John is her Mother and Hanna with Ed Haskell. Rushing over she almost knocks them over, Deanna can't believe her eyes that they've come.

"Glad to see you too, sweetheart." Her mother says sarcastically.

"Why don't we all sit down and calm down before you both ruin your makeup," suggests Ed.

"You better start to explain Mother, but first give me a big hug." Deanna throws her arms around her and Hanna again, now that her initial shock is over.

"Well we decided after we got your letter, but having only come once I was not sure how to go about making the arrangements. So I got hold of Ed, and he booked us the flight to get us here tonight, but it landed in Orlando at three thirty. Our problem was how to get here from there in time for the Banquet. We wanted to surprise you." Jenifer explains to her

"So how did you get here from Orlando?"Asks Deanna

"Ed was postponed in Washington on business, and couldn't be there to pick us up when the plane landed. He had your friend Jamie, who came and picked us up. He's a very nice man, and I can see why you would be interested in him. He drove us and got us to our hotel. He waited until we got dressed, than proceeded to bring us here." Her mother replies.

"Mother was he going home to change after he brought you here," Deanna asks?

Hanna speaks up for the first time. "No that's what seemed odd, he said he had to go somewhere first, and he might see us later. I thought he meant he was going home to change, but now I don't think so."

Jonah comes over with Katy and Dyon upon seeing his Grandmother and Hanna.

"Grandmother, Auntie Hanna why didn't you call? It doesn't matter let me introduce you, Dyon this is my Grandmother and my Great Aunt Hanna." He proudly introduces them.

"I am really not his Auntie, I have been with Miz Jennifer since his Mama was born, and I changed his diaper a time or two." Hanna tells her, smiling and feeling proud that he would introduce her as his aunt.

"We are pleased to meet you my dear," Deanna's mother says to her. "Hanna, and I have been friends for fifty years, even before Deanna was born, we're family. I have heard much about you from Ed. It sounds like he's mighty proud of you and all you have accomplished." Deanna's mother explains as she gives Dyon a kiss. Ed Haskell is smiling as he watches his old friend hugging the young woman that he looks upon as a grand daughter. "You know we all lived in the same town in Virginia a long time ago and were like family, it's good to be together once again." My mother tells Dyon.

Dyon asks Deanna's mother, "Madam my uncle, he didn't come in with you?"

"No child he didn't, he said he had somewhere he had to go first." She answers, seeing anxiety in Dyon's face.

It's the first time Deanna has heard her refer to Jamie as her uncle. She asks Dyon where he might be going, and she said she wasn't sure. "He might be going to check on Tanner and then get dressed."

"Did he pick up his tux for the Banquet?" Deanna asks her hoping to get a clue.

Dyon replies, "He has his own, so he wouldn't have to pick one up, come to think of it, I don't remember seeing it out, and that wouldn't be like him."

"I am going to try calling him once more on his cell, this is ridiculous, why wouldn't he be here with all of you," Deanna says to her and failing to raise him on the cell, she finally attempts the house phone.

"Hello, this is Tanner." She hears his familiar voice.

"Tanner, this is Deanna have you seen Jamie?"

"No, Missy I ain't, I figured he was with you at that fancy place. You mean to tell me he ain't shown yet?" Tanner asks.

"No, he picked up my mother and dropped her off, and said he had somewhere to go first. I'm worried Tanner, this is not like him." Deanna tries to convey her fears to him.

He tells her he'll find him and not to worry.

"Dian Cecht, the great healer of the Clan Tuatha De Danann, awaits permission to enter the underground city of his father, King Dagda, I'm here to seek an audience with the Dagda, tell him it's about our kinsman." He tells the king's chamberlain.

The chamberlain returns and tells him he may enter the Kings Chambers. "Lord Cecht, the King will see you now." The old retainer opens the portal to the king's chamber.

"Welcome my son, I'm told you have news of the Redeemer."

"Aye father, I have watched as you degreed, and he has completed his tasks. The people are leaving as we speak; the gea's has been absolved, we are free, my lord."

"It has been a long time waiting for the curse to be lifted, and we can now seek peace. Our kinsman has done well; does he join with us for the journey?"

"No Father, the Prophesy said that the Celtic Angel upon the completion of his task will have the right to stay or go. I believe he will stay here on middle earth, his penitence is now done, and he has found, and restores the Children of Danu, they live once more."

"Shall you be traveling with us on the journey Lord Cecht?"

"Not yet my lord, first I must leave one more message for him and there is a spirit that will accompany me. Mary wants to see him one more time, when that is done we will come to you and cross over."

"Lord Cecht, the Tuatha owes you and your kinsman our eternal gratitude; we will await you at the crossover".....

*

Rubin and Tanner drive a ranch jeep out over the rolling grass land toward the one spot Tanner believes Jamie will be. Tanner sees a lone figure highlighted in the glare of the headlights and tells Rubin to stop. They have arrived at the private cemetery, called Fiona's Acre.

"I thought this is where he'd be, pull right up here Rubin, and you help me out than you can leave, comprende." Rubin nods and smiles as he brings the truck to a stop, He then gets out and pulls the wheel chair out of the back of the truck for Tanner.

"What are you doing here you crazy old man?" Jamie hollers at him as Rubin wheels him up to the small cemetery. "I would yell at Rubin, but I know it is not his fault, are you trying to kill yourself." He runs up and takes the chair from Rubin.

"What I want to know is, why you're here when you're supposed to be at that their dinner thing, they all waiting on you boy. Don't you care anything for them gals or Missy?" Tanner says to Jamie in that level tone he uses only when he's really pissed.

"Tanner, I was just telling her how I felt, and asking if it was alright with her. Did you know that Mary and Deanna were sisters, her mother told me today? Now I know why I felt as close to her as I did, I was seeing Mary in her. It wasn't love of her; it was Mary that stirred those old feelings." Jamie falls on his knees and laments to the old man.

"That's crap and you know it, you fell for that gal the minute you set eyes on her, it's your dam guilt that makes you talk nonsense. That gal ain't my Missy, she's a woman in her own right, and she loves you more than Mary ever did."

"What are you talking about you old fool, no one could have loved me more than Mary!" Jamie yells at Tanner, anger rising in his voice. It's the first time in thirty years he's spoken harshly to his oldest friend.

"Mary needed you for her strength, and because it was your cross to bear. You know she loved you, but it was a different kind of love, you kept her alive and for her, you were the sun, and she bathed in your warmth. Don't you see you don't have to protect Deanna? All you got to do is love her and begin living again. Mary sent that gal here for you so you could live again, and finish what you had to do. Your debt is paid, you've set them free and in so doing, you've set yourself free."

Jamie stands looking down at Mary's grave when Tanner exclaims, "What's that growing next to the headstone," and he shines a light.

Jamie looks at where he is playing the light, and he sees a yellow rose, a single yellow rose growing where it shouldn't be.

"What more proof did you need, ain't nothing but daffodils been planted here. She's telling you, go get that yellow rose, and don't let it wilt none. My Missy, she's telling you to go find that happiness. She made you promise you would, I was there. Now she is sending you a sign."

Jamie stands there looking at that rose, just the one. "Tanner let's go, we're going to a party, if she'll still have this old man!" Jamie says excitedly.

"I can't go with you, I'm not dressed for a fancy party, besides, I would embarrass my babies showing up dressed like some stable tramp." Tanner says sadly.

"Then you will get dressed and so will I. You have that dark suit I bought for you when Mary passed, you'll wear that." He calls ahead to have Theresa put out the necessary clothes and get his electric razor ready for Tanner.

Jamie takes the stairs two at a time and rushes to his room, Theresa has laid out his clothes and pressed a dress shirt. He dresses with an urgency that he never had before, when suddenly he thinks. "What if she won't have me, what if she thinks the age difference is too much, or maybe she's met someone else that she's fallen for?" With a shrug of his shoulders he decides to take his chances.

Running down stairs he yells to see if Tanner is ready. Reaching the bottom he sees Rubin, and he is all smiles, pushing out a spit and polished man he hardly recognizes.

"What kept you, we've been waiting for some time, are we going, or not?" Tanner chuckles.

"Come on old man, were burning moonlight." Tanner nods and smiles and Jamie notices, he's put his teeth in....

Driving up to Country Club Jamie throws the valet his keys as he helps Tanner from the vehicle. Entering the main lobby Jamie walks up to the concierge desk and asks for directions to the banquet room. The young man at the desk tells them that dinner has been served and the entertainment is about to start. Jamie asks him who is providing the entertainment tonight, and he tells him it's Raul's band.

Jamie tells Tanner to wait by the door and asks the man where Raul's group is. The Concierge says back stage, and gives Jamie's directions.

Heading back stage to find Raul, Jamie sees him coming out of a dressing room marked employees only. He greets him warmly and Jamie tells him he has a favor to ask. Raul tells him after hearing the favor that it would be no problem. He's happy to oblige, because he was asked to play at Jamie's party that was the reason he was engaged to play tonight. Thanking him Jamie tells him what he wants him to do and hands him sheet music, Raul agrees and Jamie heads back to Tanner.

"Please take my friend in and seat him at the Los Angeles table." Jamie tells the concierge. "Tanner you go on over to the table and say nothing about me. Just tell them you couldn't find me." Jamie explains to him.

"What are you doing now boy, you ain't skipping out are you?" Tanner asks concern in his voice.

"No old friend, I'm not, just providing some entertainment for a special someone." He explains putting Tanner's mind to rest.

Deanna sees Tanner being wheeled in by the concierge and wonders if Jamie is here also. She looks about the room searching with her eyes for him.

Jamie watches her from behind the curtains to one side of the stage. She appears to be looking for someone, could it be him, Jamie wonders?

Jamie turns and heads to the other side of the stage to await Raul's entrance.

The lights go down and the curtain lifts, as Raul stands holding a microphone in his hands.

"Ladies and Gentlemen, I wish to welcome you here for the twentieth Annual Horseman's Banquet, we intend to bring you an international flavor of music tonight, for your listening and dancing pleasure. To start the night off, it's my pleasure and privilege to present a singer and song writer, who's written a song and will perform it for the first time ever in public. This song is for someone very special here this evening. Ladies and gentleman, may I present J. D. Thompson singing, Love through the Looking Glass."

Deanna gasps at the sound of his name, and looks toward where they are playing the spot light. The light illuminates a man sitting at the piano and the notes she heard that day at the Rancho are drifting out over the room. Deanna listens to the words as if hearing them for the first time. She remembers asking herself that day, could he ever love someone again as much as he loved before? Deanna reaches up and clutches the medallion that rests upon her bosom in her hand; she feels heat radiating from it as it pulses against her palm. Mel reaches over and grabs Deanna's other hand.

The entire room is silent as he sings a country love song about a man who has found his love in a mirror that turns dark with the coming of the day. It shows him a reflection of a woman that he sees only with the setting of the sun.

> Come stay with me, not just a reflection
> From the looking glass.
> Don't leave me like the fading stars.
> Stay with me, for the rest of your days,
> Let me love you, for the rest of mine.
> Let me love you, for the rest of mine.

The music ends with the last chorus and the room erupts in applause, Jamie crosses the room to stand before her and offers her his hand. Taking it, she rises to his embrace, hearing him say. "I love you, and I want you to spend the rest of your days with me, I promise to try and make you happy. It's you, I love, and there are no more ghosts. I promise you my life, because it's now mine to give." He kisses her and once again time seems to stand still, no sound except the pounding of her own heart, exactly like the first time he kissed her. The difference is, she's kisses him back and the room appears to spin, the pounding she feels now is from his heart as well as her own.

As his lips leave hers, she whispers to him, "I love you more." Taking the Medallion from around her neck, she places it around his.

Deanna looks into his eyes no longer lost, saying to him, "Only to one with a pure heart can I give mine."

Out in the garden two wraiths stand by and watch as the one dearest to both makes his choice.

"*Lord Cecht, do you believe he will be happy now?*"

"*Yes, Mistress Mary he will be happy now, for he embarks on his life's quest. He will find more of the Children of Danu and guide them to fulfillment as was prophesied long ago.*

"*All the children, will they be alright?*

"*Yes, he will retain the power to restore. The descendants gather about him now.*"

"*I don't understand, are there more like him?*"

"*Yes, there are those that carry the Tuatha blood, like Roberto, Eduardo and Dyon.*

It is time for us to depart, our people wait at the crossover for the last journey home. Come Mistress, we've tarried to long as it is we must not miss the Gateway.........

Well, that's the story, you might not believe it, and by the look on some of your faces, I can tell that you don't. I swear to you, tis true every word, for it was I, Thomas Scanlon that bore witness to this with them.

The young lass Tara asks me, "What happened to the other's Father, what of Dyon and Jonah and the girls and all the others what became of them? There wasn't really an angel was there?"

Father Tom answers her with a smile. "Ah, they're stories for another time and another place and as to whether Angels walk among us; my answer is, only if you believe."

Index

Agnes Benacourt- Tom Collin's receptionist
Angel- Adopted American Bulldog, Mary's former dog
Cerbon- Partner in Southwest Properties
Dagda- King of the Tuatha De Danu
D.C.- Dyon's palomino show horse
Deanna Gaynor- Reporter for The Palm Beach Pro Horseman's Photo Magazine
Deanna Quinn- Deanna Gaynor's maiden name
Dian Cecht- Jamie's ancestor and Lord of The Tuatha De Dana
Dr. Winmen- Katy Gaynor's court appointed therapist
Dr. Paterson- Deanna's Veterinarian
Duenas- Spanish for female chaperone
Dyon Thompson- Jamie Doyle's ward
Eduardo Sanchez- Jamie's ranch foreman and Rosa's husband
Edward Haskell- Ex U.S. Senator, financier and Father-law of Jamie Doyle
Esteban- One of Jamie's vaqueros at the ranch
Fiona Thompson- Jamie's deceased younger sister
Father Tom Scanlon- Ex priest and long time friend of Jamie Doyle
Frank Collins- Editor of Palm Beach Pro Horseman's Magazine
Gila- Marta's sister and Rosa's cousin
Hanna- Deanna's old Nanny and her mother's companion and friend
Irene O'Neil- T. J.'s mother and Tom Scanlon's housekeeper
Jake Clayton- Owner of Jake's Place and ex rodeo champion
Jamie Doyle- Owner of Rancho de Los Angeles
Jefe- Spanish for Boss or Headman

Jennifer Quinn- Deanna's mother
John Ellsworth- Owner and Publisher of Palm Beach Pro Horseman's Photo Magazine
Jonah Flynn- Deanna Gaynor's son
Katy Gaynor- Deanna Gaynor's daughter
Ken Axelrod- Palm Beach attorney and friend of John Ellsworth
Marianna Davidson- One of the State Children in Jamie's program
Marta- Another of Rosa's cousins
Marty- Security police from the magazine
Melody Ellsworth- Wife of John Ellsworth and friend to Deanna Gaynor
Miguel- Jamie's vaquero that was killed in the ambush at the Rancho
Moina McCann- Married Edward Haskell Jennifer Quinn's best friend
Nation Horse Show- One of the premier equestrian events in U.S held each year in Wellington FL.
Pita- Rosa and Eduardo's daughter
Rancho de Los Angeles- Name Jamie Doyle's ranch in Wellington
Raul- local band leader and friend of Rosa's
Red Fox Farm- Deanna's home in Lynchburg VA.
Reverend Small- Jennifer Quinn's pastor in VA.
Robert Quinn- Deanna's father and friend of Edward Haskell
Roberto Diaz- Head of the Columbian Riding Team
Roger Montgomery- English horse trainer and jumper interested in Deanna
Roger- Security police from the magazine
Rosa Sanchez- Jamie Doyle's household manager
Rubin- One of Jamie's vaqueros at the ranch
Rufus Tanner- Jamie's blacksmith and oldest friend
Segundo- Second in command or Forman
Southwest Properties- Land speculators and developers
Steve Gaynor- Deanna's ex husband
Storm- Jamie's Tennessee Walking Horse
Sweetbriar College- Top equestrian college in VA
T. J O'Neil- One of the State children in Jamie's program.
Theresa- Rosa's friend and cousin from Mexico
Thomas Flynn- Jonah's father killed during the Gulf War

Tia Rivera- One of the girls placed in Jamie's program
Tim Manning- Deanna's Photographer for Photo Magazine
Trinity Lopez- Jamie's first wife and barrel racing champion
Vaquero- Cowboy or ranch hand in Spanish
Wade Davis- Jamie's mentor and friend in his rodeo days
Williams- Partner in Southwest Properties

About The Author

Wallace Jan Ecklof grew up in a one square mile honky-tonk community on the Jersey shore, and graduated high school in 1965 during the height of the Viet Nam War.

He started working as a Roller Derby skater, a lobsterman, and then a cowboy in South Dakota for two years on a horse and cattle ranch. He then attended college studying for a degree in business and literature. His father wished he follow the path of other male family members and work for Prudential Insurance Company, while his mother wanted him to pursue something scholarly in Art or Literature.

Being married while still in college and the birth of the first of three sons, Shawn, Shannon, and Patrick put his college career on hold: His need to support his family would mean the pursuit of literary interests would have to wait.

He worked in retail and insurance, obtained his real estate license then managed a large real estate office in Middletown N.J. for twelve years. During this time his marriage ended in divorce.

A new chapter emerged in his life. Wallace ran into his childhood sweetheart who encouraged him to pursue his real calling, writing and his intense love of animals. He then remarried and decided to take a chance and purchase a small bankrupt pet store in Red Bank N.J. He used his education in literature and love of animals to write interesting ad copy and his company soon became a small chain. The company extended from New Jersey to south eastern Florida and in 1988 he relocated to Palm Beach County, Florida.

Wallace retired in Nineteen Ninety Six. Since arriving in Florida he had been involved with Horses for the Handicap and experienced what these big beautiful animals could do for people with disabilities especially children. It was at this juncture in his life that the inspiration for the Last Celtic Angel came to him. Training people with physical and emotional handicaps plus his years as a ranch hand and a life long love of everything equine all combined to inspire his writing.

For twenty five years Wallace lived in Wellington, Florida where he honed his equine skills by competing in the many horse events held in one of the nation's top equestrian areas. With the demise of his wife in 2006 he then returned to New Jersey, where he now resides.